A
Demon's
Rebellion

THE RISE OF LILITH

(A Crimson Alliance novel)

ACKNOWLEDGEMENT

To the readers who journeyed through the stars with me… thank you.

This story was written for those who believe in the power of rebellion, the strength of unlikely friendships, and the beauty of fire-forged bonds. If you love daring escapes, skyborne battles, shadowy warriors, and queens with wings… this was always meant for you.

Science fiction and fantasy have long been the places where imagination becomes reality, where myth and meaning collide. I'm honored you chose to step into this world with me.

Stay curious. Stay brave. And never stop turning the page.

A
Demon's
Rebellion

The Rise of Lilith

K.A. Dunlap
(A Crimson Alliance novel)

A Demon's Rebellion
The Rise of Lilith

Address any inquiries to:

K.A. Dunlap

Email: KADunlap@TheCAU.net

ISBNs
Hardcover: 979-8-9929819-0-2
Paperback: 979-8-9929819-8-8

Published by: Green Quill Media

Cover Design: Green Quill Media

Interior Formatting: Green Quill Media

First edition.

Table of Contents

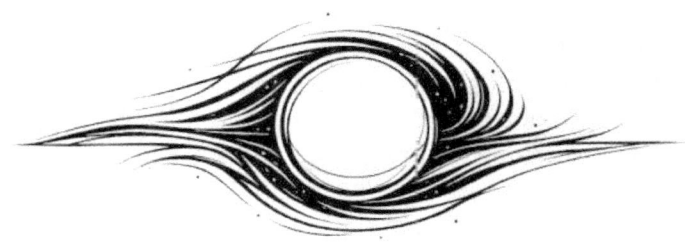

Chapter 1:

The Weight of Her Wings

Lilith stood at the edge of a volcanic plain in the Hellish Realm, the scorched earth trembling beneath her feet as if in recognition of her presence. Overhead, a sky burned with a perpetual crimson haze. It was unending and suffocating and interlaced with tendrils of dark smoke that curled like dying embers. She spread her massive crimson-and-ebony wings wide, feeling the searing, sulfurous winds whipping around her. The flickering glow of the realm's eternal twilight danced along the black edges of her wings, a cruel, molten beauty that once fueled her ambition.

At seven feet tall, crowned with a pair of intricately curled horns adding another ten inches, Lilith had long been a figure both revered and feared. Born the youngest female Scion of Belzoth and Isolde, she was fated to enforce the relentless justice of the Hellish Realm. For three hundred and fifty-two agonizing years, she had carried out the brutal punishments that defined her world. Now, amid the anguished cries of the damned echoing over rivers of boiling blood and molten rock, the weight of her destiny had become a crushing burden.

A hot gust, laden with the stench of burning flesh and sulfur, swept past her. Lilith closed her eyes and inhaled the

1

bitter air deeply before exhaling in a harsh, pained sigh. "I can't bear this much longer," she murmured to the unyielding sky. In that moment, a spark of rebellion which lay long dormant stirred within her. No longer could she ignore the yearning to break free from a cycle of endless torment.

Turning away from the edge of the volcanic abyss, she strode along a narrow, jagged ledge toward the training grounds. Here, in the heart of the Hellish Realm, lesser demons honed their dark arts amid glowing embers and towering basalt pillars.

LILITH

As always, Lilith was expected to oversee their brutal drills. Though duty and habit bound her to these grim routines, a part of her longed to cast off the chains of her role, to unfurl her wings and vanish into the fiery skies for good.

Within the training arena, set at the base of a vast crater, the clamor of clashing claws and bursts of infernal magic filled the air. The lesser demons, molded by the cruelty of their realm, froze at the sight of her imposing form. Once, their wide-eyed awe had fueled her sense of superiority. Now, it only deepened her melancholy.

"Continue," she barked, her voice echoing over the din. "You're here to train, not to gawk."

The demons scattered to resume their fierce routines. Yet, each clash of weapon and arcane burst seemed to puncture the hardened mask she wore. Memories of her days, so fiercely spent wielding her twin blazing two-handed swords in the service of punishment, now felt empty. Each tortured scream from the River of Torment below was a reminder of the price of her legacy.

As she paced the crater's rim, thoughts of her father, Belzoth, and his vast, oppressive infernal court invaded her mind. In that court of black stone and dancing flames, she had once fought, and excelled, to win his sparse nod of approval. But now, every victory felt hollow, every scar a reminder of the endless cycle of cruelty. Deep inside, a persistent question had begun to fester: *Was this unending torment all there was to her destiny?*

Her heart, heavy with centuries of enforced cruelty, now pounded with a dual purpose. Not only did she long to flee the oppressive confines of the Hellish Realm, but she also envisioned a mission beyond its fiery borders, to cross into the Material Realm and halt the malignant resistance of Necra, a force that threatened to unravel the very fabric of many worlds.

Her reverie was shattered by a sudden crash on the training grounds. Two demons, caught in a reckless maneuver, had collided violently, slamming into a basalt pillar. Lilith's wings unfurled in alarm as she strode forward.

"That wasn't controlled, it was reckless!" she chastised. In the frightened eyes of the demons, she recognized the same raw determination that had once defined her youth, a time when passion had ruled over doubt.

"No more of this," she softened her tone. "Train properly or not at all."

Standing alone on an outcropping of obsidian that overlooked the River of Torment, she muttered bitterly, "Three hundred and fifty-two years… wasted."

Her eyes fell on her sheathed flaming dual two-handed swords, the very instruments of her authority, etched with runes of ancient power and the legacy of her bloodline. Now, they seemed less like symbols of triumph and more like chains that bound her to an existence of endless suffering.

A skeletal messenger emerged from a swirling plume of ash, its voice grinding like ancient bones. "Scion Lilith. I bring word."

Annoyance flickered across her features as she regarded the errand-runner, a servant of the realm's higher powers. "Speak quickly," she ordered.

"General Malakar summons you to the Infernal Pits. He wishes to discuss your current standing."

At the mention of Malakar, a master strategist whose reputation was both feared and respected, a shiver ran down her spine. Though part of her dreaded his scrutiny, another small flame of hope was kindled. Rumors had whispered that Malakar's reach extended far beyond the Hellish Realm; perhaps he could offer a means to harness her burgeoning potential, maybe even a path to freedom.

"I see," she replied, her voice carefully neutral. "I will attend."

As the messenger melted back into the darkness, Lilith lingered on the ledge, her mind swirling with conflicted emotions. The summons was a reminder of duty and yet it carried the faint promise of a pathway to liberation. With one last, sorrowful glance at the tormented landscape below, she spread her wings and launched herself into the churning, fiery skies. Each beat of her mighty wings became a deliberate, defiant step toward a destiny that might someday span not only the Hellish Realm but also the promise of the Material Realm.

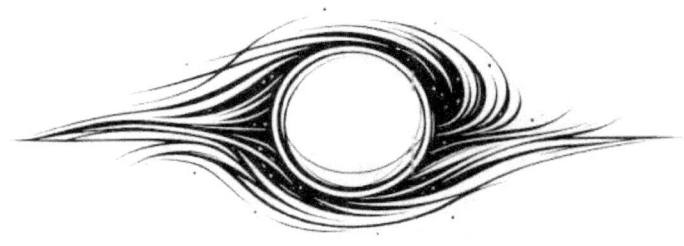

Chapter 2:

Forging a New Path

Lilith now faced the Hellfire-class scout. It is a sleek, dagger-shaped vessel that promised to train her to escape from the ceaseless torment of the Hellish Realm and train her to be able to pass to the Material Realm. Its black-and-crimson hull shimmered with ancient infernal runes and bore the emblem of a long-oppressive legacy. Though modest in size compared to the monstrous warships that filled the Infernal Pits, the craft pulsed with quiet, predatory power. Mastering it was not merely about flight; it was the key to leaving behind an existence of perpetual suffering and to challenging the malignant resistance of Necra that threatened worlds beyond.

General Malakar, standing at a massive 7 feet 8 inches wearing well-worn armor, stood behind her in the vast hangar. This is a place filled with the low hum of infernal machinery and stone-faced laborers tending to the grim fleet. "Are you frozen in place?" his deep voice reverberated through the cavern. "You said you were ready."

Lilith tore her gaze from the imposing vessel and squared her shoulders. "I am," she declared, though her heart thundered with both trepidation and hope. With determined strides, she approached the boarding ramp, her immense wings shifting restlessly – a silent testament to the mix of burden and resolve that had driven her to this moment.

Into the Engine of Escape

Inside the cockpit, the Hellfire-class scout revealed itself as a compact hub of engineered dark metals, illuminated control panels, and digital readouts. Every lever and gauge flickered with precise indications, and the wraparound dashboard displayed sleek symbols reminiscent of advanced schematics she had studied during her early training.

GENERAL MALAKAR

General Malakar took his place in the cramped co-pilot station beside her, his tone a blend of stern instruction and measured encouragement.

He observed Lilith as she ran her fingers over the wide, responsive dashboard. "Begin by familiarizing yourself with these controls," he instructed. "Remember, your input drives every function of this ship. The systems here respond immediately to your commands. A firm, deliberate touch will yield precise maneuvers – too aggressive, and you risk overloading the engines; too tentative, and you may miss your opportunity to react."

Lilith's eyes settled on the central interface panel – a sleek, cool surface that formed the heart of the ship's control system. With measured determination, she pressed her palm against it. The panel vibrated gently in response, confirming that the ship's systems were fully calibrated to her touch.

"This is your core interface," Malakar explained. "Every command you transmit here is processed and distributed to the ship's various subsystems – navigation, propulsion, weapons, and shields. It's designed to make the vessel an extension of your own precision. Mastering this will give you the freedom to pilot the scout with absolute control."

A spark of possibility lit within her. *If I can master this craft,* she thought, *I can finally break free of this oppressive realm. Beyond these burning skies lies the Material Realm – a universe where I can challenge the forces that threaten our future.*

With that resolve, Lilith began her calibration tests, her eyes fixed on the wide display as she adjusted the throttle and toggled the lever to experiment with the dual-control mode. The ship responded smoothly, each function coming to life under her confident touch. In that moment, every light and gauge confirmed one undeniable truth: she was one step closer to escape and to a destiny beyond the confines of the Hellish Realm.

The First Flight

Taking a deep, steady breath, Lilith initiated the start-up sequence. As her hand pressed firmly against the core interface, she channeled a measured surge of demonic energy into the vessel. Instantly, the control panels blazed with an eerie glow and a deep, mechanical hum resonated throughout the cockpit as the engines synchronized with her very essence. "Steady," Malakar cautioned. "Let the ship merge with you."

Within moments, the displays shifted from a tentative amber to a confident green. Malakar gestured to a lever by the throttle. "Gently now," he intoned. Lilith gripped the throttle and nudged it forward. The scout shuddered, then gracefully lifted off the hangar floor, riding columns of shimmering, red-tinged exhaust. As the confines of the Infernal Pits receded, her wings tensed not only against the physical forces but in eager anticipation of the freedom that lay ahead.

"Take us out," Malakar ordered, his tone both precise and unyielding.

Steering the vessel toward the massive exit gate – a colossal barrier pulsing with infernal energy – Lilith watched as the craft pierced a flickering force field. Beyond, the searing heat and choking fumes of the Hellish Realm gave way to a landscape both brutal and mesmerizing: boiling rivers of molten rock, jagged peaks bathed in a perpetual crimson glow, and swirling ash clouds that whispered of ancient sorrows. *I have flown these skies on my own wings,* she thought, *but never like this… with the promise of escape and a chance at renewal.*

High above the volcanic plains, the ship's sensors began to register a subtle shift in ambient energy – a thinning of the boundary between realms. In that fleeting moment, the oppressive weight of the Hellish Realm seemed to lift, replaced by a fragile, beckoning hope. The Material Realm lay just beyond the veil.

Testing the Limits of Freedom

Malakar's next command was clear: "Ascend and test its vertical thrust." With resolve, Lilith pushed the throttle further, sending the scout surging upward. The vessel soared past jagged spires and billowing columns of ash. Turbulent gusts battered its frame as it climbed, each jolt a reminder of the delicate balance between raw demonic power and precise control.

Even as superheated rock grazed the hull and the protective wards flared in defiance, Lilith's focus sharpened. "This is... exhilarating," she murmured, a rare smile crossing her lips despite the danger. Yet Malakar's steady voice reminded her, "Do not let the thrill cloud your judgment. Discipline must always guide your instinct."

Under his vigilant tutelage, Lilith executed a series of demanding maneuvers: sharp turns, rolls, climbs, and controlled descents. Each adjustment was a dialogue between her will and the arcane design of the craft. Gradually, the scout began to move as if it were an extension of her very soul.

After several flawless glides over the volatile plains, Malakar raised the stakes further. "Fly through that canyon," he commanded, pointing to a narrow chasm flanked by towering basalt walls. "Prove that you can navigate even when the forces of this realm conspire against you."

A knot of apprehension tightened in her stomach as she directed the scout toward the canyon's mouth. The passage was perilously narrow, its walls rising like jagged teeth from molten earth. Fierce winds and swirling ash threatened to hurl her off course. Drawing on centuries of experience and her newfound mastery of the vessel, Lilith steeled herself. Every twist and turn demanded unwavering focus. Her fingers clutched the controls as the ship weaved between basalt columns; each precise movement was a battle against nature's fury.

Midway through, an unexpected updraft slammed into the craft. The vessel pitched violently upward, its hull scraping the canyon ceiling and showering sparks throughout the cockpit. Alarms blared as warnings flashed across the display. In that heart-stopping moment, with her wings drawn tight in a reflexive grip, Lilith stifled a surge of panic. "Focus!" Malakar roared.

Summoning every ounce of her inner strength, she channeled her demonic energy into the core interface. Gradually, the scout steadied leveling off just inches from the scorched ceiling and resumed its cautious passage. When the craft finally emerged into a broad, lava-lit valley, a wave of relief and quiet triumph washed over her. The alarms faded, and Malakar observed, "Clumsy, but salvageable. You adapted under pressure."

Though his praise was sparse, Lilith sensed the grudging respect in his tone; a small victory in a realm where every triumph was paid for dearly.

Underworld Rumors

Between flight sessions, Lilith continued her covert inquiries about the Scorpion, a ship she has heard could take her to the Material Realm. She ventured into the shadowy markets in the lower reaches of the Infernal Pits, where contraband goods and forbidden knowledge were traded. Hooded figures huddled around smoldering braziers, exchanging secrets in hushed voices. The air was thick with the stench of rot and pungent alchemical concoctions.

"Tell me about the Scorpion," she whispered to a cowering imp behind a rickety stall. She had tossed it a small pouch of gleaming stones infused with demonic essence – a valuable currency in these circles.

The imp peered around nervously. "They say it's captained by a half-demon and half-angel. Others say a shapeshifter. No one knows. It shows up in obscure docking bays, takes on passengers or cargo, then vanishes into the nether realms."

Lilith's pulse quickened. "Where does it dock? I need details."

The imp shook its head, eyes bulging with fear. "No set schedule. The crew is unpredictable. But… I've heard rumors it was last seen near the sixth circle. Try the abandoned docks there."

Lilith exhaled, trying to contain her excitement. So, there was a lead. A bit slender, but real. She paid the imp extra, ensuring its silence, and slipped back into the warren of stalls.

"The Sixth Circle," she mused. That area was riddled with lava-choked canyons, fiercely guarded by Cerberus-like creatures. It was also known for the presence of her father's more fanatical enforcers – an extra layer of danger if she was caught snooping around. But her decision was made. Once she felt confident in her piloting skills, she would see if the Scorpion truly existed.

A Confrontation with the Past

Weeks became months. Lilith's transformation did not go unnoticed. Rumors spread among the lesser demons that Princess Lilith was no longer content with her duties. Some whispered that she sought to usurp her father; others suggested she had gone mad. Despite the gossip, no one dared to challenge her openly, not with Malakar backing her training.

Still, tension simmered in the fortress. One evening, a cadre of demonic captains, individuals outranked only by the generals, cornered Lilith in a corridor lit by the dim glow of molten rock.

"Princess," one of them sneered, a tall demon with spiked armor. "We hear you're dabbling in flight. Are you planning to abandon your post?"

Lilith's wings flared, and the corridor's temperature

seemed to spike. "Would it matter to you if I did?" she shot back.

The demon laughed, joined by his cohorts. "It might. Such an action would be considered a slap in the Dark Lord's face. Are you truly prepared to provoke him?"

Lilith felt the sting of the truth in the question. She clenched her fists. "My affairs are my own," she said, her voice dangerously low. "If you wish to make an issue of it, you can answer to me… and to Malakar."

She left them standing there, uncertain whether she had made an enemy or simply postponed a confrontation. Either way, it served as a warning: her path to freedom was fraught with peril.

Final Preparations

Eventually, Malakar declared her proficient enough to pilot a wide range of vessels. "You've exceeded my expectations," he said one day in the simulator chamber. "Your greatest foe now is not technique, but the doubt in your mind."

Lilith stepped away from the simulator cockpit, wiping sweat from her brow. The illusions of cosmic debris and swirling wormholes faded from the console. "I won't doubt myself," she said, forcing confidence into her voice.

The general studied her, arms folded over his broad chest. "Then you are prepared to face what lies beyond these caverns. Remember: the secrets of flight and the knowledge of the cosmos you now hold are dangerous tools if wielded improperly."

Lilith nodded, her heart thrumming with anticipation. She sensed that he had given her all he could. This was the limit of training within the confines of Hades. To push further, she would have to venture out, perhaps even beyond Hell's borders.

"I appreciate what you've taught me," Lilith said, a rare note of sincerity edging her voice.

Malakar gave a curt nod. "Your gratitude is unnecessary. But if you ever find your convictions wavering, recall this training. Discipline, awareness, and controlled will. They will guide you better than blind rage."

She lingered for a moment, tempted to tell him of her plan to seek out the ship called Scorpion – unsure if he would aid or condemn her. In the end, she kept her counsel. *Best not to risk it,* she reasoned.

The Path Forward

Lilith left the Infernal Pits with a renewed sense of purpose. For the first time in her existence, she had a skill that wasn't tied exclusively to oppression. Piloting demanded discipline, creativity, reflex, and intellect – a realm of mastery distinct from the routine cruelty of punishing souls.

She returned to her personal quarters; a suite carved high into a basalt cliff overlooking the River of Torment. The old Lilith might have taken pride in the screams echoing far below, but tonight, she barely heard them. She was focused on her next move: traveling to the Sixth Circle to confirm if the Scorpion was there.

Yet, even as she packed what few personal artifacts she needed – essence crystals, enchanted bindings, a protective cloak for her swords – she couldn't shake the sense that she was crossing a threshold. If she truly meant to leave Hades, she would be alienating herself from everything she had once known. Would her sisters condemn her as a traitor? Would her father hunt her down to make an example? The questions weighed on her, but not enough to stop her.

"I have to see this through," she murmured, strapping her swords to her back. Their flames hissed softly, as though in agreement… or perhaps farewell.

Seeking the Scorpion

The journey to the unknown port was fraught with peril. Lilith had navigated through the volatile outskirts of the Sixth Circle, where molten geysers erupted from deep fissures and predatory, demonic beasts lurked in every shadow. Each obstacle – whether a vicious creature or a jagged spire of scorched rock – only honed her newfound agility and steeled her resolve. Now, after hours of tense navigation, she emerged at a secluded, little-known port carved into the side of a jagged cliff.

A rusted, partially open gate marked the entrance to a weathered landing platform, its surface scarred by the relentless assault of time and flame. The place was dimly lit by a few flickering torches whose light danced uneasily across the polished black stone. The pungent stench of burning tar filled the air, and every sound – distant clanging metal, the soft hiss of cooling rock – spoke of a forgotten realm of smugglers and outcasts.

Lilith's pulse quickened as she slipped through the gate. She had heard rumors of vessels hidden in such forsaken places, and she hoped against hope that one of those legends might offer her a way out of this eternal torment. If the whispers were false, she would be met only with disappointment – and perhaps the sting of betrayal. But if they were true, her future might very well begin tonight.

Her eyes roamed the dock until they fell upon it: a battered, patchwork spacecraft, its hull marred by scorch marks and hastily welded plates of mismatched metal. Even in its rough-hewn appearance, something in its presence exuded a resilient defiance. Faded lettering along its side proclaimed the name "The Scorpion," and for a heartbeat, Lilith's breath caught. Could this be the vessel that carried the promise of escape? A ship that could whisk her away to the Material Realm?

Approaching cautiously, she found herself confronted by two figures standing at the base of a lowered ramp. One was a tall, wiry being with metallic skin that gleamed dully under the sparse light; the other, an avian creature with piercing yellow eyes, watched her with guarded intensity. Their stances were tense, as if prepared to act at a moment's notice.

"Hold there," the metallic figure demanded, raising a strange, rifle-like weapon. "State your business, Hellbourne."

Lilith squared her shoulders and let her voice ring clear and unwavering. "I am Princess Lilith, and I'm here to negotiate the purchase of this vessel," she declared. "I've heard that this ship can cross the boundaries between our realm and the Material Realm. I intend to use it to leave this place – and I'm prepared to buy it outright if necessary."

The avian creature's eyes narrowed as it replied in a low, measured tone, "And what would a demon princess want with a ship capable of such a feat? You seek escape, but such passage does not come without a price."

Without flinching, Lilith replied, "I do not seek chaos. I seek freedom. I have endured centuries of torment, and I have trained beyond the limits of what many demons could ever dream. I offer not only my coin but my skills as a pilot. I will ensure that this ship serves a purpose far greater than mere transport; it will be the means to forge a new future in the Material Realm."

A tense silence fell as the two figures exchanged skeptical glances. The metallic one finally spoke, "This vessel is more than metal and bolts; it carries a legacy. It is not simply sold on a whim. We must be sure you understand that owning it means you bear the burden of its history, and once you leave this realm, there is no simple return."

Lilith's gaze hardened. "I know my own legacy, and I have grown weary of serving a realm that offers nothing but unending cruelty. I am prepared to take on that burden. I want out, and I will pay any price to make that happen."

The avian figure then tilted its head, as if considering

her words with deliberate care. Finally, a third figure emerged from the shadowed interior of the ship – a lean individual with a face partially hidden beneath a worn hood. Their eyes, dark and assessing, fixed on Lilith. "Speak your final terms," the hooded figure said quietly, commanding a respect that silenced the murmurs around them.

Taking a steady breath, Lilith continued, "I demand the ship be sold to me. I intend to leave this cursed realm and cross into the Material Realm. Let it be known that once I take possession, I will be solely responsible for its course – and for ensuring it serves to bring about change."

For a long, charged moment, the hooded figure regarded her in silence. Then, with a slow, deliberate nod, they spoke, "Very well. You shall have the Scorpion – but know this: once you leave, your return, if ever possible, will come at a cost greater than you can imagine. Are you certain of your decision?"

Lilith's eyes blazed with unyielding determination. "I am certain," she replied, her voice resolute as it echoed across the dock. "I have nothing left but chains here. I will board this ship, claim it as mine, and use it to escape this realm forever."

The hooded figure gestured for her to step onto the ramp, and as she did, the metallic and avian beings lowered their weapons. With one final, decisive stride, Lilith boarded the Scorpion. In that moment, as the transfer was sealed and the ship became hers, she felt the oppressive weight of centuries begin to lift. Whatever lay ahead – be it danger, discovery, or the battle to free the Material Realm – she would face it as a free being, unbound by the chains of her past.

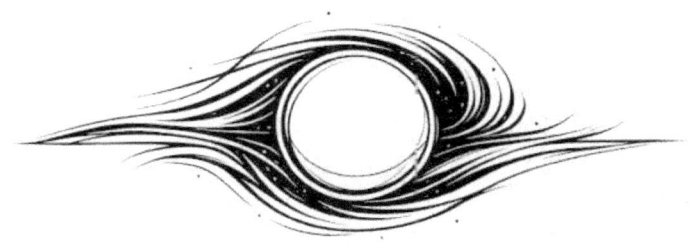

Chapter 3:

Grilka's Rise

Valkorr was a planet forged in hardship. Two brilliant yellow suns scorched the terrain by day, while frigid winds swept across jagged cliffs by night. Beneath those imposing cliffs, cut into the very face of the rock, lay the humble village where Grilka drew her first breath. The settlement was modest, no more than a few rows of ramshackle huts and carved tunnels, but its green-skinned people possessed unbreakable spirits. They had to. On Valkorr, survival demanded both grit and might.

Grilka's earliest memory was the abrasive scrape of rough stone beneath her tiny feet and the tang of metal in the hot, dry air. Even as a toddler, her orange eyes glinted with a fierceness beyond her years. The villagers whispered among themselves that she would be a force to reckon with, an impression only strengthened by her early feats of strength. By age six, she was hauling water buckets up the narrow cliff paths without pause, her very rare orange hair blazing in the sunlight like a beacon of raw determination.

A Child of Two Worlds

Her parents could not have been more different. Her father, Skran, was a blacksmith renowned for shaping unyielding Valkorrian steel into exquisite tools and weaponry. The forge kept reverberating with the clang of hammer against anvil, while molten metal cast flickering shadows across his stern face. Skran's hands were calloused, and his temper quick, but beneath his brusque exterior lay a deep love for his only child.

GRILKA - YOUNG

Her mother, Naela, was the village healer, skilled in using Valkorr's rare herbs to mend injuries and cure illnesses that struck during the punishing nights.

Where Skran's eyes burned with the fires of the forge, Naela's gaze reflected patience and empathy – qualities she tried to instill in her headstrong daughter. By Naela's side, Grilka learned that strength was not just brute force but also the willingness to protect the vulnerable.

Standing Up for the Weak

Long before she even thought of formal combat training, Grilka's fierce disposition and physical prowess caught the attention of her peers. Children twice her size found themselves bested in friendly scuffles. What started as typical playground tussles morphed into small competitions, with older kids pushing her to see how far her strength could go.

Yet Grilka's rough edges came with a surprising gentleness toward the underdog. When local bullies picked on a scrawny boy named Talrek – tearing at his clothes and mocking his small stature – Grilka intervened. She stepped between Talrek and the bullies, her fists clenched, her orange hair whipping in the desert wind.

"You wanna fight?" she barked at them. "Pick on someone who'll fight back."

They laughed at first, a group of three older kids with more bravado than brains. But the laughter turned to shock when Grilka unleashed a flurry of blows that left them sprawled in the dust, bruised and whimpering. Talrek stared at her, wide-eyed and trembling, but Grilka merely extended her hand to help him up.

"You're okay," she said, her voice gruff but kind. "Next time, don't let them push you around."

Word of her actions spread, and soon the village elders took notice. Among them, the retired gladiator Halkor stood out. Decades earlier, he had captivated Valkorr's grand arenas with his prowess, but an old injury had forced him into a quiet life in this village. Upon hearing how a mere child had singlehandedly routed three bullies, he grew intrigued.

Lessons in the Sparring Pits

Grilka's father had hoped she might someday inherit his smithing skills, while her mother envisioned her as a compassionate caregiver. But Grilka's heart yearned for the crack of knuckles against flesh and the exhilarating rush of emerging victorious in a fight. When Halkor offered to train her, both parents hesitated, fearing the path of violence would overshadow the morals they strove to teach her.

"She needs discipline," Halkor insisted, meeting Skran and Naela in their humble home. "If I don't train her properly, her anger and strength could go unchecked."

Reluctantly, her parents agreed.

From that point on, Grilka's life revolved around sweat, bruises, and endless drills. Each morning, she ran the treacherous cliffside trails, her legs pounding against the rock as the two suns rose over the horizon. The ascents tested her stamina to its limits, while the descents demanded balance and cat-like reflexes. Afternoons were for combat drills in a makeshift pit near the village center – little more than a circular clearing of compressed sand bordered by flat-topped boulders.

There, Halkor taught her the intricacies of grapples, throws, and submission holds. He emphasized technique over raw power, though he never discouraged her from utilizing her considerable strength. Indeed, he found pride in her ability to overpower almost any sparring partner.

"Strength alone won't guarantee victory," he would remind her, wiping sweat from his brow after a demanding session. "Learn to read your opponent – watch their stance, their eyes, their breathing. Predict their movements before they strike."

Grilka took those lessons to heart. She noticed that while she could often bulldoze an adversary with sheer force, a well-timed maneuver or feint could break even the strongest defenses. Nothing thrilled her more than the moment when her opponent realized her cunning matched her physical might.

Champion of the Harvest Festival

By the time Grilka reached fifteen years old she was already 6 feet tall. Rumors of her fighting skills circulated beyond the village. At the annual Harvest Festival – an event drawing participant from surrounding regions – she stood in the center of the celebration's wrestling pit: a child facing older, larger competitors.

Her first match was against a boy three years her senior, regarded locally as a rising star. The crowd buzzed with anticipation, expecting to see the unstoppable boy crush a mere upstart. But Grilka's cunning and relentless spirit took everyone by surprise. She dodged, weaved, and used her opponent's weight against him, eventually pinning him to the ground in a breathtaking display of power. The crowd erupted in cheers.

This victory impressed many, but none more than Halkor. Later that evening, he found her resting against a crate, sipping water.

"You fight like a force of nature," he said, voice low with admiration. "But it's your focus, your heart, that sets you apart."

Grilka shrugged off the compliment, but she couldn't hide her excitement. In that moment, she realized she wanted more than just local renown; she wanted to face the greatest fighters on Valkorr... and someday, beyond.

From Village Hero to Rising Star

As the years passed, Grilka traveled to small towns across the cliffs, challenging anyone who would fight her. Sometimes, she earned a little money for her trouble. Other times, she fought merely for the respect it brought. Slowly, her name became known throughout the region, whispered by children in awe and grown men in grudging admiration.

Despite her expanding fame, she never lost her instinct to protect the weak. In every settlement she visited, she intervened whenever she saw someone bullied or oppressed. That fierce compassion earned her as many friends as her fighting prowess did. She became a folk hero, a symbol of defiance against those who used strength to brutalize rather than to protect.

"Fight for yourself," Halkor reminded her one day, "but remember why you fight. Strength is hollow if it doesn't serve a cause."

Grilka answered with a wolfish grin. "I fight for anyone who can't stand up on their own. That's the only cause I need."

It was this philosophy – equal parts aggression and empathy – that crystallized Grilka's identity on Valkorr. Her father grumbled about her neglected smithing lessons, and her mother fretted over the bruises and scars that now dotted her body. Yet neither could deny their daughter's unyielding passion. They watched with a mix of worry and pride as Grilka transformed into a warrior revered across the planet's harsh landscapes.

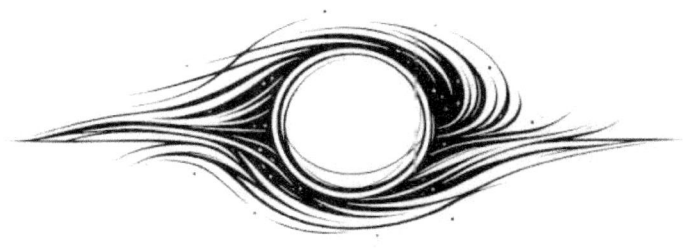

Chapter 4:

Beyond the Yellow Skies

Despite the adoration she received at home, a restlessness gnawed at Grilka. She had proven herself on Valkorr, but the stories of off-world arenas and cosmic mercenaries stoked a yearning for bigger challenges.

Her break came in her mid-forties (young by Valkorrian standards), when a traveling interstellar trader arrived in Kaeloria – the planet's bustling capital. The trader, an eccentric alien with too many arms to count, regaled the crowd with tales of distant worlds where warriors tested their mettle against strange, deadly creatures.

Grilka barged into the trader's presence at a local tavern, the rest of the patrons eyeing her suspiciously. "You talk of savage battles and fearsome foes," she said, hands planted on the table. "Take me with you, and I'll protect your caravan in exchange for off-world passage."

Intrigued by her reputation, the trader agreed. Her parents, torn between pride and anxiety, could only watch as she packed what little she owned – mostly weapons and gear hammered by her father, plus herbal tonics from her mother's collection – and boarded the rickety starship headed for the unknown.

A Galaxy of Trials

Thus began Grilka's life as a wanderer. From the moment she felt the lurch of a hyperspace jump, she knew she had entered a far larger and more perilous place than anything on Valkorr.

One of her earliest off-world battles took place in a zero-gravity ring, where opponents flew about in a dizzying spin. Grilka found herself grappling with a four-armed alien who could cling to the arena walls like an insect.

GRILKA

Though the environment was disorienting, she adapted quickly using her powerful arms to capture two of the alien's limbs and twisting with enough force to slam him against the ring's boundary. The crowd roared, stunned that a "primitive from Valkorr" had outmatched a species evolved for zero-g combat.

But not every job was a glamorous showcase of skill. She worked as a guard for merchant vessels, fending off space pirates who materialized from hidden asteroid belts. She served as a bouncer in seedy spaceport bars, breaking drunken brawls among a dozen alien races, each with its own brand of chaos. Everywhere she went, she adhered to an unspoken code: protect those who couldn't protect themselves.

That code was tested when one mercenary crew tried to conscript local villagers into forced labor. Grilka singlehandedly dismantled their plan – literally – by breaking arms and legs until the mercenaries fled. She helped the grateful villagers rebuild their homes, proving she could be as compassionate as she was fearsome.

Desert Moon Ordeal

Her most harrowing trial came after winning three consecutive rounds in a Hex fight on Threx Prime. As she and other combatants traveled home aboard a transport ship, they came under attack, forcing Grilka to evacuate in an escape pod that crashed on a nearby desolate moon. Stranded alone with a damaged transmitter, limited supplies, and the relentless heat, she survived for nearly three weeks by conserving every resource she had and adapting to the unforgiving environment.

On the brink of collapse, she was finally rescued after her failing transmitter signal was detected by a passing freighter. By the time they reached the nearest outpost, Grilka was thinner, scarred, but unbroken. That moon had tested not just her strength but her will to live.

Return to Valkorr

Though she accumulated countless scars – some from fights, others from betrayal – her spirit remained unshakeable. After nearly a decade of interstellar wandering, she found herself yearning to visit home. She returned to Valkorr with new confidence in her eyes and a new depth to her character. The girl who had daydreamed about distant arenas was now a seasoned warrior, tempered by the galaxy's cruelties but still guided by a fierce moral code.

Her homecoming was monumental. Locals who once teased her for her ambitions now hailed her as a legend. She accepted a public match against the region's mightiest wrestler, a hulking brute named Krogar who towered over everyone else in the village. The two squared off in a rocky amphitheater carved into the cliffside. The fight was brutal – a relentless exchange of bone-crunching holds and fierce strikes. In the end, Grilka triumphed by lifting Krogar clean off his feet and slamming him into the dust amid thunderous cheers.

Arrival at The Maw

Her journey led her to Valkorr's sprawling capital, Kaeloria, a neon-lit maze of towering spires and narrow alleys where traders, mercenaries, and wanderers of every stripe converged. There, she caught word that a demon woman – Lilith – had landed at the local spaceport and was making inquiries about a fighter named Grilka.

Following the rumors, Grilka found herself at The Maw, a notorious establishment known for its underground fighting pit. Illuminated by flickering lights, it was a den of raucous patrons, disreputable gamblers, and hardened warriors. The smell of sweat, cheap liquor, and old blood hung in the air.

Grilka, dressed in an orange fighter's outfit that showcased her formidable musculature, was already in a mid-brawl when Lilith entered. Grilka had taken on two Valkorrian men simultaneously in The Pit, each significantly larger to her size. They sneered at her, believing her to be a mere showboat. Within minutes, she had hammered one into unconsciousness. The second lasted longer, but Grilka eventually pinned him, her adrenaline-fueled roar echoing in the crowded space.

Breathing heavily and relishing the cheers of onlookers, she turned then her gaze locked on a seven-foot tall, red-skinned, horned figure with dark crimson skin and fiery black-and-red wings. Immediately, Grilka recognized the power in that stance, the unwavering confidence in that flaming gaze.

Lilith met her eyes from across the pit, offering a nod of silent respect before settling at a corner table. Intrigued, Grilka ended her match and headed to the bar to collect her winnings. Her manager, a short, nervous man, paid her with a trembling hand.

"I – I've never seen you fight quite so viciously," he stammered. "Why all this aggression tonight?"

Grilka scoffed, pocketing the Valkorrian credits. "People like that should know better than to provoke me." Then, glancing toward Lilith's corner, she smirked. "Besides, it looks like we have an interesting guest."

Kindred Spirits: The First Meeting

Grilka approached Lilith's table, ignoring the stares and whispers. She was used to being gawked at… and this demon woman likely was, too. The closer she got, the more she felt an odd, electric tension in the air, as though she were walking into the aura of a coiled tempest.

Lilith gestured at the seat across from her. "Impressive showing in The Pit," she said in a smooth, resonant voice.

Grilka pulled back a chair with a loud scrape and plopped down, crossing her muscular arms. "If that was just for show, you should see me when I'm truly motivated."

A faint smile touched Lilith's lips. "I've heard tales of your skill… and your sense of justice. I admire that. This galaxy has enough bullies."

Grilka nodded, feeling a spark of camaraderie. "Bullies," she echoed, her tone thick with disdain. "I've dealt with my share, on Valkorr and beyond. I don't tolerate scum who pick on the weak."

Lilith leaned forward, her fiery eyes keen. "Then we have a common cause. I'm recruiting warriors. Strong ones, sure, but ones who understand there's more to life than endless violence for violence's sake."

Grilka paused, sipping the Valkorrian ale a server had placed in front of her. It was bitter, but she found its bite oddly refreshing. "A demon with a conscience? That's a new one," she remarked, half-teasing, half-serious.

Lilith's eyes flashed with humor. "I could say the same for a Valkorrian fighter who stands up for the little guy. Sounds like we might be cut from similar cloth."

A Test of Strength

Their conversation was interrupted when the bar's ring announcer seized a microphone and bellowed for all to hear: "We have a new challenger in The Pit! Lilith, the Crimson Demon, has arrived on Valkorr! Word is that she seeks a match with none other than our undefeated champion, Grilka!"

Grilka's brow furrowed. She hadn't planned to fight again that night but the crowd, whipped into a frenzy by the announcer's words, began chanting her name. She cast a sidelong look at Lilith. "Is this part of your recruitment pitch?"

Lilith shrugged, unruffled by the scene. "I never back down from a good challenge. And if you're as good as they say, I want to see it firsthand."

A surge of excited tension rippled through the crowd

as both women stood. Grilka finished her ale with a swift gulp, her heart pounding in anticipation. She had faced countless fighters, but something about Lilith felt different. There was a sense of dignity and hidden pain in the demon's fiery gaze – a reflection, perhaps, of her own complicated path.

The Fight that Forged a Bond

The audience pressed in on all sides, forming a ring around the makeshift pit. Torches flared, casting dancing shadows across the sand. Grilka rolled her shoulders, sizing up her opponent. Lilith, in turn, slowly folded her black-and-red wings against her back, stretching her arms as the crowd's chants grew louder.

"Hope you're ready to get roughed up," Grilka said, cracking her knuckles.

"I can handle rough," Lilith replied with a confident smirk.

At the signal, Grilka charged, dust kicking up behind her. She swung a massive fist at Lilith's face only for Lilith to duck gracefully and counter with a lightning-fast left-handed uppercut to Grilka's ribs. The impact stung, but Grilka reveled in the challenge.

They exchanged blows in a punishing dance of fists and feet. Grilka's technique was raw power refined by years of discipline, her punches capable of toppling giants. Lilith countered with fluid speed and cunning, using her wings for bursts of momentum. At one point, Grilka managed to seize Lilith by the arm, intending to slam her into the sand, but Lilith twisted in midair, flipping free.

The crowd roared with its approval. Blood trickled from Lilith's lip, and bruises formed on Grilka's forearms, but neither gave an inch. They fought with an intensity that seemed to electrify inside the pit.

Then came a pivotal moment. Grilka, determined to end it, locked Lilith in a headlock, her biceps clamping down

31

like a vise. Lilith's face reddened as she gasped for air, her fiery eyes flickering with defiance. It looked like Grilka might force a submission, but in a sudden surge of demonic strength, Lilith unfurled her wings and shot upward, lifting Grilka off her feet. The crowd collectively held its breath as both fighters soared for a moment and then crashed back to the ground with a resounding thud.

Sand exploded in all directions. Grilka took the brunt of the impact, groaning as the air was knocked from her lungs. Lilith pinned her, arm pressed to Grilka's throat. The champion struggled, but the demoness held her down with surprising force. Pain radiated through Grilka's ribs, yet an odd sense of exhilaration and respect filled her chest.

"Yield," Lilith commanded, her voice hoarse but steady.

For a heartbeat, Grilka resisted. Then a broad grin split her bloody lips. She relaxed her muscles, conceding the fight with a faint laugh. "Fine," she rasped. "You've won."

Mutual Respect

Lilith released her hold, offering Grilka a hand. As Grilka rose to her feet, the raucous crowd erupted in cheers, half in astonishment that anyone had bested their champion. Both women stood amid the swirling dust, chests heaving, eyes locked in an unspoken recognition of each other's strength – both physical and moral.

Lilith wiped blood from her lip. "You put up one hell of a fight," she said, her words tinged with genuine admiration.

Still panting, Grilka nodded. "I've never met anyone who could do that. I... respect you."

Lilith extended a forearm in Valkorr's traditional gesture of camaraderie. "Join me, Grilka. I'm assembling a team to take on forces far worse than any local bully. Help me stand up for those who can't protect themselves."

For a moment, Grilka closed her eyes, feeling the

sting of her injuries and the fire in her soul. She thought of all the times she had fought for the powerless – on Valkorr, across the galaxy, on that desert moon. This was the next step, perhaps the greatest she would ever take.

"I'm in," she said finally, gripping Lilith's arm. "But don't think I'll go easy on you next time."

Lilith's laugh cut through the cheers and the torchlight. "I'd expect nothing less"

Aftermath and a New Path

As the crowd dispersed, some clapped Grilka on the shoulder, others stared at Lilith in awe. Grilka gathered her meager possessions, a worn duffel with gear and personal mementos, knowing she was about to leave Valkorr again. But this time, there was no trace of reluctance. She had found a reason, a cause that fused her love of combat with her drive to protect.

That same night, Grilka boarded the Scorpion with Lilith, stepping onto the starship's ramp under the neon glow of Kaeloria's skyline. The engines hummed, the ship vibrating with the promise of distant stars and uncharted dangers. Standing beside Lilith, Grilka felt a surge of anticipation.

"So," she muttered, glancing at the demon's crimson skin and imposing horns, "where to?"

Lilith's fiery gaze gleamed. "Wherever the fight needs us most."

With that, the Scorpion's doors sealed shut, and they lifted off into the swirling yellow skies leaving Valkorr behind but carrying its warrior spirit with them. Grilka looked out a porthole, watching the only home she'd ever known shrink beneath her. A pang of nostalgia twisted in her gut, but she reminded herself that she fought for more than memories now. She had aligned herself with a demon princess and, strangely enough, had found a kindred spirit.

Together, they would challenge the universe's

greatest threats. And for a woman who had dedicated her life to standing up for the little guy, Grilka couldn't think of any cause more worthy.

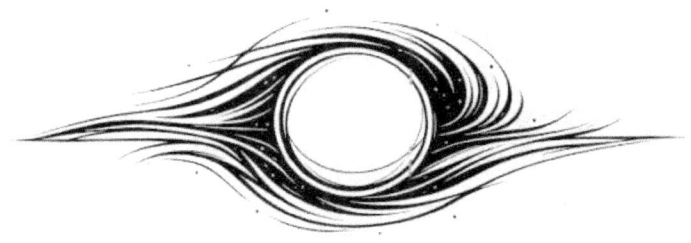

Chapter 5:

Frost and Friction

A low, moaning wind swept through Icelandia's capital city of Frostholm, carrying flecks of ice and snow across the grand causeways. Under the perpetual half-light of this frigid world, spires of crystalline ice rose like organ pipes towering toward the wintry sky. The sounds of daily life – merchants hollering, children laughing, scholars debating – reverberated through corridors carved directly into immense glaciers. At the city's center stood the Palace of Snowreach, a breathtaking structure hewn from solid ice and fortified by centuries of frost-crafting tradition.

Standing on one of the palace's high balconies, Freija – a young 115-year-old princess – inhaled the biting cold air as if it were a tonic. Her cobalt-blue wings, lined with white ice crystals, pressed against her back to protect her from the wind. She was petite, barely reaching five-foot-two, but emanated an aura of confidence that belied her stature. Her short, nearly white hair whipped across her cheeks, stinging her skin. Icelandia was unforgiving in its climate, but it was home and, in her eyes, a beautiful prison.

A few steps behind her, a second figure arrived with footsteps as soft as falling snow: Frigid, her identical twin sister except for having long white hair and being 10 minutes older. Physically, they were mirror images – same icy-blue skin, same silvery eyes – yet in temperament, they could not have been more different. Where Freija chafed at tradition, Frigid embodied duty. Where Freija's passions burned hot, Frigid's emotions were cool and measured.

Freija

Frigid stepped out onto the balcony, her own blueish-white wings folded neatly, the frost glinting along their edges. The swirl of her long ceremonial robes indicated she had just come from a council session.

"You've been standing out here since dawn," Frigid began quietly, her breath misting in the chill air. "Mother and Father noticed your absence at the court assembly."

Freija didn't turn around. She gripped the railing,

gazing toward the glacial plains that extended to the horizon. Beyond them, she imagined open skies, foreign worlds, and the possibility of a life not bound by a crown. "I know," she said finally, her voice steady but colored by frustration.

"You're supposed to attend these sessions, Freija." Frigid moved closer to her twin sister, her tone carrying more worry than reproach. "They're preparing us. Both of us. Ruling Icelandia will be our duty someday."

Freija's lips twitched in a half-smile. "Your duty, maybe. Not mine."

Twin Princesses, Divergent Paths

The tension between the sisters was an old tale in the palace. From infancy, they had been raised with the same tutors, the same physical training, the same expectations – *two* future monarchs, presumably in harmony, to guide Icelandia's destiny. Yet the older they grew over the decades, the clearer it became that their personalities diverged along a glacial fault line.

Frigid excelled at palace life: she navigated council debates with calm logic, could recite the genealogies of every aristocratic family by heart, and possessed a stoic presence that reassured subjects of her readiness to lead. Though not lacking in physical prowess – she, too, had inherited the kingdom's famed frost-based powers – Frigid used her gifts sparingly, preferring diplomacy over confrontation.

Freija, on the other hand, was famously restless. She thrived in combat drills and soared to unimaginable speeds with her wings. She trained with her twin ice-forged swords until her hands bled. She could outfly nearly anyone on the planet, darting like a blur with supersonic speeds across the Icelandic sky. But when it came to royal formality – council sessions, political alliances, or tedious banquets – she chafed at every turn.

No matter how often Frigid reminded her that duty to

their people was paramount, Freija heard only the faint call of distant worlds. *Somewhere out there,* she told herself again and again, *someone needs a warrior like me.*

A Kingdom of Frost and Tradition

Icelandia prided itself on a monarchy believed to be as unbreakable as the glaciers that dominated the planet's surface. King Frostran, their father, was a formidable ruler who had warded off several invasions in his youth. Queen Glaciana, their mother, was revered for her mystical abilities to shape and reinforce the ice structures that formed the bedrock of Icelandic civilization.

From childhood, the twins had been schooled not only in statesmanship but also in the unique frost-magic that ran in their royal blood. They could channel the raw cold into protective barriers, conjure ice shards as projectiles, and endure subzero temperatures that would kill most species. But while Frigid absorbed this training to fortify the realm, Freija felt the stirring of a different calling – a desire to test her might and discover her identity beyond the confines of frosty duty.

A Morning of Doubt

"Brooding," Frigid repeated softly, echoing an accusation often thrown at Freija. "You might deny it, but you can't hide your frustration." She placed a gentle hand on Freija's shoulder, ignoring the wind that rushed between them. "Talk to me, sister."

Freija exhaled slowly, pivoting to face Frigid. "I suppose I *am* brooding," she conceded, "but it's more than that. Sometimes, I feel like these glaciers are walls pressing in on me from all sides."

Frigid frowned, her eyes reflecting concern. "You know I don't want you to feel trapped. This is our home."

Freija gestured to the city below. "It's your home. It

is *my* home, too – but I'm not built to stay. I see these spires, the council halls, and all I can think is: *I'm wasting time.*"

Frigid folded her arms, hugging herself against the cold. "*Wasting time* doing what? Father says we have negotiations with the clans on the Southern Continent next week. There's a shortage of ice crystals in that region, and they want our help. It's an important matter for the stability of the entire planet."

Freija shrugged, unappeased. "And that's important for you, I know. But for me? The entire universe is out there, Frigid. Did you ever wonder if this monarchy, these politics, are just... too... too small?"

A flicker of hurt passed through Frigid's silver eyes. "You think our kingdom is *small?*"

"I think the galaxy is enormous," Freija responded gently, "and we know little about it. There are rumors – dark tidings of a war brewing in star systems beyond our sight. I've heard the name 'Necra' repeated in hushed whispers among traveling merchants."

The mention of Necra made Frigid purse her lips. "I heard those rumors too. But they're just that... rumors. Even if someone named Necra is conquering distant worlds, Icelandia has always stayed neutral. Our planet is hardly on anyone's chart."

Freija brushed her hand through her short hair. "Neutral until trouble finds us. We might be remote, but no place stays untouched forever. You said yourself we need to keep the clans of the Southern Continent satisfied or risk internal strife. What if an external threat – someone powerful – decides to claim our resources? We should be the ones out there gathering allies, not cowering behind ice walls."

The Council Summons

Before Frigid could respond, a palace guard approached, bowing low. "Your Highnesses, the royal council is requesting your presence in the main chamber.

King Frostran and Queen Glaciana require your input on new trade agreements."

Freija exhaled, glancing at Frigid. "You go," she said, her voice hollow. "I'll be there soon."

With a sympathetic nod, Frigid turned to leave. "All right," she said softly, "but please don't be long. Father hates it when you're late."

Freija watched her sister depart, feeling a pang of guilt. She knew she was shirking the responsibilities she was born into, yet her heart pounded with a longing she couldn't ignore. Standing alone, she closed her eyes and let the wind envelop her, imagining for a moment that she was already free – soaring above starlit realms, fighting for a cause she had yet to name.

In the Hall of Elders

The council chamber was an immense oval room carved out of dark blue ice, illuminated by hovering crystal lanterns that refracted light into patterns on the walls. Rows of council members – aged dukes, wise advisors, and a few younger nobles – were seated around a tiered arrangement of seats. At the center there were two ornate chairs reserved for the princesses.

Frigid was already seated by the time Freija arrived. Their parents presided over the affair from a raised platform. King Frostran's posture was as rigid as a glacier, radiating authority, while Queen Glaciana's serene composure spoke of unshakeable confidence in her rule.

Freija approached her seat, conscious of the stares. She settled next to Frigid, steeling herself for the monotony of political discourse.

One of the council elders, an older woman with icicle-like hair, rose to speak. "Majesties, we have an urgent matter regarding trade routes with the clans in the Southern Continent. Their resources have dwindled, and they request additional shipments of infused ice crystals."

Frigid leaned forward, her voice calm. "Have we assessed if our stores can accommodate their request without depleting our own supply?"

The elder nodded. "Yes, Princess Frigid. We estimate we can provide the shipments, but it would require rationing in Frostholm. Citizens might experience a short-term strain."

King Frostran glanced at Freija. "What say you, my daughter? We must be of one mind in this."

Freija hesitated, feeling a mix of discomfort and annoyance at being put on the spot. "We could, um, negotiate terms... possibly ask them to um... supply us with additional raw materials from their region to offset our own usage?"

The suggestion was not unwise, but it was delivered without Freija's usual spark of conviction. Sensing her hesitation, the King's brow furrowed. "You don't sound certain."

Freija shifted, her cheeks warming. "I'm not. This isn't where my strengths lie, Father."

A hush fell over the chamber. The King and Queen exchanged a subtle glance, concern etched on their faces.

Queen Glaciana addressed her gently. "We value your input. Both of you are destined to rule. You must learn this side of governance, Freija, just as you've mastered the sword."

Freija tensed, her wings were quivering. *Must I?* she thought bitterly. Her mind drifted to the rumors she had heard about cosmic battles, unstoppable foes, and heroes who rose to face them. *I'd rather fight a horde of invaders than endure another moment of these negotiations.*

Still, she gave a tight nod. "I understand, Mother."

The meeting dragged on for over an hour, topics ranging from border disputes to ice-harvest quotas. Freija's mind wandered, her boredom intensifying. Finally, the session ended. As the council members filed out, King

Frostran beckoned both daughters to remain.

He fixed Freija with a stern look. "My child, you are strong – and we love you for it. But a ruler must also be patient and diplomatic. You cannot dismiss these duties."

Freija's eyes flicked to Frigid, who stood quietly at her side, head bowed respectfully. She felt resentment welling up: *Frigid is good at this. I'm not.* Yet, she couldn't voice that frustration without sounding childish.

"I won't fail our people," Freija said at last, though her tone lacked enthusiasm. "But… I'm not Frigid."

Queen Glaciana stepped forward, placing a cool hand on Freija's cheek. "No, you're not. You are yourself, and you have gifts that your sister does not. We just want you to embrace all aspects of royalty, not run from them."

Freija managed a faint smile. "I'll try."

Frigid offered a reassuring nod, but the worry in her gaze was clear. She knew Freija well enough to sense that her sister's compliance was half-hearted at best.

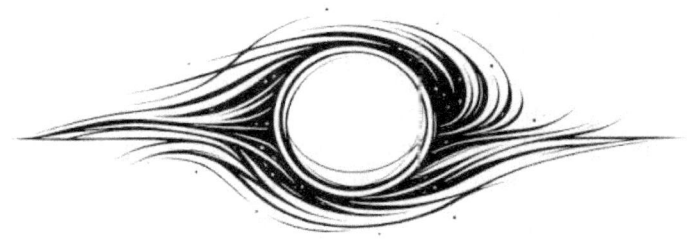

Chapter 6:

A Demon's Arrival

Word spread quickly among the palace staff that an off-world merchant ship had landed outside Frostholm. Visits from foreign travelers were not unheard of, but they were rare enough to stir curiosity. As was custom, the King and Queen dispatched a guard to greet the newcomers, to determine if they posed a threat or brought interesting trade goods.

Freija heard the commotion from her private quarters – chatter among servants about "strange visitors" who carried a foreboding air. She pressed her ear to the frosted window, straining to catch the rumors.

"They say one is a tall demon with crimson skin and black wings…"

"The other is a green-skinned warrior with fiery orange hair… I heard she's as strong as five men!"

Freija's heart thrummed. *Demon with black wings? On Icelandia!?!* The notion sounded like something from old legends. Most interstellar travelers who came here were mere traders or explorers. She had never heard of a demon among them.

Without a second thought, Freija grabbed her twin ice swords, strapped them to her back, and rushed out of her room. She navigated the palace corridors swiftly, ignoring the startled looks from guards who bowed as she passed.

She arrived at the palace courtyard, where a handful of Icelandic warriors stood, spears at the ready. Opposite them, at the wide gates, were two imposing figures indeed: one a towering seven-foot-tall female demon with horns and wings tinted black and red and the other a six-foot tall muscular, green-skinned woman with wild orange hair.

King Frostran and Queen Glaciana were also present, both wearing neutral expressions that concealed their wariness. At a respectful distance stood Frigid, her wings partially unfolded, a subtle indication of readiness for combat if it came to that.

Freija pushed through the small crowd. "Mother, Father," she said, her voice catching as she took in the sight of the strangers, "who are these people?"

Queen Glaciana answered without taking her eyes off the visitors. "They call themselves Lilith and Grilka. They come from beyond our star system, seeking an audience."

A Stranger's Entreaty

Lilith stepped forward removing a thick coat. Even at a glance, Freija recognized an air of tremendous power and a hint of weariness around the demon's fiery eyes. Lilith bowed with surprising grace, wings folding behind her. Grilka crossed her thick arms, eyeing the palace guard with an almost dismissive confidence.

"King Frostran, Queen Glaciana," Lilith began, her voice resonant, "and your esteemed princesses. We apologize for arriving unannounced. Our journey brought us here in search of potential allies... or at least a worthy warrior with a particular skillset."

A murmur swept through the courtyard. King Frostran's brows furrowed. "Worthy warrior? For what purpose?"

Lilith exchanged a glance with Grilka, who gave an almost imperceptible shrug. The demon turned her attention back to the monarch. "To stand against a grave threat named Necra, who is amassing power across multiple sectors. We are recruiting fighters – people of extraordinary ability. In our search, we came across rumors of a princess in Icelandia with wings that can shatter the sound barrier. A warrior adept with ice-forged blades."

Freija's heart pounded in her chest. *They're talking about me.* She felt Frigid's gaze from the side, a mix of alarm and curiosity shining in her sister's eyes.

"I've heard the name Necra," King Frostran said, stroking his chin. "But our kingdom remains neutral in most off-world conflicts."

Lilith inclined her head. "Neutrality is admirable until neutrality becomes impossible. Necra's dominion grows. Eventually, if she isn't stopped, there may be no corner of the galaxy safe from her reach."

The words fell like stones in the hushed courtyard. Some guards shifted uncomfortably; others maintained a stony facade. Queen Glaciana's expression was unreadable as she weighed these claims.

Frigid interjected, her voice collected yet firm. "We appreciate the warning. But Icelandia has endured many threats in its history without stepping beyond our planetary defenses."

Lilith's eyes flicked to Frigid, then to Freija. "We won't force you. We only ask that you'll consider our cause. If your famed warrior Freija, is as... is half as skilled as rumor suggests, she could be pivotal in saving countless lives."

Freija's fingers curled around the hilts of her swords. Lilith's words struck her with electrifying resonance, as if someone had peeled back the layers of her frustration to reveal a path she'd been yearning for. To fight for a cause *beyond* Icelandia. To protect not just her homeland but perhaps entire worlds.

King Frostran's voice cut through her reverie. "Our princesses are valuable to us. We do not give them up lightly to off-worlders with unverified claims."

At that, Grilka spoke for the first time, her tone edged with impatience. "Look, your majesty, we didn't come here to cause trouble. We're simply telling you the truth. If you want to bury your heads in the sand… or rather… in the ice and pretend none of this affects you, fine. But Necra's no joke."

A ripple of offense traveled through the guards, but Lilith laid a calm hand on Grilka's arm. She looked again at Freija, eyes narrowed as if gauging her mettle.

"Perhaps," Lilith said softly, "Freija can speak for herself?"

A Sister's Dilemma

All eyes turned to Freija, who stood with her wings partially flared, torn between deferring to her parents and leaping at the chance that shimmered before her like a sunlit glacier. Her throat tightened.

Frigid broke the silence. "Sister don't be rash," she warned quietly, stepping to Freija's side. "We know nothing of these people except rumors. They could be leading you into a war you're not prepared for."

A spark of rebellion flared in Freija's heart. "I've *craved* to be prepared for something greater, Frigid. You know that."

She turned to her parents, mustering the calm that had always eluded her in palace affairs. "Mother, Father… you've both taught me to use my strength to protect Icelandia. If these travelers are right… if Necra's threat is real… then I can protect Icelandia by going out there and confronting it before it arrives at our doorstep."

King Frostran's jaw tensed. "It's too dangerous. We cannot let you vanish into unknown realms from the word of strangers. We have our own methods of defense."

Freija's gaze darted to Lilith, who remained poised yet earnest. Something in the demon's eyes told Freija that this threat was no mere bedtime story. She could *feel* the sincerity, the urgency.

"But Father," Freija persisted, "every story we've heard from off-world travelers says the same: Necra conquers systematically, leaving ruin behind. Would you have Icelandia become an isolated fortress, waiting for trouble to come? Let me do what I was trained to do… fight."

A heavy silence fell. The King and Queen exchanged troubled looks.

The Twins Speak

Frigid inhaled, trying to remain the voice of reason. "Freija, I understand your desire to explore and do something meaningful, but you'd be out there alone with them. You barely know them."

Freija laid a hand on Frigid's arm. "I know your worries, sister. But you've also known me all our lives. I can handle myself. And this… this might be my chance to do more than shuffle paper in council halls."

Tears glinted in Frigid's silver eyes, though none fell. "I don't want to lose you."

Freija's heart was clenched. "You won't. I'll always be your sister. But I can't stay here, waiting. I have to *act*."

The tension thickened until Queen Glaciana raised a gloved hand. "We shall speak privately as a family," she declared. Turning to Lilith and Grilka, she added diplomatically, "We appreciate your honesty. Give us time to consider."

Lilith gave a slight bow of her head.

A Family Divided

That evening, Freija joined her parents and sister in

a secluded sitting room. A soft, bluish glow emanated from ice chandeliers overhead, casting gentle light on the velvet drapery that insulated the space. King Frostran's visage was stern, Queen Glaciana's thoughtful, and Frigid's torn between loyalty and dread.

"Freija," the Queen began, "do you truly wish to leave Icelandia with these strangers?"

Freija clasped her hands together. "Yes. I believe it's the right choice… for me, and our kingdom. If Necra is as formidable as rumors say, we can't just hide."

King Frostran frowned. "You assume we'll be overrun. We have centuries of proven defenses. Perhaps they will never come, and this demon – Lilith – merely wants to exploit your skill for her own ends."

Freija shook her head. "That's possible. But I've weighed the alternative. Doing *nothing* is a greater risk, in my eyes. If Lilith is lying, I can always return. But if she's telling the truth and we refuse to help, we may regret it when it's too late."

Frigid spoke up, her voice subdued. "Is there nothing I can say to change your mind, Sister?"

Freija's gaze softened. "You know me better than that."

A long pause passed. Then Queen Glaciana rose from her seat, approaching Freija. "Your father and I have considered everything. While we disagree with your methods… and fear for your safety… we will not chain you here. If your destiny calls you beyond Icelandia's skies, we won't stand in the way."

King Frostran's expression tightened in silent disapproval, but he nodded. "A monarchy that stifles its heirs' true path does more harm than good. But be warned: if you leave with them, we cannot guarantee your safe return. Nor can we use the kingdom's resources to aid you in distant star systems."

Freija nodded. "I understand."

Frigid's eyes glimmered with unshed tears. She lunged forward, pulling Freija into a trembling embrace.

"Promise me you'll be careful," she whispered, the words catching in her throat. "Promise you'll come back... if it grows too dangerous. Please."

Freija held her just as tightly, as if trying to memorize the moment. Her voice cracked under the weight of everything she couldn't say. "I promise."

And with that, her fate – like frost forming on still water – was sealed.

The Final Night in Icelandia

News of Freija's impending departure rippled through the palace. Some of the staff whispered that she was abandoning her birthright, while others admired her courage. Freija spent her last night gathering supplies: a small bag of personal items, a set of specialized ice crystals used for healing, and her beloved twin ice swords. She hesitated over a few keepsakes – like a carved ice figurine Frigid had made in their youth – but decided to keep her load light.

In the hours before dawn, Freija found Frigid pacing in the corridor outside her chambers. The elder twin wore a look of deep worry.

"Can't sleep," Frigid admitted. "I keep thinking of all the ways this could go wrong."

Freija offered a reassuring smile. "I know. Believe me, I'm anxious too. But I have to do this."

Frigid reached into a pouch at her waist, pulling out a small amulet fashioned from pure, transparent ice. At its center, a swirl of frost shimmered faintly. "Take this," she said, pressing it into Freija's hand. "It's a Frostheart charm. The palace artisans crafted it for me, but I want you to have it. It's said to protect the wearer in the harshest storms."

Freija's throat constricted. "Frigid, I – thank you."

Frigid swallowed hard, tears threatening to spill. "I'm not sure it'll help against cosmic wars, but... if there's any piece of Icelandia that can keep you safe, this is it."

They embraced, clinging to each other in silent farewell. Neither spoke of the possibility that they might never see each other again.

Dawn Flight

The morning arrived with a pale gray sky. A swirl of snow drifted down as Freija, accompanied by Frigid, made her way to the courtyard where Lilith and Grilka waited by their ship. King Frostran and Queen Glaciana looked on from the palace steps, faces set in regal composure despite the emotion simmering underneath.

Lilith inclined her head in polite greeting. "Princess Freija, are you certain of this path?"

Freija stepped forward, her chin held high. "I am."

Grilka, arms folded, gave a curt nod. "You've got guts, kid. I like that."

With a final glance at her family – her father's stoic pride, her mother's composed sorrow, her sister's bright tears – Freija unfurled her cobalt-blue wings. She let out a long exhale, feeling both fear and exhilaration churn within her. *This is it,* she thought. *I'm leaving everything behind to protect it.*

She turned toward Lilith and Grilka with tears in her eyes. "Let's go."

The three boarded the Scorpion amid the hush of onlookers. Engines roared, and the ship lifted from the icy ground. As it rose, Freija moved to a viewing port, pressing a hand against the cold glass. In the courtyard below, she could still see Frigid – small and solitary, wings folded, gazing skyward.

"Goodbye, sister," Freija whispered, tears running down her face. *I'll return one day, stronger, braver, and with the power to keep you safe.*

Moments later, the Scorpion shot through the cloud-filled sky, leaving behind the spires of Frostholm and the only life Freija had ever known.

An Oath of Purpose

As the craft ascended into the upper atmosphere, Freija felt the planet's gravitational pull lessen. She spread her wings slightly within the confined space, as if testing the air of freedom. Lilith piloted the ship with practiced ease, while Grilka monitored readouts at a weapons console. The synergy between them hinted at many shared battles.

Freija took a seat in the only remaining seat – the co-pilot's, her swords clinking gently. Her entire body buzzed with a mix of dread and excitement. She thought about the rumors of Necra, of unstoppable armies, of star systems on the brink of destruction. *This is no longer a daydream. This is war.*

Yet she did not regret her decision. For the first time, she felt a sense of alignment between her abilities and her purpose. *I'm not a stateswoman,* she reminded herself. *I'm a warrior. It's time to fight for something that really matters.*

A moment later, Lilith glanced over her shoulder, her voice low and earnest. "Freija, I sense your resolve. Know that once we pass beyond your home star system, there may be no going back until we face Necra. Are you ready for that?"

Freija looked up, meeting Lilith's fiery gaze. "I am," she replied, adrenaline surging. "I don't care how tough Necra's armies are. If they threaten innocent lives, if they threaten Icelandia or any other planet, I'll do whatever it takes to stop them."

Lilith's lips curved into a small, satisfied smile. "Then welcome to the cause."

From the weapon's console, Grilka shot a wry grin. "Don't think it's all glory, kid. We'll be up to our necks in danger. But if you can fight half as well as you can talk, we might just stand a chance."

Freija matched her grin. "Danger is what I'm best at

handling."

Reflections

As the ship accelerated, shimmering lines of starlight streaked past the viewports. Freija caught her own reflection in the glass: a young woman with frost-blue skin, short white hair, and wings that glowed faintly in the cosmic light. She thought of the responsibilities she had left behind and the new burdens she had taken up. The Frostheart amulet given by Frigid dangled at her neck, reminding her of home.

Was this the right decision? The question gnawed at her. Yet she also felt a deep calm, as if this path was the only one that had ever truly called her. She had no illusions that the battles ahead would be easy, but at least now she fought on her own terms.

Within a few minutes, the Scorpion left Icelandia's orbit, plunging into the star-speckled void. The planet shrank in the distance until it was just another icy dot. Freija closed her eyes, etching the image of Frostholm's spires into her memory. She prayed silently that her family would remain safe, that her sister would thrive as the future ruler, and that someday she could return with victory in hand.

Farewell, Icelandia. Until we meet again.

With that final thought, she exhaled and opened her eyes to the vast universe. For the first time, her relentless longing for "something more" felt sated. She was forging her destiny among the stars, no longer caged by the weight of a crown, but free to wield her blades in a cause that spanned solar systems.

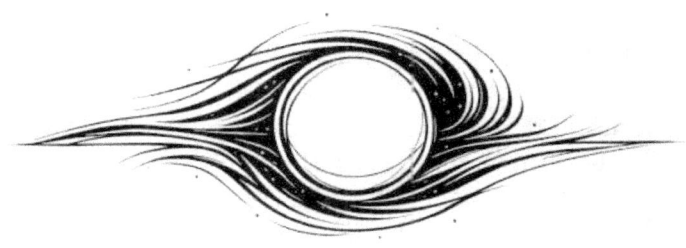

Chapter 7:

Wings of Ice and Fire

The Scorpion soared in silent flight through the star-filled vacuum. Its hull being a mix of dark metals and patchwork repairs. Inside the cockpit, Lilith guided the vessel with practiced hands, her black-and-red wings folded behind the pilot's seat. Grilka monitored sensor readings at a weapons console, her orange hair glowing under the subdued cabin lights.

At the rear of the cockpit, Freija hovered on the threshold, arms folded, wings tucked close to her petite frame. It had been mere hours since she had left Icelandia behind, but her mind was already racing ahead – toward the challenges awaiting them in the cosmos. She still wore the Frostheart amulet from her twin sister, Frigid, as a tangible tie to home.

Lilith, sensing Freija's hesitation, glanced over her shoulder. "Are you alright?"

Freija exhaled, forcing a smile. "I'm fine, just… adjusting."

Grilka tapped a few buttons and turned her gaze. "Adjusting to space travel, or adjusting to leaving your royal life behind?"

"Ummmm… both," Freija admitted.

Inside the Scorpion

The ship's interior was more spacious than Freija expected for the three of them with corridors leading to a small armory, a communal lounge, a kitchen, a small one-person bathroom, a small cargo bay, and sleeping quarters comprising of two bunk beds and two chairs bolted to the floor. Though the Scorpion's design carried a hint of infernal influence, evident in the runic etchings and the warm glow of the engine core, it wasn't wholly bad. Freija suspected Lilith had scavenged or modified it from various missions.

Lilith leaned over to Freija who was sitting to her right. Lilith stated, "You are sitting in the co-pilot's seat which also includes communication and navigation. Since you're with us, you might as well familiarize yourself with the basics. There will be times when there are all hands on deck. Plus, we need to ensure we don't get lost in the huge cosmos."

Freija turned to Lilith. "I'm new to starships," she admitted, "but if it's anything like a battlefield, I'll manage."

Lilith grinned. "Spoken like a true fighter. We have a modest arsenal – plasma cannons, and short-range missiles. She can explain those better than I can."

Freija ran her finger across a series of glowing glyphs on a side panel. "Each symbol is a rune?"

Lilith nodded. "They correspond to different ways to navigate through hyperspace without colliding with any other ships or planets. That is a pretty important step when you are traveling faster than light and everything in the galaxy is constantly moving."

Freija's pulse quickened at the notion. Even after leaving Icelandia, the prospect of real combat – on foreign ships or unknown planets – still felt surreal. But it also invigorated her. *This is what I wanted: a chance to make a difference.*

Charting a Course

After Freija familiarized herself with the console, and the ship on auto-pilot, they moved to the lounge. Lilith pulled out a holographic image device. She turned it on, and a holographic star map projected into the room. Pinpoints of light represented known systems, many labeled with cryptic or ominous notes: "Hostile territory," "Necra's incursion," "Alliance outpost," and so on.

Lilith tapped a control, zooming in on a cluster of star systems. "We have a lead on Necra's forces around the Archon Corridor. Rumor says she's subjugated three planets in that sector. One of the main ones is a planet called Jaze."

Grilka muttered a curse under her breath. "Three more than last time we heard. She's expanding fast."

Freija studied the map intently. "And what's our plan? Charge in, guns blazing?"

Lilith shook her head. "We're outnumbered if we do that. We need more allies. That's part of why we came to Icelandia. We hoped to recruit not only you but perhaps some of your best warriors."

Freija grimaced, recalling how resolutely her parents defended Icelandia's neutral stance. "My people are… cautious. You're lucky I joined."

A wry smile from Lilith. "Indeed. We'll gather more allies elsewhere, but at least we have you, Grilka, and me. Three strong fighters are better than none… or one."

Grilka folded her arms. "We should also see if we can track down others who hate Necra's tyranny. Mercenaries, freedom fighters… anyone crazy enough to stand with us."

Lilith nodded, shifting her gaze to Freija. "You said you can fight at incredible speeds in open air. How does that translate in a no gravity?"

Freija pressed her lips together. "I've trained in low temperatures and high altitudes, but never in the void of space or in low gravity. My wings are powered by my frost energy and physical strength; I'm not sure how they'll function without atmospheric lift."

Grilka snorted. "Might want to suit up before you try stunts outside the hull."

A flicker of annoyance crossed Freija's face. "I'm not suicidal. I plan to adapt, not just fling myself into open space."

Lilith raised a hand to forestall any bickering. "We'll figure something out. If we end up in a ground skirmish on a planetary surface, your speed will be invaluable. If we face boarding parties, you can outmaneuver them in corridors. One step at a time."

Freija nodded, reassured by Lilith's calm authority. She appreciated direct leadership as someone who could see the bigger picture. *Good,* she thought. *I might actually belong here.*

Bonding Over Sparring

Their first day traveling together ended with an impromptu sparring session in the ship's cargo hold. Lilith insisted they get a feel for each other's fighting styles. Grilka was enthusiastic, she always enjoyed a chance to brawl, and Freija yearned to test her new allies' capabilities.

The cargo bay was a wide-open space, littered with crates of supplies. Lilith cleared a section by pushing crates aside effortlessly, revealing a decent patch of floor. She drew her black-flamed swords, their infernal fire dancing along the blades.

"I'll go first with Freija," Lilith announced. "Grilka, watch and give pointers. Then you can jump in."

Freija unsheathed her twin ice swords. Their edges shimmered with frost, the near-freezing aura causing steam to rise from the warmer ship's air. She spread her wings, bracing for a quick leap if necessary.

Lilith took an opening stance, demonic wings half-spread. "Ready?"

Freija nodded, lunging forward faster than expected. She pivoted on her lead foot, aiming one blade in a thrust toward Lilith's midsection. Lilith parried with a flick of her flaming sword, sparks of ice and fire colliding in a hiss of steam.

They exchanged a rapid series of blows – Freija's smaller frame darted around Lilith's tall form, while Lilith countered with strong, well-placed strikes. Whenever Freija tried to exploit her own speed advantage, Lilith shifted her wings for a burst of momentum, meeting her head-on.

"She's quick," Grilka observed from the sidelines, arms crossed. "But Lilith's got the reach."

A grin flickered across Freija's face. "Time to use that *speed*," she muttered. Summoning her frost energy, she dashed around Lilith's flank, delivering a flurry of slashes that forced Lilith to pivot rapidly. Frost crystals formed in the air around them, colliding with embers of infernal flame.

Lilith responded by unleashing a small surge of demonic power, momentarily intensifying her blades. The heat forced Freija to recoil. "Nice trick," Freija admitted, stepping back to shake off the sudden warmth that threatened to melt the frost on her arms.

With a final clash, Lilith locked blades with Freija. Their faces were inches apart, one set of eyes blazing red, the other shimmering silver. They smiled at each other, acknowledging a mutual respect.

"Well done," Lilith said, lowering her swords. "Your technique is polished, and your speed is incredible. You'll do fine."

Grilka clapped slowly. "My turn?"

Lilith smirked. "Sure. But let's switch it up – Freija and I together against you."

Grilka's eyebrows rose. "Ganging up on me? Fine. Don't hold back."

Freija shot Lilith a sidelong look, exchanging a nod. The two advanced on Grilka, who cracked her knuckles with a grin. Within seconds, the cargo hold filled with the clang of steel, the sounds of fists on armor, and the swirl of cold and heat. Freija found herself weirdly exhilarated. This was her new life – sparring with a demon princess and a green-skinned bruiser, forging bonds in the crucible of combat.

By the end, they collapsed onto crates, sweaty and laughing, each bruised but unbroken.

"You both are insane," Freija said, catching her breath. "And I love it!"

Grilka wiped her brow. "Welcome to the team, ice princess."

Revelations of War

Later, the three sat around the ship's small lounge table, nursing drinks – hot tea for Freija, something far stronger for Grilka, and an unknown demonic brew for Lilith. The overhead light flickered, as though uncertain whether to remain steady or yield to the darkness.

Lilith pulled up a holographic screen from the table's built-in projector. It displayed images: star systems ravaged by war, shattered planets, fleets of battered ships. Freija's eyes widened at the scope of destruction.

"These are from worlds Necra has already attacked?" Freija asked quietly.

Lilith nodded, sipping her brew. "She doesn't always destroy a planet outright. Often, she conquers it, forces its inhabitants to serve. Those who resist are made examples of. Entire cities left in ruin."

Grilka chimed in, her voice grim. "We've been to some of these worlds or… what was left of them. We've saved who we could and fought where we had the advantage. But Necra's armada grows larger than ours. We need more warriors, more resources."

Freija felt a chill that had nothing to do with her frosty powers. The worlds beyond Icelandia were far harsher than she ever imagined. She pictured her sister, safe behind the palace walls, and was relieved Frigid had chosen to remain. *Still, how long until danger knocks on Icelandia's door?*

"What do we know about Necra herself?" Freija asked.

A heavy silence followed.

"Not as much as we'd like," Lilith admitted.

Freija's grip tightened around her teacup. The idea of facing such power both terrified and intrigued her. "Do we have a plan?" she pressed. "We can't just randomly pick fights."

Lilith set down her drink, eyes narrowing thoughtfully. "Our plan is evolving. First, we'll gather intelligence and allies. Then, target Necra's operations strategically, cut off supply lines, liberate strongholds, weaken her from within. We're a small force, so we must be cunning."

Grilka's voice turned harsh with remembrance. "Cunning, yeah. Because brute force alone doesn't work. We tried that once." She gazed at Lilith, who offered a solemn nod in return.

Freija hesitated before asking, "What happened?"

Lilith exhaled. "We attacked one of Necra's outposts head-on. Our group was bigger then. A small coalition of rebels. Necra retaliated with destructive black magic, turning our own fallen against us. We barely escaped with our lives."

A hush fell. Freija realized that Lilith and Grilka had already lost friends in this war. *They don't show it outwardly, but they carry that sorrow.* A pang of empathy coursed through her.

"I'm sorry," she said softly. "I won't let you down."

Lilith offered a sad smile. "We appreciate that. But understand, Freija: we're not looking for a martyr. We need a comrade who knows when to fight and when to retreat. I sense you have the wisdom for that."

Freija straightened. "I do And I'll learn from your

mistakes and successes."

They clinked cups, a silent pact forming under the flickering light.

Training in Zero-G

Over the next few days, the Scorpion traveled through FTL lanes between star systems. To pass the time constructively, Lilith proposed another challenge: training in zero-gravity. She deactivated the ship's artificial gravity in the sealed cargo chamber, instructing Freija to adapt her fighting style to weightlessness.

Freija's wings beat reflexively as she floated off the floor. She spun awkwardly, struggling to maintain orientation. "This is... weird," she muttered, a wave of vertigo hitting her.

Lilith drifted nearby, extending her hand to steady her. Without gravity, Lilith's large black-and-red wings looked even more dramatic, floating behind her like dark sails. "It takes practice. Try using small bursts of your wings to maneuver."

Freija complied, flapping gently to propel herself across the chamber. She bumped into a wall. Grilka snickered from the corner.

"Oh, hush," Freija shot back, pushing off the wall to glide more gracefully. She discovered that focusing her frost energy could help anchor her. She conjured a small patch of ice on the floor to provide traction for a springboard leap. It worked – launching her across the chamber in a controlled arc.

Lilith nodded with approval. "Exactly. What you must do is to create makeshift gravity or friction. Not every battlefield has normal gravity. Some are in orbit, others on low-gravity moons."

Freija smirked. "I'd give anything to see Grilka do this," she teased.

At that, Grilka scowled. "Nah, I'll wait till we need

it. I prefer having my feet on the ground, thanks."

Still, the training sessions continued, with Freija rapidly improving. By the end of the second day, she could fight using her ice swords in zero-G drills without spinning wildly. It was a victory she savored, a testament to her adaptability. *I truly belong here,* she thought again, feeling the quiet satisfaction of mastering a new skill.

An Encounter with a Refugee Ship

On the fourth day, an emergency beacon drew the Scorpion's attention. A small, battered freighter drifted near an asteroid belt, broadcasting a repeated distress signal. Lilith immediately altered course.

"Might be a trap," Grilka warned. "Pirates sometimes do that."

"Or it might be genuine," Lilith countered. "Either way, we should investigate."

Freija's heart thumped. *My first real mission with them.* She strapped her swords on, readying for potential conflict.

They approached cautiously, scanning for life forms. The readings were faint but indicated a handful of survivors. The ship's hull was scorched and pockmarked, likely from weapons fire. With careful maneuvering, Lilith docked the Scorpion to the freighter's airlock. Freija and Grilka readied themselves at the hatch, while Lilith monitored from the cockpit.

The hatch opened to reveal a dimly lit corridor. The flicker of damaged lights revealed drifting debris. A hush of stale air greeted them. Freija's breath felt heavy in her chest as she advanced, each step echoing on the metal floor.

"If anyone's alive in here," Grilka muttered, "they're in rough shape."

They found the survivors – a ragtag group of aliens and humanoids – holed up in what appeared to be a storage bay. As Freija and Grilka entered, the refugees cowered, some of them raising makeshift weapons.

"We mean no harm," Freija called. "We picked up your distress signal."

A tall, gaunt alien with dusty blue skin – perhaps the captain – stepped forward. "You're… not with Necra?"

Freija shook her head. "No. We're here to help."

Relief washed across the survivors' faces. The captain slumped against a crate. "Our engines failed after a skirmish. Necra's patrol ships destroyed our escorts. We escaped, but not for long if you hadn't come."

"We have med-kits and supplies," Grilka said gruffly, "assuming you don't shoot us."

A few refugees laughed shakily, lowering their makeshift weapons. Freija's gaze swept the room. She spotted a pair of children among them – tiny figures, clinging to an older woman's arm. The stark fear in their wide eyes tugged at her heart.

"Let's get you to our ship," Freija offered gently. "We can't fix this wreck easily, but we'll provide safe passage to a better port."

The group murmured gratitude. As they gathered supplies, a battered soldier stepped forward, tears brimming in his eyes. "You don't know what this means. Necra's men would have killed us if they found us. We're just… ordinary people, trying to survive."

Freija knelt before the soldier, touching his shoulder. "You're not alone anymore."

A Taste of the Larger War

They guided the refugees into the Scorpion, settling them into the lounge and cargo bay. Lilith, after verifying that no threats remained, joined them. As she comforted the children, offering them water and food, Freija realized she was witnessing exactly why they fought: not for glory, nor conquest, but to protect those too vulnerable to defend themselves.

One of the older refugees, her face lined with sorrow, thanked Freija profusely. "When we saw your horns" – she nodded at Lilith, then at Freija's wings – "we thought you might be allied with those monsters. But you're... good."

Freija forced a smile. "There's good and bad in every realm of the galaxy, every species. We just happen to be on the side that won't let Necra terrorize the galaxy."

The woman's eyes shone. "May the stars bless you."

Freija emerged from the cockpit corridor. "Nearest friendly spaceport is two days away if we deviate from our route. Should we do it?"

Lilith studied the weary faces of the survivors. "Yes," she said. "We'll bring them somewhere safe. Our mission can wait."

Freija nodded, warmed by Lilith's compassion. She had left Icelandia to find a grand purpose, and here it was – in the battered faces of survivors who needed hope.

That evening, after the refugees were settled, Freija excused herself to the cockpit. She gazed through the forward viewport at the swirling cosmic expanse. Tiny elongated lines of light shimmered in the distance. *So many worlds; so much injustice,* she mused. It was simultaneously daunting and inspiring.

Lilith approached softly, resting her hand on Freija's shoulder. "You handled them with kindness. Are you sure you were meant to be a warrior and not a diplomat?"

Freija let out a soft laugh. "Diplomacy in a war zone, maybe. All my life, I believed my only skill was fighting. But if that skill can protect people like this, then... I finally feel proud of it."

Lilith offered a small, encouraging smile. "You'll do great things, Freija. Mark my words."

Freija's gaze never left the stars. "I intend to."

Echoes of Home

Later that night, after checking on the refugees,

Freija retired to a small bunk assigned to her. She placed her swords in a corner, carefully setting the Frostheart amulet on a small shelf. Thoughts of Frigid welled up, and a pang of longing struck her chest. *Is she doing fine? Are my parents coping?*

She remembered their parting words, the tension in Frigid's eyes, the paternal worry in her father's voice. She remembered standing on the palace balcony, complaining about feeling caged. Now, aboard the Scorpion, the entire universe felt open. *Was it worth hurting them to find freedom?*

Despite a swirl of emotion, she felt no regret. She was forging a path that served a greater cause. If that cause kept even one child from losing their home to Necra's onslaught, then it was worth the risk – and worth the sadness of leaving.

Her eyelids grew heavy. She drifted into a restless sleep, dreams filled with swirling ice and flame, images of battling undead legions, and the faint whisper of Frigid's voice urging her on.

Arrival at the Refuge

True to Freija's estimate, two days passed before the Scorpion arrived at Traxis Outpost, a frontier station orbiting a dusty, orange-tinted planet. The outpost was a modest hub for traders, mercenaries, and those fleeing conflict zones. Ringed by battered docking platforms, it bustled with haggard travelers from hundreds of races.

Lilith guided the Scorpion to a designated berth. As soon as they lowered the ramp, station medics and relief workers came aboard to assess the refugees. Freija stood by, offering reassurance. Some refugees clung to her hands, reluctant to let go of the security she and her new comrades had provided.

"You'll be safe here," Freija told them gently. "The outpost might not be a paradise, but you can recover, find work, or move on somewhere new."

The battered soldier who had wept earlier approached; posture straighter now that his wounds were bandaged. "Is it too much to ask for your name, so we can remember the one who saved us?"

Freija's cheeks colored slightly. "Freija of Icelandia. But just Freija will do."

He nodded, eyes wet. "Then thank you, Freija of Icelandia. We won't forget."

Lilith, Grilka, and Freija spent the next hour ensuring the refugees had initial funds for lodging that were pulled from the Scorpion's limited coffers and setting them up with the local relief offices. By the time everything was settled, the outpost's neon lights flickered on, painting the dock in harsh yellow and pink hues.

Exhausted, the trio returned to the Scorpion's ramp, breathing in the stale, metallic air of the docking bay. Grilka stretched, wincing at a sore shoulder. "We've done our good deed for the day. But we still need fuel, supplies, and a plan."

Lilith nodded. "Let's see if we can find any fresh intel on Necra's movements while we're here. Maybe someone's seen her fleets passing near Archon Corridor."

Freija hefted a bag of credits, gleaned from trading some Icelandic frost crystals. "Count me in. I'm ready to test out these so-called mercenaries." Her wing feathers ruffled with anticipation.

The Seeds of a Legend

They stepped onto the outpost's main promenade, a winding corridor lined with makeshift shops, flickering signs, and shadowy alcoves. Strange faces glared or regarded them with curiosity – traders, smugglers, and bounty hunters, each with a story. Freija felt a rush of excitement, tempered by the knowledge that danger lurked around every corner.

"We're definitely not in Icelandia anymore," she

quipped, half to herself.

A passing merchant overheard her eyeing her frost-tinted wings. "Icelandia, you say? Heard that's a quiet planet of ice-folk. Surprised one of you left."

Freija mustered a polite nod but said nothing more. *Yes, I left. Because I needed to fight for something bigger.* She remembered the frightened children on the refugee ship and the weariness on Lilith's face when discussing battles lost. The galaxy needed defenders, and she intended to stand among them.

Her mind flashed to Frigid, to the vow she had whispered: *I'll return someday.* The question was, would it be as a triumphant warrior who helped dismantle Necra's empire, or as a broken fighter with only regrets?

No, she resolved, *I'll come back strong and victorious.*

Lilith and Grilka led her toward a dingy bar rumored to be a good place for gleaning info. As they crossed the threshold, Freija's wings brushed the rickety doorframe, signifying her new presence in a wider world. The clang of alien music and the sharp tang of spiced liquor assaulted her senses, but she strode forward without flinching.

"Eyes up," Grilka murmured. "We're in a nest of scoundrels."

Lilith smirked. "My kind of place."

Freija's heartbeat quickened, adrenaline surging. *I'm finally living, not just existing.* She squared her shoulders, stepping into the murky haze. Whatever challenges lay ahead – betrayal, fierce battles, unimaginable horrors – she would meet them head-on. This was the life she had longed for among the glacial spires of Icelandia, and now, with new allies at her side, she was determined to make every moment count.

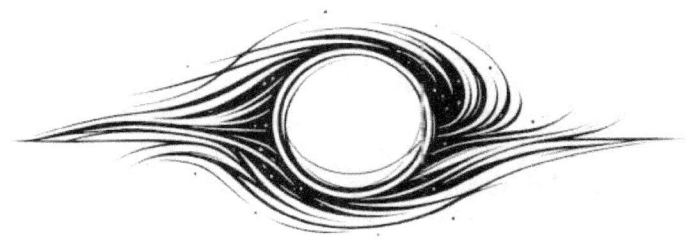

Chapter 8:

The Team's First Battle

Docking Bay E on Traxis Outpost smelled of burnt circuitry and stale air. Machinery hissed and rattled in the dim light, while overhead, rows of flickering neon panels buzzed faintly. At the center of the hangar stood Lilith, her tall frame wrapped in a black-and-crimson cloak that just barely concealed the edges of her massive wings. She regarded the ragged crowd of refugees shuffling aboard the Scorpion.

The outpost itself was a frontier hub orbiting a stormy planet named Harridan. Grilka grumbled as she stood beside a shipment of supplies they had bartered for: a pallet of energy cells, canisters of purified water, and some contraband stims gleaned from a local smuggler. Her broad, green-skinned shoulders strained against the weight of a power conduit she was hefting onto a gravity cart.

"Any chance we can get this loaded without half the station gawking at us?" Grilka muttered. "We're an odd sight," Lilith replied, half-smiling. Her black-and-red wings rustled underneath the cloak as she checked the final cargo manifest on a handheld device. "Don't mind them."

Across the bay, Freija carefully guided two wide-eyed children up the Scorpion's loading ramp. The siblings clutched battered bags and wore matching expressions of relief and exhaustion. They were among the dozen or so refugees Lilith's team had rescued from the drifting freighter only days ago. Freija's blueish-white wings lifted slightly, offering the children a sense of protective calm.

"Watch your step," Freija said gently, helping them across a creaky metal plate. Her voice was soft, but behind it throbbed an undercurrent of worry. *These kids have seen enough horror to last a lifetime*, she thought. *But at least they'll be safe with us – for now.*

Despite the swirl of engine noise, hissing pneumatic lifts, and the echo of heavy footsteps throughout the docking bay, Lilith found herself momentarily lost in thought. Each refugee boarding the Scorpion represented another life pulled from the edges of a widening conflict – a conflict spelled out in every rumor about the dark figure named Necra. Although they'd only heard fragments, each new tale painted Necra as a power-hungry conqueror ravaging distant systems. Even here at Traxis Outpost, battered survivors of unknown wars whispered the same name in hushed fear.

"Hey, demon," came Grilka's gruff voice, snapping Lilith's focus back. "We've got a problem."

Grilka jerked her chin toward the outpost's main corridor, visible through the open hangar doors. A sharp-eyed guard from the local security detail sprinted toward them, armor dented, breath labored. Alarm sirens began blaring overhead.

A Dire Warning

The guard stumbled up to Lilith, nearly doubling over to gasp for breath. "Out… outside the station… vessels approaching. *Hostiles.*"

Lilith's fiery gaze hardened. "Pirates?"

The guard's eyes flicked uneasily between Lilith's imposing horns and Grilka's hulking form. "They call themselves… the Legion of Baron. We've heard rumors they serve an overlord who wants to claim this region. They're armed to the teeth, and they're heading this way."

Baron. Lilith exchanged a tense glance with Grilka. She'd encountered the name once before – spoken by a desperate merchant they'd passed on Harridan. The merchant had lost an entire fleet to Baron's forces, describing them as "cybernetic nightmares" loyal to a self-styled "conqueror." Lilith's instincts flared with alarm.

"Where are they hitting first?" she demanded.

"They've already infiltrated sections of the outpost's outer ring," the guard coughed, wiping sweat from his brow. "Security can't hold them off much longer. We need all the help we can get."

Lilith felt the tension mount. They had intended to leave Traxis Outpost discreetly, ferrying refugees to a safer station in the next system. But if Baron's legion boarded the outpost, that plan was about to be shattered.

Grilka clenched her fists. Her jaw tightened. "We can't just let them butcher everyone. We owe the outpost for giving us supplies and medical care."

Freija hopped down the Scorpion's ramp, wings fluttering with nervous energy. "Lilith, if these are the same brutes that keep popping up all over, we have to stop them. Or at least slow them down so everyone here can evacuate."

"We're with you," Lilith told the guard, her voice low but resolute. "Show us where."

Relief flooded the guard's features. "Docking Ring C… that's where the first wave landed. Hurry!"

Into the Frey

They sprinted through the outpost's labyrinthine corridors. Flickering overhead lights revealed battered walls plastered with holographic advertisements for shady weapons dealers and cheap lodging. Residents scrambled in panic, carrying what few belongings they could gather.

Alarm sirens shrieked in a shrill chorus that echoed off the metal bulkheads.

In the corridor beyond an automated security gate, Lilith and her companions found their first glimpse of Baron's legion: a row of cybernetically enhanced soldiers marching forward in perfect lockstep. Each soldier wore black armor with inlaid glowing crimson lines. Their faces, half-concealed behind metal plates, bore no emotion. The lead soldier hefted a heavy plasma rifle, scanning for targets.

Freija halted at the edge of a corner, peeking around just long enough to catch a volley of lasers scorching the corridor walls. "They're well-armed," she hissed, wings bristling. "I can try taking them from above if I can find a vantage point."

Grilka gave her an up-nod. "You do that. Lilith and I will hold them at ground level."

Before the group could formalize a plan, a new volley of plasma bolts chewed through the security gate behind them. Station guards yelled in terror as they were thrown aside by the onslaught. Smoke filled the air. Lilith's wings unfurled in a flash, her fury igniting. *Nobody else dies if I can help it.*

"Freija," Lilith barked, "take to the rafters. Knock out their heavy guns. Grilka, with me!"

Grilka bared her teeth in a grin that was half excitement, half rage. "Let's crush 'em."

Freija dashed to a ladder leading up to a narrow maintenance ledge overhead. Her ice-forged short swords clinked lightly as she climbed. Despite her anxiety, she pushed fear aside and opened her wings, flitting across the ceiling beams with nimble grace. Once perched above the corridor, she locked eyes on the legionnaires below, searching for a weak point in their formation.

Lilith charged forward, her massive black-and-red wings flaring wide. Twin fiery swords burst into life in her hands. The nearest soldier raised a rifle… too slow. Lilith's blade cleaved through the soldier, sparks and molten metal spraying across the floor. The soldier toppled backwards, its circuits exposed.

Grilka lunged beside her, using a dented steel girder as an improvised club. She slammed it onto two more cyber-soldiers, crushing their exoskeletons with a sound like shattering glass. Fragments of armor skittered across the deck.

"Don't get cocky," Lilith warned, spotting a second squad stepping into the corridor from a side hatch. Their rifles glowed with charging plasma. "More inbound!"

Battle in the Corridors

High above, Freija inhaled sharply, focusing. *This is it, my chance to help from the skies – even if the 'sky' is just a metal roof.* She gripped her swords, conjuring a swirl of frost around the blades. With a swift pivot, she launched two razor-sharp shards of ice at the cluster of reinforcements. The shards bit deep into the corridor floor, cracking open a coolant pipe that spewed frigid vapor.

Confusion spread among the legionnaires. Frost coated their metal limbs. Their movements slowed, seizing under the sudden cold. Grilka let out a triumphant roar and charged forward, smashing them aside like frozen statues. One soldier raised an arm, trying to muster a shot, but Grilka tore the limb free, sparks flying.

Meanwhile, Lilith squared off against a particularly formidable trooper sporting heavier implants – a gleaming cybernetic eye and reinforced chest plating. The soldier rumbled forward, launching a sizzling bolt of red energy that crashed into Lilith's left wing. She hissed in pain, staggering. A wave of fury coursed through her veins. *I've endured the fires of Hell. This is nothing.*

She thrust her flaming blade forward, aiming for a joint in the soldier's armor. The trooper parried with a vibrating blade that hummed with disruptive energy. Sparks flew. Lilith twisted, swinging her second sword upward in an arc. The trooper's guard broke just long enough for her to stab straight through the chest plating. With a jolt of demonic flame, the soldier collapsed, smoking.

"Lilith, behind you!" Freija called, her voice echoing from above.

Lilith whirled, just in time to see two more troopers leap from a side passage. She deflected one volley of plasma but took a grazing hit to her arm. Pain flared. Grilka, finishing off another trooper, roared in frustration. "We can't keep this up forever! There's more coming!"

Freija soared down from her vantage in a blur of cobalt feathers, slashing in mid-flight to give Lilith a moment's reprieve. The corridor was rapidly filling with the remains of decimated legionnaires, but the outpost's flashing alarms indicated more firefights raging deeper inside.

Pushing Back the Tide

With a shared nod, the trio advanced, clearing each corridor systematically. The outpost's layout became a maze of battered bulkheads and crisscrossing catwalks. Grilka took point, her thick musculature absorbing the brunt of enemy fire. Lilith moved in tandem, swords dancing with lethal precision. Whenever a soldier attempted to circle behind them, Freija swooped down, her ice powers freezing limbs and weapons before finishing them off with swift strikes.

Yet for every squad they scattered, new combat units arrived. Over the distant roar of gunfire, Lilith could sense the stutter of heavy footsteps – like mechanical siege engines. *Artillery or mechs?* She gritted her teeth. "Freija, scout ahead. If they've got heavier forces, we need to know."

Freija nodded, breathless from exertion. "On it, Captain." With a beat of her wings, she ascended an access ladder to the overhead walkway. Swiftly weaving past flickering lights, she slipped through a partially collapsed archway leading to the next ring of the outpost.

"They're bringing in a big walker!" Freija yelled down a moment later, voice echoing in the tight corridor. "Some kind of multi-legged mech. There's a *lot* of troopers with it!"

Lilith's stomach twisted. A walker would tear through the outpost's interior. Dozens, maybe hundreds, of civilians and refugees were still pinned behind locked-down bulkheads. *We have to stop that machine before it tears the station apart.*

Turning to Grilka, she spoke quickly: "We can't handle a walker in a tight corridor. We'll funnel it into Docking Ring D – there's more open space there, near the outer hull." She raised her voice to address Freija: "Drive it to the ring if you can. We'll meet you there and take it down together."

Freija soared back, eyes wide but determined. "I'll lure them. Hurry!"

Showdown in Docking Ring D

Docking Ring D was a wide circular passage that granted access to cargo bays used by large freighters. Hazy lights flickered across the open floor, scattered with crates and half-loaded cargo containers. The walls curved around in a wide loop. A perfect place for a last stand if it came to that.

Lilith and Grilka arrived first, using the reprieve to catch their breath behind a towering column of sealed cargo. Lilith flexed her bruised wing, wincing. "This better work," she muttered, voice tight with pain. "If that walker blasts the hull open, we're all vented into space."

Grilka wiped sweat and grime from her brow. "We got no choice, demon. We fight here or watch them slaughter everyone."

Before Lilith could respond, the ring trembled with the thunderous steps of approaching metal legs. Freija darted into view, pursued by a wave of troopers and an eight-legged mech walker that clanked and hissed with lethal grace. Its main cannon glowed hot with charging plasma.

"Get behind something!" Freija shouted, landing near Lilith and Grilka. "That cannon's about to…"

A high-pitched whine split the air as the walker fired. A massive energy beam streaked across the docking ring, scorching the floor and punching a hole in a stack of crates. Fragments of superheated metal rained down. Lilith shielded her face with a wing, grateful for Grilka's quick action in pulling her behind cover.

The legion troopers spilled out in formation around the mech. Their rifles whirred, unleashing another barrage. Lilith clenched her jaw, adrenaline surging anew. "Together, we take out that walker first. Freija, freeze its legs. Grilka, help me carve a path."

The Final Push

Freija sprang upward, wings flashing. She circled around the mech, dodging plasma bolts. With each swoop, she shot blasts of frost aimed at the walker's jointed legs. Ice crackled, slowing the mech's movement. It fired wildly, beams ricocheting off the ring's curved walls. One shot blew a chunk out of the ceiling, showering sparks across the battlefield.

Meanwhile, Grilka stormed forward, ignoring the stinging blasts that peppered her shoulders and back. She barreled into the line of troopers, slamming them aside with a steel cargo strut. They toppled like dominoes, metal limbs clanging on the deck. "I've got your back, Lilith!" she roared.

Lilith charged in behind Grilka, swords flaming with demonic intensity. She deftly cut through the troopers Grilka knocked aside, ensuring they stayed down. Her heart pounded like a war drum. *Just a few more steps until we're in strike range of that mech…*

74

Freija's freezing blast finally built up enough layers of ice around the walker's joints to jam its motion. The multi-legged beast twisted, trying to free itself, but the thick frost held. Its cannon flared, then dimmed as the internal coolant system seized.

"Now, Lilith!" Freija yelled from above.

Lilith sprang, using Grilka's broad shoulder as a launchpad to vault higher. She soared in a swift arc, wings beating furiously. With a growl, she plunged both flaming swords down at the mech's central power module – a glowing sphere on top. Metal shrieked as the blades penetrated. A wave of heat pulsed out, forcing Lilith to yank her swords free and fling herself clear.

Sparks flew, and the walker's legs convulsed. The cannon sputtered once, then exploded in a burst of red-orange fire. Grilka shielded her eyes, the shockwave nearly throwing her off her feet. Freija wobbled in midair as the station deck rocked.

But it was enough. With a tortured groan, the walker collapsed, its metal carcass smoking, half-frozen and half-melted. The few remaining troopers scrambled to regroup – but Grilka, her chest heaving with triumph, roared at them, brandishing her battered cargo strut. They turned and fled into the labyrinth of corridors, leaving their shattered war machine behind.

Victory and Departure

Silence finally fell over Docking Ring D, broken only by the crackle of small fires and the echo of distant alarms. Lilith sagged to one knee, breathing hard. "That... that should buy time for the outpost to evacuate," she said, her voice husky.

Grilka leaned against the smoking mech, wincing from various burns and cuts. "Hah... Next time we charge for these rescue missions. My shoulders are killing me."

Freija touched down gently, folding her wings. Her

face glistened with sweat, but a tentative smile curved her lips. "We did it," she breathed. "The outpost can make a stand now."

They heard pounding footsteps and turned to see the same guard from earlier approach with a handful of battered security officers. Relief and awe shone in their eyes. "You saved the outpost," the guard said, voice quavering. "We've already begun evacuating civilians who can't fight. The rest of us will hold off any stragglers."

Lilith nodded, though her expression remained grim. "We can't stay. Too many refugees are counting on us to get them off-station. But if Baron's behind this, he won't stop. Be prepared."

They retraced their steps to Docking Bay E, weaving through corridors littered with debris. At times, they spotted groups of frightened families huddling in side passages, waiting for rescue or an all-clear. Lilith paused to point them toward the security bunkers, noticing the weary acceptance on their faces. *They've seen more violence than they ever asked for,* she thought.

When the trio arrived at their hangar, the Scorpion's engines were already warmed, thrumming in readiness. The refugees on board gazed out from windows or peered down the ramp. Some looked terrified, but the children Freija had helped earlier waved excitedly, relieved to see their protectors return alive.

"Close up the bay," Lilith ordered. "We're lifting off now."

Grilka quickly sealed the cargo holds, while Freija guided the last lingering outpost staff away from the ship's ramp – no more passengers could fit. The Scorpion had reached capacity.

As the ramp hissed shut and the docking clamps released, Lilith moved to the cockpit, ignoring the stinging burn on her wing. She settled into the pilot's seat and flicked switches overhead. "Everyone, brace yourselves."

The outpost's hangar doors groaned open, revealing the star-flecked darkness of space. With a roar, the Scorpion shot forward, leaving Traxis Outpost behind amid swirling lights and drifting debris. Inside, the refugees clung to whatever handholds they could find. Grilka dropped into the copilot's seat, glaring at the radar readouts. "No pursuit – yet" she noted.

Freija exhaled, leaning against the cockpit doorway. "We might have slowed them, but I doubt Baron's legion is beaten. We're just one step ahead, for now."

Lilith guided the ship onto a safe jump vector, the tension in her shoulders easing slightly. "We'll deliver these people to safer territory," she murmured, "then we'll see what else we can do to stop Baron's expansion."

A hush settled among them. Outside the viewscreen, the stars stretched into streaks as the Scorpion engaged its faster-than-light hyperdrive. Traxis Outpost, once a precarious haven, receded into the cosmic distance.

"This fight is far from over," Lilith said softly, her voice resolute.

Grilka nodded, pounding a fist into her palm. "We'll be ready."

Freija's wings folded behind her, the corners of her lips set in a determined line. "We always are."

Their hearts were heavy with the knowledge of the battles to come, yet steady in the conviction that they fought for those who couldn't fight themselves. For now, they had won one more victory by shielding one more corner of the galaxy from oppression. And so, the Scorpion flew onward, carrying the new team into a new horizon of danger and hope.

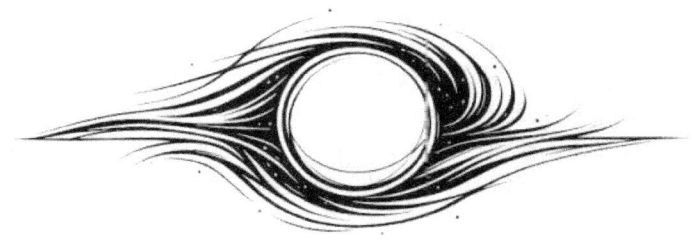

Chapter 9:

The Path to Earth

After dropping off the refugees at a neighboring outpost, Lilith sat in the pilot's seat, taking a look at the holomap aboard the Scorpion, arms folded, wings partially unfurled in the confined space. An image flickered above the device – a small, blue-green planet labeled Earth. Soft overhead lighting cast wavering shadows across her black-and-crimson wings, lending a somber weight to her announcement.

"There's a rumor about a ninja fighter on this planet," Lilith said, her voice low but purposeful. "A smuggler on Traxis Outpost claimed she could take down an entire squad of mercenaries on her own. If it's true, we might gain a valuable ally for the battles ahead."

Across from her, Freija leaned in, her ice-blue wings twitching with interest. "Earth, huh?" she mused, resting a slender hand on the edge of the holomap. "I've heard of it. Should we head there next?"

Lilith gave a small shrug. "If someone can hold off off-world attackers with little more than instinct and grit, that's someone I want on our side."

Grilka, arms folded over her broad chest, glowered at the rotating hologram of Earth. "I won't argue about adding more muscle," she said in a deep, direct tone. "But there's talk of an asteroid belt or debris field blocking the fastest route. Seems like it's more trouble than it's worth."

Lilith's jaw tensed. That same concern had weighed on her mind. "From everything we've heard, the standard routes to Earth are slow and controlled by the Federation's bureaucracy. We don't have the time or resources for a prolonged detour. But this direct path..." She paused, her gaze flicking toward the star-laden viewport. "It's scattered with debris from old orbital outposts and broken asteroids. The local name for it is the Belt of Vinedar. According to charts, few captains have tried to cross it safely."

Grilka exhaled a rough breath. "I hate tiptoeing around hazards we can't just smash. Rocks, debris, it's all random. One miscalculation, and the Scorpion gets turned into scrap metal."

Freija pursed her lips, her cobalt eyes darting over the digital readout of the belt's density. "I'll be honest – I'm not thrilled about weaving through a mess of floating boulders. But this might be our only shot at a quick route. If the ninja rumor is true, we can't pass it up."

Lilith nodded, feeling tension through her body. "Exactly. We need every edge against the threats we're facing – Necra, Baron, and whoever else emerges."

Freija drummed her fingertips on the console. "So we fly in carefully, yeah?"

Grilka let out a humorless laugh. "Yeah, carefully. Because that's never gone wrong before."

A brief silence followed, each of them replaying old battles in their minds – victories that were always overshadowed by the lingering threats on the horizon. Finally, Lilith straightened, her wings rustled.

"It's settled then. We aim for Earth. If I can pilot us through that field, we might just find our next teammate."

A hint of a grin tugged at Grilka's lips. "You sure you're up to it, demon? I remember that near-miss in the

Gorgal Nebula."

Lilith bristled, half in mock annoyance. "You're never letting me live that down, are you?"

Grilka smirked. "Definitely not. But we trust you anyway."

With that, Lilith stepped away from the holomap, exhaling to steady her racing pulse. The conversation resolved, they set a course, each aware that the next few hours could be as dangerous as any firefight they'd faced. A hush of anticipation and apprehension spread across the ship as they initiated the journey.

Approaching the Belt of Vinedar

The Scorpion slid through the star-speckled darkness, guided by Lilith's hand on the pilot's yoke. Freija and Grilka hovered behind her, scanning readouts and sensor data. The engines vibrated through the metal deck with a steady hum, but the tension within the cockpit was unmistakable.

Lilith's eyes flicked from the viewport to the console displays. "We're closing in. The debris field is massive – chunks of old stations and big asteroids colliding over millennia."

Grilka grunted. "I see a chunk of hull plating from a tanker, maybe. Perfect. Let's try not to add our hull plating to that drift."

Freija forced a lighthearted tone, though her wings twitched with nerves. "I'm sure Lilith's got this. She's basically a pro by now."

The jab – equal parts genuine encouragement and teasing – brought a ghost of a smile to Lilith's lips. "Let's hope so."

In the forward viewport, swirling shapes gleamed in distant starlight. Dust clouds drifted between jagged asteroids. Twisted wreckage glinted – a grim testament to those who had attempted this route and failed. Lilith's heartbeat quickened. She refused to let fear seize her, though doubt gnawed at her mind: *I learned to pilot out of necessity, not love. Do I truly trust my skills here?*

She swallowed the doubt. *We have no choice.*

Into the Fray

From the navigation array from the co-pilot's seat Freija's voice rose as she examined the sensor panel. "The belt's outer edge has a cluster of mid-sized asteroids spinning at weird angles. We might want to skirt that area. Going through the center is suicide."

Lilith licked her lips, nodding. "Alright, we'll try hugging the perimeter." She toggled a thruster control. "Adjusting course."

Still, when the Scorpion entered the debris zone, it was like wading into a cosmic minefield. Metal shards and shards of rock pelted the deflector shields with a persistent ping. Lilith's wings shuffled behind her, a silent expression of her tension.

Grilka frowned at the weapons array screen. "We've got a big chunk up ahead, rotating at some nasty velocity. If it swings the wrong way, we'll be eating vacuum."

The proximity alarm shrieked. Lilith hissed, flicking off the alarm and jerking the ship to starboard. An elongated asteroid tumbled past, close enough for them to see pitted craters along its surface.

Freija gripped the console seat, wincing at the near miss. "That was... very close."

A forced laugh escaped Lilith. "No problem. Piece of cake." Then, more quietly, "We can't keep that up for every rock."

Grilka tapped a control, scanning the rotating patterns of the asteroids. "Look for a gap. Once we find a corridor, accelerate and pray we don't get hammered by any stray chunks."

Lilith exhaled hard. *Praying isn't exactly my style,*

she mused inwardly, but she nodded. "Freija, keep an eye on that top drift. If you see anything crossing our path."

Freija was already scanning a rotating mass of smaller fragments drifting overhead. "Copy that. They're unpredictable. I'll shout if we need to swerve."

A Brush with Disaster

The corridor Lilith aimed for seemed momentarily clear. She nudged the throttle, pushing the Scorpion into a quiet pocket flanked by two large asteroids. For a heart-stopping instant, everything seemed fine – then the sensors wailed. A battered piece of space station, still bristling with twisted beams, careened into view from behind the nearest rock.

"Lilith!" Grilka barked.

Lilith rammed the controls, pivoting the ship. The fragment whirled with terrifying speed, and a jagged metal spar scraped across the port side shields, showering the viewport in sparks.

Grilka yelped as she nearly toppled against the console. "Deflectors are failing on that side!"

Lilith's breath caught. She hammered a sequence to reroute shield power. "Hold together, hold together!"

With a sizzle, the chunk of debris spun away, leaving the Scorpion battered but intact. The onboard lights flickered and then steadied. A wave of relief washed over Lilith, though her hands shook on the yoke.

"Damage?" she asked tersely.

Grilka scanned the readouts. "Shields down to fifty percent. Hull plating's dented, but no cabin breach."

Freija exhaled, a half-laugh, half-sob. "Okay. Everyone's alive. Let's not do that again."

Lilith managed a grim nod. "Agreed."

Threading the Needle

They pressed on, the interior of the belt becoming increasingly choked with swirling rock. Lilith spotted a swirl of dust coalescing around a massive asteroid that had smaller chunks orbiting it like a deadly halo. She felt a flash of panic. *I'm not good enough for this.* But she forced it down. If she balked now, they'd get pinned between hazards.

She inhaled and spoke quietly: "We'll circle wide around that big one. Stand by for thruster adjustments." She gently eased the yoke, feeling the Scorpion tilt. Her wings pressed painfully into the seat's back, but she couldn't worry about comfort now.

Grilka's gaze flickered between readouts and the swirling darkness beyond. "We can do this, demon," she said, her voice firm. "We've done worse."

Freija braced herself while sitting in the co-pilot's seat. "At least with robots and foot soldiers, I can fight back. Hard to freeze an asteroid."

"Focus, you two," Lilith murmured, though a small smile tugged at her lips. Their banter, anxious as it was, reminded her that they weren't alone. *We're the Crimson Alliance,* she told herself. *We've survived so many battles. I won't let a few drifting boulders kill us now.*

Carefully, she angled the ship around the large asteroid's spin. For a few agonizing minutes, time seemed to slow. The only sounds were the hum of the engines, the distant ping of smaller debris on the shields, and the ragged breathing of three anxious warriors. Every so often, Lilith would tap the thrusters, weaving them through clusters of drifting chunks. Freija pointed out stray fragments that threatened the flank while Grilka monitored engine output.

When at last they maneuvered clear of the swirling halo, a patch of open space emerged – stars shining unobstructed. Freija let out a gleeful laugh, her wings fluttering as though she might take flight there in the cockpit. "Yes! That's the last big cluster, right?"

Lilith squinted at the scope. "One more thick band up ahead, but it's smaller – just smaller rocks. We can handle it."

Grilka let out a breath like a half-snort of relief. "Then let's get it done."

Breaking Free

It took another tense fifteen minutes to pass that final band of debris. The Scorpion twisted, pitched, and thrummed as Lilith coaxed it through the final labyrinth. At last, the proximity alarms fell silent, and the swirling mass receded behind them. The belt glimmered in the rear camera view, a cosmic ring of chaos that they'd managed to conquer.

Lilith sagged in the pilot's seat, her shoulders trembling from the overload of adrenaline. "We made it," she whispered, half in disbelief.

Grilka rubbed her neck, exhaling like she'd just lifted a mountain. "Damn straight we did. Knew you had it in you."

Freija practically danced over to Lilith, clasping her on the shoulder. "Nice flying, demon. I'd almost call that graceful... Almost."

A breathy laugh escaped Lilith. "Could do without the near-death adrenaline, but thanks." She flexed her wings, wincing at the aches from tensing for so long. "Let's never do that again if we can help it."

Freija leaned back in her seat, wings folding neatly behind her. "One can dream. I'm just glad we're not space dust. Now we can focus on this Earth ninja rumor, right?"

Lilith set a course on the nav console, ensuring they'd have a clean jump to Earth's orbit. "Yep. Short jump, then we'll be scanning Earth. If the outpost's intel is right, we'll find our warrior soon."

Grilka arched an eyebrow. "It'd better be worth it after all this."

Lilith chuckled. "If it isn't, then we drag him back through that belt as punishment."

Freija smirked. "Harsh, but fair."

Toward Earth

With the Belt of Vinedar behind them, the Scorpion cruised in relative calm. Lilith allowed herself a moment to relish the star-filled view beyond the cockpit. Her heart rate finally slowed, replaced by a trickle of excitement about the next step – finding a ninja on a planet could be a challenge itself.

The overhead lighting flickered softly, signaling the Scorpion's readiness for faster-than-light transition. Grilka confirmed the coordinates, and Freija strapped herself in ready for the jump. Lilith glanced over her shoulder at them.

"Hold on. We'll need all our luck. But I've got a good feeling."

Freija grinned. "We overcame bigger odds before. Let's see how this so-called Earth ninja stacks up."

Grilka cracked her knuckles. "If they're half as good as rumored, she'll be a huge asset. If not..." She shrugged. "We move on."

Lilith keyed in the final commands and then pressed the lever that initiated the jump. Stars elongated into bright lines, and the Scorpion hummed with a rising pitch. Everything outside blurred, leaving only the promise of Earth ahead.

In the hush that followed, Lilith closed her eyes, exhaustion mingling with triumph. They had survived the Belt... her biggest challenge yet as a pilot. Now a fresh challenge beckoned: recruiting an unknown warrior on a distant world. If they succeeded, they might become a team that she was calling the *Crimson Alliance*, strengthening their cause against cosmic tyrants like Baron and Necra.

We can do this, Lilith thought, letting the star-streaked view calm her. *We're unstoppable when we work together.*

As the Scorpion soared onward, her heart lifted with

a spark of renewed purpose. The future was uncertain, but with each hurdle they overcame, the team grew stronger. Earth, and whatever fierce ally awaited them there, was now only a single jump away.

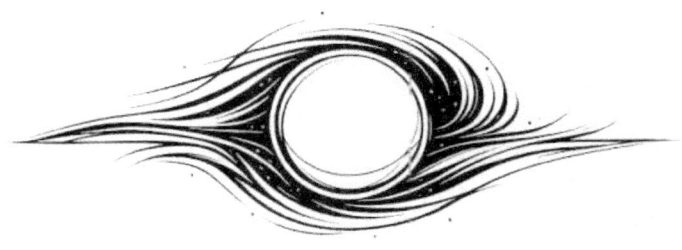

Chapter 10:

Kimiko's Early Days

Kimiko was born on a crisp autumn morning on the outskirts of Kyoto in the year 2288. Her parents lived in a modest home bordered by ancient, moss-covered walls – an architectural relic of an era long past. Despite neon skyscrapers gleaming nearby and hover-vehicles zipping across the skyline, within those walls lingered echoes of Japan's feudal heritage. It was here that Kimiko's father, Takeshi, upheld the traditional ways of the samurai by day and, in secret, embraced the clandestine arts of the ninja by night.

A Longed-for Son

From the moment she could understand words, Kimiko sensed her father's silent disappointment. He had yearned for a son to carry on his lineage – someone to inherit the sword and the code of bushido he had cherished since his youth. Yet, fate gave him only a daughter. In the outside world, many viewed a daughter as equally capable, but Takeshi was bound by centuries of family tradition. Over time, his reservations yielded to acceptance, though it was not an easy transition.

Kimiko, small and wide-eyed, would watch him from the corner of the training yard starting at a mere 4 years of age. Dawn often brought with it the clack of wooden swords or the whisper of arrows cutting the air. Takeshi tried to ignore his daughter's curious stares, but her fascination was palpable. She hovered near the wooden gate, heart pounding when he practiced katas under lantern light. Even then, she wanted to join him, to mimic every stance and strike.

KIMIKO - YOUNG

Initially, Takeshi forbade it. The unspoken rule in their lineage was that daughters did not don the samurai's blade. But the quiet determination Kimiko exuded chipped away at his resolve. Eventually, he offered to teach her the basics – "strictly to discipline her body," he insisted. However, that small concession would shape Kimiko's destiny more profoundly than anyone foresaw.

The Mother's Influence

If Takeshi was the stern instructor, Kimiko's mother, Mariko, was the bedrock of the family. She had no samurai lineage of her own; her strengths lay in wisdom, empathy, and a fierce protective instinct. Yet she was no stranger to self-defense. Mariko came from a line of female martial artists skilled in jujutsu, wrestling, and other practical fighting forms. She encouraged her daughter to break free from traditional molds.

While Takeshi taught Kimiko sword forms in the courtyard, Mariko quietly supplemented her daughter's regimen with lessons in grappling and footwork. Kimiko was small for her age, but a lively determination shone in her eyes, and Mariko saw potential. When father and daughter sparred, Kimiko would try a sudden throw or sweep, something gleaned from her mother's private sessions. Takeshi, startled at first, recognized the balance and agility behind those moves. He did not scold her. Instead, he nodded, seemingly approving that she could blend multiple disciplines seamlessly.

That mix of influences – samurai swordsmanship, maternal wrestling prowess, and the hidden lessons her father guarded even from the public eye – nurtured a formidable spirit in Kimiko. Their household might have looked unremarkable from the outside, but behind closed doors, it brimmed with secrets and ambition.

The Hidden Legacy

Unknown to most, Takeshi's lineage was not purely samurai. He belonged to a covert family branch that had, for

91

centuries, walked the razor's edge between honor and subterfuge. They served as spies, scouts, and – when needed – assassins for powerful lords. Takeshi's father had taught him the silent arts of infiltration and stealth, forging him into a living paradox: a warrior of strict honor who also dealt in deception.

Over time, Takeshi saw glimpses of that same paradox in Kimiko. During their training, she displayed a calculating calm that belied her young age. She rarely wasted movement, studying her opponent's weaknesses with sharp, cold eyes. While she seldom smiled, there was no cruelty in her – the stoicism served her as a tool, allowing her to focus on the discipline of each technique.

At night, once the rest of Kyoto slumbered beneath neon lights, Takeshi began teaching Kimiko the clandestine arts. He showed her how to move through corridors without a whisper of noise, how to blend into a crowd while staying undetected, and how to use simple objects – like a hairpin or a short stick – as lethal weapons if cornered. Kimiko soaked in every lesson with silent eagerness.

"Your path must remain unseen," Takeshi would say, glancing about as though the walls might hear. "Honor in public, stealth in darkness. Never forget who you are – nor what you must protect."

Blossoming Skills

By the time Kimiko turned fifteen, the fruits of her relentless training were evident. The old school gymnasium, overshadowed by more modern facilities, became her proving ground for martial arts tournaments. At first, her opponents scoffed at her slender build, but she outmaneuvered them with fluid grapples and sudden takedowns. Each victory added to her growing reputation. *How does a girl that small pin her opponents so quickly?* Spectators wondered.

Then came the archery tournaments: Kimiko, with

calm detachment, drew her bow, ignoring the crowd's chatter. She breathed in, slowly exhaled, and released arrows that found the bullseye with uncanny accuracy. It wasn't merely her father's samurai teachings guiding her aim – she had also adapted her mother's sense of timing and body alignment.

Swordsmanship, however, remained her pride and her father's lingering challenge. Takeshi pushed her hardest with the katana, insisting on perfect posture, controlled breathing, and unwavering discipline. In private, he let slip more advanced techniques than he'd never taught his own students, pressing Kimiko to refine blade angles and footwork that took a lifetime to master. She'd rise at dawn, practicing each kata a hundred times, sweat soaking her training clothes until her muscles trembled.

Yet, even with all these formal skills, Kimiko's secret ninja training never ceased. Whenever she wore the simple dark garb Takeshi provided, the rest of the world faded away. On nights lit only by the city's neon glow, she tested her stealth amid alleyways and abandoned warehouses. To her father's cautious pride, she climbed walls without hesitation, vanished into thin air, and perfected silent takedowns on shadowy practice dummies.

Father and Daughter

Behind each milestone, an unspoken tension lingered: Takeshi's initial longing for a son. Kimiko sometimes sensed it in the way her father's praise never came with open warmth, or how he studied her in the training yard as though searching for flaws. Still, she strove to exceed every expectation. Over time, the disappointment in Takeshi's eyes softened. He recognized that Kimiko wasn't a stand-in for a hypothetical son – she was a force all her own.

One evening, after an exhausting sparring session, Takeshi spoke words that Kimiko would never forget:

"Kimiko, your skill surpasses that of most young warriors I've known. You embody bushido's honor and the shadows' cunning. I once believed I needed a son to uphold our legacy, but you have proven me wrong."

Those were the closest to affectionate words he'd ever uttered. Though her expression remained stoic, Kimiko felt a subtle warmth stirring within.

On the Cusp of Destiny

At seventeen, Kimiko stood poised for a future that few could predict. She was a star martial artist in her local circuit, often underestimated until she pinned opponents twice her weight. She excelled with the bow, her arrows rarely missing a mark. Her swordsmanship was disciplined and lethal, sharpened under her father's uncompromising gaze. And in the unseen hours of the night, she crept across rooftops, a wrath mastering the arts of infiltration, sabotage, and silent dispatch.

In many ways, she was still a child – grasping at fleeting shards of normalcy: small friendships, an occasional laugh with her mother, or a rare day trip away from the city's sprawling masses. But overshadowing every moment was the knowledge that she was being shaped into something dangerous. One day, her father's secret vow to an ancient lineage might demand her prowess in ways neither of them could foresee.

Regardless of what lay ahead, Kimiko's path was set. She was the daughter of a samurai who wore two faces – honorable warrior and hidden assassin – and she carried both legacies in her every breath. Whether in a training studio under bright gym lights or slipping like a phantom through the darkest alleys, Kimiko was prepared to stand unyieldingly. Hers was a tale of silent footsteps, unblinking resolve, and a destiny that would echo in both the sunlit world of honor and the moonlit domain of secrets.

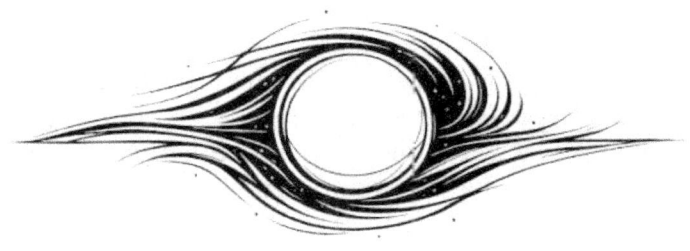

Chapter 11:

The Assassination of Daichi

Tokyo in the year 2317 shimmered with neon splendor, but beneath its polished exterior pulsed a darker undercurrent. Towering skyscrapers pierced the night sky, their colored billboards and holograms reflecting on the wet pavement below. Yet high above the bustle – far from prying eyes – Kimiko prowled among the rooftops. She wore a sleek, midnight-black ninja gi tailored for both agility and silence. Her twin katanas crossed over her back, and a pair of dark sai hung tightly at her hips. She had no time for the city's lights or its fleeting pleasures.

Tonight, she hunted.

A Calculated Mission

An assignment from the Federation had brought her here – to root out a renegade monk known as Daichi, rumored to dabble in forbidden powers. Though the Federation's name meant little to her, Kimiko's lethal reputation ensured she was the one they dispatched for high-risk tasks. She found herself perched on a rooftop overlooking the Shukujō Monastery in Tokyo's outskirts.

Her eyes, cold and watchful, scanned the monastery

grounds. Lantern light danced over tranquil gardens that belied the corruption within. Reports suggested that Daichi was twisting fellow monks to his cause, creating a nest of dangerous disciples. It would not be a simple infiltration. Still, Kimiko did not hesitate; her mind was already orchestrating possible entry points and escape routes.

She dropped from the rooftop, landing in the cover of an alley. Without a sound, she navigated the winding streets until she reached the forested hill behind the monastery.

KIMIKO

The path leading up was draped in mist, faintly lit by moonlight. *A shame this place has become a haven for traitors*, she mused, tracing a finger along one of her katanas.

I will purge them quickly.

Silent Infiltration

At the outer wall, Kimiko scaled the ancient stone as though it were a mere ladder, her gloved fingertips finding purchase with unerring precision. Her breath was even, controlled – each movement measured to avoid detection.

Peering over the parapet, she spotted two guards posted near the courtyard gates. No conversation passed between them; they simply stood, rigid and vigilant.

They won't last long, Kimiko thought, her expression devoid of pity.

She removed both sai, calculating the guards' positions. Timing her throw between pulses of a lantern's glow, she hurled the weapons in twin arcs. The two sai found their marks with surgical accuracy, striking the guards at pressure points. The men collapsed soundlessly, shocked unconscious before either could cry out. Kimiko slid down the wall, retrieving her two sai and putting them back in their sleeves as if it were a mundane chore.

Inside, she moved among the shadows that traced the courtyard's edges. The hush was almost reverent – only the gentle clink of wind chimes stirred the stillness. Her instincts flared with caution: the serenity felt staged, a thin veil for underlying menace.

Treading Hallowed Halls

She slipped through an unguarded side entrance into the main hall's corridor. The polished wooden floors reflected her lean silhouette, while the air was thick with incense. Each candlelit alcove seemed to cloak new threats. Kimiko remained coldly focused, stepping heel-to-toe to minimize creaking boards.

She paused at a half-open door. The faintest flicker of energy, both dark and oppressive tingled at her senses.

Pressing against the wall, she angled her head just enough to peer inside.

Daichi knelt on a raised tatami mat platform, head shaved, and robes draped in ceremonial style.

Briefly, he appeared every inch the devout monk. But Kimiko perceived the swirl of forbidden power coiled around him, shimmering like a malevolent aura. A single candle burned at his side, casting elongated shadows across the walls.

He's the source, Kimiko thought, lips tightening. *It ends tonight.*

Clutching the hilts of her katanas, she advanced into the hall. Her footfalls were ghosts on the polished floor. Yet as she closed the distance, Daichi's eyes snapped open – dark orbs reflecting a twisted amusement.

"Foolish assassin," he murmured, not bothering to rise. "You believe stealth can hide you from me?"

A Deadly Engagement

Before Kimiko could reply, Daichi flicked his wrist. A pulse of invisible force slammed into her torso like a sledgehammer. She was thrown backward into a wooden pillar. Pain jarred her bones, but she didn't cry out. Her training had ingrained stoicism into her core.

She sprang up, unleashing a flurry of katana strikes. The blades hissed through the candlelit air; each cut aiming at a vital point. Daichi rose to meet them, his hands moving with eerie speed. Her steel found only his forearms or empty space – he twisted away from lethal thrusts as though he'd practiced these moves a thousand times.

"You kill with skill," he said with a sneer, "but skill will not save you from the darkness."

He thrust his hand forward, and a roiling black energy erupted, surging like a wave toward Kimiko. She leapt sideways, boots sliding on the smooth floor, evading the brunt of the attack. *He's strong,* she realized, brow furrowing. The coldness in her gaze deepened, but her mind raced. *No time for doubt. I must find a weakness.*

Circling behind a pillar, she used the geometry of the room to her advantage – striking from blind spots, never lingering in one place. Their duel became a dance of slashes and dodges, arcs of steel colliding with bursts of foul magic that threatened to crush the walls themselves.

Yet Daichi's defenses remained formidable, and the monstrous energy drained at her stamina.

With each wave of dark power, a deep chill crept across her skin. She clenched her teeth, determined not to yield.

Exploiting Weakness

A flicker of opportunity arrived when Daichi paused to gather another surge of power. His chest was unprotected for a heartbeat. Kimiko aimed a sai at him, while her mind carefully calculating angle and velocity. The throw was silent and precise. The sai impaled Daichi's shoulder, drawing a strained growl from his lips. The tainted aura surrounding him flickered, granting her a fleeting advantage.

She lunged, both katanas poised for a lethal strike. *End it now.* But Daichi, despite his wound, deflected one sword and caught the other in a vice grip, dark energy seeping into the steel. A pulse of black lightning snaked along the blade and jolted Kimiko's arm. Agony threatened to loosen her hold. She snarled and twisted free, rolling away to re-center her stance.

Daichi smirked, though blood stained his robe. "I admire your dedication, ninja. But your efforts are wasted. Soon, all will bow to the power I wield."

Kimiko's cold expression betrayed no fear, only an icy resolve. She refused to indulge his taunts with a reply. Instead, she scanned the hall for any structural weakness – anything to use as an equalizer.

Her gaze fell on the support beams crisscrossing the

ceiling. *Yes. A collapse might trap him.* She feigned a battered retreat, drawing Daichi away from the platform's center. The dark aura around him crackled ominously, but rage made him less cautious. He advanced, chanting low incantations that warped the air with an unnatural force.

At the right moment, Kimiko pitched her remaining sai upward. The weapon struck a beam overhead. Wood splintered with a deafening crack. The roof above Daichi groaned and then collapsed. Chunks of ceiling and heavy timber crashed onto him in a storm of debris.

Dust choked the room as the floor quaked under the impact. Kimiko coughed, stepping back to avoid a falling lantern. For a tense moment, nothing moved. Then a rattle of rubble revealed Daichi pinned beneath collapsed beams. His dark aura sputtered, nearly extinguished.

"This… means nothing," he rasped, voice rasping with fury. "You cannot stop what's coming."

Kimiko spared him no sympathy. She retrieved her fallen sai and holstered her weapons. The building's walls trembled, threatening a total collapse. *Time to go.* Without a backward glance, she darted through the corridor, ignoring the ache in her limbs.

A Lethal Retreat

Corridors cracked around her as supporting columns gave way. Kimiko moved fast, heart steady, each breath carefully metered as she vaulted fallen rafters and dodged plumes of dust. The final hallway led to a courtyard. She flung herself through a shattered window just as the monastery's ceiling caved in behind her, burying Daichi's final howls.

Landing outside on the slick grass, she paused to regain composure. The city lights glowed in the distance, taunting her with normalcy. She gazed back at the crumbling building. Daichi's vile presence no longer dominated the air, but his cryptic warning echoed in her mind.

You cannot stop what's coming.

Perhaps not alone, but Kimiko did not rely on faith or fear. She believed in precision, stealth, and cunning. If a new threat emerged, she would meet it with steel and silence.

As sirens wailed faintly in the distance, Kimiko slipped into the shadows at the monastery's edge. Each footstep carried her further from the ruins. Another mission was completed. Another threat was suppressed. Her expression remained impassive. The human cost or moral complexity of it all… irrelevant. Survival and success were the only metrics she measured.

Aftermath

Back in Kyoto's neon canyons, she stepped onto a deserted rooftop, pausing to wipe debris from her gi. The city's hum enveloped her once more, though she felt an unspoken detachment from its bustle. *My work is never done,* she reflected, eyes narrowed. *I remain a blade in the darkness, waiting for the next assignment.*

Seconds later, she vanished into the labyrinth of towers – an incorporeal ghost amid the luminous haze. The Federation might call again, or another power might summon her talents. For now, Kimiko moved on, her lethal presence unwitnessed, her footsteps lost in the city's constant drone.

An assassin's life was lonely. She accepted that. She had no illusions of heroism or redemption. She was a samurai acting as a ninja, royal to her kind but also cold and calculating, born to eliminate threats, unflinching before any danger.

And Daichi's final words? Let the darkness come. Kimiko would be ready.

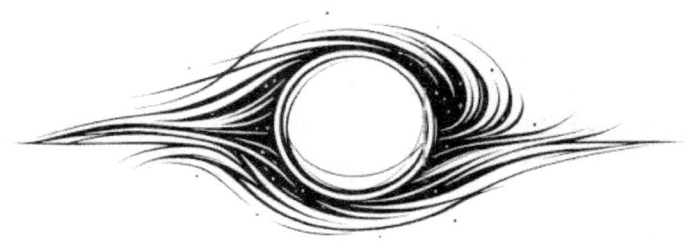

Chapter 12:

The Search for Kimiko

Lilith, Freija, and Grilka strode into a spaceport bar on the outskirts of Chicago, the neon sign above the door struggling to stay lit. Inside, dim lights flickered over dingy tables and a swirl of pungent smoke. The hum of half-muttered conversations tangled with the rattle of an ancient jukebox in the corner.

Freija tugged at the collar of her coat and tried not to wrinkle her nose at the smell. "Is... is this normal?" she asked quietly, glancing around at the mismatched chairs and scarred wooden bar. She kept one hand near the hilt of her short swords, more out of habit than threat.

Lilith, her large black-and-red wings folded tight, gave her a sympathetic look. "It's Earth. And from what I've heard, this corner of the galaxy doesn't exactly rank high on intergalactic tourist guides."

Grilka's orange braid swished as she ducked beneath a low-hanging lamp. "I've seen worse," she drawled, heading for a tiny table in the back. "But maybe next time we hit a place with decent ventilation?"

Not Quite a Princess Here

They settled down, jostling for space at a rickety table. Freija perched carefully on a stool that squeaked alarmingly under her weight. She folded her cobalt-blue wings, trying to avoid brushing a sticky patch on the wall behind her. "I'm not used to these conditions," she whispered, glancing at the haze of questionable smoke.

"I recall your grand halls of Icelandia," Lilith murmured, swirling an odd greenish drink in her glass.

"Must be a bit of a shock. Nobody's bowing to you here, Princess." Freija let out a gentle sigh. "I was never too fond of all that bowing, to be honest. Still, a little courtesy wouldn't kill them, right?" She caught the bartender giving her an uninterested glance and tried for a regal nod. He rolled his eyes. Freija frowned. "See? Zero recognition."

Grilka smothered a smirk. "Welcome to Earth. Try not to break your fragile royal heart." Her tone was teasing, but Freija caught the hint of camaraderie underneath.

Eavesdropping on Ninjas

A few tables away, a scruffy human trader entertained a couple of reptilian patrons with tall tales of Earth's warrior traditions. Lilith's keen hearing picked up choice phrases: "stealth assassins," "ancient arts," and especially "Kimiko."

Ninjas. The word made Lilith's wings twitch in interest. She leaned toward Freija and Grilka, lowering her voice. "He's talking about ninjas. Something about Earth's shadow-warriors. Listen."

Freija's eyes sparkled with curiosity. "Shadow-warriors? Good. I was hoping we'd meet people who don't sanitize their streets every day," she quipped, referencing her memory of pristine walkways back home.

The trader raised his voice, letting them catch the gist: "...and *then* there's this one ninja, Kimiko. Master of infiltration, martial arts, you name it. Rumor says she can slip into a fortress, take out a legion, and vanish without a trace."

Grilka gave an approving grunt. "That's the type we need in our fight. If we can recruit her…"

Lilith nodded. "Exactly."

Freija tried to stand gracefully, but her stool squeaked like a dying rodent. She froze, her cheeks coloring faintly when no one gave her a respectful bow. "Let me go chat with that trader," she muttered, heading over with practiced poise.

Tips from the Trader

Freija approached with a friendly but confident smile. "Excuse me," she said, her wings tightly folding behind her back so as not to whack the reptilian patrons. "I overheard you mention a ninja named Kimiko. Mind sharing a bit more?"

The reptilians gave her an appraising look. The human trader set down his drink, eyeing Freija's swords. "Sure. She's a bit of a legend. If half the stories are true, she's unstoppable. Word is, she's held up in Tokyo, on the other side of the planet. But good luck tracking her – lots have tried, and none come back with proof they've met her."

Freija inclined her head, hoping to appear worldly. "Would you say she's… open to new alliances?"

The trader chuckled grimly. "If you can find her, maybe. I hear she doesn't take kindly to uninvited guests." He shrugged. "That's all I've got, Miss."

Freija thanked him with a polite bow, an old habit from Icelandia, then returned to Lilith and Grilka. "We're heading to Tokyo. That's all we know."

Heading for Tokyo… via Space Junk

They left the bar soon after, ignoring the human

bartenders who couldn't care less about Freija's lineage. Outside, the night sky glowed with the lights of Chicago, but the trio headed straight for their battered but loyal ship, the Scorpion.

"This planet is so advanced in some way, but still has random piles of space debris," Lilith grumbled, studying the nav console. "We'll have to break the atmosphere again and circle to Tokyo from orbit. There's an old ring of junk floating around Earth's low orbit."

Grilka rolled her shoulders. "Rocks, metal scraps... we've done worse. If you can pilot us without scuffing the hull, we'll be fine."

Freija found a seat in the cockpit, still quietly amused by the complete lack of bowing from the Earth ground crew as they taxied out. "No red carpet. No royal fanfare," she sighed in mock disappointment. "Just lumps of metal spinning in the void."

Lilith's lips twitched. "I'll see if I can manage to keep your royal self safe while flying." She engaged the engines, and the Scorpion roared skyward, leaving Chicago behind.

Night Lights of Tokyo

They angled the Scorpion down, blazing through Earth's atmosphere. City lights emerged below, stretching as far as the eye could see. Tokyo's luminous sprawl glowed in multi-colored brilliance; a tapestry of old temples nestled among futuristic skyscrapers.

They settled on a discreet landing pad on the outskirts. Once the engines powered down, Freija hopped onto the tarmac, brushing imaginary dust from her jacket. "At least this spaceport looks a little more... official."

Grilka snickered, scanning the busy lanes where Earth and alien travelers mingled. "Tell me you don't miss being recognized as a princess."

Freija pursed her lips. "I mean... a tiiiiny bit. A fancy

parade would be nice. But I'll live."

Lilith tapped at a handheld device. "Alright, let's keep a low profile. We're rumored to be looking for a hidden ninja. That means we can't exactly show up with a marching band. Let's see if local bars have leads."

The Shadow's Edge

Tokyo's labyrinth of streets, all flashing neon signs and towering advertisements, dazzled Freija. She stared wide-eyed at holographic billboards showcasing everything from VR concerts to alien restaurants. "I... wow," she murmured. "Nobody ever prepared me for a city like this."

Lilith gently tugged her arm when Freija gawked at a sign depicting a cartoonish alien sushi chef. "Focus. I know it's mesmerizing, but let's not get lost."

They ventured into Shinjuku's lively district, where an alley sign reading "The Shadow's Edge" pointed to a narrow doorway. Inside, the bar was hushed and dimly lit by red lanterns. Hardened mercenaries and shady dealers sipped from chipped mugs, eyeing the newcomers suspiciously.

Freija paused near the entrance, half-hoping to play her usual role of "diplomatic princess." But not a single person batted an eye in acknowledgment. She disguised her discomfort with a polite cough. *Huh, guess I am just another random traveler here.*

Lilith approached the bartender, wings folded as unobtrusively as possible. "We're looking for someone named Kimiko," she said quietly.

A flicker of alarm crossed the bartender's features before he resumed a cool façade. "Kimiko... not a name people say out loud. She's known to appear – if she wants to. If you're wise, you'll drop it."

Grilka set a few credits on the bar, each coin stamped with an off-world insignia. "We're not known for dropping things. We'd appreciate a lead."

The bartender let out a subdued sigh. "Try the old

quarter, near the remnants of the Edo-era dojo. She's rumored to train there sometimes, after midnight. But tread lightly – she's… selective about visitors."

Off to the Dojo

Back on the street, Freija shook her head. "Selective about visitors, huh? Does that mean we set up a picnic and hope she drops by?"

Grilka gave a short laugh. "I'll pass on picnics. Let's just do what we do best: show up, show we're not pushovers, and see if she decides we're worth noticing."

Lilith nodded, tucking her wings in as they navigated more crowded alleyways. Signs in Japanese script glowed overhead, and the aroma of fried food wafted from corner stalls. "We might have to prove ourselves," she mused. "But if Kimiko's truly the best ninja around, she might be the perfect ally."

Freija's wings shivered with excitement. "I do love a good challenge. At least in Icelandia, people recognized me – maybe that impressed them. But here, no one cares. That might be… freeing?"

Lilith smiled at her friend's statement. "Glad to hear it. Now we just must earn Kimiko's respect, too."

Grilka cracked her knuckles. "Respect or fear. Either works for me."

The trio headed deeper into Tokyo's neon-washed night, a swirl of thrumming signs and shifting shadows guiding their steps. Each of them felt a hint of anticipation building. So far from their comfort zones – one a demon from the Hellish realm, one a green-skinned bruiser from Valkorr, and one a princess from icy Icelandia with no recognition in this bustling metropolis – they were about to face a silent master of Earth's hidden arts.

No fanfares, no bows or curtsies, just a quest to find Kimiko and persuade her to join them. They pressed on, determination lighting their faces, stepping into the unknown with a mix of nerves, humor, and curiosity.

Around them, Tokyo continued as though nothing extraordinary was about to happen. To everyone else, they were simply three more strangers disappearing into the crowd.

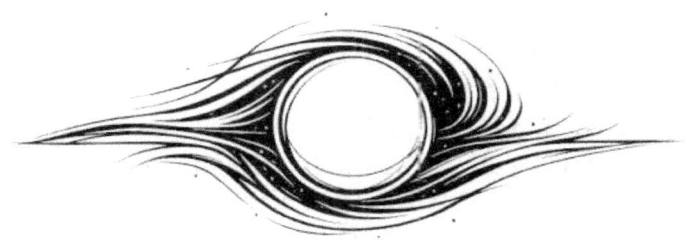

Chapter 13:

Finding Shinjuku

The old quarter of Tokyo carried a quiet mystique. Lantern-lit streets meandered under low-hanging eaves, and the distant hum of modern skyscrapers felt like another world entirely. Here, Lilith, Freija, and Grilka – came in search of a person whose reputation preceded her: Kimiko, a ninja rumored to outmatch entire armies with swift and silent skill.

They moved past ancient gates into a courtyard lined with cherry blossoms, their petals drifting across worn stone tiles. At the far end stood an unassuming dojo – its wooden doors slid open just enough to reveal a lit interior. Voices and the dull thuds of martial practice filtered out.

"Quiet place," Freija murmured, her icy wings folding behind her. She noted how meticulously the grounds were maintained. "But for all we know, Kimiko's behind every shadow."

Grilka rolled her shoulders, scanning the courtyard. "If she's half as secretive as people say, she might already be watching." Her voice was pitched low, laced with a readiness to fight if ambushed.

Lilith's black-and-red wings shifted, a subtle sign of her own vigilance. "Then let's not waste time," she said.

"We'll ask inside."

The Dojo's Greeting

They stepped through the sliding doors and entered a modest training hall. Rows of students practiced in hushed concentration, striking wooden dummies or pairing off in fluid sparring. The air smelled of incense and polished cedar. At the far side, an elderly sensei, clad in simple robes, took note of their arrival. He approached, offering a small bow.

Freija inclined her head politely – a remnant of her royal upbringing – though no one here recognized her as a princess. "We seek Kimiko," she said in a measured tone. "Word is she trains here sometimes."

The sensei's posture was calm, eyes keen. "Indeed, Kimiko visits on occasion, but she chooses her own hours. May I ask your intentions?"

Lilith answered simply. "We want her help. Our team needs a warrior of her skill to confront a threat spreading across the galaxy."

The sensei's face remained neutral. "Kimiko does not respond to summons. She guards her privacy as fiercely as she wields a blade." His gaze flicked to the group's unusual appearances: Lilith's wings, Grilka's massive frame, and Freija's poised alertness. "If Kimiko wishes to speak with you, she will. But I cannot promise when – or if…she will appear."

Grilka exhaled, keeping her voice low. "So, we wait?"

Before the sensei could answer, a shuffle of footsteps approached. A young student, having overheard the conversation, tapped hurriedly at a small device. His eyes darted between the newcomers and the sensei, sending a covert message. Lilith noted the movement but chose not to confront him. *He might be alerting Kimiko,* she thought, *exactly what we want.*

They each bowed and thanked the sensei and left the

main hall, stopping near the dojo's entrance corridor. A few paces away, the hush of night settled, broken only by the whisper of a breeze through the trees.

Waiting in the Shadows

Freija and Grilka found a bench near a paper lantern, while Lilith paced along the wooden deck. The flickering glow cast restless shapes on the walls.

"Standing around like this grates my nerves," Grilka muttered. She flexed her hands, each big enough to crush a grown man's skull. "We usually take action."

Freija tried for a light remark. "Patience is a virtue, isn't it? I recall reading that somewhere."

Grilka snorted. "Says the one who used to be a – what was it? Princess?"

Freija spread her wings slightly in a show of mock offense. "Former princess. I'm not recognized here, remember? No line of bowing admirers."

Lilith's gaze traveled to the moonlit garden outside. "We've done our part. If Kimiko's as skilled as rumored, she'll sense us. She either chooses to come… or not." She paused. "At least we'll know soon."

Unbeknownst to them, a figure observed from above the rafters: Kimiko, drawn by the student's message. Despite her petite stature – barely over five feet – she carried herself with quiet authority. Clad in black, and a tight ninja gi, she watched the trio for signs of deception.

An Unceremonious Introduction

In the stillness, Kimiko made her move. A near-invisible shift in the air, then a sudden rasp of steel. Before Lilith could react, Kimiko yanked one of Lilith's curved horns back, pressing a gleaming katana to the demon's throat. The motion was impeccably controlled – enough to show she meant business without severing Lilith's neck outright.

"Who are you," Kimiko said in a calm, low voice, "and why do you want me?"

The group froze. Freija's hands drifted near her short swords; Grilka half-rose, muscles coiled. Lilith gave a short hiss of surprise but forced herself to remain still. The blade's edge pressed lightly onto her skin.

"Easy," Lilith said, her voice steady. "We're not here to cause trouble, Kimiko."

Kimiko's dark eyes shifted, analyzing the three. She kept her blade level. "Use my name again without explaining who fed it to you, and I'll reconsider letting you speak."

The iron-cold professionalism in Kimiko's tone left no room for pleasantries. She was a world apart from the typical brash mercenaries who boasted of their kills. This was someone who did her work methodically and precisely.

Freija stepped forward slowly, wings half-spread to show no immediate aggression. "We came from beyond Earth seeking your skills. We have a mission – one that needs a fighter like you."

Kimiko's gaze flicked over Freija, then to Grilka, who stood near the bench, tense but refraining from an open attack. "I've no interest in off-world drama," Kimiko said. "State your case. Quickly."

The Pitch

Lilith, still pinned, inhaled. "We face a looming threat named Necra. An enemy who conquers worlds and builds unstoppable armies. We barely survived our last encounter. We need someone who can operate in ways we can't. You come highly recommended by… well, everyone we've asked."

For a beat, Kimiko kept the katana pressed close to Lilith's throat. Then she released Lilith's horn, stepping back just enough to maintain an advantage. Her blade hovered at an angle, ready to strike if needed.

"And if I refuse?" Her voice was cool, more curious than defiant.

Freija ventured forward another step. "Then we leave you in peace," she said. "But trust us: if Necra continues unchecked, Earth won't remain off her radar forever. You might be forced to fight anyway."

Kimiko's expression remained inscrutable, her stance unchanged. She measured their words. "I'm not in the habit of trusting strangers. Especially those who disturb my training ground."

Grilka rumbled low, crossing her arms. "We're not a typical bunch. But we don't lie. If we wanted you dead, we'd not walk in openly."

A moment stretched in the silence. Kimiko's eyes flicked from Lilith's horns to Grilka's imposing build, then to Freija's poised readiness. Each had a unique aura of capability.

She eased the katana away, sheathing it in a single fluid motion. "Continue talking. Briefly."

Lilith exhaled, stepping out of sword range. She rubbed the back of her neck. "We aim to assemble warriors with specialized skills. We overcame one foe, Baron, but barely. Now, another threat looms, bigger than anything we can handle alone."

Freija nodded. "Your name came up again and again. If you're half as adept in stealth, infiltration, and silent takedowns as rumored, you could shift the tide."

Kimiko listened, postured upright, with a calm expression. Her eyes betrayed no excitement, only a flicker of guarded interest. "This war... it's not local, correct?"

Lilith shook her head. "It spans multiple systems. Eventually, every planet becomes a target. We'd like to avoid letting that happen to Earth."

The ninja gave a slight, almost imperceptible tilt of her head. "So you're asking me to abandon my base, risk my life on foreign battlefields, and place trust in three off-worlders I've just met."

"Uhm… Yes," Freija said simply.

Grilka let out a quiet chuckle. "We're persuasive like that."

Kimiko said nothing for several heartbeats. The distant chatter of dojo students echoed softly down the corridor. Finally, she turned, motioning them to follow with a curt nod.

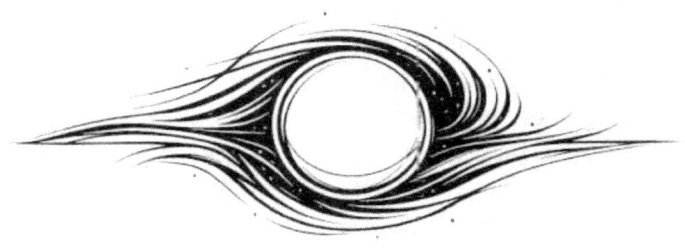

Chapter 14:

A Shadow Among Them

The cramped Scorpion rested quietly in its slot in the spaceport. The ship's small barracks, or sleeping quarters, consisted of two bunk beds pushed against cold metal walls. Lilith lay sprawled on the top bunk on the right bunk, her crimson and black wings draped over the edge. Her lower legs hung off the edge of the bed which was meant for someone about 6 feet tall. Her chest rose and fell heavily with each breath, a faint glow of embers flickering in the dark.

Below her, Grilka's hulking frame dominated the bottom bunk, snoring loudly enough to rattle the wall paneling. On the opposite bunk, Freija muttered something indistinguishable, her icy breath forming frost patterns on the edge of her blanket.

The ship was silent except for the rhythmic sounds of sleep.

Kimiko stood on the dock at the edge of Tokyo's spaceport, half-hidden behind a stack of cargo crates. Ahead rested the vessel called Scorpion, its hull chipped and scuffed from countless voyages. Two days had passed since she'd briefly met Lilith, Grilka, and Freija in a quiet dojo in old Tokyo. They claimed to need her expertise to combat some off-world menace. She didn't trust them. Truthfully, she didn't trust anyone. Yet curiosity, or perhaps a sense of looming obligation, had drawn her here.

She kept the hood of her dark ninja gi pulled low, concealing her face from any roving port cameras. A faint breeze ruffled the stray wisps of her hair. In the distance, neon lights flickered across the city skyline, but the spaceport itself lay in hushed twilight.

The Scorpion was small – surprisingly so. A vessel of that size would hardly accommodate a robust crew, which matched what little she knew of the three women she'd encountered. She observed from a distance for nearly an hour, analyzing the ship's basic security patterns. The doors sealed, a mild motion-activated sensor near the main ramp, likely some kind of minimal detection around the hull. Nothing advanced enough to deter a skilled infiltrator.

I need to see if they're truly worth my time, Kimiko told herself, recalling Lilith's wings, Grilka's brute strength, and Freija's quiet composure. She decided on a test. If their craft was as vulnerable as it looked, it wouldn't take long to bypass.

No Weapons, No Sound

She removed her swords and two sai – her primary weapons – to a secluded corner behind stacked cargo. Carrying them might hamper her ability to squeeze through vents or compromise her silhouette. She placed them in a hidden compartment she'd discovered upon scanning the docking bay. The overhead lighting created shifting shadows across her gi. After a final glance at her stowed blades, she slipped away.

Approaching the Scorpion, she pressed her palm to the hull, feeling for vibrations. The engines were offline; the interior seemed still. A faint beep emanated from the main ramp's access panel, but she ignored it, creeping around the side. A vent grate jutted out, just wide enough to admit a slender figure. Perfect.

In a fluid motion, Kimiko removed the metal grate's screws with a small tool from her belt. No alarms triggered; she deduced the ventilation system wasn't integrated with the main security. Exhaling softly, she pulled herself inside. The narrow duct was cool, carrying a faint draft of recycled ship air.

Too simple, she thought. *They rely on the ramp sensors instead of defending every potential entry. Not wise*

She began her crawl through the vent, each movement measured to avoid scraping metal.

Through the Vents

Inside, the ventilation shaft was tight. Kimiko pressed forward slowly, arms and legs braced against the metal to avoid scraping. Periodically, she paused to listen for footsteps. Only a distant hum of machinery sounded and some snoring, but no sign of an alert.

Too easy, she told herself. *They either underestimate infiltration or have placed all their faith in that external ramp sensor.*

At a junction, she heard a faint snore echo through the duct – resonant enough to vibrate along the metal. This must be near the sleeping quarters, she concluded, remembering the trio from the dojo: Lilith, the horned demon; Freija, the small-winged ex-princess; and Grilka, the hulking green fighter. *Which one snores like that?* she wondered, stifling a near-smirk.

Quiet Corridor

The vent opened into a corridor with low overhead lights. Kimiko dislodged the grating and dropped soundlessly onto the deck. She scanned for cameras – found nothing more than a corner sensor likely aimed at the main door. This path was clear.

Following the distant, almost comically loud snoring, she advanced toward the sleeping quarters. The corridor was narrow, strewn with scuff marks and personal clutter. Small crates, a half-open tool chest, and what looked like a piece of wing-sheathing for Lilith lay scattered about. *They live casually,* Kimiko thought, *not the tight discipline of a professional unit.*

Soon, she reached a hatch left ajar, through which the snoring intensified. It resonated in heavy waves, like a beast in a cave. Kimiko raised an eyebrow. *Must be Grilka,* she decided. *No one else from that trio likely produces that kind of roar.*

She slipped inside.

Observing the Sleeping Warriors

The room was dimly lit by a single indicator lamp near the bunks. Two bunk beds were pressed against opposite walls in a cramped arrangement. Two chairs sat against the far wall.

Kimiko's gaze moved to the top bunk on the right. Lilith slept there, her dark, crimson-edged wings hanging over the side. Even in sleep, her expression remained serious, her lips turned downward as though scowling at a dream.

Below her lay Grilka. Kimiko recognized her immediately by the booming snore that rattled the overhead shelf. The powerful Valkorrian was sprawled across the mattress, orange hair spread over a pillow that looked far too small. Every inhale produced a deep rumble that rolled through the cabin before ending in a sputtering snort. The metal floor beneath Kimiko's feet vibrated ever so slightly.

Across the aisle, Freija occupied the lower bunk. She had curled into a tight ball, her wings wrapped around her shoulders like a blanket. A delicate crust of frost shimmered along the edge of the bedding, betraying her icy nature even in sleep.

Kimiko studied each of them in silence. For all their fearsome reputations, they appeared strangely vulnerable now. The cabin was quiet except for Grilka's relentless snoring. *If I were a killer, this would be trivial,* she thought. *But that isn't why I'm here.* She had come to identify their security weaknesses and study them up close.

A Quiet Foray into the Kitchen

She exited the room to continue her exploration of the ship. In front of her, to a slight left, she noticed a living room next to a small kitchen. She decided to explore the kitchen.

Pushing open a half-closed sliding door, she entered the ship's tiny kitchen. One overhead light flickered lazily, casting her shadow in wavering shapes across the floor. Cabinets lined both walls, interspersed with a compact fridge unit and a battered food dispenser. She opened a random cupboard, listening carefully to any alarm. None sounded.

Inside, she found metal canisters labeled in various alien scripts, plus a couple in Earth languages. A row of ration packs featuring a stylized alien figure caught her attention. The packaging boasted some promise of "complete protein." Kimiko had tasted worse. She selected one, turning it in her hands to read the label. *High-calorie survival rations.* Good enough.

She rummaged further, discovering a small plastic pouch that seemed to contain dried fruit or something similar. Curious, she tore open the seal carefully. A sweet, tangy aroma wafted out – likely some exotic produce from an off-world orchard. She tried a piece, chewing thoughtfully. *Not bad.*

Satisfied, she pressed the fridge door open. The interior revealed more haphazard storage: a sealed jar of pickled something, an unmarked tub, half-filled with an unknown paste. Kimiko wasn't eager to experiment. She closed it softly, then turned on her heel, the ration pack in hand.

I'll see how they react if they find me casually eating their supplies, she thought, a hint of amusement flickering behind her otherwise impassive eyes.

Exiting the galley, she retraced her steps, each footfall meticulously placed to avoid the slightest sound. The snoring from the sleeping quarters grew louder. She recognized the pattern: inhalation in three beats, exhalation in a rumbling gust. *Definitely the green one, Grilka,* she assumed, recalling the imposing, green-skinned woman.

Re-entering the Sleeping Quarters

The room smelled of three distinct presences: a trace of sulfur from Lilith's demonic lineage, a faint earthy musk from Grilka's alien physiology, and the crisp tang of ice that clung to Freija's aura. All breathing deeply, lost in slumber.

Kimiko drifted inside. None of them stirred at her presence. She discovered two small seats in the center of the room, likely used to lace boots or set gear. With a deliberate grace, she crossed the cramped floor, stepping around a stray boot and an oversized gauntlet. At no point did her footsteps produce more than a whisper.

She sank onto a chair, opening the ration pack. The content's sweet smell teased her senses. Carefully, she took a bite, analyzing the taste: part fruit, part synthetic protein. It wasn't unpleasant. She methodically chewed, swallowing without expression. Despite the improvised meal, her gaze remained alert, flicking around the room. *If they awaken, how will they respond?*

Grilka's snoring hit a new crescendo, practically roaring. The bunk vibrated under her. Kimiko blinked, continuing to eat calmly, unaffected by the noise. *At least one threat is loud enough to be noticed from orbit,* she thought sarcastically.

Lilith Awakens

Her wait paid off. Lilith, perched on the top bunk to her left, stirred with a groan. Her wings flexed, half-extending. Groggily, she lifted her head, squinting at the figure in the corner. Kimiko continued chewing, her posture relaxed, the ration pack in her right hand.

Lilith stiffened, her fiery eyes snapping fully open. She half-rolled off the bunk, wings flaring instinctively. "Who ... Kimiko!" she hissed in a hushed tone, mindful not to wake the others. "How did you ...?"

Kimiko raised a finger to her lips to ask for silence. "You'll rouse your crew," she said quietly, her voice devoid of warmth.

Lilith's wings twitched in agitation. She shot a glance down at Grilka, who, ironically, did not need "rousing." The green woman's snore might as well have been an alarm siren. The demon let out an exasperated sigh. "You couldn't just knock?"

Kimiko didn't bother answering right away. She took another measured bite of the ration. "This was simpler," she said at last, wiping a stray crumb from her lip with near-clinical precision. "I wanted to see if your security lived up to your bragging."

Lilith pressed her mouth into a hard line. "And your conclusion?"

Before Kimiko could respond, Freija stirred on the opposite bunk, blinking away the haze of sleep. The small princess-like figure, who once commanded a frozen kingdom, regarded Kimiko with a wide-eyed stare. "What's going ...?"

Kimiko kept her tone dispassionate. "I slipped in through your vents. Ate a snack from your kitchen. And decided to watch you sleep. You didn't notice a thing."

Freija sat up, raking a hand through her short, frosty hair. "That's... thorough. We should improve some measures." She glanced at Lilith, who looked irritated but didn't object. "We expected you might show up unexpectedly, but we didn't think you'd do it at …" She squinted at a small clock. "Four in the morning?"

A low, snorting rumble from the bunk below Lilith heralded Grilka finally stirring. She jerked upright, nearly hitting her head on Lilith's bunk. "Who's talkin'…?" Her orange hair stuck out at odd angles, and she wore a scowl of confusion. Then her gaze locked on Kimiko. "You're… the ninja. On our ship?"

Kimiko nodded, unflustered, and took another bite of the ration bar. "Yes."

Grilka's expression flickered from shock to irritation. "You rummaged through our stuff? Wait – did you eat *our* food?"

Kimiko held up the half-eaten ration. "If that's a problem, consider it the price of a security inspection."

Lilith gave a small growl, more at the situation than at Kimiko personally. "You're awfully sure of yourself. We could've attacked you."

Kimiko's dark eyes remained cold. "You would have to wake up first – and you didn't. I was here long enough to rummage the kitchen, come back, and enjoy a snack in your quarters."

Freija tried to mask a smile, somewhat amused. "Alright, point taken. We'll upgrade our perimeter checks. But … why are you here, exactly?"

A Pragmatic Assessment

Kimiko brushed off a crumb and rose from the chair. Her posture exuded rigid composure. "I said I'd consider your proposal. I wanted to confirm you're not incompetent liars. Your lack of advanced security is… concerning. But the supplies in your galley, the star charts I glimpsed, your personal items – none of it suggests you're bluffing about a serious mission."

Grilka grabbed a blanket to cover her exposed

shoulders. "If your infiltration is a test, we get it. Don't think we're totally sloppy – just exhausted."

The ninja dipped her head in a half-shrug. "Exhaustion won't matter in real conflict. If you truly aim to face a galactic-level threat, you'll need vigilance at all hours. War doesn't wait for better mornings." Her voice was clipped, matter of fact.

Lilith flexed her wings, annoyance simmering in her gaze. "We can't be on guard all day. No one can. But fine, we'll do better."

Kimiko tossed the empty ration wrapper onto a nearby shelf. "Satisfactory enough. I'll remain in contact. For now, consider me... provisionally on board." She paused, letting a heartbeat of silence pass. "But if I sense incompetence or hidden agendas, I leave. Understood?"

Freija stood, letting her small wings unfold. "You'll find we're serious. We've seen enough horror to know what's at stake. We appreciate your caution."

Kimiko stood, letting her gaze flick over them all. "This was a test," Kimiko said coolly. "I wanted to confirm if you're truly serious about this war you spoke of – or if you're a group of slackers who sleep with no alarm systems."

Grilka bristled, crossing her arms. "Most people use a door." Her voice rumbled, laced with both embarrassment and annoyance. "You could've told us you were coming."

"Where's the challenge in that?" Kimiko countered with a thin edge.

Lilith drew a slow breath, evidently reining in her irritation. "All right, point taken. Next time, we'll post a guard."

A hush fell as the trio processed her words. Freija's eyebrows rose, a trace of relief or excitement lighting her features. "You'll fight alongside us?"

Kimiko nodded once, almost curtly. "For now. Until I see reason to depart. And if you disappoint me or hide something crucial, I leave without warning."

Grilka exhaled, tension leaving her bulky shoulders. "Fair enough. If we know we can count on your skills in a fight." Then, glancing around the cramped bunk room, she half-muttered, "We'll figure out sleeping arrangements, I guess."

Lilith's wings relaxed fractionally. "We appreciate it. Seriously. We need a stealth specialist." She paused, scanning Kimiko's unreadable expression. "What changed your mind?"

Kimiko tore her gaze away, stepping toward the corridor. "Nothing changed. I just confirmed you're not lying. You have real star charts, a real ship, and evidently a real threat if you go this far. Also, if Necra is as vast as rumored, leaving Earth unprepared isn't an option." She let a beat of silence pass. "I'll gather my gear."

Lilith nodded. "All right. We can discuss details in the morning – well, later this morning."

Grilka yawned mightily, "Finally, a reason to sleep again… if you're done rummaging," she said, a half-hearted grin tugging at her lips.

Kimiko's tone remained cool, though something akin to dry amusement flickered in her eyes. "Yes. I found your ration packs quite… passable. Next time, lock them up if you don't want guests sampling."

Freija, still perched on her bunk, let out a soft laugh. "We'll keep that in mind."

Joining the Crew

Moments later, Kimiko dropped onto the landing bay floor outside. The cool night air greeted her. She walked to her hidden stash behind the cargo crates, retrieving her shivered katanas, she twirled them around magnetically attaching them to her back. She then picked up her two sai, reattaching them to her belt in practiced motions. Her expression never wavered.

She glanced once more at the Scorpion's hull, faintly illuminated by the overhead dock lights. *I've seen enough. They're naive in some ways but determined.* The plan now was to embark with them and see if their mission truly justified the risk. *Better to control the situation from the inside,* she reasoned.

Kimiko then headed toward some local shops to pick up some supplies and rations. Within an hour she had returned to the dock and approached the Scorpion approaching it from the front. The sensor beeped softly at her presence, but she tapped a small override on the panel. The door slid open with a hiss.

Inside, the corridor lights remained dim. Lilith stood there, arms folded over her chest, wings slightly spread as if braced for confrontation. Behind her, Freija and Grilka peered over, still looking a mix of groggy and guarded.

"You're back... with weapons and supplies this time," Lilith observed, scanning the katana's hilt and the pack in her left hand. Her tone carried only mild caution now, not outright hostility.

Kimiko inclined her head. "I prefer them close. If I'm to ride this ship, I'll do so on my terms." She let her gaze drift to Grilka, who gave a curt nod, and to Freija, who offered a faint half-smile.

Freija gestured toward the corridor leading to the main cabin. "We have a spare bunk, but it's something." She paused. "If you want it."

Kimiko weighed the offer, then shook her head once. "I'll keep watch until morning. Let's just say I'm used to being awake when others sleep."

Lilith relaxed her stance, wings folding behind her. "Fair enough. We'll get some rest, then. Try not to scare the maintenance crew if they show up."

Grilka snorted, the rumble echoing down the hall. "Says the demon with fiery horns," she teased lightly. Then, more seriously, "Glad you decided to stay."

Kimiko didn't smile, but her posture softened by a fraction. "So am I." She let her eyes glide around the cramped interior. *At least it's functional,* she thought. *We'll see how it fares in real conflict.*

Freija yawned, nodding. "It's late – early, I suppose. Welcome aboard, Kimiko." Her voice held sincerity, even if it lacked the formalities one might expect for a princess to greet a new ally.

"Thank you," Kimiko replied, tone clinical. "I'll stand watch up near the cockpit."

Lilith, Freija, and Grilka shared a look of acceptance before turning back to their bunks, resigned to the fact that a stealthy ninja was now part of their crew. They retreated to the sleeping quarters. Meanwhile, Kimiko pivoted down the corridor, heading toward the cockpit lights glowing faintly in the distance.

Settling In

Behind her, Grilka's enormous snore resumed, reverberating faintly even through the closed bunk hatch. Kimiko shook her head silently. *I'll have to endure that noise if we're truly traveling together.* But the thought barely fazed her. She'd endured harsher conditions, and more irritating companions, on past missions.

Kimiko initially went to the armory where she stowed her swords and sai. She set her back on one of the seats in the living quarters and headed back to the cockpit.

In the dim glow of the cockpit console, she settled into the copilot's chair, crossing her arms. The star charts flickered across the main display, revealing far-flung systems marked in bright lines. *So many worlds out there. And they want me to help protect them from an enemy named Necra.*

She couldn't say she believed in their quest entirely yet, but she recognized the scale. If Necra was real, and the threat as dire as claimed, then ignoring it was tantamount to waiting for disaster. Better to act preemptively, and if these three needed her unique talents, so be it.

At least they're not fools, she told herself again, remembering Lilith's constrained irritation, Freija's earnest calm, and Grilka's unapologetically loud existence. *They'll learn quickly or perish in the attempt. So, will I.*

Eyes fixed on the star map, Kimiko leaned back, letting the hum of the ship's systems lull her into a semi-meditative state. In the morning, they'll talk. In the morning, they'd plan. For tonight, she kept vigil – unflinching, composed, and ready to cut ties if needed. That was how she survived.

Yet something about this group felt oddly... complementary. Enough to make her want to stay.

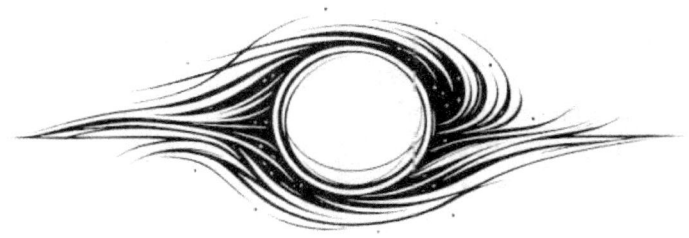

Chapter 15:

Star Pilot's Gamble

The bar's dim neon lights flickered as Adrian sauntered in, the scent of stale alcohol and burned-out dreams mingling in the air. Adrian's life was one of sharp turns, relentless sarcasm, and the ever-present allure of danger.

The Maverick Pilot

Born in the orbital colony of Astoria Alpha, Adrian had always been drawn to the stars. His human mother died when he was very young, meaning he was raised as a single child by his father. His human father, a decorated military pilot, had instilled in him a love of flying and a disregard for rules. While his father's career was defined by discipline, Adrian's path diverged sharply. By his late teens, he was already tinkering with secondhand ships and running smuggling operations for local traders.

"You're wasting your talent," his father had told him once, standing in the doorway in their modest home. "You could've been great."

Adrian smirked, flipping a wrench in his hand. "Greatness is boring. I'll stick with fun."

Despite his rebellious streak, Adrian's natural skill as a pilot was undeniable. He could navigate asteroid fields blindfolded, dodge patrol ships with pinpoint accuracy, and coax life out of engines others would have deemed scrap. By the time he was twenty-five, he was a name whispered across star ports, both revered and cursed.

The Gambler

Adrian's penchant for risk extended beyond the cockpit. He was infamous for his love of gambling, his cocky grin a staple at underground card tables.

ADRIAN FLYNN

On one such night in Lusona's Drift, a bustling

outpost in the Zaran quadrant, Adrian found himself in a game that would change the course of his life.

The table was crowded with an assortment of rogues, traders, and mercenaries, their faces illuminated by the pale blue glow of the cards. Adrian leaned back in his chair, his twin disruptors holstered loosely at his sides, his leather jacket creaking with every casual movement.

"Raise," he said, sliding a stack of credits forward. His voice was smooth, but his sharp eyes studied his opponents' every move.

Across the table sat Jarek Vorn, a notorious arms dealer with a temper as explosive as his merchandise. Jarek narrowed his eyes, his hand hovering over his own stack of credits. "Bold move, Flynn. You sure about that?"

Adrian's grin widened. "Bold is my middle name."

The final card was dealt; the tension at the table thickened. Adrian's heart raced as he glanced at his hand – almost perfect. But almost wasn't good enough, and he knew it. Jarek leaned forward, his gaze predatory.

"Show your cards," Jarek growled.

Adrian's mind worked quickly. A loss here wasn't just about credits – it was about survival. He needed to bluff, and bluff big. He leaned back, a picture of confidence, and revealed his hand.

The table erupted in chaos as Adrian's cards didn't just win – they obliterated Jarek's. Jarek's face darkened, his fists clenching. "You cheated."

Adrian shrugged, standing and collecting his winnings. "Or maybe you just lost."

Jarek lunged across the table, but Adrian was faster. He grabbed his credits, bolted out of the room, and made a beeline for his ship – a sleek two-seater he called the Starlight Shadow. Jarek's men were close behind, disruptors firing as Adrian dove into the cockpit pitching his winnings into the co-pilot's seat and powering up the engines.

"Guess I won't be visiting Lusona's Drift anytime

soon," Adrian muttered, pulling the ship into a sharp ascent as disruptor bolts streaked past. Credits were flying all across the cockpit with such a sudden ascent.

A Debt to Pay

The incident with Jarek wasn't an isolated one. Adrian's gambling habits and sharp tongue had earned him enemies across multiple star systems. While he prided himself on his ability to slip away from trouble, the debts and grudges were piling up. His ship, though fast and reliable, was constantly in need of repairs, and his credits rarely lasted beyond the next port.

On one particularly rough day, Adrian found himself in the Tarnis Station, bartering with a surly mechanic named Milo. The Shadow's engines were sputtering, and Adrian's funds were dangerously low.

"Look, Milo," Adrian said, leaning against the counter, "you fix the engines, and I'll bring you back a crate of that Corellian ale you love. Deal?"

Milo scowled. "You've got three outstanding tabs with me, Flynn. Why should I trust you?"

Adrian flashed his signature grin. "Because I'm charming?"

Milo snorted but relented. "Last time, Flynn. Next time, you're paying double."

As Adrian left the shop, his comm buzzed. It was a familiar voice, one he hadn't heard in years – Commander Elaine Lopa, a former ally from his smuggling days.

"Flynn, we've got a job for you," the purple-skinned Elaine said, her tone brisk. "Big payout. High risk."

"High risk? My favorite," Adrian replied. "What's the target?"

Elaine hesitated. "Not over comms. Meet me at the Crossfire Bar on Andaris V."

A Fateful Meeting

Adrian's journey to Andaris V was uneventful – no bounty hunters, no engine failures, just the quiet hum of the Starlight Shadow as it slipped through hyperspace. When he arrived at the Crossfire Bar, the atmosphere was as he expected: smoky, dimly lit, and buzzing with quiet danger.

Elaine was waiting in a booth at the back, her sharp features illuminated by the soft glow of her data pad. She looked up as Adrian approached, her expression a mix of relief and annoyance.

"Flynn," she said, motioning for him to sit. "Still alive, I see."

"Barely," Adrian replied, sliding into the seat. "So, what's the job?"

Elaine leaned in and her voice was low. "There's a growing threat in this sector. A warlord named Necra is consolidating power, taking over planets, stripping them of resources. She's got loyalists everywhere, and she's dangerous."

Adrian raised an eyebrow. "Sounds like you need an army, not a pilot."

Elaine smirked. "We need both. But the job I'm offering is reconnaissance. You get in, gather intel, and get out. Clean and simple."

"Simple, huh?" Adrian leaned back, considering her words. "What's the payout?"

Elaine slid a data chip across the table. "Enough to cover your debts many times over."

Adrian studied her for a moment, his grin fading slightly. "What's the catch?"

Elaine's expression darkened. "If you get caught, you're on your own. No backup. No rescue."

Adrian's grin returned. "Sounds like my kind of job."

The Mission

The metallic hum of the Starlight Shadow's engines filled the small cabin as Adrian leaned back in the pilot's seat, boots propped up on the console. The weight of Elaine's mission loomed over him like a shadow. This wasn't a simple fly-and-grab job. It was deep reconnaissance on one of Necra's fortified outposts. High risk, high reward. Adrian's specialty.

Elaine's purple-skinned face lingered in his thoughts, her tone sharp and measured when she had explained the job. "You're going to infiltrate Necra's secondary outpost. Get past her loyalists, retrieve the schematics for their shield disruptors, and leave without a trace. This isn't about bravado, Flynn – it's about precision."

Adrian smirked at the memory. "Bravado and precision are my middle names," he muttered to himself as the Starlight Shadow exited hyperspace and the dusty red planet of Kaelus-7 came into view.

The Landing

The outpost was situated in the middle of a rocky wasteland, its tall, fortified walls gleaming under the harsh sunlight. Adrian brought the Shadow down carefully on a nearby ridge, keeping the ship hidden behind jagged rocks. He grabbed his toolkit, a data pad, and his twin disruptors before stepping out into the arid air.

The heat pressed down on him, but Adrian paid it little mind as he approached the outpost's perimeter. A handful of humanoid guards patrolled lazily near the entrance, their yellowish skin glinting in the light. Adrian crouched behind a boulder, surveying the scene.

"Looks like these guys didn't get the memo about situational awareness," he muttered, activating the small holographic projector on his wrist. A miniature display of the outpost's layout appeared, courtesy of Elaine's intel.

The weak spot was a ventilation shaft on the eastern wall, just wide enough for someone of Adrian's size. It was unguarded – probably considered too small to be a threat. *Perfect.*

The Infiltration

Reaching the vent was a delicate operation. Adrian moved silently across the rocky terrain, timing his movements to the guards' lazy patrol patterns. At one point, a small pebble dislodged under his boot, clattering noisily. After ducking behind a crate, he froze as one of the guards glanced in his direction, their yellow eyes narrowing.

Adrian held his breath, gripping his disruptor tightly. The guard hesitated for a moment before shrugging and continuing their patrol. Adrian let out a slow exhale, smirking to himself. "They're not sending their best."

He reached the ventilation shaft, unscrewing the grate with practiced efficiency before slipping inside. The narrow space was cramped and stifling, the metallic walls amplifying every movement. Adrian crawled forward, the faint hum of machinery growing louder as he approached the heart of the outpost.

Data Retrieval

The control room was just as Elaine's intel had described – a small, heavily secured chamber at the center of the facility. The shield schematics were stored in a terminal, guarded by a pair of loyalists who looked more bored than vigilant.

Adrian perched above them in the ventilation shaft, carefully removing the grate. He dropped silently into the room, landing behind the guards with feline grace. Before either of them could react, he raised his disruptors and fired two stun blasts, dropping them instantly.

"Too easy," he whispered, stepping over their

unconscious forms. He plugged his data pad into the terminal, the screen flickering as it began downloading the schematics. A progress bar appeared… agonizingly slow.

"Hurry up," Adrian muttered, glancing at the door. His fingers drummed against the console as the bar crawled toward completion.

Suddenly, the sound of footsteps echoed down the hallway. Adrian tensed, his hand hovering over his disruptors. A squad of four loyalists entered the room, their eyes widening as they took in the scene.

Adrian grinned with his disruptors already drawn. "Hey, fellas. Fancy seeing you here."

The room erupted into chaos as Adrian fired, the blasts ricocheting off walls and consoles. He dove behind a terminal, narrowly avoiding a volley of return fire. One by one, he picked off the loyalists, their bodies crumpling to the floor in a heap.

The data pad beeped, signaling the download's completion. Adrian grabbed it, shoving it into his jacket pocket as he sprinted toward the exit.

The Escape

The alarms blared as Adrian navigated the labyrinthine corridors, his breath coming in quick bursts. He was looking at the holographic schematics of the interior with each corner that he took. More guards poured into the facility, their disruptors firing wildly. Adrian darted into a storage room, locking the door behind him as he took a moment to catch his breath.

"Alright, Flynn," he muttered. "Time for Plan B. Or C. Or… whatever letter we're on."

He spotted a maintenance access ladder leading to the roof. With a quick glance at his holographic schematic, he realized it led to a small landing pad where several vehicles were parked. If he could grab one, he could make it back to the Shadow in no time.

The climb was grueling, but Adrian reached the roof just as a fresh wave of guards spilled onto the landing pad. He ducked behind a parked speeder, formulating a plan. His eyes locked onto the largest vehicle – a cargo ship with its engines still running.

"That'll do nicely," he said, pulling a small detonator from his belt. He tossed it toward the far end of the landing pad, the explosion rocking the facility. The guards scattered, giving Adrian the opening he needed.

He bolted for the cargo ship, firing over his shoulder as he ran. He vaulted into the cockpit, slamming the door shut behind him. The engines roared as he powered up the ship, lifting off just as the guards regrouped and opened fire.

The cargo ship soared into the sky, Adrian steering it toward the ridge where the Starlight Shadow waited. He landed the stolen ship haphazardly. He quickly activated the ship's self-destruction system and darted toward his ship. He jumped onboard and began transferring the schematics to the Shadow's secure system before igniting its engines.

His ship took off as a couple of other ground crews were making it to the stolen cargo ship before it erupted with an intense explosion, taking out all the pursuant guards.

The Starlight Shadow shot off vertically, shooting beyond orbit within seconds. He then launched the ship into hyperspace.

The Aftermath

Adrian didn't relax until the Starlight Shadow was safe in hyperspace. He leaned back in his seat, letting out a long breath as the adrenaline faded.

"Another job well done," he said, pulling the data pad from his jacket. The schematics gleamed on the screen – a critical piece of the puzzle in the fight against Necra.

He met up with Elaine and debriefed her on his successful mission. After receiving his rewards, he knew that he wanted to have a drink ... ideally a very strong one –

and maybe a card game.

He set the coordinates for Earth and more particularly the Spaceport Bar in Los Angeles, a familiar grin spreading across his face. Whatever trouble awaited him next; Adrian was ready.

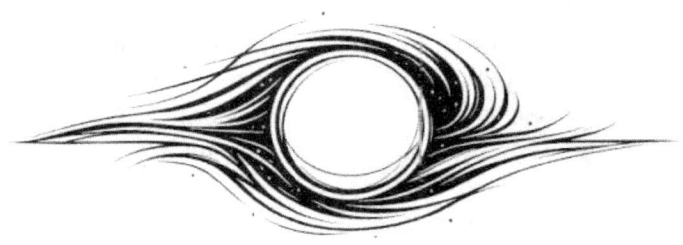

Chapter 16:

The Pilot Search

Tokyo's skyline glimmering under the late morning sun, neon lights still burning from the previous night, a city that never truly sleeps. In a small café tucked between towering buildings, the group occupy a corner table. Locals coming in for takeout bow politely, more out of habit than recognition of these off-world visitors. The café smells of brewed tea, rice, and sizzling street-food style pork.

The four women have drawn as little attention as possible, though a few curious patrons keep glancing at Lilith's black-and-red wings and her large 10-inch horns. A hush of admiration trails behind Grilka's towering frame when she moves, while Freija's slight blueish-white wings fascinate a couple of kids at a nearby table. Kimiko, always poised and distant, sits with her back to the wall, eyes steady.

A young 10-year-old Japanese boy recognizes Grilka and hesitantly approaches her for an autograph. He is obviously a fan and couldn't believe that his favorite wrestler was in Tokyo, of all places. Grilka is happy to sign an autograph while the boy's parents are very apologetic about their son's interrupting their lunch. Grilka grins, bows slightly to the parents and takes the wrestling magazine the boy was holding and turns the magazine to an article written about her with a picture of her receiving a prize for beating a hulking orange creature. She signs it and then gives the boy a reassuring pat on the head. The boy smiles hugely and takes the signed photo back to his parents with a huge amount of glee on his little face. A moment he will forever remember.

Grilka returns her attention to the group.

Freija smirks. "So, you have a groupie. Even all the way out here on Earth?"

Grilka confidently replies, "What can I say, people know me."

A modest lunch assortment decorates their table: bowls of steaming miso soup, a few onigiri (rice balls) stuffed with unfamiliar fillings, and tea so hot it sends up little clouds of steam.

Lilith picks up a rice ball with practiced caution. She's not fully at ease with Earth cuisine, but she'll try anything once.

Grilka devours a bowl of stir-fried vegetables and rice with gusto with her fingers. She discovers she likes bold flavors.

Freija sniffs the miso soup, her breath exhaling a faint frost. She tastes it carefully, eyes widening at the salty-savory combination. "This is… different," she murmurs, stirring the soup.

Kimiko sits composed, half-finished tea by her hand. She nibbles on a plain rice ball in near silence, scanning the café.

At first glance, they could be strangers just sharing a table – except for the hush of energy around them.

Lilith sets her tea down, turning to Kimiko. "You said we need to go to Los Angeles? Today?" while keeping her voice low.

Kimiko nods, brushing a stray grain of rice from her lip. "My contact there gave me a lead on a pilot. We can't face Necra's domain without a pilot who has top-tier navigational skills." Her tone is clinical, as always.

Freija raises an eyebrow, swirling her soup. "Didn't realize Earth had so many big cities. Tokyo… Los Angeles. Must we keep traveling?"

Grilka shrugs, big shoulders rolling. "If it means we get a pilot worth their salt, let's do it. Tokyo's been interesting enough." She glances around at the neon signs outside.

Kimiko sips her tea. "I only know this: the bar is near Los Angeles' spaceport. My contact says many skilled pilots pass through there. We'll have to do a bit of searching."

Lilith looked at them all, picking up the last piece of her rice ball. "Finish your food. We leave within the hour."

Freija grimaces playfully at the half-eaten onigiri in front of her. "I'm still not used to… fish flakes for lunch." She takes a measured bite anyway.

Grilka chortles. "I'll finish yours if you can't handle it."

Freija huffed, but offered a wry grin, passing her leftover to Grilka. Kimiko eyes them quietly, the corners of her mouth barely curved in what might be a smirk.

Onward to Los Angeles

An hour later, they exit Tokyo via an intercity shuttle. Billboards in Japanese script flash overhead, advertising everything from VR gaming to specialized alien cuisine.

Soon they are back on the Scorpion. Ready to put in the coordinates of the Spaceport Bar. Kimiko rests in the lounge while Lilith, the pilot, Freija, the co-pilot, and Grilka at weapons, take the short flight from Tokyo to Los Angeles. They arrive at about 8:00 at night.

Walking through the chaotic streets, they find a directions kiosk pointing them to the Spaceport Bar, a known watering hole for off-world travelers. Kimiko leads with swift steps, weaving between pedestrians. Freija, unnerved by the clamor, stays close to Lilith. Grilka's imposing figure parts the crowd easily.

A flickering neon sign reading "Spaceport Bar" greets them at the entrance: letters half-burned out, but legible enough.

Adrian and Lopeth

Adrian sits in a corner booth near the flickering neon signage. He's a lean figure, with dirty blond unkempt hair, and a battered leather jacket that's seen better days. On the table in front of him: two upsides down and three additional shot glasses, each filled with tequila. He's savoring them – or procrastinating, it's hard to say.

He'd been in L.A. two nights, drifting aimlessly. He calls himself a pilot, gambler, and occasional scoundrel. The bartender knows him only as that 'space jockey' who pays in half-torn credit chits. Adrian is halfway watching the bar's door, half ignoring the rest of the world.

Enter Lopeth – a broad man with a scar across his temple, wearing a heavy coat. Lopeth stomps in and glances around. The hush that usually greets him is stifled by the bar's hum, but Adrian notices. He smirks, swirling one of the tequila shots.

"Lopeth," Adrian mutters under his breath. "Didn't expect to see you in this corner of Earth."

Lopeth notices Adrian almost instantly, scowling. He strides over, glaring. "Flynn," he growls. "Fancy finding you here, losing yourself in cheap drinks. I hoped to never smell your stench again."

Adrian quirks a brow. "Now, Lopeth, that's no way to greet an old associate. Pull up a seat, I might let you share my tequila… assuming you can cover half the tab."

Lopeth's lip curls. "I'd rather pay triple for good liquor than drink your swill. Last time we met, you left me high and dry. I won't forget that."

"Suit yourself," Adrian says, lifting a shot in a

mocking salute. "But do me a favor – take a breath. All this bitterness can't be good for your blood pressure."

Lopeth's eyes narrow. He slides onto the opposite seat, but not too close. "One day, Flynn, you'll choke on that sarcasm."

Adrian laughs lightly, downing one shot. It burns fiercely. "Until that day, I'll keep talking. So, what brings you to Earth? I thought you did your dirty dealings in the frontier zones."

"Trying to pick up a new contract," Lopeth mutters, scanning the bar. "Looking for something easy that pays well."

A crooked grin tugs at Adrian's lips. "Maybe you should stay away from card tables this time."

Lopeth bristles but doesn't retort. The tension between them simmers, not quite at boiling.

The 4 Enter

The door slides open, revealing Lilith, Freija, Grilka, and Kimiko. The bar quiets for a moment and all eyes swivel to the imposing group. Adrian notices the hush, and leans to glimpse them, too. He sees black-and-red wings, a giant green figure, and one other with lesser wings and a silent aura. *What in the cosmos?* Adrian thinks, eyebrows shooting up.

Lopeth also noticed, frowning at their outlandish appearance. The group strides to the bar, ignoring the stares. The bartender greets them with a wary nod.

Freija speaks first, her voice firm but not loud. "We're seeking a pilot. We have urgent business off-world."

The bartender scratches his chin, unimpressed. "A pilot, huh? You must be more specific. Plenty of folks come in claiming to fly. Did you want cargo hauling or …?"

Lilith leans in, face stern, wings partially open. "We need someone skilled with unpredictable routes, maybe dogfights, and not afraid of high stakes. And we need them soon."

The bartender chews at his lip. "Well, not many around here this early in the night. I got one or two mercs popping by… that fella Lopeth is some sort of pilot, I guess, though mostly muscle. He's the orange guy sitting over there next to the guy in the leather jacket." He points with a nod. "Take your pick."

They follow his gaze: indeed, Lopeth sits at a corner booth with another man. Lopeth spots them looking and immediately waves them off with a dismissive sneer, turning his attention back to his glass. Clearly uninterested.

Freija exhales, disappointed. "He's not even giving us a chance."

Lilith's eyes flash. "He can keep his disinterest." She strides a step closer to approach, but Lopeth pointedly turns away, raising his drink in a gesture of 'buzz off.' Kimiko remains silent behind them, observing.

Adrian, from his vantage, snorts and calls out, "He's all bark and no throttle, ladies."

All four women glance at the voice. They see a lean man with messy hair, brandishing a half-smile behind a lineup of shot glasses. The demon-lady raises a brow. "And you are?"

Adrian sets his drink down and slides out of the booth, ignoring Lopeth's glare. "Adrian Flynn. And you must be part of the traveling carnival. Gotta say, your style is… eye-catching." He motions vaguely at their wings, armor, and silent ninja gear.

Grilka bristles slightly, but Freija, though serious, can't help a wry grin. "We're not a carnival," she says flatly.

"Coulda fooled me," Adrian quips. Then he shrugs. "But if you're looking for a pilot, you can skip old Lopeth there. He can't fly worth a damn. Probably just runs guns or contraband. Me, on the other hand …" He spreads his arms in a theatrical gesture. "I'm a real star pilot."

Lilith narrows her ember-colored eyes at him. "And

how would we know that, Adrian? Or that you won't waste our time?"

Adrian smirks, casting a glance at Lopeth, who smolders in silent frustration. "Because if I were incompetent, Lopeth would have no problem humiliating me right now. Instead, he's sulking – 'nuff said." He looks back at the quartet. "You need skill. I've got skill. Let's talk terms."

Freija steps forward, her voice grave: "We have a mission – urgent, potentially involving combat. Pay is negotiable. But first, can you handle... unconventional routes?"

Adrian chuckles. "Unconventional is my middle name, right after 'Danger'." The sarcasm oozes out of him.

Lilith sighs, though amusement briefly flickers in her eyes. "We'll see. We have to confirm you're not just talk."

Kimiko says nothing, but her gaze is intense, as if evaluating Adrian's every twitch.

"Just talk, eh?" Adrian retorts. "I'll show you if you earn it. But first, I have a condition." He taps the bar twice, signaling the bartender. "Shot of tequila for me and each of these lovely ladies, courtesy of him," pointing to Lopeth who doesn't notice. "Make these top shelf."

Tequila Trials

Freija frowns. "Tequila? Why would I ..."

Adrian grins mischievously, raising an eyebrow. "Gotta share a toast before I sign onto anything. My personal tradition. No shot, no pilot." He shrugs. "Take it or leave it, Frosty."

Grilka snorts. "That's ridiculous, but fine. I'm game for a drink."

Lilith glared at him, her wings twitching in annoyance. "If it's that important to you. But this better not be a joke."

"Would I joke?" Adrian calls for four more shot

glasses. The bartender lines them up, pouring the top shelf tequila into each of the five glasses. Freija wrinkles her nose, while Kimiko stands a step behind, arms crossed, silent.

Freija picks up a shot, sniffs it, and nearly gags. "It's vile. Smells like a chemical spill."

Adrian lifts a shot in cheers. "Correct. Some call it rocket fuel, or paint stripper. But trust me, it's an Earth tradition." He tips his glass to the group, smirking. "Down the hatch, ladies."

Grilka grabs her shot, eyes gleaming. "I've tried some strong brews. Let's see." She knocks it back in one gulp, grimaces momentarily, then lets out a satisfied gasp. "That stings … but good." She bangs the empty glass on the bar, asking for another with a quick nod.

Freija sips hers hesitantly. The fiery liquid hits her tongue, and she sputters, wings flaring slightly. "Ugh, that's… disgusting!" She coughs. "By my home's glaciers, who drinks this for fun?"

Lilith stares at the shot then raises the glass. She locks eyes with Adrian as she swallows it in one swift motion. Her face twists for half a beat – though she tries to mask it. "Better than sulfur fumes, I guess," she mutters. "Still awful."

Finally, all eyes turn to Kimiko. She stands stiffly, her shot glass untouched. Her dark, neutral gaze flickers from the liquor then to Adrian. He simply arches a brow, as if to say, *Well?*

Grilka, emboldened by her second shot, nudges Kimiko gently with an elbow. "Go on, ninja. Nothing kills you faster than fear." She laughs, swirling her own refill.

A hint of vexation crosses Kimiko's face. She lifts the shot, sets it to her lips, and drinks. Her posture remains utterly poised, though the flush at her throat betrays the burn. She grimaces – tiny but noticeable. Then she sets it down, taking a steady breath.

Adrian claps once, delighted. "Excellent. Now we're

all partners in crime, right?" He waves his glass in a triumphant flourish. "Bartender, a round of applause for these troopers."

A few patrons glanced over, unimpressed. The bartender simply rolls his eyes.

Sealing the Deal

Lilith recovered from the tequila burn, her voice returning to that stern tone. "Alright, we did your little ritual. Now, name your price, pilot."

Adrian folds his arms in mock contemplation. "Mmm, let's see. Hazard pay, plus living expenses, plus a bonus if this job is half as dangerous as you imply. I can't be undercut. Also, I have the final say on flight routes. You want me to steer you to victory, you trust my instincts."

Freija, still reeling from the taste, sighs. "You drive a hard bargain for a random stranger in a bar."

He gives a flippant shrug. "Random or not, I'm your best bet. Otherwise, Lopeth can step up – oh, wait." He points to Lopeth, who glowers from a distant table, refusing to look their way.

Lilith exchanged a glance with Kimiko, who nodded minutely. Then Grilka sets down her second empty shot, wiping her mouth. "We can pay well enough. We're funded by certain allied networks. As for trusting your route, we'll see… just don't bail on us halfway."

Kimiko finally spoke, her voice low but firm. "And if you try to betray us, no second chances." She levels a cool stare at Adrian.

He meets her gaze with a crooked smirk. "Understood, ninja-lady. I'm not suicidal. Betraying a group with wings, horns, and giant muscles isn't my style."

Freija straightened, placing a hand on Lilith's arm as if to calm any residual tension. "We depart soon. We'll send you the coordinates of our ship. Meet us at dawn tomorrow for a test flight. If you pass, we move out."

Adrian stands, pushing the empty shot glasses aside. "Dawn? That's… rather early, but I'll manage." He fishes a few credits from his pocket, slapping them on the bar to cover the drinks. "Deal. Adrian Flynn, star pilot, at your service… for a price."

He winks. "Now, if you'll excuse me, I might need to find a bed where I can crash before you people drag me into an interstellar war."

Exiting the Bar

At that moment, a restless hush ripples through the bar again. People sense that the confrontation or conversation is wrapping up. Lopeth eyes them one more time, as if reconsidering whether to start trouble with Adrian. But the presence of the four formidable women makes him think twice.

Grilka stretches her green arms, letting out a contented sigh after the strong liquor. "Huh, I like Earth drinks. Who knew?"

Freija still with the awful taster in her mouth says, "Well, I for one hope we never do that again."

Lilith rubbed her temple. "For once, I agree with Freija. Let's get out of this place." She pivoted toward the exit, wings twitching restlessly. Kimiko, silent as ever, slips behind her with graceful, near-invisible steps.

The four women pause at the threshold. Lilith looks over her shoulder at Adrian. "Tomorrow. Dawn. Don't be late… or you lose this chance."

Adrian offers a casual salute, leaning against the bar. "Bright and early, got it."

Freija, holding her stomach from the aftertaste, just shakes her head and exits. Grilka gives Adrian a friendly, if slightly tipsy, nod. Kimiko spares him a final, cold glance before slipping out.

Adrian's Reflection

The door slides shut behind them, leaving Adrian once again in the smoky gloom of the L.A. Spaceport Bar. He rubs a hand over his stubbled chin, mind churning. *A winged demon-lady, a green amazon, a frosty princess, and a silent ninja.* Not exactly the typical crew. But they're paying.

He glances at Lopeth, who remains at his table like a coiled snake. *That's one old grudge I'd like to avoid.* A job off-world might be the perfect escape. Standing, Adrian tosses the bartender a lopsided grin. "Thanks for the tequila, friend. I might be out of your hair soon." He slides another credit chit across the counter for good measure.

The bartender shrugs. "Your funeral, pilot. Though I guess it's worth a shot if you're lucky."

"Luck is my middle name," Adrian quips, pivoting away. In truth, he's half-sure this is a monumental gamble. But that's his style. *High risk, high reward,* he thinks. If the group stands a chance against interstellar tyranny, being their pilot could be more profitable than any petty smuggling job.

He steps out into the neon-lit Los Angeles dusk, the sky a swirl of orange and pink against distant skyscrapers. A faint breeze rustles his hair, still carrying the tang of cheap tequila on his breath. *Tomorrow, a test flight at dawn.* Usually, Adrian hates early mornings. But for a decent paycheck – and maybe some cosmic glory – he'll drag himself out of bed.

A grin tugs at his lips. *They wanted to see if I can handle unusual routes? They've never flown with Adrian Flynn.* He imagines Freija's recoil at more Earth liquor, Lilith's unwavering scowl, Grilka's bullish enthusiasm, and Kimiko's silent intimidation. *What a crew,* he muses, *and I'm about to join them.*

In the back of his mind, a flicker of concern: what if this job is bigger and badder than anything he's known?

Necra. A name whispered among travelers, describing entire worlds subjugated. The wise part of him says he should run the other way. But that wise part is drowned out by the gambler's rush. *Potentially huge pay. Epic battles. Better than rusting in some Earth back alley.* Indeed, life's too short not to roll the dice.

He hums a tuneless melody as he meanders down the street, heading back to his ship. *At least if tomorrow goes sour, I'll have the memory of forcibly feeding them tequila. That alone might be worth the risk.* He laughs to himself.

And so, Adrian heads off, preparing for dawn's uncertain promise… another shot of chaos, courtesy of the unstoppable, improbable group.

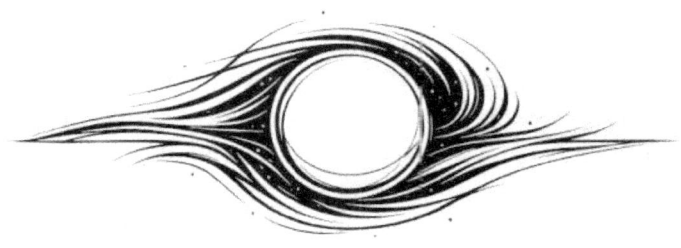

Chapter 17:

The Ship's Tour

As it so happens, Adrian's ship was in the same spaceport as where he was supposed to be meeting his new shipmates. He was just one dock away. That was rather convenient.

Adrian approached the Scorpion in a haphazard skip, his boots clinking on the metallic floor of the hangar as he took in the sight of the ship. He tilted his head, squinting at its dented, rusted hull and uneven landing gear. The grey paint job was faded in places, with scorch marks hinting at close calls in the past. He stopped, placing his hands on his hips.

"So, this is it, huh? The mighty Scorpion," he said, his voice dripping with sarcasm. He turned to Lilith, his smirk widening. "Looks like it's held together with spit and prayers. Let me guess, Demon Captain – she's a 'work in progress'?"

Lilith's fiery wings flared slightly as she folded her arms. "She's… functional. That's all that matters."

Adrian gave an exaggerated shrug. "Functional? Sure. Until you're in the middle of a firefight and a panel falls off." He walked closer, tapping the hull. A dull clang echoed. "Yep, just as I thought. She's been through some things."

Freija stepped up, her icy wings twitching with excitement. "Oh, come on! She's got character! Let me show you around... you'll see." Without waiting for a response, she grabbed Adrian's arm and led him toward the ramp.

The interior of the Scorpion wasn't much more impressive than the exterior, but Freija's enthusiasm made up for it. She pointed out the various spaces, starting with the cockpit.

"This is the pilot's section," she said, gesturing dramatically. "Three seats: pilot on the left, co-pilot on the right. That lever right there switches control from one to the other in case of emergencies. And the third seat back there?" She spun to face him. "That's for weapons and shields."

Adrian examined the setup, nodding slowly. "Not bad. Compact but efficient. I've seen worse... barely."

Freija ignored the jab and moved to the next area. "Now, this is the bathroom. Tiny, but functional. One person at a time, obviously."

"Obviously," Adrian muttered, peeking inside. "Cozy."

They continued to the barracks. Freija pushed open the door to reveal two bunk beds lining the narrow room. The beds were clearly built for standard six-foot people, with no extra frills or space.

"This is where we sleep," Freija announced. "Four beds, all the comfort you need."

Adrian leaned against the doorway, looking at the room, then back at Freija. He counted on his fingers theatrically. "One, two, three, four... and now me, that makes five. Do we rotate? Draw straws? Or does someone sleep on the floor?"

Freija grinned. "Oh, don't worry. You can always curl up in the cockpit if you don't like it. Or maybe Kimiko will teach you how to meditate while standing."

Lilith's voice cut through the banter. "We'll figure it

out. Focus."

Adrian gave her a mock salute. "Yes, Demon Captain. Whatever you say."

The next stop was the living space, equipped with four leather chairs arranged in a semicircle. The walls bore signs of wear, but it was clear this area was meant for downtime. In the middle was a table with wings that could be pulled out to provide an eating service.

"And this is where we relax," Freija said, plopping into one of the chairs. "What do you think?"

Adrian looked around, then sank into one of the chairs with exaggerated effort. "I think… it'll do. Barely."

Next to the living area was a small kitchen that could barely fit one person comfortably.

Kimiko, who had been quiet during the tour, spoke up from the doorway. "If you're as good as you claim, the ship shouldn't matter. Or are you going to back out now?"

Adrian's grin returned. "Oh, I'm in. I just like giving Demon Captain here a hard time."

Freija pointed to two more doors. One of them leads to their armory and the other to a cargo bay. On each side of the ship was a docking port so an additional two ships could dock with the ship. This would be how Adrian would dock his ship while in flight.

Lilith rolled her eyes. "Enough is enough. The tour is over. Let's move on. Grilka and I have a stop to make."

Arming Up Grilka

Lilith and Grilka made their way to the nearest weapons store, a large, bustling establishment filled with racks of advanced firearms. The walls were lined with everything from sleek disruptors to heavy-duty plasma rifles. Grilka's eyes lit up as she surveyed the selection.

"It's been too long," she said, running her fingers over the grip of a plasma rifle. "This feels right."

Lilith watched as Grilka picked out two disruptors, a

155

leather belt with dual holsters, and a plasma rifle with a shoulder strap. As they approached the counter, Lilith finally spoke. "Do you miss it? The shooting, I mean."

Grilka paused, her expression turning serious. "Sometimes. It's what I'm good at, you know? But this mission… is different. Bigger than anything I've done before. What about you? Do you miss leading your own kind?"

Lilith's fiery gaze softened. "Every day. But this…" She gestured vaguely, as if encompassing their current mission. "This is where I need to be. Where we all need to be."

Grilka nodded, a rare moment of quiet understanding passing between them. "Let's make it count, then."

Getting Personal

Back on the Scorpion, Adrian, Freija, and Kimiko were seated in the living space, each settling into their roles. Freija was her usual lively self, gesturing animatedly as she talked about their mission and the adventures so far.

"And then Lilith nearly flew us into an asteroid! I swear, I thought we were done for," Freija said, laughing.

Adrian raised an eyebrow, his grin teasing. "And you still haven't found a better pilot until now? Lucky me."

Kimiko, sitting cross-legged, spoke in her usual cold, calculating tone. "Luck has nothing to do with it. You're here because we need someone with your skills. To prove you're worth it."

Adrian's expression turned mock serious. "Ouch. Cold as ice, huh? Don't worry, sweetheart. I'll prove myself when it counts."

Freija laughed. "You two are going to get along great. I bet by the end of this you two will be best friends."

Kimiko didn't respond, her focus already shifting to sharpening one of her katanas. Adrian leaned back in his chair, watching her with interest before turning his attention to Freija.

"So, I've got to ask," he said. "What's it like working with the Demon Captain? Is she as intense as she seems?"

Freija's smile widened. "Lilith? She's… passionate. And very serious about the mission. But once you get past the wings and the horns, she's a good leader."

Adrian chuckled. "Good to know. I'd hate to get on her bad side."

"You're probably already there," Kimiko muttered, earning a laugh from Freija.

The banter continued, the three of them gradually finding a rhythm. For all their differences, there was a growing sense of camaraderie – a foundation for the battles ahead.

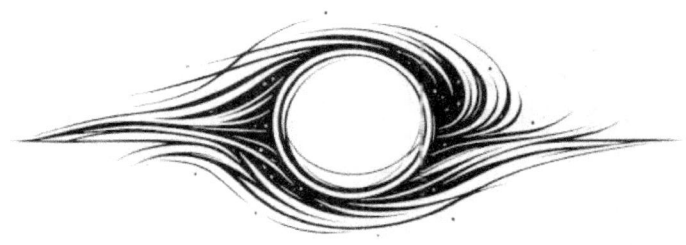

Chapter 18:

A Native American's Spirit

The sun dipped below the horizon, casting a fiery glow across the vast plains of the Great Wakasa Reservation. Rainstorm stood at the edge of a towering cliff, her long, Native American black hair whipping in the wind, her twin braids adorned with feathers and beads that glimmered in the twilight. Her ceremonial tomahawks rested in their sheaths at her sides, and her arm bore the tattoo of her spirit guide: a majestic hawk with wings outstretched in eternal flight.

Rainstorm, born Tala Redhawk, was the only daughter of Chief Eshona of the Wakasa people. Her community was one of the few remaining tribes that managed to preserve their traditions and sovereignty while also embracing modern times.

As the chief's daughter, she was both a symbol of her people's heritage and a fierce defender of their lands.

A Spiritual Legacy

From an early age, Tala exhibited a unique connection to the spiritual world. The tribal elders often said that she walked in two realms – one of flesh and one of spirit. At the age of fifteen, during her Vision Quests, she had fasted and meditated alone in the sacred canyon for three days. On the final night, under a canopy of stars, the hawk had come to her, its piercing gaze locking with hers before it soared into the heavens. The elders interpreted this as a sign that Tala was destined to be a guide and protector for her people.

Her father, Chief Eshona, was a proud but pragmatic leader. He saw the weight of responsibility Tala carried and tried to balance nurturing her spirituality with preparing her for the harsh realities of leadership.

RAINSTORM

"The stars may guide us," he often said, "but we must still walk the earth with steady feet."

Tala embraced her dual nature, honing both her spiritual and physical skills. She trained relentlessly with the tomahawk and short staff, her movements fluid and deliberate, each strike accompanied by a prayer. To embrace modern technology, she was also taught the use of a disruptor to ensure she could be accurate from a distance, if that were needed. She excelled in all three weapons.

The elders taught her the ancient chants and ceremonies, while her father instructed her in diplomacy and the art of war.

Her mother taught her the use of herbs and how to read nature and its plants. She was taught the basics and advanced healing techniques that she could use to not only heal herself while in combat, but also any other warrior injured.

She was even taught alien physiology in case she needed to mend the wounds of others who were from distant planets.

The Regal Warrior

By the time she reached adulthood, Tala had become a figure of awe and respect among her people. Her regal bearing and quiet strength made her a natural leader, while her deep connection to the spiritual realm earned her the title of Rainstorm, a role that signified her as a bridge between the divine and mortal worlds.

Despite her lofty position, Tala never shied away from the struggles of her people. When outsiders attempted to encroach on their lands to mine rare minerals, she led the resistance, using her skills in combat and strategy to drive them away. In one particularly tense standoff, she faced a group of heavily armed mercenaries, her tomahawks gleaming in the sunlight. Her unflinching resolve and commanding presence forced the intruders to retreat without a single drop of blood spilling.

Her victories only deepened her people's reverence

for her, but Tala carried the weight of her responsibilities with humility. She often sought solitude in the sacred canyon, where she would meditate for hours, seeking guidance from her spirit guide. The hawk remained a constant presence in her visions, a reminder of her purpose.

A Call to the Stars

As much as Tala loved her people and her land, she often found herself gazing at the stars with a sense of longing. Her spirit guide's flight into the heavens during her Vision Quest had left an indelible mark on her, planting the seed of a destiny that stretched far beyond the plains of Wakasa.

Her father noticed this restlessness and confronted her one evening as they sat by the fire. "Your heart is not content to stay here," he said, his tone both understanding and wistful.

Tala hesitated with her gaze fixed on the flickering flames. "I feel the call of the stars, Father. There is a great battle coming. A darkness that threatens not just our people but all people. I cannot sit idly while others fight to protect the balance of the universe."

Chief Eshona regarded her silently for a long moment before nodding. "If this is the path the spirits have chosen for you, then you must walk it. But remember, no matter where you go, you carry Wakasa with you. You are Rainstorm and your people will always look to you for strength."

The Transition to Rainstorm

The plains of Wakasa glistened under the light of the setting sun, the rain from earlier that day still clinging to the tall grasses. Tala stood atop the Cliff of Spirits. She was no longer the same young woman who had taken up arms for her people in that fateful battle. The storm that had raged both in the skies and within her heart had reshaped her into something more – a warrior known not only for her strength but for her spirit. The name Rainstorm, given to her by the elders, had spread far beyond the Wakasa Plains, a symbol of her unyielding resolve.

Rainstorm had embraced the name, but with it came a profound sense of duty. The weight of her people's trust was not a burden she carried lightly. She had spent the years following that first battle deepening her connection to the spiritual world, meditating in the sacred canyon where her vision quest had taken place. Each time she entered the canyon, she felt the presence of her spirit guide, the hawk, its piercing gaze reminding her of her purpose. The elders often called upon her to lead ceremonies, her prayers and chants weaving seamlessly into the fabric of her warrior identity.

The Call of the Stars

Despite her connection to her people, Rainstorm couldn't shake the feeling that she was meant for something more. Necra's growing influence in the galaxy had reached even the Wakasa, her name whispered in hushed tones by traders and travelers who passed through. Rainstorm listened intently, her heart stirring with the knowledge that a great battle was on the horizon. The plains of Wakasa had forged her into a warrior, but she knew her skills may be needed elsewhere.

Her father, Chief Eshona, sensed the change in her. One evening, as they sat by the fire, he spoke with the wisdom and clarity she had always admired. "You are restless, Rainstorm," he said, his voice calm but knowing. "Your heart belongs to the Wakasa, but your spirit seeks the stars."

Rainstorm hesitated, the flickering firelight casting shadows across her face. "I feel it, Father. There is a darkness spreading, one that will not spare us if left unchecked. I cannot ignore the call."

Chief Eshona nodded, his expression was both proud and bittersweet. "The spirits chose you for this, Tala. You are Rainstorm, not just of the Wakasa but of all who need your strength. If you must go, go with honor and carry Wakasa with you wherever you fight.

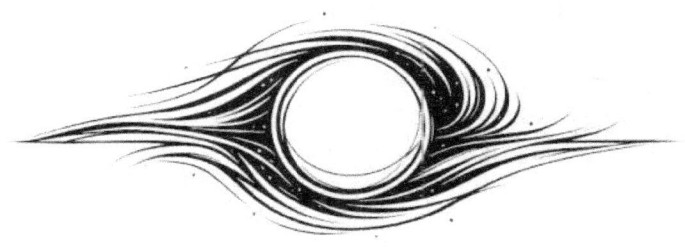

Chapter 19:

The Search for Rainstorm

Adrian leaned against the cockpit controls, watching the terrain below. "You know," he said, his tone laced with sarcasm, "I'm starting to think our little group of misfits might be biting off more than we can chew. Armies, intergalactic enemies, and what? Five of us?" He glanced at Lilith, smirking. "Even with Demon Captain here, it's a stretch."

"You have a suggestion?" Lilith asked, her fiery eyes narrowing slightly.

Adrian's grin widened. "Actually, yeah. Ever heard of a woman named Rainstorm? She's a warrior – Navajo, strong as hell, and more in tune with the spiritual world than anyone I've ever heard of. If you're looking for someone who can hold her own, she's the one."

Kimiko, seated at her usual spot sharpening her katanas, paused. "Rainstorm? I've heard of her. She's known for her skill with tomahawks and her precision with throwing weapons. If she's as good as they say, she'd be a valuable addition."

Lilith nodded, her wings shifting behind her. "Where do we find her?"

Adrian gestured out the window. "We're close. She

lives on a reservation not far from here. But..." He hesitated, scratching his chin. "Finding her may not be easy. She's not exactly the welcoming type."

Kimiko had to interject, "Neither was I."

Lilith nodded in agreement.

The Scorpion descended over the red sands of Arizona, its engines humming against the stillness of the desert landscape. The early morning sun cast long shadows over jagged rock formations and sparse vegetation, creating a scene both serene and mysterious. The Crimson Alliance had arrived, their search for the next addition to their team beginning in earnest.

With Adrian as the pilot and Lilith as the copilot, the Scorpion landed in a clearing near the reservation.

Adrian, Kimiko, and Lilith disembarked, the dry heat of the desert air greeting them as they stepped onto the sandy ground. Ahead, the reservation's modest structures were nestled among the rocks, blending seamlessly with the natural surroundings. A few residents eyed them curiously but said nothing.

The three made their way through the reservation, taking in the serene atmosphere. Elders sat outside their homes, carving intricate designs into wood or beads, while children played under the watchful eyes of their families. The air was rich with the scent of sage and cedar, and an underlying stillness seemed to permeate the entire settlement.

Their first stop was the community center, where they hoped to gather information. Inside, a group of locals sat in a circle, engaged in quiet conversation. An older man, his long hair tied back, his face lined with wisdom, noticed their arrival and approached them with measured steps.

"You've come a long way," he said, his voice steady. "What brings you here?"

Lilith stepped forward. "We're looking for a warrior named Rainstorm. We need her help."

The elders' sharp eyes moved over each of them, lingering briefly on Adrian's disruptors and Lilith's wings. "Rainstorm is a protector of our people. Her path is guided by the spirits. What do you seek her for?"

Adrian, uncharacteristically serious, answered. "We're fighting a battle that's bigger than any of us. We need someone with her strength and her connection to the spiritual world. This isn't just about us. It's about everyone in the galaxy."

The elder considered this, his gaze unwavering. Finally, he nodded. "Rainstorm trains by the stream at dawn. Follow the path through the rocks, and you will find her. But approach her with respect. She is not easily swayed."

The three followed the elder's directions, winding their way through the arid landscape. The sun's rays grew stronger as they walked, but the sound of running water eventually broke the silence. As they approached the stream, the landscape shifted subtly, becoming cooler and greener. Towering boulders and sparse trees created a secluded haven, and the sound of birds added to the tranquil atmosphere.

Kimiko, who had been silent for most of the journey, raised a hand to halt the group. "There, on the left," she whispered, nodding toward the water's edge.

Rainstorm stood with her back to them; her long black hair braided into two thick plaits that reached halfway to her waist. She wore a traditional woman's headdress, adorned with feathers and beads, and her cheeks were streaked with war paint. Her off-white training outfit sported a leather belt with two tomahawk holsters and a short staff on her back. On her arm was a large tattoo of a hawk, its fierce eyes seemingly alive, etched into her arm. Around her neck hung a necklace of beads and carved symbols, which swayed slightly as she moved.

She was in the middle of training, her tomahawks slicing through the air with precision and power. Her

167

movements were fluid, almost hypnotic, as she struck a series of targets fashioned from bundled sticks and animal hide. Each strike landed with a solid thunk, the force of her blows sending splinters flying.

Lilith started to step forward, but Adrian placed a hand on her arm. "Careful," he whispered. "She's not someone you just walk up to."

Kimiko moved ahead instead, her approach measured and respectful. "Rainstorm," she called softly.

Rainstorm stopped mid-swing, her sharp eyes snapping to the group. She lowered her tomahawks but didn't let her guard down. "Who are you?" she asked, her voice steady and commanding.

Kimiko inclined her head. "My name is Kimiko. These are my companions. We've come to ask for your help."

Rainstorm's gaze swept over them, lingering on each one. "Help with what?"

Lilith stepped forward, her wings folding neatly behind her. "We're fighting a war. The enemy we face threatens not just our worlds but every world. We need warriors – the best warriors – to stand with us."

Rainstorm studied Lilith, her expression unreadable. "Why me?"

Adrian spoke up, his tone earnest. "Because you're strong. Because you've got the skills and the heart to make a difference. And because we can't do this without you."

For a moment, Rainstorm said nothing. Then she set her tomahawks down and walked to the edge of the stream, staring into the water. "The spirits guide my path," she said softly. "If they will it, I will join you. But you must prove that your cause is just."

"How?" Kimiko asked, stepping closer.

Rainstorm's expression tightened, and she took a step back, shaking her head. "I've sworn an oath to protect my people," she said firmly. "They are my priority. Why should I leave them to fight in a war I know nothing about?"

Kimiko stepped closer, her voice softer but more resolute. "Rainstorm, I understand your hesitation. You've dedicated your life to protecting your people, but this war isn't just about us. It's about everything. If we fail, your people will face the same threat we're fighting against – but they'll face it alone. Joining us could be the very thing that saves them."

Rainstorm's eyes narrowed, her skepticism clear. "And you think you can promise their safety? What do you know of my people... of their needs?"

Kimiko again stepped closer, her gaze unwavering. "I know what it means to fight for something bigger than yourself. Your skills, your strength, your connection to the spirits – they're needed now more than ever. If we're going to stop this enemy, we need someone with your heart and your conviction. You wouldn't just be fighting for us – you'd be fighting for them."

Adrian, leaning casually against a nearby tree, chimed in. "She's right, you know. Besides, these guys?" He gestured toward the group. "They're not half-bad. And hey, if you don't like us, you can always come back and toss us into the nearest canyon."

Rainstorm's lips quirked briefly, almost a smile, but her serious demeanor returned. She turned to the stream, kneeling at its edge. "I will meditate," she said quietly. "The spirits will guide my decision. Wait here."

The team watched in silence as Rainstorm closed her eyes and sat down cross-legged, her hands resting lightly on her knees. The sound of the water seemed to grow louder, the air around them stilling. Minutes passed; the weight of her deliberation settled over them. She began to chant an ancient stream of words.

Finally, Rainstorm opened her eyes and stood. Her expression was calm but resolute. "The spirits have spoken. I will join you," she said. "But understand this: I fight for my people and the spirits. If your cause proves unworthy, I will leave."

Lilith nodded, her fiery gaze steady. "We wouldn't expect anything less."

With an unusual sense of wanting to be funny and serious at the same time, Kimiko chimed in, "I said the same thing two days ago."

Adrian was quick not to be out humored while shaking his head up and down, "Me too about two hours ago."

Rainstorm Tours the Scorpion

Back at the Scorpion Freija – bubbly as ever – eagerly took on the role of tour guide, leading Rainstorm through the ship. "It's not much, but it's home," she said with a grin. "This is the cockpit. Three seats: pilot, co-pilot, and weapons control. Over here is the galley…"

Adrian followed, adding his own commentary. "Modest living quarters. Four beds for six people. Hope you like sharing."

Rainstorm raised an eyebrow. "I've slept in worse places."

"See?" Adrian said with a laugh. "She'll fit right in."

As the tour continued, the team's camaraderie began to grow. Rainstorm's presence brought a new strength to their ranks, and for the first time, they felt like a force truly capable of taking on the battles ahead.

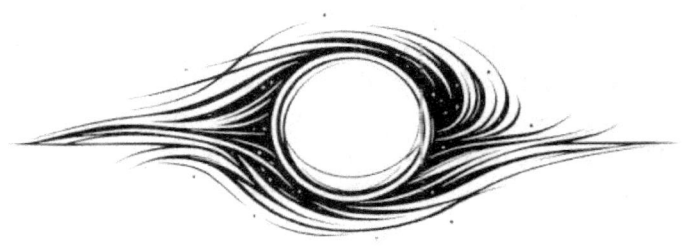

Chapter 20:

Nefertari's Path

The sands of Akhenai, an ancient desert oasis, shimmered under the heat of the sun of northern Africa. Golden dunes stretched endlessly, interrupted only by the towering spires of the Temple of Bastet, a sanctuary dedicated to the goddess of protection and war. Inside its cool, shadowed halls, Nefertari knelt before a statue of the feline goddess, her long black hair damp with sweat from the morning's training.

Nefertari was no ordinary inhabitant of Akhenai. Born to the royal bloodline of the House of Amara, she was a warrior chantress, raised with both the privileges of royalty and the unrelenting demands of her heritage. Her title came with expectations: to protect her people, to lead them in times of strife, and to embody the virtues of their ancient traditions. Yet Nefertari had always carried a heavier burden... one she embraced without question. Her people revered her, not just for her lineage but for her unmatched skill on the battlefield and her unwavering sense of duty.

Regal Upbringing

From the moment she could walk, Nefertari's life

was steeped in discipline. Her mother, High Priestess Sahmira instilled in her a deep sense of responsibility to their people, while her father, High Priest Khafra, honed her body and mind. Lessons in diplomacy were followed by hours of combat training, her days filled with both the grace of a diplomat and the ferocity of a warrior.

NEFERTARI

By the age of ten, Nefertari had already mastered the use of the khopesh – the curved blade that symbolized the royal warriors of Egypt. Her father often brought her to the training grounds, where seasoned soldiers tested her abilities. Though small in stature compared to the towering men she faced, Nefertari's agility and precision made her a force to be reckoned with.

Not only was she skilled with the blade, but she was also a sharpshooter with energy guns and rifles. When she reached her teens, she partook and was often placed in the top three of any contests.

"Strength is not enough," her father would say as she practiced. "A true warrior must fight with their heart and mind as well as their blade."

Her regal training extended beyond physical. Nefertari was immersed in the ancient texts of Akhenai, studying the legends of their ancestors who had fought to unite the desert tribes. These stories ignited a sense of duty within her, a belief that her life was not her own but belonged to her people and their future.

The Desert Trials

At eighteen, Nefertari faced the Desert Trials, a rite of passage for Akhenai's royal heirs. The trials were designed to test not only physical endurance but also mental fortitude and spiritual connection to the goddess Bastet. For five days and nights, Nefertari journeyed alone through the unforgiving desert, carrying nothing but her khopesh, a 2-liter water pouch, and the blessings of her people.

The trials were grueling. Sandstorms battered her, and the scorching heat of the day gave way to the freezing chill of the night. Yet Nefertari pressed on, her resolve unyielding. On the second night, she encountered a wild desert beast – a massive lion with eyes that glowed like embers.

The creature lunged at her, but Nefertari did not falter. She sidestepped its charge and struck with her khopesh, her movements as fluid as the winds that shaped the dunes.

When the beast fell, Nefertari knelt beside it, whispering a prayer of gratitude to Bastet. In that moment, she felt a profound connection to her goddess and her destiny.

For sustenance, she ate the beast's highest protein meat areas raw. She drank the beast's blood for more nutrients until it was time to return home.

By the time she returned to the temple, weary but victorious, her people greeted her as a true leader – a warrior blessed by the divine.

A Leader in Battle

As Akhenai faced increasing threats from off-world raiders seeking to plunder its treasures, Nefertari proved herself not only a capable fighter but a brilliant tactician. She led her people in skirmishes against invaders, her khopesh cutting through the enemy ranks with unrelenting precision. Her bravery on the battlefield inspired her soldiers, and her tactical acumen earned her the respect of her generals.

One of her greatest victories came during the Siege of Anubet, when a band of raiders armed with advanced technology stormed the sacred city. Nefertari, outnumbered and outgunned, devised a daring plan to use the city's intricate network of tunnels to outflank the enemy. Her forces struck with precision, overwhelming the raiders and driving them out of Akhenai. The people celebrated her as the Shield of Akhenai, a title that cemented her place in their history.

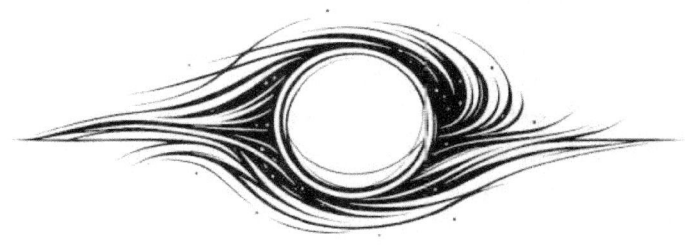

Chapter 21:

A Trip to Egypt

The six of them were gathered in the Scorpion's modest living quarters. The atmosphere was serious, despite the cramped space and Adrian's usual smirk. He and Freija stood near the doorway while the others sat in the well-worn leather chairs. Adrian crossed his arms, his expression unusually thoughtful.

"Alright, let's be real here," he began, his tone both serious and laced with his trademark sarcasm. "Two winged women, a space cowboy, and three ground warriors against armies? Yeah, that's not gonna cut it. We need one more. Someone fierce. Someone who can actually give us an edge. Probably a master technician, no offense, Lilith."

"Very funny, Adrian. But you're not wrong," Lilith admitted, her wings shifting slightly as she sat forward. Her fiery gaze swept over the group. "We've made progress, but we're still outnumbered. Who do you have in mind, Adrian?"

Adrian shrugged, leaning against the wall. "Not me this time. Let's hear from the rest of the dream team."

Rainstorm, sitting quietly, glanced up. Her expression was thoughtful. "I've heard stories," she said slowly. "Of a fierce woman warrior in Egypt. A chantress.

Her name is Nefertari."

The room grew very quiet as everyone turned to her.

"What is a chantress and what else are we talking about?" Freija asked, her icy wings twitching with curiosity.

Rainstorm's voice grew stronger as she continued. "A chantress is like a princess elsewhere. However, she is not the kind who sits on a throne all day. Nefertari is a true warrior. They say she's stronger than any man she's faced in battle. There's a story about her..." She paused, glancing around the room. "Four men challenged her in mock combat. She bested all of them in three rounds."

Grilka leaned back in her chair, a sly grin spreading across her face. "Sounds like my twin sister," she quipped, earning a few chuckles from the group.

Rainstorm's expression remained serious. "If the stories are true, she's exactly what we need. She's agile, powerful, and skilled with a sword. I've also heard she trains others in the art of combat. Her knowledge alone would make her invaluable."

Kimiko nodded. "A warrior who can both fight and teach would be a strong addition. If she's willing to join us."

Lilith stood, her wings unfurling slightly. "Then it's settled. We'll find her."

With Adrian and Lilith taking the helm and Grilka at the weapons console, the Scorpion soared through the skies toward Cairo. The journey was quiet, each member of the team mentally preparing for what lay ahead. The red sands of Egypt came into view, and soon the bustling city of Cairo stretched beneath them, a mix of ancient architecture and modern sprawl.

The Scorpion landed discreetly near the palace grounds, its imposing structure standing tall against the horizon. Lilith, Rainstorm, and Kimiko disembarked, leaving the others to stay with the ship.

Hello Nefertari

The palace was a marvel of design, with golden domes and intricate carvings depicting scenes of battles and victories. Guards in traditional armor stood at the gates, their spears crossed as the trio approached.

"State your business," one of them commanded.

Rainstorm stepped forward, her voice steady. "We're here to see Chantress Nefertari. We've come a long way and need to speak with her."

The guards exchanged glances before one nodded. "She's in the arena, training. Follow me."

They were led through the grand hallways of the palace, the air filled with the scent of incense and the faint echo of sparring weapons. Finally, they emerged into the open-air arena. The sound of clashing metal and shouts of exertion filled the space.

Nefertari stood at the center, her long black hair glistening with sweat. She wore traditional gold and blue metal woman's armor and a matching loincloth, her muscular frame radiating strength. In her hands, she wielded a khopesh sword with deadly precision, demonstrating techniques to a group of young men and women.

"That's her," Rainstorm said quietly, her tone tinged with admiration.

The group watched as Nefertari moved with a combination of grace and power. She corrected the stances of her students, her voice firm but encouraging. When the lesson ended, she turned and caught sight of the visitors. Her expression was unreadable as she approached, the crowd parting for her.

"Who are you?" Nefertari demanded, her voice commanding.

Lilith stepped forward, her wings half extended. "We're here to ask for your help. We're assembling a team to fight an enemy that threatens not just our worlds, but all worlds. We've heard of your strength and skill. You would be an invaluable ally."

Nefertari's brow furrowed. "And you think I would leave my people for your war? Why should I trust you?"

Kimiko stepped forward, her voice calm but firm. "Because this isn't just our fight. If we fail, your people will face the same danger – but without a chance to prepare. You've trained your warriors to be strong. Imagine what you could accomplish with us."

Nefertari studied them, her dark eyes piercing. "Words are easy. Show me your strength." She gestured to the arena. "Choose one among you. If they can strike me three times before I strike you three times, I will consider your offer."

Lilith opened her mouth but before she could make a sound, Kimiko stepped forward without hesitation, her katanas already in hand. "I accept."

Nefertari smirked, clearly intrigued. The two warriors stepped into the arena, the crowd of trainees forming a loose circle around them. Each woman took off their swords and picked up two training wooden bokken swords. The air grew tense as the two women sized each other.

The first clash was swift and brutal. Nefertari's wooden sword sliced through the air, aiming for Kimiko's head. Kimiko ducked, the blade missing by inches. Nefertari followed up with a low slash toward her legs, but Kimiko flipped backward, evading the strike and landing lightly on her feet. Nefertari pivoted, swinging a heavy strike, but Kimiko sidestepped and retaliated with a quick slash toward Nefertari's side. The bokken grazed her armor, drawing the first touch.

Nefertari's expression hardened, a glimmer of respect in her eyes. "Again."

The second round opened with Nefertari lunging forward, her strikes coming faster and more aggressively. Kimiko dodged, ducking low and spinning on her heel to avoid the bokken slicing toward her ribs. Nefertari pressed forward, forcing Kimiko to backflip out of range. Landing gracefully, Kimiko used her smaller frame to her advantage, darting under Nefertari's next attack and slashing upward. The blade grazed Nefertari's shoulder, earning the second touch.

"Impressive," Nefertari said, her smirk deepening. "Again."

The third round was fierce, both combatants were fully immersed in the fight. Nefertari's brute strength and agility kept Kimiko on the defensive, each strike forcing her to retreat or dodge with precision. Nefertari feinted left before spinning into a powerful downward strike. Kimiko narrowly avoided the blow, tumbling to the side and rolling back to her feet. Nefertari seized the momentum, aiming a wide arc at Kimiko's midsection. Kimiko leapt high into the air, twisting mid-jump to avoid the blade.

As Kimiko landed, Nefertari changed her tactics, using a quick combination of slashes that pushed Kimiko back toward the edge of the arena. With no room left to retreat, Kimiko dropped low, sliding beneath Nefertari's next strike. She spun around, her bokken flashing in the sunlight as she aimed for Nefertari's leg. Nefertari countered, blocking the strike with her bokken and forcing Kimiko to disengage.

The crowd murmured in awe as the two warriors continued their duel, their movements like a deadly dance. Nefertari finally broke the stalemate, feinting high and sweeping low with her blade. Kimiko jumped, but not before Nefertari's bokken grazed her side, earning the first strike for Nefertari.

Now it was 2-1.

Kimiko reset her stance, her breathing steady despite the exertion. Nefertari advanced, her strikes relentless. Kimiko deflected one blow, then another, her bokken making loud thuds against the other bokken. Seeing an opening, Nefertari swung hard, aiming to finish the duel. Kimiko dropped into a low crouch, sliding beneath the swing and popping up behind Nefertari. With a quick pivot, she delivered a light tap to Nefertari's back, sealing her third and final touch.

The arena fell silent before erupting into cheers and murmurs of admiration. Nefertari turned, lowering her weapons as she studied Kimiko with newfound respect. "You are skilled," she said, a proud smile spreading across her face. "I accept your offer."

The Team is Complete

Later, as the group escorted Nefertari back to the Scorpion, the princess paused, eyeing the ship with a raised eyebrow. Its worn, dented exterior and scorch marks didn't inspire confidence. She crossed her arms and looked at Lilith. "This is the ship you're relying on?" she asked, her tone both skeptical and amused.

Lilith's wings flared slightly, but her response was calm and unyielding. "It's functional. That's all that matters."

Nefertari gave a slight smirk but said nothing more as they climbed the ramp. Inside the Scorpion, Freija, Grilka, and Adrian waited, curiosity etched on their faces. Freija immediately stepped forward, her icy wings twitching with excitement.

Rainstorm gestured toward Nefertari. "This is Chantress Nefertari, our newest recruit. And, might I add, Kimiko bested her in a duel to bring her on board."

Adrian gave a mock clap. "Well done, Kimiko. I always knew you had it in you to take on a chantress. But tell me, Nefertari, do all royalty come with combat skills, or are you the exception?"

Nefertari tilted her head, studying Adrian. "I am the standard to which others should aspire."

Freija giggled. "I like her already!" She extended a

hand to Nefertari. "I'm Freija. I'm kind of the positive energy around here, and I can't wait to show you around."

Adrian stepped forward, giving a dramatic bow. "And I'm Adrian, pilot, sharpshooter, and your personal guide to the quirks of this ship. Welcome aboard."

Freija took Nefertari's arm eagerly. "Come on, I'll start with the cockpit!"

"This is where the magic happens!" Freija exclaimed. "Lilith and Adrian handle the piloting, and Grilka mans the weapons. I mostly hang around to offer moral support."

Adrian leaned casually against the co-pilot's seat. "Moral support is code for 'backseat flying,' in case you were wondering."

Freija stuck her tongue out at him. "Ignore him. He's just jealous he doesn't have wings."

The tour continued to the barracks. Nefertari frowned slightly as she took in the cramped quarters. "And these are for...?"

"Seven of us," Adrian said with a grin. "Four beds. Don't worry; we're still working out the logistics of the rotational sleep schedule."

Freija nudged him. "He's joking. Sort of. It's not the most luxurious setup, but it works."

Next was the galley, a tiny area with a table and four bolted-down chairs. "This is where we eat," Freija said brightly. "When we're not too busy saving the galaxy."

"And by 'eat,' she means fight over the last protein bar," Adrian added. "It's like a game, really. Survival of the hungriest."

Nefertari's expression remained impassive, though a hint of amusement flickered in her eyes.

"Or for arguing over who gets to sit where," Adrian quipped. "Pro tip: Avoid Lilith's chair. It's the one with the scorch marks."

Nefertari allowed herself a small smile. "It's...

quaint."

Freija beamed. "Exactly! Quaint, but full of heart."

As the tour concluded, Nefertari seemed more at ease. Though the Scorpion was far from regal, its crew and their camaraderie made it clear she had joined something greater than herself.

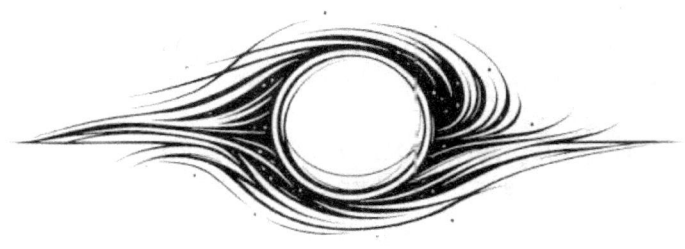

Chapter 22:

The Bonding Before the Battle

The Scorpion – with Adrian's Starlight Shadow attached – was silent, the hum of its engines the only sound as it hovered in the stillness of deep space. Adrian had just finished piloting through a tense stretch of asteroid debris, and the crew, though relieved, remained tense. They had succeeded in gathering their team, but the enormity of their task against Necra loomed ahead.

Lilith called for everyone to meet in the ship's living area. It wasn't an order, but the weight of her voice made it clear this wasn't optional. The Scorpion was large enough for privacy when needed, but tonight, Lilith wanted her team together.

The Gathering

Lilith stood at the entrance of the room, her crimson wings partially furled, her fiery presence both commanding and oddly comforting. The others filtered in: Freija with her light steps sitting in Lilith's spot on the left. Nefertari, with her regal composure, was sitting next to Freija. Grilka was sitting on the floor with her usual bluntness, Adrian was sitting next to Nefertari holding a cup of something strong and wearing a smirk, Rainstorm, with her quiet grace, sat in the last seat, and Kimiko slipping in almost unnoticed, her eyes sharp and observant sat on the armrest of Rainstorm's seat.

Lilith looked at each of them in turn. "We've come together for a reason. We all know that. But I need more than warriors. I need trust. I need unity. We can't win this fight if we're all carrying secrets and doubts."

Adrian quipped, "Sounds like we're about to share our darkest secrets. I'll go first: I snore. Ask Grilka."

Grilka snorted. "That's the least of your problems."

Lilith's serious gaze silenced the room. "This isn't just for me. This is for all of us. We need to know who we're standing beside. What drives us. What we're willing to fight for."

Nefertari's Resolve

Nefertari spoke first, her tone steady and regal. "I am Nefertari, Chantress of Akhenai. My people called me the Shield of Akhenai for defending our lands from raiders who sought to plunder our sacred sites. I left my home not because I wanted to but because I had to. My people are strong, but I saw that the galaxy is vulnerable. If this Necra succeeds, her reach will eventually extend to Earth and my people."

She paused, her voice softening as she continued. "I was raised to protect what is sacred, to wield my khopesh not for glory but for duty. Leaving my people was the hardest decision I've ever made, but I know it was the right one. If we don't stop Necra now, there may be no Akhenai left to protect."

Her dark eyes met Lilith's. "I fight for my planet, but I also fight for the stars. If I don't stand against Necra, everything I've protected could be destroyed."

The room was silent, allowing the weight of her words to settle over them. Nefertari shifted slightly in her seat, her regal composure unbroken, but her vulnerability clear to those who looked closely.

Adrian's Mask Slips

Adrian leaned back in his chair, the smirk fading from his face. "You all probably think I'm just some sarcastic pilot tagging along for the ride. And you'd be half-right. But before all this, I was a nobody – a guy flying smuggling runs and trying to survive one job at a time."

He paused, swirling the drink in his cup. "Then Necra's forces came to a planet I used to visit. Decent people, nothing special, but they were wiped out because they had resources she wanted. No one stood up for them. I didn't, either. I was just passing through. But I've hated myself for it every day since."

His gaze dropped to the floor, his voice quieter now. "I've spent most of my life running from things – responsibility, danger, guilt. Joining this team… it's the first time I feel like I'm running toward something instead."

He looked up with a tear in his eye, his tone lightening as he added, "Plus, someone's gotta keep this ship in one piece, and I'm the best pilot here. No offense, Lilith."

Lilith rolled her eyes but allowed herself a small smile.

Rainstorm's Quiet Power

Rainstorm's voice was calm but resonant. "I am Rainstorm, daughter of Chief Eshona of the Wakasa people. My spirit guide is the hawk, and it has led me to this fight. My people taught me that we don't fight for glory; we fight for balance. I've seen what happens when darkness tips the scales."

She hesitated, her fingers brushing the feathers in her hair. "Leaving my people was the hardest decision I've ever made, too. But this fight isn't just about me or you. It's about all the lives Necra has touched and destroyed. I'm here to make sure the balance is restored."

Her gaze softened as she added, "I don't know what will happen tomorrow, but I know that I was meant to be here. With all of you. My hawk spirit guide has never led me astray."

Grilka grunted approvingly. "You talk fancy, but you fight like a warrior. That's what matters."

Freija's Honesty

Freija spoke next, her voice light but sincere. "I'm Freija, Princess of Icelandia, though I haven't lived like a princess in a long time. My twin sister, Frigid, stayed behind to rule our people. She always believed in tradition, but I wanted something more. I wanted freedom, adventure… a purpose." She began to fumble with the Frostheart charm around her neck.

She glanced at Lilith with a small smile. "I didn't expect to find purpose with a demon and her ragtag crew, but here we are. And honestly? I think this is where I'm meant to be."

Her wings flickered faintly as a tear came out of her eyes; she continued, "I know I've got a lot to prove. But if you trust me, I won't let you down."

Kimiko's Shadowed Truth

Kimiko sat silently for a moment before speaking. "I'm Kimiko, from Tokyo on Earth. I've spent my life fighting as a Samari and as a ninja hiding in the shadows, training to be the best at what I do. And I am the best."

Her voice was sharp but softened as she continued. "I've always worked alone. Trust doesn't come easily to me, but in the short time I've been here, I've seen something I didn't expect – a team that fights not just with skill, but with heart."

She paused, her sharp gaze meeting Lilith's. "I don't promise loyalty lightly. But if I'm here, it's because I believe in what we're doing."

Grilka's Simplicity

Grilka stretched, her orange hair catching the light. "You all talk a lot. I'm Grilka. I'm strong, I fight, and I don't usually lose. That's why I'm here."

A rare smile crossed her face. "But... I've been in a lot of fights, and I can tell you this is different. I'm not just fighting for myself anymore. I'm fighting for all of you. So don't mess it up!"

Lilith's Leadership

Finally, all eyes turned to Lilith. Her fiery wings glowed faintly as she spoke. "I've been called many things – Hellbourne, demon, even monster. I've made mistakes, some I'll never forgive myself for. But the one thing I've never stopped believing in is that I was meant for more than destruction."

She looked at each of them in turn. "You've all trusted me enough to join this fight, and I won't let you down. Together, we're stronger than Necra ever expected. And we're going to prove it."

A Moment of Unity

The room fell silent for a moment, the weight of their shared truths settling over them. Then Adrian broke the tension with a smirk. "So, who's taking first watch? Because I think I've earned some sleep after all this emotional bonding."

Freija laughed, and even Kimiko smiled faintly. Rainstorm reached over to clasp Nefertari's hand briefly, a gesture of quiet solidarity.

Lilith nodded, her voice steady. "Get some rest.

Tomorrow, we start planning. Necra won't know what hit her."

As the team dispersed, there was a sense of something unspoken but understood. They weren't just warriors anymore – they were a family. And together, they were going to become unstoppable.

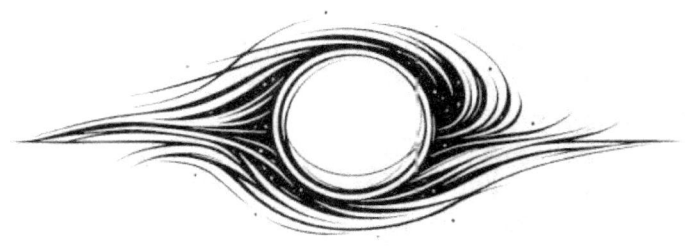

Chapter 23:

Training In the Cockpit

Adrian, Kimiko, and Freija sat together in the cockpit of the Scorpion as the ship, on autopilot, orbiting Earth. Adrian, as usual, was at ease, leaning back in the pilot's chair with one arm casually draped over the console. Kimiko and Freija sat in the weapon's stations, and co-pilot's station respectively their expressions were more serious.

Adrian glanced sideways at Freija, his tone light but his question pointed. "So, have you ever flown a ship before?"

Freija shook her head firmly. "No. Never."

Adrian raised an eyebrow, his smirk widening. "Not even once? Not even a little solo joyride?"

Freija's expression remained steady. "My people don't have ships. Our battles are fought on the ground, or we can fly ourselves."

"Good to know," Adrian muttered, turning his attention to Kimiko. "And you? Any experience with this kind of firepower?" He gestured toward the weapons console.

Kimiko's dark eyes flicked over the array of controls. "I'm familiar with handheld weapons. Swords. Knives. However, I can adapt."

Adrian let out a low whistle, rubbing his chin. "Adapting is good, but let's make sure you don't accidentally blow us out of orbit while you're 'adapting,'" he said, using finger quotes.

Kimiko's expression didn't change, but there was a faint twitch at the corner of her lips, almost like a smile.

Adrian leaned forward, his usual sarcasm giving way to a more serious tone. "Alright, listen up. Here's the deal. Everyone needs to have at least a basic knowledge of these controls. We're going into situations where things can get hairy, and if I'm down – or worse – someone needs to step up. Same goes for all of us."

Freija and Kimiko exchanged glances, both nodding in agreement.

Adrian pointed to the console in front of Freija. "This is the co-pilot's station. It can mirror the pilot's controls for most functions, so if you need to take over, it's all here. Throttle, pitch, yaw, roll – you name it. That lever right there," he pointed, "switches full control between the pilot and co-pilot. Got it?"

Freija leaned forward, studying the controls carefully. "Got it."

Adrian nodded, pleased with her focus. He then stood up and walked over to Kimiko's station. "And you, ninja warrior, this is the weapons console. Shields are here," he tapped a glowing blue section of the panel, "and offensive weapons are here." He tapped a row of buttons marked with various targeting symbols. "Disruptors, missiles, and – if we're desperate – a very experimental plasma cannon that I'm pretty sure will explode if we ever use it, given the condition of what I see with this ship."

Kimiko arched an eyebrow. "Noted."

Adrian grinned, leaning back. "The targeting system is mostly automated, but you'll need to lock on to your targets manually if the computer gets jammed. Those toggles," he pointed to a cluster of switches, "are for switching between defensive and offensive modes. Defensive mode focuses on shields and countermeasures; offensive lets you go full Rambo."

Freija tilted her head. "What or who is Rambo?"

Adrian chuckled. "An old Earth soldier with a habit of solving problems by firing guns ten times his size at them."

Kimiko studied the controls, her fingers hovering just above the buttons. "Understood."

Adrian leaned back in his chair, folding his arms across his chest. "Look, I'm not trying to turn you into ace pilots or gunners overnight, but if something happens, I need to know you two can handle this. We're a team, and that means having each other's backs."

Freija nodded solemnly. "You have my word. I'll learn."

Kimiko gave a curt nod as well. "I'll do what needs to be done."

Adrian's smirk returned as he leaned forward, tapping a button on the console that brought up a holographic diagram of the Scorpion. "Good. Because the last thing I want is this ship going up in flames because someone hit the wrong button... No pressure, of course."

Kimiko and Freija exchanged faint smiles, their tension easing slightly. Adrian leaned back, satisfied.

"Alright, ladies," he said, standing and stretching. "That's your crash course. We'll do some hands-on practice soon, but for now, just don't touch anything unless I say so."

Freija tilted her head slightly, her tone light. "I thought you wanted us to be prepared."

Adrian chuckled. "Touché. Fine... you can practice. But if you fire a missile into a friendly ship... you're buying the drinks at the next port... and you're having a top-shelf shot of tequila with me, to boot."

Kimiko allowed herself a small smirk. "Deal."

As the three settled into their roles, Adrian suddenly

pointed at a large red button on Kimiko's console in the far upper right corner with an image of a circle and a lot of lines going off in all directions. "Do you see that button?" he asked, his tone unusually serious.

Kimiko's gaze followed his finger, and she nodded. "I see it."

Adrian leaned in slightly, his expression deadpan. "That is the self-destruct button. Don't push that button… Ever."

Kimiko arched an eyebrow, her tone equally deadpan. "I'll try to resist the urge."

Freija, sitting at her console, couldn't help but let out a quiet laugh. "Good advice. Noted."

Adrian's smirk returned as he stood up, brushing off his serious tone. "Alright, that's enough for now. Let's not accidentally blow ourselves up before the real fight begins."

As the three settled into their roles, the atmosphere in the cockpit grew lighter. Despite the gravity of their mission, there was a growing sense of camaraderie – a bond forged in preparation for the challenges ahead.

Back in the sleeping quarters, Lilith was sound asleep in the top right bunk. Grilka, unusually quiet, snored lightly in the bottom right. Nefertari was sound asleep in the bottom left bunk, and Rainstorm slept softly in the top left, whispering in her sleep.

Shift Change

About six hours later, the hum of the Scorpion remained steady as Lilith, Nefertari, and Grilka entered the cockpit to relieve the three tired crew members. Adrian, still in the pilot's chair, stretched and turned to face them.

"Right on time, Captain," Adrian quipped, though his voice carried a hint of exhaustion. "We've kept everything in one piece for you."

Lilith nodded, her wings shifting slightly as she took the pilot's chair. "Good work. We'll take it from here."

Before leaving, Adrian leaned against the console, his tone becoming serious. "Lilith, we need to train everyone on the basics of piloting and weapons. If something goes wrong, we can't afford anyone being completely clueless."

Lilith met his gaze, her expression firm. "Agreed. We'll make it a priority. I will make a list on training on who and where and a time for us to run drills and practice."

Adrian nodded, satisfied. "Good. They've got potential, but they need more hands-on experience."

As he stepped back, Kimiko and Freija followed him out of the cockpit, their exhaustion evident but their movements steady. Walking toward the barracks, Adrian couldn't resist breaking the silence. "Alright, ladies, about those sleeping arrangements... I call the bottom bunk. Who's joining me?"

Kimiko shot him a sharp look, half-serious and half-amused. "Not in this lifetime."

Freija smirked but said nothing, brushing past him to the barracks. Adrian chuckled, shaking his head as he muttered, "Tough crowd."

Freija called out, "I'll take the other bottom bunk after I shower."

Kimiko said, "Fine with me. I like being high up."

With that, the first watch settled into their sleeping spots.

Night Watch Part 2

Back in the cockpit, Lilith settled into the pilot's seat, Nefertari taking the co-pilot's station and Grilka positioning herself at the weapons console. Lilith glanced at Nefertari. "Nefertari, I'll start giving you basic piloting lessons while we're in orbit. You need to know how to handle this ship in case things get tight."

Nefertari regally agreed "You've got it, Captain. I'm ready to learn."

Lilith's gaze shifted to Grilka. "Grilka, I'll update

you on more of the weapons systems. Adrian's done the basics, but I want to make sure you're fully prepared for what's ahead."

Grilka nodded, her expression serious. "Understood. Let's get to work."

As Grilka leaned over the weapons console, her sharp eyes caught something unusual. A strip of tape was stuck just below a large red button in the upper right corner, with a handwritten message scrawled in bold letters: **DON'T PUSH THIS BUTTON.**

Grilka motioned to Lilith to come over. Lilith blinked, and then a laugh burst out of her, loud and unexpected. Nefertari turned in her seat, slightly bewildered.

"What's so funny?" Nefertari asked, craning her neck to see.

Lilith pointed at the tape, her grin wide. "Adrian's handiwork. I should've known."

Grilka leaned in and smirked. "Subtle. Think it'll stop anyone from trying?"

Lilith shook her head, still chuckling. "Probably not. But it's very Adrian."

From the crew sleeping quarters, Adrian heard Lilith's loud outburst and smiled to himself. *I guess she saw my note.*

Nefertari laughed, shaking her head. "He really doesn't trust us, does he?"

"Can you blame him?" Lilith quipped, straightening. "Alright, let's focus. The galaxy won't save itself."

Grilka nodded, her expression serious. "Understood. Let's get to work."

As the ship orbited Earth, the trio began their training, the quiet hum of the Scorpion a steady reminder of the challenges that lay ahead.

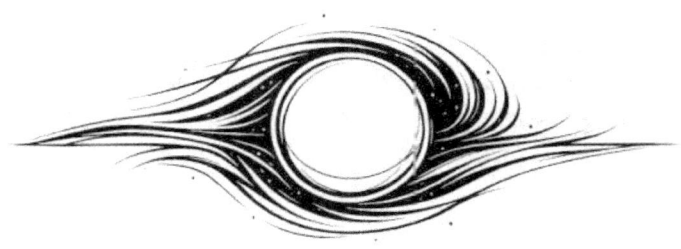

Chapter 24:

Adrian At Helm

After a few days of basic training and running drills, the Scorpion surged into hyperspace, the brilliant swirls of light streaking past the cockpit windows as Adrian gripped the controls. His usual smirk was gone, replaced by a look of intense concentration. Sitting in the co-pilot seat, Lilith monitored the navigation system, her fiery wings folded tightly behind her. Grilka was stationed at the weapons console, her hands hovering over the controls, ready for action.

"This route isn't going to be easy," Adrian said, his voice steady. "We're cutting it close to a few heavily trafficked sectors, and the gravitational pulls near those nebula clusters are tricky."

Lilith glanced at the readouts. "Tricky isn't the word I'd use. These coordinates are barely navigable. Are you sure this is the fastest route?"

Adrian flashed a quick grin. "Fastest? Definitely. Safest? Eh, not so much. But don't worry, Demon Captain. I've got this."

Lilith sighed but said nothing, her eyes scanning the trajectory. She couldn't deny that Adrian's confidence was oddly reassuring, even if his methods were unconventional.

As the Scorpion approached the first challenge, a dense asteroid field that shimmered with electromagnetic interference, Adrian leaned forward, his hands flying over the controls. "Alright, folks, this is where the fun begins."

"Fun?" Grilka muttered. "This looks like a death trap."

"Only if you're not me," Adrian shot back. He pulled the Scorpion out of hyperspace just in time to weave between a cluster of massive rocks tumbling through space. The ship's hull hummed under the strain as Adrian deftly maneuvered, banking left and then diving sharply to avoid a particularly large asteroid. All the while, electromagnetic lightning scorched the asteroid field.

"Grilka, keep an eye on the aft sensors," Adrian ordered. "If anything gets too close, I need you to give it a love tap with the aft disruptors."

"Love tap?" Grilka said incredulously. "You mean blow it to pieces?"

"Exactly!"

Grilka rolled her eyes but gripped the controls, her keen eyes fixed on the monitor. The weapons console lit up as she activated the targeting system. "Ready when you are."

The ship lurched to the side as Adrian dodged another asteroid, the motion so sudden that Lilith had to brace herself against the console. "Warn us next time!" she snapped.

Adrian chuckled. "Wasn't any time for that?"

Despite his lighthearted banter, Adrian's focus was razor-sharp. His hands moved with practiced precision, adjusting the thrusters and stabilizers to keep the Scorpion on course. The cockpit was filled with a tense silence, broken only by the occasional beep of the sensors and the hum of the ship's engines.

The asteroid field grew more chaotic as they moved deeper, the electromagnetic interference disrupting their navigational systems. Sparks danced across the control panels, and a warning alarm blared. "System recalibrating," Lilith reported, her tone clipped.

"Recalibrating or not, we're not stopping," Adrian replied, his voice firm. He yanked the controls to the right, narrowly avoiding a collision with two massive asteroids that ground against each other like angry gods. The sound of the debris scraping past the shields made the entire ship vibrate.

"Grilka, now!" Adrian barked as a cluster of smaller rocks came barreling toward them from the aft. Grilka didn't hesitate, firing the ship's rear disruptors in a precise burst that shattered the debris into harmless fragments.

"Clean shot," she muttered, her voice tense but satisfied.

Adrian grinned. "Nice work. See? I told you this would be fun."

Grilka muttered something under her breath that Adrian either didn't hear or chose to ignore. The Scorpion dove and climbed through the chaotic field, the crew bracing themselves at every sudden movement.

The debris grew denser, and smaller shards continuously pelted the shields, causing the ship to shudder. "Shield strength at 72%," Grilka called out, her fingers flying over the console to divert additional power to defenses. "We're not going to make it if this keeps up."

"We'll make it," Adrian said firmly, pushing the engines to their limit. He twisted the controls hard, pulling the Scorpion into a sharp corkscrew maneuver to evade a cluster of massive rocks spinning wildly in the void. The gravitational forces threatened to tear the ship apart, and warning lights blared across the cockpit.

"This is madness," Lilith muttered, gripping the armrests of her seat. "If you miss even one of these turns..."

"I won't miss," Adrian interrupted, his voice calm but determined. "Trust me."

Lilith shot him a skeptical glance but said nothing

more, her eyes fixed on the navigation readout. "Approaching the edge of the field," she announced. "If we don't clear this in thirty seconds, we're going to get caught in a gravity well."

"Then I guess we better clear it," Adrian said, pushing the thrusters to maximum. The Scorpion roared forward, dodging and weaving through the remaining asteroids. Grilka fired another precise burst, clearing a path just wide enough for the ship to slip through.

As the ship finally cleared the asteroid field, the crew let out a collective sigh of relief. But there was no time to celebrate. Ahead of them loomed the swirling clouds of a massive nebula, its electric storms pulsing with dangerous intensity.

"This is the nebula cluster," Lilith said, her tone grim. "If we lose control here, we won't get it back."

Adrian leaned forward, his eyes narrowing. "Alright, buckle up. This is going to get bumpy."

Adrian then announced over the intercom. "Everybody not on the bridge, get to the living quarters and buckle up. You have 15 seconds!"

Kimiko, Freija, Grilka, and Nefertari each jumped out of their bunks and bolted to the living quarters to strap themselves into their seats.

The Scorpion entered the nebula, and immediately, the turbulence hit. The ship lurched violently, and the view outside was an overwhelming swirl of colors and lightning. The gravitational anomalies threw the ship off balance, and Adrian fought to keep it steady. Lose items inside the ship began to feel the intense gravity fields of the nebula.

"Stabilizers are struggling," Lilith reported, her voice tight. "We need to adjust power distribution."

"Already on it," Adrian replied, flipping switches and turning dials. The Scorpion groaned under the strain, but the stabilizers held – for now.

"Watch those energy bursts!" Grilka shouted as a

massive bolt of lightning arced through the nebula, narrowly missing the ship.

Adrian rolled the Scorpion sharply, dodging another burst. The ship spun and dipped, the engines screaming as Adrian pushed them to their limits. Every movement was precise, calculated, and just barely enough to keep them alive.

"Debris incoming, two o'clock!" Grilka called out.

Adrian looked up to his left and then twisted the controls, pulling the Scorpion into a sharp climb. The debris shot past them, grazing the shields. Sparks erupted from the console, and the ship shook violently.

"Shields at 54%," Grilka reported, her voice tense. "We can't take much more of this."

"You keep telling me that but noted!" Adrian said through gritted teeth. He adjusted their trajectory, aiming for the clearer path ahead. But the nebula was relentless, throwing wave after wave of turbulence and danger their way.

Finally, after what felt like an eternity, the Scorpion broke through the edge of the nebula. The swirling clouds gave way to the vast emptiness of open space, and the cockpit was filled with heavy silence. Adrian leaned back in his seat, his hands still gripping the controls tightly with whitened knuckles.

"And that," he said, his voice shaky but triumphant, "is how you fly a ship."

Lilith exhaled slowly, her fiery gaze fixed on him. "You're reckless, Adrian. But I'll admit, you're good."

"I bet you are now glad that you took that shot of tequila with me back on Earth," Adrian replied with a weak grin.

Lilith smiled, "I am."

Grilka let out a low chuckle, her tension finally easing. "You're insane, you know that?"

"Insane people don't know they're insane," Adrian

said, finally releasing the controls. "But hey – results are results."

The Scorpion re-entered hyperspace, the swirling lights once again filling the viewport. The tension in the cockpit eased, but the weight of their mission remained. Adrian glanced at Lilith, his smirk fading slightly.

"We'll get there in time," he said, his tone uncharacteristically earnest. "Necra won't know what hit her."

Lilith nodded, her expression softening. "Let's hope you're right."

Freija entered the cockpit. "I guess we couldn't just fly over it on that one."

Everyone in the cockpit broke out into insane laughter. Adrian quipped, "Not on that one."

Lilith entered their final destination into the ship's navigation system and set the ship on autopilot.

As the Scorpion hurtled toward their destination, the crew prepared themselves for the battle ahead. The stakes were higher than ever, but with Adrian and Lilith at the helm, they knew they had a fighting chance.

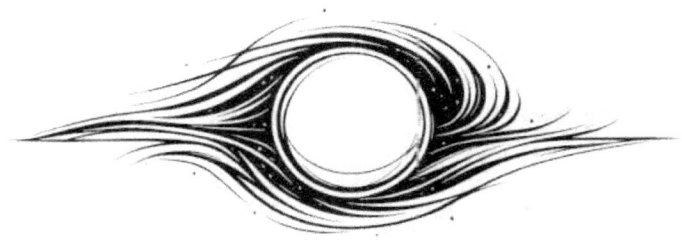

Chapter 25:

Training the Team

The Scorpion cruised steadily through hyperspace, its hum a constant reminder of their impending mission. In the quiet after the chaos, Adrian and Lilith gathered the team in the living quarters to outline their next plan.

"We need to make sure everyone on this ship can handle the controls. I know we have already spent a week, but nobody becomes an expert overnight," Adrian began, leaning casually against the wall. "In a fight, anything can happen. If I'm down – or anyone else for that matter – someone must step up and be ready to take on heavy duties."

Lilith nodded. "Freija, Nefertari, you'll continue learning the basics of flying the Scorpion. Adrian will take the lead, but I'll assist to ensure you both understand the fundamentals."

Nefertari's eyes gleamed with interest. "I've always relied on the strength of my body in battle. This will be... different."

Freija's wings fluttered slightly. "I'm ready. Let's see if I can fly something other than myself."

"Grilka," Lilith continued, turning to the orange-haired warrior, "you'll continue to train Rainstorm and Kimiko on weapons and shields. They need to know how to divert power between systems and operate the defenses if it comes to that."

Grilka nodded. "I'll make sure they're ready." She glanced at Rainstorm and Kimiko, her expression firm. "Don't think I'll go easy on you."

Kimiko smirked, her cold demeanor softening slightly. "I wouldn't expect you to."

Adrian led Freija and Nefertari to the cockpit, gesturing to the array of controls. "Alright, ladies, welcome to your next crash course in starship piloting. This is your lifeline in space. Screw up here, and its game over for all of us."

Adrian directed Freija to the pilot's seat and Nefertari to the co-pilot's seat.

Freija leaned forward, her icy-blue eyes scanning the controls. "Straight to the point. I like it."

Nefertari crossed her arms, her warrior's stance unyielding. "Show me what needs to be done."

Adrian grinned. "That's the spirit." He pointed to the main console. "This is your throttle – controls your speed. The stabilizer keeps us steady, but you'll have to adjust it manually in rough patches. This lever here switches between autopilot and manual control. Got it?"

Both women nodded, their focus unwavering. Adrian spent the next hour walking them through basic maneuvers, explaining how to adjust course, monitor the engines, and interpret the navigation systems.

"Your turn," Adrian said, stepping back. "Freija, you are in the pilot's seat. Nefertari, you're co-pilot. Don't worry about perfection; just get a feel for the controls." Adrian then disengages the autopilot.

Freija adjusted her posture in the pilot's seat, her wings folding tightly behind her. She gripped the controls and, under Adrian's guidance, executed a series of basic turns and adjustments. Nefertari monitored the navigation readouts, calling out coordinates and engine levels as instructed.

"You're a natural," Adrian said, his tone genuinely impressed as Freija adjusted the stabilizers to compensate for a simulated gravitational pull.

"Maybe it's not so different from flying myself," Freija replied, her tone light.

Nefertari smiled faintly. "This requires a different kind of discipline, but I see its value."

Adrian then flips the switch allowing Nefertari to have full control. They rehearse the other person's roles until both women have a basic knowledge of piloting a ship.

Meanwhile, Grilka led Rainstorm and Kimiko to the weapons console. "Alright, listen up," she began, her tone no-nonsense. "These controls operate the shields and the disruptors. Your job is to know when to switch power between them. Shields protect us, but too much power weakens our weapons. Balance is everything."

Kimiko studied the console with sharp precision. "Understood. What's the range of the disruptors?"

"Depends on the target," Grilka replied. "But don't think of this as swordplay. You're aiming for precision, not flair."

Rainstorm, holding a steady gaze, asked, "What about emergencies?"

Grilka nodded approvingly. "Good question. If we're under heavy fire, divert all power to the shields. It's better to survive than to attack recklessly."

Over the next few hours, the trainees practiced under Grilka's watchful eye, learning how to target incoming threats and manage the ship's power distribution. By the end, both women showed a good understanding, their movements more precise than before.

None of the ladies ask about the "DON'T PUSH THIS BUTTON" that was taped next to a large red button in the upper right corner.

Creating a Plan

Adrian leaned back on one of the worn leather seats in the Scorpion's living quarters, his smirk tugging at the corners of his mouth. Across from him, Lilith sat upright, her crimson and black wings draped like a regal cloak. The gravity of their mission ahead was evident in their expressions, but this moment was all about preparation.

"We've got two ships," Adrian began, gesturing with his hands. "My fighter is fast and nimble, perfect for distracting their forces or making precision strikes. The Scorpion, though, is the heavy hitter and the command center."

Lilith nodded, her fiery gaze meeting him. "We'll split roles. I can lead the air assault with Freija. That leaves Nefertari, Grilka, Rainstorm, Kimiko, and you to manage the Scorpion and lead the ground team."

Adrian leaned forward. "Nefertari should pilot the Scorpion. She's shown a knack for quick thinking and adaptability. Rainstorm's focus and precision make her perfect for weapons."

"That puts Grilka and Kimiko on the ground," Lilith concluded. "They're the most suited for direct combat."

Adrian tapped his fingers on the armrest, his smirk fading into a more serious expression. "The world we're heading to, Luthor, isn't your typical backwater. They've got advanced tech, but they haven't breached spaceflight yet. It's like handing a loaded disrupter to someone who doesn't know the stakes or the firepower they are holding in their hands."

"Necra's forces will exploit that," Lilith said, her tone sharp. "They'll use the planet's resources and tech against them."

Adrian nodded. "Exactly. We know Necra has one of her generals there leading the operation. Taking him out, along with his top lieutenants, is crucial. It'll destabilize their command structure and will buy us time. Plus, we need to start to gather intel on their operation"

Lilith leaned back, her wings shifting slightly. "This is why we need one of the lieutenants or the general alive. We'll extract whatever intel we can about Necra's plans and movements."

Adrian grinned, the smirk returning. "Nothing like a good old-fashioned kidnapping in the middle of a battle. Let's just hope the team's ready for it."

Lilith's expression hardened. "They will be. Failure isn't an option."

With their plans laid out, the two leaders prepared to brief the rest of the team, knowing the challenges ahead would test them all.

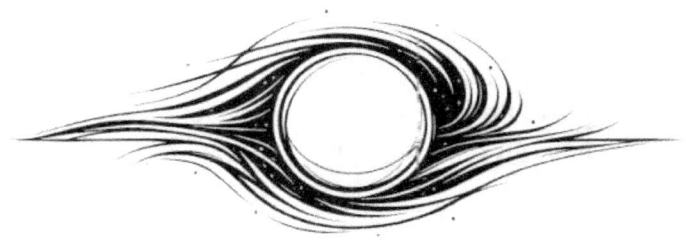

Chapter 26:

Into the Atmosphere

The Scorpion's cockpit hummed with energy as Nefertari adjusted the pilot's controls. Her steady hands maneuvered the ship with growing confidence while Freija, seated in the co-pilot's seat, carefully monitored the readouts. Rainstorm was stationed at the weapons console, her focused expression revealing her readiness for any incoming threats.

In the armory, Grilka strapped extra rounds into her belt, her practiced hands inspecting her twin disruptors and testing the rifle's scope. Kimiko, silent and intent, ran a whetstone along her katanas, their dark blades having no reflection at all under the ship's lights.

Adrian entered the common area, his boots clicking against the metal floor. He wore his trademark leather jacket and an almost relaxed demeanor, though his eyes betrayed a sharp focus. "Lilith, you ready to play recon?" he asked, glancing at the towering demoness adjusting her gear and her twin two-handed swords now strapped to her back.

Lilith nodded, her wings shifting as she secured her harness. "We'll fly out once we're in the atmosphere. Freija will scout ahead while we take a closer look near their main headquarters. Keep comms open."

Adrian grinned. "Always."

As they reached the planet's atmosphere, the Scorpion began to rumble under the strain of entry. Nefertari's jaw tightened as she adjusted for turbulence. Freija reached out to steady the controls. "We've got this," she said calmly.

"Approaching target altitude," Nefertari announced. "Freija, you're up."

Freija unbuckled her harness and opened a small airlock on the starboard side. With a quick flick of her wings, she shot out of the Scorpion like a bullet, her speed quickly breaking the sound barrier. The supersonic echo of her departure left the crew momentarily stunned before they refocused on their tasks.

"She's crazy fast," Rainstorm murmured, her hands steadying the weapon's console. The sensors tracked Freija's movements as she darted over the surface, scanning the area for key locations.

"Contact made," Freija's voice crackled over the comms. "Necra's forces are concentrated near a massive industrial complex – looks like their command center. Sending coordinates now."

"Good work," Lilith replied, her fiery wings unfurling. "Adrian, let's go."

As Freija returned to the Scorpion, Adrian and Lilith climbed aboard his fighter attached to the cargo bay on the port side. The smaller, sleeker ship detached from the Scorpion, its engines roaring to life. Nefertari steadied the larger ship as Adrian and Lilith sped toward the surface.

"We'll circle wide and get eyes on their troop movements," Lilith said, her tone clipped but determined.

"Try not to steal all the glory," Adrian joked, though his hands moved expertly over his controls.

The mission was underway, and the team was ready to strike.

As Adrian's fighter approached the boundary of the

industrial complex, he slowed the ship. The hum of the engines softened, and he turned toward Lilith. "This is where we split. Try not to make me look bad out there."

Lilith smirked, her crimson and black wings stretching as she prepared to launch. "Stay safe, Adrian. I'm counting on you to get us out of this."

"Counting on me? Never thought I'd hear that." Adrian winked before opening the airlock.

With a powerful leap, Lilith launched into the air, her wings catching the current and propelling her high above the battlefield. The fighter's engines roared back to life as Adrian banked sharply, heading toward the complex's perimeter.

Meanwhile, Nefertari guided the Scorpion to a landing zone just outside the complex's boundary. The ship's engines powered down with a low whine as the team prepared for their next moves.

Freija was the first to exit, her wings shimmering as she took flight once more, scouting the immediate area for potential threats. Rainstorm stayed at her console a moment longer, scanning for any signs of enemy activity before joining Grilka and Kimiko near the ramp.

Grilka adjusted her belt, her voice steady. "Let's keep this clean and fast. The less noise we make, the better." She tapped the rifle that was slung across her back. "But if things get messy, we're ready."

Kimiko nodded, her voice cold and precise. "We'll do what we must. No hesitation." She sheathed her katanas with a fluid motion, her sharp eyes scanning the horizon.

Rainstorm stepped forward, her expression serene but focused. "We have a duty to the lives on this planet. Let's not lose sight of that."

Grilka smirked. "You're always the philosopher, huh?"

Rainstorm didn't answer, her gaze fixed on the distant complex.

Kimiko broke the silence. "We should move. Time is against us."

The three women exchanged brief nods before the first two were about to be heading out, their movements synchronized and deliberate. Freija's voice crackled over the comms. "Perimeter looks clear for now, but don't get comfortable. There's heavy patrol activity near the east gate."

"Noted," Rainstorm replied. She glanced at Grilka and Kimiko. "You two take positions and be ready for anything."

Grilka and Kimiko exchanged a glance as they moved to exit the Scorpion. Rainstorm stood by the ramp's hatch, her expression calm but resolute. As they reached the threshold of the exit, she placed a hand on Grilka's shoulder.

"Stay sharp," Rainstorm said, her tone carrying the weight of a silent prayer.

Grilka gave a confident nod, adjusting the strap of her rifle. "You worry too much, Rainstorm."

Kimiko, already stepping down the ramp, turned her head slightly. "Time is wasting."

Rainstorm smiled faintly and waved as they stepped onto the barren ground. "Good hunting," she said, closing the hatch behind them.

Returning swiftly to her position at the weapons console, Rainstorm rechecked the monitors, her fingers flying over the controls. The ship's systems hummed steadily, ready for action at a moment's notice.

As the team dispersed, the mission was in motion. Adrian's fighter circled the complex, his sharp eyes scanning for weak points in the enemy defenses. Lilith soared high above, her fiery form a silent sentinel. The battle to disrupt Necra's forces was beginning.

Freija soared high overhead, her keen eyes scanning the landscape far below. The industrial complex stretched out like a jagged scar on the terrain, brimming with enemy activity. Spotting an ideal vantage point, she hovered in place, signaling Lilith with a quick motion of her hand.

Lilith, already circling at a lower altitude, caught the signal. With a powerful beat of her fiery wings, she ascended to join Freija. The two hovered high above the complex, their silhouettes barely visible against the thin clouds, far too high to draw attention from the ground below.

"They're spread out," Freija said, her voice calm but edged with concern. "The central area is fortified, but there's a weaker spot near the western boundary. That's where their officers are moving."

Lilith nodded, her sharp eyes narrowing as she scanned the scene. "We'll need to act quickly. Taking out their leadership is key. If we strike hard and fast, the rest will falter."

Freija pointed to a cluster of movement near a poorly guarded entry point. "There's one – a lieutenant, I believe. Looks isolated. We could extract him for intel."

Lilith's lips curved into a faint, determined smile. "Good eye. Let's keep an eye on him for now." She reached for her communicator. "Adrian, come in."

Adrian's voice crackled through the comms, tinged with his usual nonchalance. "Right here, Demon Captain. What's the plan?"

"Freija's found a weak spot," Lilith explained. "A lieutenant or possibly a major is patrolling alone near the western boundary. It's unguarded. We need you to meet us there for a quick extraction."

"Sounds like my kind of party," Adrian replied. "I'll be there in three."

Freija glanced at Lilith, her wings steady against the high-altitude winds. "I'll keep watch from above. You head down and coordinate with Adrian."

Lilith's fiery eyes glimmered as she nodded. "Keep your distance. If anything changes, let me know… immediately."

Freija gave a quick nod and adjusted her altitude, maintaining a silent vigil. Lilith angled her wings and began a controlled descent toward the western boundary, her imposing figure cutting through the sky like a comet. Below, the Scorpion settled into its position.

The mission was entering its next critical phase. The team's cohesion and strategy would soon be tested as they moved to eliminate Necra's forces piece by piece.

Grilka and Kimiko took their positions near the southern boundary of the complex, carefully avoiding patrols as they advanced. Kimiko, stealthy as ever, moved ahead, her katanas sheathed but ready for a quick draw. Grilka followed at a distance, her rifle at the ready, scanning the area for potential threats. Their objective was clear: create a diversion and capture the lone officer.

Kimiko slipped into the shadows, approaching the southern border undetected. Grilka kept her distance but maintained a clear line of sight on her partner. "I've got your back," she murmured over the comms, her voice calm but resolute.

Kimiko's reply was a soft whisper. "Approaching the target. Stand by."

Meanwhile, Lilith soared high above, her sharp eyes locked on the officer. She readied herself to swoop down the moment Kimiko made her move. From her vantage point, Freija monitored the perimeter, her keen gaze scanning for unexpected activity. "All clear for now," she reported. "But don't linger. Patrols are shifting."

Adrian's fighter circled above, providing overwatch. "I've got you covered," he said, his tone more serious than usual. "Let me know if things heat up."

Kimiko reached the officer's position, her movements silent and precise. She unsheathed one of her katanas. In a fluid motion, she stepped behind the unsuspecting officer and pressed the blade lightly against his neck. "Not a sound," she hissed.

The officer froze, his hands slowly raising in surrender. Kimiko signaled Grilka, who moved in quickly to secure the target. Just as Lilith began her descent to retrieve the officer, chaos erupted.

From the shadows, a squad of heavily armed troops emerged, their weapons trained on Kimiko and Grilka. "It's a trap!" Grilka shouted, raising her rifle and firing the first shot. The blast took down one soldier, but the rest quickly returned fire.

"Lilith, abort extraction!" Freija's urgent voice crackled through the comms. "We've got heavy resistance!"

Lilith adjusted her trajectory, swooping low and grabbing the officer in a powerful grip. Her fiery wings flared as she launched vertically into the sky, narrowly avoiding a barrage of gunfire. "Officer secured," she reported. "Heading to the rendezvous point."

On the ground, Kimiko and Grilka were overwhelmed. Kimiko fought fiercely, her katanas flashing in a deadly dance of precision and power.

Seven soldiers closed in on her. She jumped forward into a front shoulder roll while unsheathing both katanas as she rose to her feet and swung both swords with deadly accuracy, taking out three soldiers. She immediately did a cartwheel, closing the distance on the remaining four soldiers.

Kimiko now stood in the center of the four soldiers, all of whom were momentarily dumbfounded by how quickly she'd got in. She smirked at the guard to her left – he fired, but she ducked instantly. His shot struck one of his own teammates.

Without missing a beat, Kimiko swung both swords in opposite directions, slicing down two more. One guard remained at her left rear. He tried to raise his weapon – too slow. She spun and sliced upward, cutting through him in a single, decisive strike.

Nearby, Grilka tried to cover Kimiko, blasting away

with her rifle – but the enemy kept coming in overwhelming waves. When the barrage grew too thick, she switched to close combat, her disruptors spitting rapid-fire bursts.

One soldier lunged at her with a knife. Grilka blocked the strike with the butt of her gun, then drove a bone-crushing kick into his chest, sending him sprawling. Another grabbed her from behind – but she hurled him over her shoulder, slamming him into another soldier with brute force taking them both out.

Her fists took over from there, raw strength turning each blow into a takedown. But even Grilka couldn't hold back the tide forever.

Forty more guards came rushing in.

"We're surrounded!" Kimiko shouted over the comms. "Grilka, fall back!"

"I'm not leaving you!" Grilka growled, switching back to her disruptors but her disruptors started to run dry. She fought with brute force, using her fists and wrestling moves to take down enemies in close combat. Despite her strength, the sheer number of troops began to overwhelm her. She was battered and bleeding, but she refused to back down.

Above, Adrian's fighter dove into the fray, its disruptors cut through enemy lines with surgical precision. He targeted clusters of troops, buying precious moments for Grilka to retreat. "Hang on, I'm clearing a path!" he shouted. The fighter's engines roared as Adrian swooped low, strafing the area with calculated bursts. He spotted a heavy weapons emplacement and took it out with a direct hit, creating a brief window for Grilka to fall back.

Amidst the chaos, Freija descended from the skies, her icy-blue wings cutting through the smoke. Her twin ice swords gleamed as she landed silently behind a group of soldiers advancing on Grilka. With swift, deliberate strikes, she froze and shattered their weapons, disarming them before delivering sharp, debilitating blows. One soldier turned to aim at her, but Freija spun gracefully, her blade slicing through his weapon and sending him sprawling.

Another two soldiers came in to take on Freija, but she fully extended her wings knocking them off balance. She used her ice swords to take them each out while they were stunned.

"Keep moving!" Freija called to Grilka, holding off more enemies with a flurry of strikes. Her ice swords left trails of frost in the air, creating a cold mist that slowed the advancing troops. Another soldier lunged at her, but Freija countered with a freezing slash that immobilized him instantly.

About thirty feet away Kimiko was meeting even more overwhelming odds. She had already taken out nearly thirty troops single-handedly but more continued to come in.

They tried to surround her. She used one of her signature moves when fighting overwhelming odds. This was to go to the ground and start attacking legs as she spun around in rolls and twists from the ground. Taking out every leg that she could, followed by a shoulder roll to keep advancing. Even though these were not killing shots, they were enough to take down the enemies. This also allowed the enemy themselves to be the ones who gave her cover as they had to climb over their own wounded.

After twenty more enemies fell, she noticed that she had no way to move forward. Too many injured fighters piled up so high that she couldn't move forward or backward. She had blocked herself into a corner so that she could not recover.

Kimiko, realizing her dire situation, made a split-second decision. She sheathed her katanas and raised her hands in surrender. "Grilka, go!" she yelled. "I'll hold them off!"

"No!" Grilka roared, but she was forced to retreat as more troops closed in. With a final, desperate burst of strength, she fought her way out, her battered body barely making it to cover.

Adrian, still overhead, watched helplessly as Kimiko was captured. "They've got her," he said grimly over the comms. "I can't get a clear shot without hitting her."

Freija realizing there was nothing else that she could do, launched herself supersonically into the air creating a small sonic boom within seconds.

The Scorpion, under Nefertari's control, fired at the southern border to cover Grilka's escape. Rainstorm manned the weapons, blasting away at ground forces and incoming fire. The ship shuddered under the strain of the assault but held firm.

Grilka stumbled back to the Scorpion, her body bruised and bloodied. She climbed aboard, her face a mixture of pain and fury. "They took Kimiko," as she spat blood onto the floor and then collapsing into the co-pilot's seat. "We need to get her back." The Scorpion then took off to meet at the rendezvous point.

The remaining team regrouped at the rendezvous point, a secluded area a few miles outside of the line. Lilith landed with the captured officer, his yellow face pale with fear. Before anyone could speak, Adrian stormed over to him, his eyes blazing with anger. Without hesitation, he punched the officer square in the face, sending the man reeling, light green blood coming out of his nose and lip. "Where did they take her?" Adrian shouted, his voice raw with emotion.

The officer groaned but said nothing, his defiance only fueling Adrian's rage. Adrian grabbed him by the collar, shaking him. "Answer me! Where are they taking her?"

Lilith unfurled her wings with a menacing snap, her fiery gaze locking onto the captive. She barked, her voice sharp and commanding, "Enough, Adrian! Step back." For a moment, Adrian hesitated, his fists clenched tightly, but he relented, stepping away to let Lilith take over.

Lilith crouched in front of the officer – now

recognized as a captain – her towering presence made all the more intimidating by the glow of her crimson wings. Her twin two-handed swords immediately went to full blaze reflecting off her inner wings. "You'll want to answer us," she said, her voice cold and deliberate. "Not just about our teammate, but about Necra's plans. Start talking, or this will get much worse for you."

The captain glared at her, stubborn and silent. Lilith's patience wore thin. She let a stream of fire spark from her fingertips, the heat singeing the air between them. "This is your last chance," she growled.

Freija, now standing to the side, crossed her arms, her icy demeanor sharp enough to cut. "You're not in a position to resist," she said softly. "Speak now, or you'll wish you had." The combined force of Lilith's fire and Freija's frost created a chilling tension that filled the air.

The captain finally shifted, his bravado cracking under pressure. "Alright, alright! They've taken her to the interrogation chamber near the central compound," he said, his voice shaking. "She's a valuable hostage. They'll interrogate her – maybe worse – if you try anything."

Lilith stood tall, her expression unreadable. "What about Necra's generals? What's their plan here on Luthor?"

The captain hesitated, his loyalty battling against his fear. Adrian stepped forward again, his voice lower but no less dangerous. "Don't make us ask twice."

"The generals... they're consolidating forces," the captain stammered. "They want to strip this planet of its resources. They've got orbital drills coming in – huge machines to rip the core apart. If you're planning to fight them, you're already too late."

The group exchanged grim glances. Rainstorm standing just outside the circle said, "We'll need to move fast. Kimiko can't wait... and neither can this planet."

Lilith's fiery eyes burned with determination. "This isn't over," she said, her voice cold and steady. "We'll get her back… and we'll make them pay."

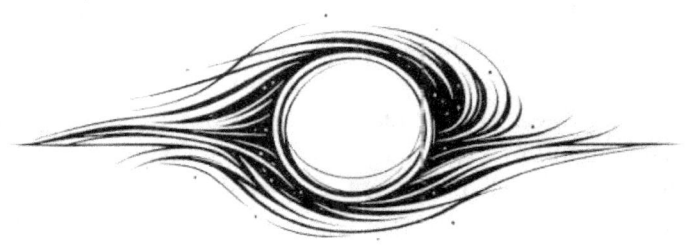

Chapter 27:

Kimiko's Interrogation

The room was silent except for the faint hum of the fluorescent lights that flickered intermittently, casting uneven shadows on the dull grey walls. Kimiko sat motionless, handcuffed to a cold metal table in the center of the stale square room. Her face bore the marks of the brutal fight she had endured – a swollen lip, a bloody nose, and cuts lining her arms like a macabre map of battle. Yet her eyes, sharp and unwavering, stared straight ahead, refusing to betray even a flicker of emotion.

Across from her stood two yellow-skinned humanoid men, their appearance alien yet unsettlingly familiar. Their eyes, small and calculating, bore into her as one of them slammed his fist onto the table, the sound echoing in the confined space.

"We'll ask you again," the first interrogator snarled, his voice low and gravelly. "Who are you, and what was your mission?"

Kimiko remained silent, her gaze fixed on an indeterminate point on the wall behind them. Her stoic demeanor only seemed to inflame the interrogator's temper. He leaned closer, his face mere inches from hers.

"You think this is a game?" he growled. "You and

your team are nothing but insects, interfering in matters far beyond your comprehension. Speak, or things will get worse for you."

Kimiko's lips curled slightly, almost imperceptibly. It wasn't a smile – more a subtle acknowledgment of their futility. For a brief moment, her eyes flicked to meet his, a calculated gesture that carried a quiet defiance with a hint of power aimed to cause fear.

The second interrogator, broader and more composed, stepped forward. He placed a hand on his companion's shoulder, easing him back. "She's a trained operative," he said in a measured tone. "She won't crack so easily. Let's try a different approach."

He turned to Kimiko, his demeanor shifting to one of feigned concern. "You don't need to suffer like this," he began, his voice soft but insidious. "Tell us what we want to know, and we'll make sure you're treated well. Cooperation can be… rewarding."

Kimiko's head tilted slightly, her expression unchanged. She blinked once, deliberately, before resuming her blank stare. The interrogator's smile faltered, frustration creeping into his features.

"Perhaps you need a reminder of your situation," the first interrogator interjected, stepping forward again. He grabbed a metal chair, dragging it noisily across the floor before sitting directly in front of her. "You're alone. Your friends can't save you. And unless you cooperate, your suffering will only deepen."

Kimiko's eyes shifted, locking onto him for a fraction of a second. The weight of her gaze was unsettling, even for a seasoned interrogator. The silence stretched, heavy and oppressive.

"What are your team's plans?" the second interrogator pressed. "What do you know about Necra's operations?"

Still, Kimiko said nothing. Her hands, though

restrained, rested calmly on the table. Her breathing remained steady, a stark contrast to the growing tension in the room. The interrogators exchanged a glance, their patience thinning.

The first one stood abruptly, slamming his hands on the table. "Enough of this!" he roared. "You think your silence protects you? We have ways of making you talk."

Kimiko's head turned slightly, her gaze shifting to the corner of the room where a small camera was mounted. Her lips parted just enough to reveal the faintest smirk, a deliberate act that seemed to mock their efforts. It was as if she were silently saying, *I've endured worse than you could ever imagine.*

The first interrogator's face was contorted with rage. He reached for a nearby baton, but the second stopped him with a firm grip.

"We can't break her spirit like this," the second said through gritted teeth. "But everyone has a breaking point. Let's give her time to reflect."

He leaned close to Kimiko, his voice dropping to a menacing whisper. "We'll leave you for now. But when we return, I promise you'll wish you'd spoken."

The two interrogators exited the room, the door slamming shut behind them. The stale, metallic air seemed to thicken in their absence. Kimiko exhaled softly, her body still composed. Her mind, however, raced. She cataloged every detail – the layout of the room, the positioning of the guards she had seen, the faint sound of footsteps echoing through the adjacent corridors.

She shifted her wrists subtly, testing the strength of her restraints. The cuffs were tight, and the table was bolted to the floor, but Kimiko's resolve remained unshaken. Her weapons were in the next room, just out of reach, but her greatest weapon was her mind.

The fluorescent lights flickered again, casting brief, erratic shadows. Kimiko straightened in her chair; her gaze fixed on the door. *Let them come,* she thought. *I'll be ready.*

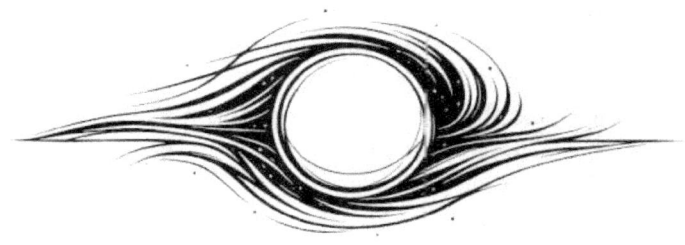

Chapter 28:

A Plan of Deception

Back at the Scorpion, the team regrouped in the makeshift camp just outside the ship after they gleamed all the information that the captain knew. The captured captain, now bound and gagged, had been handed over to a local rebel ally who promised to keep him secure. The air was thick with tension as Rainstorm knelt by Grilka, carefully applying a poultice of local herbs to her wounds. The scent was sharp and earthy, mingling with the metallic tang of blood still smeared on Grilka's skin.

"You're lucky it wasn't worse," Rainstorm said quietly, her hands steady as she worked. "These herbs should help with the pain and stop infection."

Grilka winced but managed to smile a weak smile. "Lucky? I'd say it was skill, not luck. They'll need more than brute force to take me down."

Rainstorm didn't reply, though a flicker of respect crossed her face. She tied off the bandage and gave Grilka a pat on the shoulder. "Rest while you can. We'll need you soon."

Nearby, Adrian, Lilith, Nefertari, and Freija were deep in discussion, their voices hushed but intense. Freija gestured to a hastily sketched map of the stronghold that

Adrian had drawn in the dirt.

Lilith addressed the small group, "If their setup is typical and from what we were able to gleam from the captain, there should be multiple entry points here and here," she said, pointing to the southern and western perimeters. "But they'll be heavily guarded."

Adrian leaned back, rubbing his chin thoughtfully. "We'll need to blend in, get close without raising suspicion. If we can disguise ourselves as their soldiers, we might be able to infiltrate."

Lilith's fiery gaze fixed on him. "How do you propose we do that? They'll recognize we're outsiders immediately."

Adrian grinned, the hint of a mischievous glint in his eyes. "Simple. We use their own tricks against them. I'll take the captain's badge and uniform. Rainstorm, Nefertari, and I can dye our skins with some of that yellow herb paste we found. They'll dress in local attire to look the part."

Freija arched an eyebrow. "And Grilka?"

Adrian's grin widened. "That's the biggest part. We'll pretend we've captured her. Say she's a rebel we need to bring in for interrogation. They should already recognize her from when she and Kimiko were fighting them."

Lilith crossed her arms, considering the plan. "It's dangerous, but it's our best shot. We need to move quickly. Every moment we waste, Kimiko is in greater danger."

Nefertari chimed in, "I'll do it. If it gets us closer to Kimiko, I'll play the part."

Rainstorm joined in and said unknowingly asked, "What are you guys talking about?"

Freija replies, "Rescue Kimiko."

Rainstorm replies, "Then I am in. Whatever it is I am sure it is going to be a good plan."

Nefertari continued with the previous train of thought, "But we'll need to be convincing. One slip, and it's over."

"Don't worry," Adrian said, his tone lighter but still focused. "I've got a knack for improvisation. Just stick to the plan, and we'll get her out."

A little while later, the team finalized their disguises. Rainstorm, Adrian, and Nefertari applied the yellow dye to their skin, the earthy paste staining them a near-perfect match to the enemy soldiers. Adrian donned the captain's uniform, adjusting the badge on his chest. Grilka grumbled as her wrists were loosely bound with rope, her gruff demeanor lending authenticity to the act. Rainstorm takes off all of the bandages so her injuries will help sell the capture.

"We go in from the west wing," Adrian instructed. "The story is simple: we caught this rebel outside the perimeter. We're taking her to the interrogation wing to join the other prisoner. No embellishments, no overacting. I will do all of the talking. Got it?"

Rainstorm nodded. "Straightforward. Let's do this."

The group moved under the cover of darkness toward the stronghold's west entrance. Two guards stood at the gate, their weapons slung casually over their shoulders. Adrian stepped forward confidently.

"Caught this one sneaking around," he said, nodding toward Grilka. "Orders are to take her to the interrogation for questioning."

The guards exchanged glances, their eyes lingering on Grilka's defiant scowl. "Where's your patrol unit?" one asked, suspicion creeping into his voice.

"Spread thin," Adrian replied smoothly. "They're securing the perimeter while we handle this. You want to explain to the general why we're late?"

The mention of the general silenced any further questions. The guards stepped aside, motioning them through. Adrian gave them a curt nod and led the group inside.

The interior of the stronghold was dimly lit, its metallic walls echoing with the distant sounds of machinery and voices. A soldier escorted them down a narrow corridor, stopping at an office door. "Captain Harrek will take it from here," he said before stepping back.

The door opened, revealing a yellow-skinned officer seated at a desk. Kimiko's weapons were laid out neatly in front of him, their black blades lay ominously under the harsh light. Rainstorm and Nefertari exchanged subtle glances, noting the location of the weapons.

Captain Harrek eyed the group suspiciously. "Another prisoner? What's the story?"

Adrian shrugged. "Caught her near the southern fence. She's got information, but she's not talking. Figured you'd want her in the same cell as the other one."

Grilka barked a string of curt, convincing insults, her voice laced with venom. She ended with a snarl: "You'll regret this… *all of you!*"

Harrek smirked, leaning back in his chair. "Feisty. I like that. Fine, take her to the other interrogation room."

He waved them off dismissively, his attention returning to the weapons on his desk. The soldier led them to the second interrogation room, first stopping outside a door with a small observation window. Through the glass, Adrian caught a glimpse of Kimiko, still cuffed to the table, her expression unyielding despite her injuries. Adrian slowed his pace and turned to the guard. "What's the story with this one?" he asked, his tone casual.

The guard shrugged. "Another rebel. She was trying to attack from the south a little while ago, Sir."

Adrian raised an eyebrow, glancing back at Kimiko through the window. "Ah, makes sense. This green one," he motioned toward Grilka, "was her companion. They're a pair, huh?" The guard gave a brief nod before motioning them further down the hall.

Adrian's jaw tightened, but he forced himself to stay calm. "Let's move," he said quietly to Grilka.

The group continued down the hall to the next room,

their steps measured. Every detail of the stronghold etched itself into their minds, the plan taking shape with each passing second.

They were led into another interrogation room next door, the door clicking shut behind them. Adrian looked around the room briefly before addressing the guard. "We'll need cuffs and a key," he said, his tone authoritative. "If we're going to interrogate both prisoners, we need flexibility to work them properly."

"Yes Sir," the soldier responded.

Within a few minutes, the soldier returned, handing Adrian a pair of cuffs and a key. Adrian nodded, gesturing for Nefertari and Rainstorm to bring Grilka forward. Grilka, still playing the role of the defiant prisoner, cursed loudly and struggled as she was dragged toward the table.

Adrian grabbed her shoulders and shoved her into the chair, his expression hard. "Sit down and shut up," he barked, slapping the table for emphasis. Nefertari and Rainstorm, playing their parts, forced Grilka's arms onto the table. Both ladies notice the camera from the side of their eye.

Adrian took the cuffs and locked them around her wrists, but with careful sleight of hand, he pretended to secure the chain to the lock on the table. Instead, he adjusted the chain just enough to give Grilka the slack she'd need to break free, if things went sideways. He then pulled the ropes off her wrists and dropped them dramatically onto the table.

The guard watched with faint amusement before stepping out of the room, the door clicking shut behind him.

Adrian took a seat across from Grilka, leaning back casually as he began his act. "Alright, you stubborn, green-skinned nuisance. You're going to tell me everything I want to know," he growled, his tone sharp.

Grilka sneered, her voice dripping with venom. "You'll get nothing from me, you sniveling traitor!"

Adrian slammed his hand on the table, the sound

echoing through the room and down the hall. "I'm not playing games here! You've already lost. Now, talk!"

Grilka responded with a string of insults so loud that anyone within four or five rooms could hear her defiance. She leaned forward, her eyes blazing. "I'll never talk, you cowardly fool! You think you can break me? Try harder!"

Nefertari and Rainstorm stood nearby, their expressions grim as they maintained the illusion of captors. Rainstorm occasionally adjusted her grip on the disruptor at her side, adding to the performance. Nefertari's eyes flicked toward the door briefly, ensuring no one was listening too closely.

Grilka's voice rose again, filling the hallway with her angry shouts. In his office, Captain Harrek smirked at the commotion. *Sounds like that one's putting up a fight.* he muttered to himself. After a moment, his smile widened and whispered to himself, *I need him over with that other prisoner. Let's see if he can get anything useful from her.*

Grilka's defiant shouts softened momentarily, her shoulders slumping as she let out a resigned sigh. She glared at Adrian, her voice dripping with venom. "Fine. You want answers? I'll talk."

Adrian leaned in, his expression intense. "Finally. Start with how many others are working with you."

"Dozens," Grilka spat, her tone laced with false conviction. "We've infiltrated every sector of this operation. We know all your patrol routes and weaknesses."

Adrian nodded slowly, pretending to take her words seriously. "Where's your main camp?"

Grilka's lips twisted into a smirk. "In the northern forests, hidden so well you'll never find it. Even if you sent an army, you'd be ambushed before you got close."

Adrian glanced at Nefertari and Rainstorm, who maintained stoic expressions, and then back to Grilka. "And your mission objectives?"

"To destroy everything you've built," Grilka sneered.

"To liberate this planet from your filthy hands."

Adrian's jaw tightened, his act unwavering as he fired off more questions. Grilka continued to answer with a mix of lies and exaggerations, her performance just believable enough to sound convincing to an outsider. He nodded occasionally, his face betraying no sign of skepticism.

After several minutes of this back-and-forth, Adrian pushed back from the table, letting out a dramatic sigh. "You're impossible, you know that?" he muttered, shaking his head. "But at least I've got something to work with."

Adrian rose from his chair and moved to the door, stepping into the hallway where Captain Harrek was waiting. The yellow-skinned officer smirked as Adrian approached. "Any luck?"

Adrian shrugged, his tone casual. "She's stubborn, but she's talking. A lot of it might be nonsense, but I can piece together some intel from it."

Captain Harrek chuckled. "They always crack eventually, Captain."

Adrian crossed his arms, his expression calculated. "What about the other prisoner? Any progress?"

Harrek's smirk faded slightly. "Not a word from her. Silent as a rock."

Adrian tilted his head thoughtfully. "Maybe I can get through to her. If she's anything like this one, I've got a few tricks that might work."

Harrek considered this for a moment before nodding. "Fine. She's in the next room. Give it your best shot. If you can get her to talk, you'll save me a lot of time and effort."

Adrian's lips curved into a faint smile. "Gladly. I'll handle this personally."

Satisfied, Harrek motioned to a soldier. The soldier opened the door to Kimiko's interrogation room. The air inside was tense and still, the only sound the faint hum of the overhead lights. Kimiko remained motionless, her gaze fixed forward, her expression unchanging. She didn't flinch or acknowledge the door opening but did notice Adrian, Nefertari, and Rainstorm through her peripheral vision. She did fully hear Grilka's dramatic performance through the walls and decided to play along with whatever was coming next.

Adrian nodded to Nefertari and Rainstorm. "Wait outside," he said curtly, stepping into the room and closing the door behind him. He walked to the table, pulled a chair across from Kimiko, and slammed it down noisily. The metallic clang reverberated through the room.

"Alright!" Adrian shouted, his voice filling the space. "You think you're tough? Let's see how tough you really are."

Kimiko didn't move, her face an unreadable mask of calm defiance. Adrian first winked where Kimiko could see but out of sight of the cameras.

Adrian's eyes then narrowed, and he leaned forward, slamming his palms on the table for effect. "Do you even understand the trouble you're in? Huh? Say something!" He then winked at her again, giving her the cue to start her own dramatic performance.

For several moments, Kimiko remained utterly silent, her expression unwavering. Then, almost imperceptibly, she shifted her gaze slightly, her lips parting just enough to whisper a simple sentence. "I'm listening."

Adrian's eyebrows shot up, and he leaned back in his chair. "Oh, she does talk!" he exclaimed, the sarcasm heavy in his tone. "How about a name, then? You've got one of those, don't you?"

Kimiko hesitated, calculating her response. Finally, she lied, "Mika."

Adrian smirked, his eyes narrowing as he leaned forward. "Mika, huh? Alright, Mika. Let's start with the obvious: what were you and your big green friend doing near the southern fence?"

Kimiko tilted her head slightly, her gaze remaining calm. "We were scouting," she said simply, her voice low but steady.

"Scouting? For what?" Adrian pressed, his tone sharp. "Intel? Weak points? Or maybe you were planning something bigger?"

"Weak points," Kimiko replied, keeping her answers brief. "Your defenses are sloppy."

Adrian raised an eyebrow, playing along. "Sloppy, you say? Care to elaborate?"

Kimiko's lips twitched almost imperceptibly. "Your patrols are predictable. Too much focus on the perimeter, not enough on internal security."

Adrian feigned a scoff. "Internal security, huh? Well, we've managed just fine so far. And your camp – where is it?"

Kimiko's expression hardened, but she didn't hesitate. "Northern forests," she said, echoing Grilka's lie. "Well hidden."

Adrian leaned back, nodding slowly. "Interesting."

Adrian glances toward the door as if irritated. He slapped the table suddenly, making Kimiko blink for the first time. "Alright, fine. Let's change the subject. What exactly is your objective here? Why risk so much for such a poorly planned attack?"

Kimiko hesitated just long enough to sell her next response. "Distraction," she said evenly. "To keep you busy while the real operation happens elsewhere."

Adrian narrowed his eyes, leaning in closer. "Real operation? Care to enlighten me?"

Kimiko's gaze didn't waver. "No."

Adrian grinned, shaking his head. "Of course not. You've got guts, I'll give you that." He stood abruptly, pacing the room with a show of frustration before slamming his fist on the table again. "You know what? I'm done for now. We'll see how long you can keep up this act."

Adrian leaned forward again, his eyes narrowing as he studied her. "Mika, huh? That's what we're going with? Fine." He let out a mocking laugh. "Well, Mika, I hope you like long conversations because you and I are going to have a lot of them."

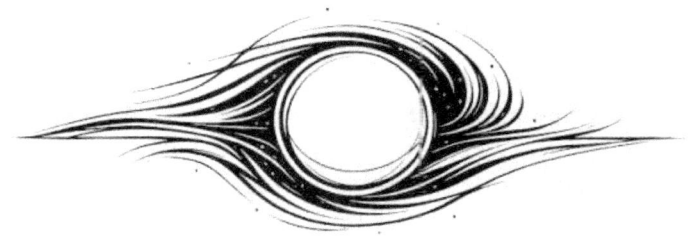

Chapter 29:

Solitary Plans

Adrian exited the interrogation room with a confident stride, his face a mask of calm determination. Outside, Captain Harrek stood waiting, his yellowish skin catching the dim light of the corridor. Adrian didn't waste time.

"I want both of these prisoners put in solitary confinement," Adrian said firmly. His tone carried the weight of authority, leaving little room for argument.

Captain Harrek's brow furrowed slightly, skepticism flickering in his gaze. "Solitary? That's a bit extreme, don't you think? They're already secured."

Adrian leaned closer, his voice lowering conspiratorially. "They're playing us, Captain. The green one won't stop yelling, and I'm not taking chances with the other one suddenly clamming up again. Separate them, and we'll see who cracks first."

Harrek tilted his head, considering the suggestion. Adrian pressed on. "Look, I've gotten more intel out of them in one session than anyone else has. Let me do my job. You'll get results. And, by the way, that is an order."

After a moment, Harrek nodded reluctantly. "Yes Sir. But I want a report on anything new you learn."

"You'll have it, Captain," Adrian assured him, before continuing, "I'll take both to solitary myself. No need to waste anyone else's time."

Harrek raised an eyebrow but seemed satisfied. "Yes, Sir."

Adrian nodded curtly, then motioned for the door to be opened. As the door swung wide, his eyes landed on Kimiko's weapons lying on the captain's desk. He pointed sharply at them. "You two," he said, directing his command to Rainstorm and Nefertari. "We're taking those to evidence. Grab them and follow me." He stepped back into the interrogation room where Grilka sat, her wrists cuffed, and a scowl firmly planted on her face.

Rainstorm picked up two sai and Nefertari picked up the two sheathed katanas.

"Time to move," Adrian announced, his tone sharp and commanding. Grilka shot him a glare but grumbled under her breath as he grabbed her by the arm and pulled her to her feet. She barked out a few choice insults including some yellow-skinned racial slurs which were loud enough to echo down the hallway, adding to the performance.

Adrian stood Grilka up, his grip firm on her arm. He unlocked one of the cuffs, the metallic click echoing in the room, and rotated the cuff with a deliberate show. He then moved both of her arms behind her back and snapped the cuff on the same wrist ensuring the echo of a locked cuff could be easily heard. He tapped a finger on her other wrist to let her know what he just did. Grilka's scowl deepened, adding to the performance.

Adrian led Grilka into the corridor and he handed her over to Nefertari, who was still holding the two swords in one hand. Grilka's insults grew louder and more theatrical. As they exited, Kimiko's calm demeanor shifted just enough to deliver a sharp remark aimed at Grilka. "Traitor," she spat, her voice cutting through the air like a blade.

Grilka whipped her head around, glaring at Kimiko.

"What did you say?" she growled, pretending to struggle against her cuffs. "If I wasn't restrained with these cuffs, I'd rip off her damn head!"

Kimiko tilted her head slightly, her tone mocking. "In your dreams," she said with a faint smirk, adding, "Good thing you're fully restrained, huh?"

Grilka snarled, her performance ramping up as she tugged at her faux-secured cuffs. "Keep talking, you coward! I'll make you eat those words!"

Adrian barked at both of them and then slamming his hand on the wall for effect. "Enough! Both of you!" His sharp tone silenced the verbal altercation, though Grilka continued to grumble under her breath. Kimiko, ever composed, sat perfectly still, her gaze calm and measured. Adrian met her eyes with a stern look. "You too," he barked and motioned for her to stand.

Kimiko rose slowly, deliberately, her hands still cuffed in front of her. Adrian took her arm and, mimicking the same procedure as with Grilka, unlocked one cuff with a loud click, moved her arms behind her back, and cuffed the handcuff to the same wrist and again touched a finger on the opposite wrist. His grip on her arm was firm, his movements deliberate. "Let's go, Mika," he said gruffly, as if handling a troublesome prisoner.

Adrian handed the cuffed Kimiko to Rainstorm, who was holding the two sai in her other hand.

With both women in tow, Adrian led them down the hallway toward the solitary wing. Harrek stood at the end of the corridor, observing the procession with a smirk of satisfaction.

"You're good at this, Captain," Harrek remarked. "Keep up the pressure, and we'll get what we need."

Adrian responded with a curt nod. "Count on it." He kept walking, ensuring his demeanor stayed convincing.

As Adrian was leading the two mock-prisoners down the hall and around a few corners, he was looking at the nearest maps on the wall. As they walked down the corridor, he scanned for exit routes and the guard placements. His sharp eyes caught sight of a glowing green exit sign at the end of an unguarded hallway. He slowed his pace, subtly motioning toward it.

"This way," Adrian muttered under his breath, his voice just loud enough for Grilka and Kimiko to hear. The women didn't visibly react but registered the instruction.

The hallway was long and eerily quiet, with only the hum of the facility's lights to accompany their footsteps. Adrian maintained his commanding demeanor, his pace steady and deliberate. As they turned the corner, the exit door came into view. Adrian glanced around, ensuring no one was watching.

"Move," he whispered sharply, quickening his pace.

The group was making their way to the door when suddenly, two officers in each in a major's uniforms entered from the opposite end of the corridor. Their boots echoed off the steel walls as they strolled in, completely unaware of what was happening – until one of them caught sight of Adrian's uniform. His gaze lingered, recognition dawning.

"This way," Adrian ordered under his breath, pivoting sharply to the left.

Without hesitation, the team turned with him, disappearing down an adjacent corridor before the officers could fully register what was happening. For a brief moment, it seemed as though they had avoided detection – until the blaring wail of the alarm system shattered the tense silence.

"Escaping prisoners!" the officer's voice roared through the intercom.

A deep, resonant alarm thundered through the hallways as red lights began flashing along the ceiling panels.

Adrian exhaled sharply. "I guess this means Plan B."

Nefertari, running at his side, shot him a glance. "And what, exactly, is Plan B?"

"Plan B?" Adrian gave a sharp grin despite the chaos erupting around them. "Get out as fast as possible before we get riddled with holes!"

The loudspeaker crackled to life, an urgent voice filling the corridors: "Prisoners escaping in Section B-12! Again, prisoners in Section B-12! All security personnel, converge immediately!"

The warning sent shockwaves through the facility. The once-empty hallways erupted with the sound of pounding boots – troops mobilizing from every direction.

"We've got about one hundred yards to go!" Rainstorm shouted, glancing at the map on her wrist device. "Three turns. Keep moving!"

Just as the team rounded the next corner, they were met with the worst-case scenario – troops converging from multiple directions.

Five soldiers barreled toward them from ahead, their weapons raised and ready. From a branching hallway on the right, ten more appeared, and from another hall on the left, at least eight heavily armed guards emerged in perfect formation.

"Looks like we've been expected," Kimiko muttered.

"We don't have time for this!" Adrian barked.

Rainstorm wasted no time. In one fluid motion, she sheathed the twin sai she still held in her hands and drew two disruptors from her belt. Instead of turning, she tossed them over her shoulder, sending them into a perfect backward arc.

Grilka, with inhuman reflexes, leaped into the air, twisting mid-jump to catch the disruptors before landing on one knee. Without missing a beat, she opened fire down the right corridor, dropping three of the closest guards before they could react.

Rainstorm, her hands now free, whipped out the sai and charged forward into the incoming soldiers, slicing through their ranks with lethal efficiency.

Nefertari moved quickly, her golden eyes locking onto Kimiko. With precision, she threw the sheathed twin katanas into the air.

Kimiko's body was already in motion before the swords even reached her.

She leaped forward, caught both weapons in midair, and fluidly spun the sheaths – each sheath swinging outward in an elegant arc as they locked onto her back in a single, practiced movement.

The moment the swords clicked into place, she drew the first katana in a single, sweeping motion. A second later, the second blade slid free in an equally seamless strike.

In one breath, she twisted into a whirling blur of steel, meeting the six incoming guards from behind with absolute, deadly precision.

Nefertari, meanwhile, dropped into a low roll across the floor, coming up on one knee. Her disruptors were already drawn as she unloaded controlled bursts down the left corridor, firing off headshots with unnerving accuracy.

Behind Rainstorm, Adrian pulled out his own disruptors and vaulted over a fallen guard, planting himself directly over Rainstorm as he rained suppressing fire down the length of the hall. Any guard who made it past the first few waves was quickly met by Rainstorm's flashing sai.

"We have to push forward!" Adrian yelled.

Kimiko, now fully in control of her battlefield, moved like a wraith, striking down the remaining soldiers before kicking off the wall and rebounding forward.

The others followed, racing down the corridor as gunfire and alarm sirens filled the air.

"Attention! The prisoners have made it to Section B-13! Repeat, B-13!"

More guards. More weapons. More resistance.

The group barely slowed, fighting through incoming waves of troops with relentless precision.

Adrian noticed troops moving in from a side hall far

ahead, cutting off their final turn before the exit.

"Keep going!" he ordered. "We can't let them box us in!"

They rounded the last corner, slamming into the emergency exit door.

As soon as Rainstorm threw it open, gunfire erupted from the guards stationed outside on the walls.

"I'm the sharpshooter here," Grilka growled, moving forward.

Rainstorm barely glanced at her. "So am I."

Without hesitation, Grilka dropped low onto her stomach, while Rainstorm remained standing above her.

"I take left, you take right," Grilka muttered.

"Agreed," Rainstorm confirmed.

With that, the two women unleashed a hailstorm of disruptor fire.

Rainstorm's disruptor fire ripped through the enemy ranks while Grilka took careful, devastating shots at the rooftop snipers. *One. Two. Three down.*

Adrian shoved the door wider and pointed toward a cluster of crates stacked fifteen feet away.

"We need cover... there! Move!"

Kimiko and Nefertari wasted no time, sprinting across the open ground as Grilka and Rainstorm covered them.

Adrian, waiting for the right moment, charged next, dodging gunfire before sliding behind the nearest crate.

Kimiko took point, her twin katanas slicing through any soldier foolish enough to get close. Nefertari backed her up, sending well-placed disruptor shots into their enemies' weak points.

Grilka did a quick shoulder roll landing on her feet and raced to the crate.

Rainstorm was last out, kicking the heavy steel door shut behind her. Without missing a beat, she flipped a switch on her disruptor and fired a concentrated beam, welding the door shut.

Then, she was off, sprinting across the battlefield to join the others.

Gunfire rained from above, but Grilka moved like a machine, switching between rooftops and ground troops with seamless efficiency.

"We need to move!" Adrian called out. "We're still too exposed!"

The team advanced, fighting tooth and nail toward their only viable escape point.

Finally, they made it – a cargo ship stationed next to a chain-link fence.

As they reached the cargo ship they looked up at the chain-link fence. The towering 12-foot barrier loomed before them; its barbed wire curled outward like the fangs of a beast.

Adrian reached for his comms and pressed the button to connect with Lilith and Freija, who were waiting nearby in the Scorpion. "We are almost clear. Head to the rendezvous point to pick us up," he said, his tone calm but urgent.

Lilith's reply crackled through softly and confidently. "Copy," she said, her voice steady and composed.

Kimiko was already assessing it, eyes scanning the structure. "This is actually simple," she said, sheathing her katanas. "The barbed wire faces outward, making it easier to scale. We climb, reach the top, jump, and roll. No need to climb down."

Adrian, halfway through a sarcastic retort, turned away to take out a soldier with a well-placed shot. "Right, because …"

By the time he turned back, Kimiko was already on the other side, crouched in a defensive stance, katanas drawn, waiting for the others. All in less than a few seconds.

The rest of the team just stared.

Grilka blinked. "Did she just …?"

Rainstorm scoffed, still firing at approaching troops. "Achieved before we even planned to achieve. Typical."

Nefertari, snapping out of her stunned moment, slung her rifle over her back and began climbing. With her long, fluid movements, she made short work of the ascent. As soon as she reached the top, she stood on the thin railing and jumped over and landed on the ground with a simple forward roll.

Meanwhile, Rainstorm, Adrian, and Grilka were still covering their escape, laying down suppressing fire while soldiers rushed toward them from the main gate.

Grilka was next, climbing fast with practiced strength. When she reached the top, instead of immediately jumping, she turned and took down three more soldiers from her vantage point.

"Anytime now," Adrian called up, returning fire toward the courtyard.

"Covering your slow asses," Grilka muttered as she finally leaped down.

Rainstorm vaulted up next, moving quickly as disruptor fire whizzed past her.

Adrian groaned, firing one last shot before slinging his disruptor. "At this rate, Freija's gonna have dinner ready before we all make it over."

"Not my fault you all move like snails," Kimiko sai deadpanned from the other side.

With the last of their enemies momentarily suppressed, Rainstorm finally made the jump.

Now it was Adrian's turn – and the enemy was closing in.

"Last one over buys drinks!" he called out as he climbed.

Grilka rolled her eyes. "Move it, flyboy, or you're gonna be the last one *shot* instead."

Adrian quickly climbed the fence and jumped to the

other side with a shoulder roll.

They all gave each other a nod and started to run toward the hills.

The group rounded the bend, moving swiftly but carefully. Ahead, the Scorpion stood waiting, its lights dimmed to avoid drawing attention. By the entrance to the ship, Lilith and Freija stood watch, their silhouettes sharp against the muted glow of the vessel's interior.

Nefertari was the first to emerge from the bend, her posture straight and her weapon at the ready. Rainstorm followed close behind, her eyes darting to the surrounding area for any signs of pursuit. Kimiko came next, her movements fluid despite the intensity of their escape. Adrian and Grilka brought up the rear, their steps deliberate as they scanned for any lingering threats.

As soon as Freija saw Kimiko, her face lit up with relief. She dashed forward; her usual energy was amplified by the tension of the moment. Without hesitation, she wrapped Kimiko in a warm hug. "Thank the stars you're okay," Freija said, her voice bright and heartfelt. "We were so worried about you."

Kimiko stiffened slightly, unaccustomed to such overt displays of emotion, but a faint smile tugged at her lips. "It'll take more than this to keep me down," she said quietly, her tone softening as she acknowledged Freija's concern with a soft hug in return.

Lilith stood by the entrance, her fiery gaze scanning the horizon. "Get inside," she commanded, her tone calm but firm. "We'll debrief once we're in the air."

Freija gave Kimiko a final squeeze before pulling back, her eyes sparkling with genuine warmth. "Come on," she said, motioning toward the ship. The group wasted no time filing into the Scorpion as the hatch began to close behind them.

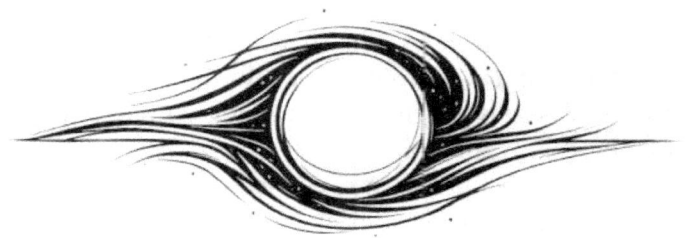

Chapter 30:

The Debrief

The Scorpion soared through the atmosphere, its engines humming steadily as the team gathered in the living quarters. The tension of their escape lingered in the air, but for the first time since their mission began, there was a sense of relief. Rainstorm sat cross-legged on one of the leather seats. She took a deep breath, glancing around at the group before beginning her recount of the mission.

Lilith says, "Let's catch everyone up on this last mission to rescue Kimiko. Rainstorm, I know you won't embellish. Tell me your side of the story."

"Alright," Rainstorm started, her tone calm but purposeful. "Let's go over what just happened from the beginning."

Freija, perched on the edge of another seat, immediately interrupted, her wings twitching with excitement. "Can we just talk about how amazing it was when we saw you all come around the bend?" she said, her voice bubbling with enthusiasm. "I mean, I knew you'd make it, but seeing it was so much better!"

Rainstorm raised an eyebrow but smiled faintly. "Yes, Freija, it was a good moment. But let me get through this, okay?"

Freija nodded quickly, though her grin suggested

she'd have more to add soon.

Rainstorm continued, her gaze settling on Kimiko. "First off, I have to say, your silence during the interrogation was impressive. They couldn't get a single thing out of you, and that kind of resolve is rare."

Kimiko's expression remained cool, though a slight nod acknowledged the compliment. "It was necessary," she replied simply.

Rainstorm leaned forward, her eyes narrowing slightly as her excitement grew. "And Grilka, you were incredible. The yelling, the over-the-top threats, making up an entire story on the fly? It was like watching a theater performance. It's no wonder that the captain and those guards bought every word."

Grilka grinned, crossing her arms smugly. "Well, I'm not just muscle, you know. I have range."

Adrian smirked. "Range, huh? Like the part where you threatened to rip off Kimiko's head?"

Grilka chuckled. "It worked, didn't it?"

Kimiko let out a small smile.

Rainstorm laughed softly before continuing. "And Kimiko," she said, turning back to the ninja. "Your ability to pick up on Grilka's story and feed right into it without hesitation? That was genius. You even added details that made it sound more believable. I don't think anyone could have guessed it was all fake."

Kimiko's lips twitched slightly into what might have been a smile. "It's important to stay adaptable," she said quietly.

Nefertari, unable to contain herself, burst out, "And then the captain! Oh my stars, when Adrian faked him out and we made it to the exit? That was such a power move!" She gestured dramatically. "You were like, 'Let me take them to solitary,' but you were really like, 'I'm just going to walk out of here with everyone.' It was perfect!"

Adrian leaned back in his chair, a smug grin

spreading across his face. "What can I say? I'm good under pressure. And let's not forget how well everyone followed my lead."

"Oh, please," Grilka interjected, rolling her eyes. "If anyone deserves credit for making it believable, it's me. My performance was what sold it."

Rainstorm raised a hand to calm the playful banter. "Let's not forget the escape itself," she said. That was teamwork in action. We used our sharpshooter skills to lay down the cover fire so that we could begin our escape. This took precision and teamwork. Every person acted together to get out of that stronghold."

Freija practically bounced in her seat. "I still can't believe how amazing it all was. Can we do it again?"

The group groaned in unison, though laughter followed quickly. Even Lilith, standing silently by the doorway, allowed a small smirk.

"You all did well," Lilith said finally, her voice calm and steady. "But don't let your guard down. Necra's forces won't stop because of one victory. There's more to come."

The room fell quiet for a moment, the weight of Lilith's words settling over them. Then Freija, unable to resist, broke the silence. "Okay, but can we also celebrate just a little? Because that was AWESOME!"

Rainstorm shook her head but couldn't suppress her smile. "Fine. A little."

As the group began to relax, Freija launched into a vivid reenactment of their escape, complete with exaggerated sound effects and dramatic gestures. Despite themselves, the team couldn't help but laugh, and the tension from their mission finally began to lift.

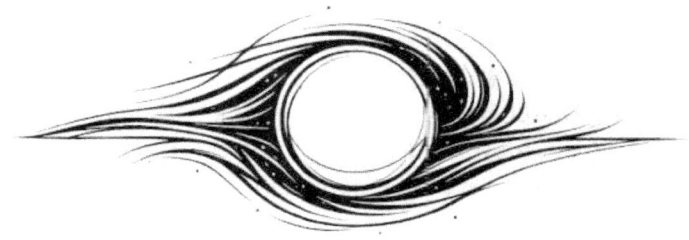

Chapter 31:

Tactical Groundwork

The Scorpion hummed quietly in a low orbit around a nearby planet in Luthor's solar system, its hull blending into the darkness of space. Inside the ship's living quarters a holomap flickered to life above the central table, casting a pale blue light across the faces of the Crimson Alliance. Everyone was tense and focused.

Lilith stood at the head of the table, wings folded neatly behind her, the tips of her claws tapping rhythmically on the edge of the holomap as the layout of Luthor's stronghold expanded into view.

"Three hours ago," she began, "we intercepted a transmission from a low-ranking officer contacting someone back on Luthor. The message was short, but clear – Necra has fortified a central compound on Luthor. We believe it houses key strategic intel: communication logs, command protocols, possibly even her next targets."

Rainstorm stood near the viewport, arms crossed, her gaze fixed on the flickering planet below. "How secure is this location?"

"Very," Kimiko replied. She moved a hand across the display, isolating three towers and a series of defensive trenches surrounding the structure. "Based on aerial recon, the stronghold is embedded into a canyon wall. It's covered by high-range anti-air batteries and reinforced bunkers. Direct assault would be suicidal."

Grilka scoffed. "Then let's be smart about it. You want intel? We hit them where it hurts, but we don't make it look like a raid. We sow chaos, extract the data, and disappear."

Freija, lounging against the wall with one foot on the wall, smirked. "So, a smash-and-grab, but with a little finesse."

"Something like that," Adrian added, sitting backward in his chair, arms crossed on the backrest. "Except we need the data intact. No fried circuits, no incinerated logs. That means no blowing everything to hell – at least not right away."

Nefertari stood to the side, arms behind her back in a regal stance. "I'll remain with the Scorpion. We can't afford to lose our ship. If something goes wrong, I'll be standing by for rapid extraction."

Lilith turned toward the team. "Here's the plan."

The holomap shifted, highlighting two paths into the stronghold – one via a maintenance tunnel beneath the southern cliffs, and another via an overlooked cargo route near the south tunnel that is used during late-night resupplies.

"Kimiko and Rainstorm, you'll infiltrate the compound through the cargo corridor. It's tight, but it'll put you close to the server bay. Grilka and Freija, you'll loop in from the south tunnel. Use the canyon walls for cover and draw any patrols away. Adrian, you'll stay in low orbit in the Starlight Shadow – ready for a hot pickup if needed, or air support if things get messy."

"What about resistance?" Grilka asked. "Because you know there'll be plenty."

"There will be," Lilith confirmed. "That's why we hit fast, hit hard, and get out before they realize what we're after."

Adrian gave a lazy salute. "And if things do go sideways?"

Lilith's eyes glinted with quiet resolve. "Then we burn everything on the way out."

The group fell into a brief, heavy silence before Rainstorm spoke again. "Any sign of the generals?"

Lilith shook her head. "They haven't resurfaced since the last push. But I doubt they've gone far. If they're coordinating the next phase of Necra's campaign, they'll be close to that data."

Freija grinned, tightening the strap on her harness. "Then let's get in there and rip the truth out from under their noses."

Lilith surveyed her team, pride hidden behind her stoic expression. "You all know what's at stake. We're not just disrupting Necra's plans – we're crippling her ability to strike first. Every scrap of intel we pull gives us an edge. And I don't need to remind you that edges are what keep us alive."

Kimiko nodded once. "We're ready."

Grilka cracked her knuckles. "Let's light the match."

The team dispersed, each moving to their stations with silent precision. The Scorpion's corridors filled with the sound of gear being prepped, boots against steel, and low murmurs of pre-mission focus. Lilith stayed behind for a moment longer, staring at the blinking cursor on the holomap as it hovered over the stronghold's command core.

For just a heartbeat, her mind drifted – flashes of the hellish realm, her father's harsh lessons, the weight of leadership bearing down like fire on her wings. But then she exhaled slowly, banishing the doubt.

"I'm coming for you, Necra," she whispered to herself. "And this time, it's personal."

She turned, her wings flicking behind her, and marched out toward the hangar.

The mission had begun.

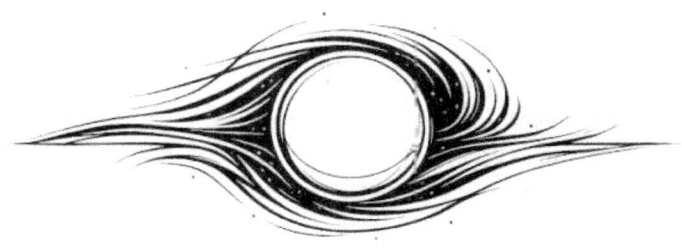

Chapter 32:

Operation Breakpoint

The Scorpion slipped through the shadows of Luthor's atmosphere, barely more than a whisper against the roiling gray clouds. Below, the twisted canyons and scorched ridges of the stronghold's outskirts stretched like veins – an intricate maze concealing the beating heart of one of Necra's war machine.

Inside the ship, the team was already moving.

"Final check," Lilith's voice echoed calmly through the comms. "All teams ready?"

"South tunnel team in position," Freija responded, crouched beside Grilka behind a jagged rock formation near the southern access point. Her icy wings were folded tight against her back. The glow of motion sensors blinked faintly nearby.

"Cargo corridor team, moving," Kimiko's voice came next. The ninja crouched low in the half-lit ventilation duct, Rainstorm behind her, silent but ready. Below them, the corridor ran dim and empty, only sparsely patrolled.

Adrian's voice crackled in next. "Starlight Shadow is on standby. Ping me the moment anyone wants a lift."

From the cockpit of the Scorpion, Nefertari's voice chimed in, steady and alert. "Telemetry locked. If someone trips an alarm, I'll be ready to clear a path."

Lilith, crouched on the rocky bluff above the stronghold, peered through the thermal scope mounted on her wrist gauntlet. Her fiery wings were folded, cloaked under a refractive shroud that made her shimmer faintly against the rocks. Below her, the stronghold bristled with motion – patrols, drones, and floodlights. But there were gaps, shadows. Weaknesses.

And they were about to become openings.

Freija and Grilka – The Southern Assault

"Two guards. Left side," Freija whispered, drawing both icy swords. "I'll freeze the one by the door. You take the heavy."

Grilka growled with satisfaction and cracked her knuckles. "Finally."

In a blur, Freija launched forward, blades sweeping outward. A cloud of frost enveloped the guard to her left, freezing him solid mid-step. Grilka charged with a roar, disruptors blazing. Her first volley slammed into the second guard's chest. He crumpled before he could hit his comm.

They breached the first checkpoint.

Behind them, the canyon echoed with the sound of distant sirens that were still far away.

Grilka set up a short-range jammer on the wall. "That'll keep this hallway quiet for a few minutes."

Freija nodded. "Move fast."

They descended into the reinforced corridor, slipping between bulkheads and steel-girder catwalks. Security cameras were disabled one by one – mostly by Freija's ice, some by Grilka's brute strength.

Finally, in a reinforced chamber near the bunker's center, they found him – General Rax, mid-transmission, barking orders over a communications console.

He turned just in time to see Freija's wing sweep upward.

"What the…" he began, but her sword hit the console, severing power.

Grilka vaulted over a table and slammed into him shoulder-first, knocking the general flat. Her fist cracked across his jaw, and the fight was over in seconds.

"Lilith, target one secured," Freija reported. "We're heading to the roof."

Kimiko and Rainstorm – The Silent Strike

The cargo tunnel was warm, narrow, and filled with the hum of servos and machines. Kimiko moved like smoke through it, her katanas already in hand. Ahead, the door to the storage center opened silently.

Inside, a cluster of guards loaded crates into armored transports. Rainstorm nodded to Kimiko. No words were needed.

Kimiko dropped from the ceiling vent and landed in a crouch. Her blades whirled. Two guards dropped before they could shout. Rainstorm leapt after her, tomahawks flashing. The other three were down in seconds.

A reinforced vault door loomed ahead.

Rainstorm whispered, "General's inside. Reading two more guards."

Kimiko touched the control panel and slid a bypass wire into the circuit. "Three seconds…"

The door hissed open.

General Zhrex turned in surprise, flanked by two elite soldiers. "You…"

Kimiko moved first. She ducked a disruptor shot, rolled forward, and swept the guard's legs. Her blade spun and took the second guard cleanly. Zhrex backed up, reaching for a sidearm.

Rainstorm tackled him through a side table, slamming her elbow into his ribs. "Told you we didn't need a distraction," she muttered, binding his wrists.

"Extraction point is the eastern loading bay," Kimiko said into her comm. "We're moving."

Lilith – The Aerial Sweep

Lilith soared low over the stronghold's northern

edge, weaving between anti-air turrets. Her blades were sheathed but charged with searing fire.

Below her, the patrols scrambled. They had no idea where to focus.

On the central tower's roof, Freija and Grilka appeared with General Rax slung between them.

"Drop point in sight," Freija called out.

Lilith banked hard. Her wings flared open, trailing fire as she descended. She landed in a crouch as Grilka tossed the unconscious general over her shoulder.

"Incoming bogeys!" Freija shouted, pointing across the ridge.

"Go!" Lilith ordered. "Adrian, I need pickup, now!"

Adrian – The Winged Rescue

The Starlight Shadow emerged from stealth like a predator breaking cover. Its twin engines screamed as it dove toward the rooftop.

"Package received," Adrian said, as Lilith hurled Rax's body onto the extended cargo ramp. Grilka jumped in after him.

Freija gave a short wave and took off again, looping back toward the western side to support Kimiko's team.

"Rainstorm, you've got troops closing in," Nefertari warned over the channel.

"I see them," Rainstorm said, crouching low behind a supply crate. "We're blocked in."

"Not for long," Adrian muttered.

He skimmed the edge of the loading bay and fired a precision shot into the hangar door lock. The metal buckled and fell away, creating a direct path to the Scorpion's rear bay.

Rainstorm and Kimiko ran, the unconscious Zhrex between them.

Guards flooded in behind, too late. They had jumped onboard.

The Scorpion's rear ramp slammed shut.

The Escape

Nefertari pulled up hard, punching the engines into full thrust. "We're out."

Adrian's voice came in, breathless but triumphant. "Starlight Shadow secure. Target retrieved. Ready to dock to the port airlock."

Lilith dropped into the cockpit beside Nefertari, her expression grim but satisfied. "We have two. That's enough for today."

Rainstorm leaned against the interior wall, catching her breath. "That was close."

Freija wiped frost from her forehead. "Too close."

Grilka cracked her knuckles. "Now let's see what they know."

Lilith nodded, her gaze burning with intensity. "Yes. Let's."

She turned toward the chamber where the two generals now lay in stasis cuffs.

Interrogations would come next.

But for now, they had won.

For now, the Crimson Alliance had struck first… and was victorious.

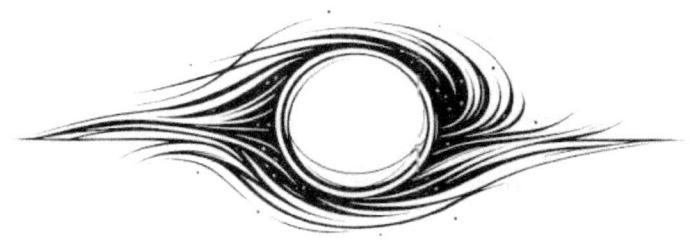

Chapter 33:

Interrogation Protocol

The Scorpion's engines pulsed steadily as it cruised silently through Luthor's upper atmosphere, its sleek black hull blending into the cold gray sky. Inside, the atmosphere was anything but calm.

The two captured generals had been separated.

General Rax lay unconscious in the cargo bay, strapped to a reinforced chair with heavy-duty stasis cuffs around his wrists and ankles. His yellowish-green skin was blotched with bruises from the brief struggle, and his uniform had been stripped down to a plain undershirt and regulation trousers. Grilka stood at his side, arms crossed, disruptor rifle slung across her back. She didn't speak – just watched, like a predator waiting for its prey to wake.

In the living quarters, General Zhrex sat slumped in another reinforced chair. He was slightly leaner than Rax, but his eyes carried more malice – sharp and calculating. Adrian lounged in the corner, pistol resting lazily on one thigh, his posture casual but his gaze razor sharp.

Lilith stood between the two chambers, her fiery wings folded tight behind her back, her expression unreadable. Kimiko and Rainstorm flanked her silently. Both were calm but alert, their hands never far from their weapons.

"They're not going to crack easily," Rainstorm said in a low voice.

"They don't have to crack," Lilith replied. "They just have to slip."

She motioned to Kimiko. "You and Rainstorm stay with Zhrex. I'll start with Rax."

As Lilith stepped into the cargo bay, the door hissed closed behind her. Grilka stepped aside but stayed close, disruptor still in hand. Rax stirred at the sound of her boots. His eyes blinked open, pupils dilating against the low light. He looked up, groggy but quickly assessing his situation. His gaze landed on Lilith and narrowed.

"You," he muttered. "A demon…"

"Have you seen my kind before," Lilith said coolly. "That'll save us time."

"I won't talk," Rax grunted. "You'll get nothing from me."

"I doubt that," she said, walking a slow circle around him. "You've already given me something: fear. That twitch in your jaw, the way your fists clench when I speak – it tells me you know you've already lost."

"You think capturing me changes anything?" Rax sneered. "Necra will wipe your little squad from the stars."

Lilith crouched in front of him, her face inches from his. "Then let's talk about Necra."

He looked away.

Lilith didn't push. Not yet. Instead, she stood and nodded once to Grilka, who turned on the nearby wall console, displaying a flickering hologram of Zhrex in the next room.

"We already know Zhrex is cracking," she said, lying smoothly. "He's been talking for ten minutes. You sure you want him deciding what story survives?"

Lilith didn't speak right away. She let Rax see it.

The display wasn't clear enough to read lips, but

Zhrex looked tense. He shifted in his chair, his posture a little too rigid for comfort. His fingers twitched once, then stilled. A bead of sweat traced down the side of his neck.

Lilith noticed the flicker in Rax's gaze.

"Strange, isn't it?" she mused, voice low. "He's been in that chair less than an hour, and already he's... expressive."

Rax narrowed his eyes. "He won't break."

"Maybe... or... maybe not," she said. "But what if he talks just enough to make you expendable? To shift the blame, to protect himself? You were both captured. Only one of you needs to be seen as useful."

She walked a slow, deliberate circle around the restrained general, her boots clicking softly against the floor. "Tell me something, Rax. When Necra sent you to Luthor, what was your mission?"

Silence.

"Because I've seen the troop concentrations," she continued. "The defensive structures, the encrypted networks, the deep bunker layouts. Luthor isn't just a holdout – it's a pivot point. You don't build a fortress like that unless you're hiding something... or preparing for something big."

Still, Rax said nothing, but Lilith saw the way his jaw clenched – harder now. His nostrils flared.

Lilith's voice dropped a little. "So, here's what I think. I think you and Zhrex were staging for a campaign. Maybe a weapons rollout. Maybe fleet movement. Maybe a test launch. I don't know yet. But I will."

She turned back toward the screen. "And when I do, if his version of events is the only one we have, then that becomes the official record."

Rax finally growled, "He doesn't know anything. I'm the one Necra trusts."

Lilith stopped. Pivoted slowly back toward him. "Go on."

He bit his lip but said nothing else.

She stepped closer again, crouching at his eye level. "Help me understand, Rax. If Necra trusted you, why were you left behind? Why wasn't there an evac plan?"

"She needed time," he said instinctively. Then stopped, catching himself.

Lilith's eyes narrowed. "Time for what?"

The general turned his head, refusing to meet her gaze.

Lilith stood tall. "We're done here for now," she said, signaling to Grilka.

As she walked toward the exit, she let her words hang like smoke in the air: "But Zhrex's version already sounds more convincing."

Elsewhere – Living Quarters

Zhrex sat upright in the same posture, sweat gathering at his collar. Across from him, Kimiko stood with arms folded. Rainstorm paced slowly before him, watching like a hawk circling prey.

Adrian sat nearby, tapping his disruptor against his boot. "So… Rax is singing," he said. "Loud."

Zhrex didn't respond, but his brow creased.

"You want to know what he said?" Adrian asked, casually. "Because he started talking about the bunker complex. The sealed level. You know, the one off-grid."

Zhrex looked up, startled. He tried to hide it.

Lilith stepped into the room just then, letting the door hiss shut behind her. She met Zhrex's eyes with calm precision.

"You were preparing something," she said. "Not just protecting territory. That complex is too secure. Too active."

Zhrex was silent.

"We know it's not a research site," Rainstorm said quietly. "There's too much traffic. Too many fuel trails. No long-range signatures, though. So that narrows it."

"You're building something," Lilith said, stepping closer, her wings flaring just slightly behind her. "Or protecting something mobile."

"I have nothing to say to you," Zhrex muttered.

Kimiko's voice was soft, but sharp. "Then we'll let Rax say it first."

Zhrex twitched. "He doesn't know everything."

"There it is," Adrian muttered.

Lilith's eyes didn't waver. "Then enlighten us."

Zhrex hesitated, jaw tight. "There's a project... under Necra's direct control. She's overseeing the final phase herself."

"Where?" Lilith demanded.

Zhrex shook his head. "If I tell you... she'll kill me."

Lilith leaned in, her voice icy. "If you don't tell me, I will."

Zhrex cracked.

"Jaze," he whispered. "She's at Jaze."

Lilith stepped back slowly. "Why?"

He exhaled shakily. "A new weapon. She's installing it herself. A mobile assault array – something long-range. Experimental. She thinks it will change the war."

Rainstorm and Kimiko exchanged a glance.

"Coordinates?" Kimiko asked.

Zhrex swallowed. "Northern plateau. They've buried it into the cliffside. You won't see it from above."

Lilith nodded. "Thank you."

"You'll never reach her in time," Zhrex added quickly. "Even if you do... you won't win."

Lilith offered a slow, burning smile. "We'll see."

Hours Later – Rebel Drop-Off

The Scorpion hovered above a secure rebel outpost hidden deep in the canyons of a nearby system. Under heavy guard, both generals were escorted onto the rebel transport. Each bore a tracker, and neither had spoken since.

Lilith watched them from the ramp as they were led away, flanked by silent guards.

"They'll be interrogated again," Nefertari said, stepping up beside her. "The rebellion can squeeze more from them."

"They gave us what we needed," Lilith replied. "The rest is justice."

She turned back toward the ship, her wings trailing sparks.

In the Scorpion's living quarters, the team reconvened. A 3D map of Jaze rotated slowly on the holo-table, its red terrain craggy and hostile.

Lilith studied it in silence. Then she looked to the team, her voice steady and commanding.

"Jaze is our next target. We're not just hunting her anymore," she said. "We're going to break her war machine."

Her hand clenched into a fist over the glowing map.

"It ends where it began."

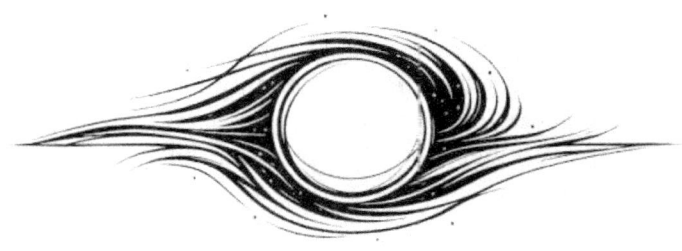

Chapter 34:

Shadows In the Hall

The fortress on Jaze stood like a wound carved into the red cliffs – hidden beneath camouflage arrays, reinforced by obsidian plating, and pulsing with the quiet menace of unfinished machinery. Far beneath the surface, in a chamber carved from volcanic rock and lit by vertical veins of molten plasma, three generals stood in a crescent around their queen.

Necra sat motionless on her throne, forged from blackened alloy and fused bone. Her figure was tall, skeletal and yet commanding, clad in dark armor etched with spirals of ancient runes. A faint mist clung to her skin like the aftermath of a storm, and her eyes glowed with pale, unnatural light.

In the silence of the chamber, a messenger knelt trembling beside the dais. He did not raise his head.

"…Captured," he whispered. "Two of our Luthor commanders were taken alive. The facility was compromised."

Necra didn't move.

The silence stretched so long that the messenger dared to speak again.

"General Rax and General Zhrex… They're in

enemy hands."

A slight shift broke the stillness. Necra's long fingers curled around the hilt of the staff resting beside her throne.

"I sent them to manage a fortress, not lose it to ghosts," she said, her voice low and smooth – like poisoned silk. "Who. Took. Them?"

The messenger hesitated. "We… We don't know. The survivors gave inconsistent reports. There was chaos – attacks from multiple directions, infiltration, coordinated strikes."

Necra's eyes narrowed. "Speak clearly."

"They described only fragments," the messenger said, more desperately now. "A blue-skinned female with cobalt wings… a massive green brute with orange hair… two human attackers – one airborne, one on foot."

He stopped, clearly hoping that was enough.

Necra stood.

The chamber dimmed.

The three generals tensed in unison.

"I have ruled this quadrant without equal," she said coldly, descending from the throne like the shadow of a god. "Every resistance has been crushed. Every whisper of rebellion – silenced. And now… some mythical pests with wings and banter manage to dismantle one of my outposts?"

Agramor, a seven-foot five-inch demon, stepped forward, his towering, horned form casting a long shadow across the floor. His crimson skin and armor bore the marks of countless battles. "My Queen, let me lead a strike force. I will find these imposters and…"

"No," said Necra, raising a hand. "You will not chase smoke while our future is still assembling here."

She turned to the second general – a woman with metallic silver skin and a visor that blinked faintly with tactical data. Her name was General Serath, commander of Necra's logistics division and silent overseer of the Jaze facility.

"They've already captured Rax and Zhrex," Serath said, her voice even. "If those two break… they could reveal Jaze's role."

Necra's eyes flickered.

"They don't know enough," said the third general, General Valthar, a lean, spectral figure wrapped in layers of scorched silk and armor. "They were not briefed on the scope of the project. Only its supporting operations."

"But they knew Jaze mattered," Serath replied. "They knew a weapon was being built here. Even that knowledge compromises our timeline."

"Then move the timeline up," Necra snapped, stepping between them. "Double the output. I want the targeting systems operational in three days."

"We need five," Serath warned.

Necra didn't answer. She simply turned to the plasma wall beside her, where a hologram of the stronghold flickered into view. She stared at it for a long moment, then reached out and touched a blinking red section labeled *Luthor*.

"Whoever they are," she murmured, "they've made a mistake."

Agramor flexed his massive hands. "Let me hunt them, my Queen."

Necra's gaze slid to him. "Soon. But when we strike, it won't be to chase. It will be to annihilate."

She turned to the messenger still kneeling, her voice quiet and sharp. "Go. Prepare the black relay. Inform our agents that if anyone shows signs of collaboration with these attackers – there will be *no trials*. Only ash."

"Yes, my Queen." The messenger bowed and fled the chamber as quickly as he dared.

Necra returned to her throne, lowering herself with regal ease. Her eyes burned softly beneath the shadow of her crown.

"They think they're hidden," she said, almost to

herself. "They think they're special."
A faint smile curved her lips.
"Let them come."

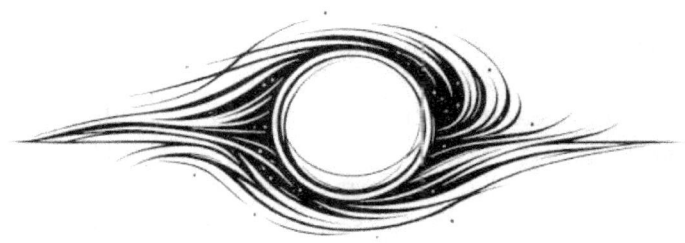

Chapter 35:

Into the Fire

The Scorpion drifted just above the upper reaches of Jaze's scorched atmosphere, cloaked in silence. Beneath its hull, the planet pulsed with a heavy tension – like something alive was waiting. In the living quarters, the Crimson Alliance gathered one more time.

Lilith stood over the central holo-table, its blue light bathing her crimson skin in a cold glow. Her wings were folded but restless, flexing ever so slightly with every breath.

"This is reconnaissance," she said, her voice quiet but firm. "We're not storming their gates. We're here for one thing: intel. Command routes, supply depots, patrol rotations, anything that tells us what Necra's doing next."

She pointed to a spidery cluster of installations on the map – black-and-red icons dotting the northern ridge of a broken canyon system.

"These relay points are newer. Unmapped. Likely hidden. We believe they're transmitting data to somewhere off-world. We take the system offline long enough to copy and intercept without alerting the entire quadrant."

Adrian leaned forward, boots up on the table. "Sounds simple enough. So, what's the catch?"

"Everything," said Rainstorm flatly. "The relay

station is buried under an old barracks surrounded by automated turrets and fresh troop movement. No obvious weakness."

Grilka stretched her neck. "Good. It wouldn't be fun otherwise."

Freija gave a small grin. "We've survived worse."

Kimiko, silent in the shadows, leaned forward. "One small change in pattern, and the whole thing falls apart."

Lilith nodded. "Which is why we're splitting into three teams. Kimiko and I will approach the relay through the geothermal vents along the east wall. Rainstorm and Grilka take the canyons from the south – there's a series of collapsed bunkers we can use for cover. Adrian and Freija, you'll draw attention away with a staged aerial sweep to the west."

Nefertari tapped a button on the wall, opening the secondary hatch. "The Scorpion will maintain high orbit. Once the data's secured, I'll swoop in for extraction. You'll have fifteen minutes, max."

Lilith's eyes swept over the team. "We go quiet. No alarms. No casualties unless absolutely necessary. If one of us goes down, the others fall back. Clear?"

Everyone nodded. Kimiko's eyes, narrow and unreadable, flicked to Lilith. "We move."

Eastern Approach – Lilith & Kimiko

The air near the geothermal vents reeked of sulfur and heated iron. Steam hissed from jagged cracks in the blackened rock, obscuring sight and muffling sound. Kimiko moved like smoke through it – silent, each step a calculated risk.

Lilith followed a few feet behind, crouched low, her fiery wings slightly unfurled. Her swords remained sheathed but burned faintly at her hips, reacting to the proximity of enemy sentries.

"Thermal sensors just ahead," Kimiko whispered.

"I see them." Lilith pointed to a blinking sensor buried in the cliff face. "Can you bypass?"

Kimiko nodded. With surgical precision, she climbed the narrow ledge, slicing wires from behind without tripping the beacon. A moment later, the blinking light went dark.

They continued forward – into a steel-plated corridor partially buried by volcanic debris. It was old tech, scavenged and fortified. But something was off.

Kimiko paused. "Heartbeat monitors."

Lilith's eyes glowed faintly "Four signatures?"

"Six," Kimiko corrected, unsheathing her blades.

The ambush came in an instant. A hidden panel slid open and plasma rounds tore through the corridor. Kimiko rolled left, cutting down the first soldier with a blur of black steel. Lilith charged forward, unsheathing both flaming swords in an arc of molten light.

The corridor was filled with smoke and fire.

Lilith parried a blow with the flat of her blade and slammed her shoulder into her attacker. Kimiko ducked a wild swipe and stabbed upward, disabling another with a flash of steel. But as the last soldier fell, an alarm blared.

Kimiko's breathing was sharp. "We're compromised."

Lilith's left arm bled from a deep gash, but her eyes stayed hard. "We keep moving. Find that relay."

Southern Canyons – Grilka & Rainstorm

Wind tore through the collapsed bunkers where Grilka and Rainstorm moved. The ruins were scorched and skeletal, the bones of an old battlefield. Drones buzzed in the sky overhead.

"Three drones, fifty meters," Rainstorm whispered, adjusting the scope on her disruptor.

"I'll get their attention," Grilka growled.

She leapt from behind a collapsed wall and opened

fire. Explosions ripped through the dust. One drone swerved to retaliate, but Rainstorm's tomahawk clipped its wing midair, sending it spiraling into the rocks.

The other two adjusted and fired. Rainstorm spun and ducked, but one blast caught her in the ribs. She collapsed against the stone with a grunt, clutching her side.

"Rain!" Grilka shouted, ducking behind a fallen support beam.

"I'm fine," Rainstorm hissed. "Just grazed."

They pressed on, weaving through the trenches until they reached the ridge. Below them, the eastern relay hummed with energy – tall towers, data transmitters glowing red, soldiers on patrol.

"This is it," Rainstorm said.

Grilka's jaw clenched. "Let's blow it."

Aerial Sweep – Freija & Adrian

High above the compound, Freija banked left, wings spread wide. Her armor glinted in the clouds, blue streaks trailing from her frost-blades.

"Drawing their attention now," Adrian said, spinning the Starlight Shadow just above cannon range.

Anti-air fire screamed upward. Freija dodged, sending a blast of frost down on a scanning beacon. It exploded in a burst of ice.

"Contact – north tower is trying to launch a tracker drone," Adrian reported.

"Not for long," Freija said, folding her wings and diving hard. She slashed through the tower's antenna before it could activate, then flared upward, nearly clipped by a grazing round.

Adrian looped behind her. "Keep going. We need five more minutes."

Inside the Relay Core

Lilith and Kimiko finally reached the relay room – a hexagonal chamber bristling with servers, sparks flying from a damaged console. A soldier lay dying nearby, one of Kimiko's blades still embedded in his side.

"We don't have long," Kimiko said.

Lilith plugged in a data spike. "Copying now."

Rainstorm's voice came over comms, pained. "Grilka's down. Took a heavy hit. She's alive, but not walking."

Lilith gritted her teeth. "Hold your position."

Alarms howled across the compound.

Suddenly, metal doors slammed open and six reinforcements poured in. Lilith turned, drawing both blades. "Buy me thirty seconds!"

Kimiko threw herself into the fray.

She parried one strike, slashed another across the leg, but a glancing shot caught her shoulder, spinning her around. Blood flew. Lilith snarled, igniting a blast from her blades that consumed three attackers in a wave of fire.

But it wasn't enough. Kimiko staggered.

Adrian's voice crackled through: "Extraction window closing. Now or never!"

Lilith grabbed Kimiko, the download was complete. "We're out."

Extraction

Nefertari brought the Scorpion in low, its belly nearly scraping the ridge. Adrian's fighter hovered above, engines flaring.

Rainstorm limped up the ramp with Grilka slung over her shoulder. Freija, bleeding from a slash to her hip, carried Kimiko in. Lilith stumbled last, her left arm useless and her face pale.

As the doors slammed shut, Lilith dropped to one

knee. The room blurred around her. Her breath came in ragged gasps. Blood soaked the fabric of her uniform.

But the data chip was intact.

And the intel was theirs.

No words were exchanged.

Just the quiet roar of escape.

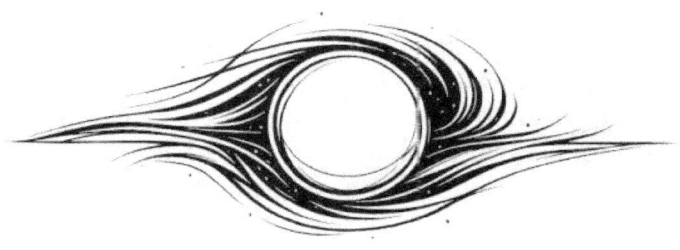

Chapter 36:

The Price of Clarity

The Scorpion streaked low through the atmosphere of Jaze, trailing heat as it fled the wreckage below. Inside, the crew of the Crimson Alliance sat slumped or staggered against bulkheads, wounded but alive. The ship's interior was filled with smoke, sweat, and the quiet groans of pain.

Lilith stood near the rear cargo bay, gripping a handrail to keep herself upright. Blood trickled from a burn on her shoulder, her armor scorched and torn. She stared at the black data chip clenched in her fist. It felt heavier than it should have.

"We're secure," Nefertari announced from the cockpit. Her voice was calm, but tight with concern. "No signs of pursuit. We'll break orbit in two minutes."

Lilith didn't answer. Her eyes remained fixed on the chip, as if trying to burn answers into it with sheer will. Behind her, the team settled into a makeshift triage.

Grilka lay stretched across a bench, her side wrapped in a temporary pressure pad. She groaned as Rainstorm adjusted the seal. "That last blast took out my armor. Ribs feel cracked. Not fun."

"You shouldn't have charged that turret alone," Rainstorm muttered, binding her own bruised forearm with a strip of cloth torn from her cloak.

"It was a distraction," Grilka hissed through gritted teeth. "We'd be dead if I didn't."

Freija limped into the chamber, her right wing partially folded and stained with blood. She flopped down beside Kimiko, who was propped against the wall, her arm in a makeshift sling.

"I still can't believe that room was a kill box," Freija muttered, exhaling slowly. "If we were two seconds slower…"

"We weren't," Kimiko said. Her voice was quiet, but steady.

Lilith finally turned, her gaze passing over them all. Every one of her teammates bore wounds except for the two pilots, Nefertari and Adrian. Every one of them had bled for her plan.

Adrian walked in from the docking corridor, his face streaked with soot. "Starlight Shadow made it back. Barely. Shields are toast. We're lucky to be breathing."

He stopped when he saw Lilith.

"You okay, Captain?"

Lilith nodded once, but it wasn't convincing.

Adrian studied her for a moment, then walked to the center table where the holomap still flickered. He activated the tactical overlay.

"Whatever that relay was protecting... this," he gestured at the chip, "was worth it. We hit a live system. Data's fresh, and the encryption is military-grade."

Nefertari's voice came over the intercom. "Decryption is underway. Give it another hour."

"You hear that?" Adrian said, glancing around. "We did it. We got in and out with the enemy's playbook."

No one answered.

Rainstorm looked up from where she knelt beside Grilka. "We did it. But at what cost?"

Kimiko's eyes flicked toward Lilith. "That plan was

razor-thin. We nearly lost three people."

"I knew the risk," Lilith said quietly. Her voice was hard to read – a mix of frustration, guilt, and stubborn pride.

"We all did," Nefertari added over the comm.

Freija raised an eyebrow. "Doesn't mean it hurts any less."

Silence fell again.

Lilith crossed to the main console and set the data chip down with care, as if it might shatter. "The information we pulled may be the only thing standing between Necra and a galaxy-wide assault. If this mission costs us..." Her voice trailed off.

Adrian stepped forward. "We made it back. That's what matters. Now let's make sure what we bought was worth the price."

Lilith nodded, but her expression was troubled. She turned away from the others and walked toward the forward viewport. Jaze's surface was growing smaller below them, the sky darkening to stars. Her reflection flickered faintly in the glass.

Behind her, her team sat bruised and broken but not defeated. And somewhere deep inside her chest, the first tremors of self-doubt began to stir.

She had led them into fire. And fire answered.

She gripped the edge of the console tightly.

They survived. But for how much longer?

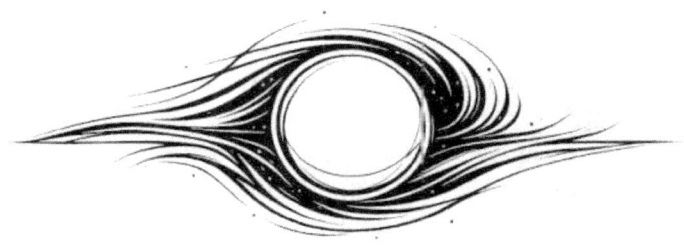

Chapter 37:

Triage

The Scorpion soared away from Jaze, its hull scarred and scorched, its engines pulsing weakly as it cut through the upper thermals of the system's outermost planet. Inside the cockpit, Nefertari adjusted the sensors with a steady hand, though her arm still throbbed from a healing plasma burn.

She had found it – a green and blue planet nestled just beyond Jaze's sun, largely unmapped and seemingly untouched. No cities, no fortresses, just open land and signs of stable oxygen and biosphere.

She tapped the console. "Rainstorm, get to nav. I may have found something."

Rainstorm hobbled in moments later, her bruised ribs stiff beneath the wrap Grilka had helped her secure.

Nefertari gestured to the display. "Remote planet. Habitable. The scans show flora and some water sources. Might be what we need."

Rainstorm scanned the readings. "It's perfect. High probability of native herbs and clean air. We can land, find cover, and begin healing."

Grilka, overhearing from the hall, leaned in. "If it's got anything better than Valkorrian fungus sludge, I'm in."

They landed in a quiet valley of golden plains

flanked by pale cliffs. The twin moons hung low overhead, casting silvery shadows across the tall grass. A stream trickled down the cliffside, winding through the field like a peaceful vein.

Lilith stood just inside the Scorpion's ramp; her shoulder still bandaged from a deep plasma burn. She watched the others disembark – Freija, wings carefully folded, one side still stiff with injury; Grilka limping heavily but upright; Kimiko silent, her thigh tightly wrapped; Adrian slower than usual, arm favoring his cracked ribs. They were broken from the impact of flying his ship's wild maneuvers.

But breathing.

Rainstorm stepped into the sun and took a long breath, then tapped her scanner. "Let's get to work."

Healing Preparations

With Kimiko, Freija, and Grilka assisting, Rainstorm collected samples of plant life and traced the water's edge until she found soft-barked trees and flowering reeds. Her datapad chimed each time it identified a promising medicinal analog.

She carefully gathered a thick red-rooted plant whose cooling gel and demon-compatible alkaloids could soothe Lilith's burns. Nearby, pale-stalked mushrooms showed properties that promoted rapid clotting and muscular regeneration for Kimiko's wounds. For Grilka, she harvested resin from the bark of a broad tree, knowing it could reduce internal hemorrhaging within the Valkorrian's dense musculature.

Adrian's injuries required something different. Rainstorm selected a yellow-leafed plant whose extract resembled willow and would help manage the pain from bruised ribs and damaged tissue. Along the shaded wall of the valley, Freija discovered frost-touched leaves with regenerative qualities suited to repairing delicate wing membranes. Finally, Rainstorm collected sap from the curled roots of an ancient tree, blending it into a treatment for herself and Nefertari that would reduce inflammation and help resist infection from their plasma wounds.

Back at camp, Rainstorm heated a smooth stone and laid out small blades, bowls, and Lilith's sword, whose infernal flame was the only heat intense enough to prepare some of the compounds. Freija organized the bundles of herbs while Kimiko quietly cut strips of clean cloth for fresh bandages.

Lilith's Vigil

Lilith walked slowly among them, her steps measured but strong. She was used to being the sharpest blade in the room, not the one nicked and dulled. Her gaze passed from Kimiko's bloodied leg to the stiff way Rainstorm winced every time she lifted her left arm. She saw Grilka pressing on her ribs between breaths, the half-hidden grimace of someone too proud to ask for help. She paused by Adrian, who kept his usual smirk but had yet to take a full breath without pain.

Freija's wing still trembled slightly with every wind gust.

Lilith clenched her fists. *They followed me… into the fire. And now they bleed for it.*

Rainstorm returned with the paste for Lilith's shoulder. "This will sting. But the gel needs to settle into the tissue to pull the heat out."

Lilith didn't flinch as the cold mass was pressed into the open wound. Steam hissed from her skin. "Don't go easy on me."

"I never will," Rainstorm said, and moved on.

Lilith sat on the crate beside her team, listening to their breathing, the slight groans as muscles were unknotted and bones wrapped. She didn't speak. But her mind churned. *I told them this was recon. Not war. And still, they bled.*

The Ceremony

Later that evening, as the moons cast a ghostly light over the plain, Rainstorm gathered them again. She built a fire ring of white stones and set the remains of their healing herbs at its center. With a careful touch, she lit it with Lilith's sword, and a slow, curling smoke rose, which was very fragrant and earthy.

"Back on Earth, we honor our pain with ritual," Rainstorm said softly. "The pain itself reminds us that we are alive. But healing – healing binds us."

They sat together in a quiet circle. Lilith watched the flames, one hand resting on the bandaged shoulder where the battle had left its mark. Beside her, Grilka leaned back on her elbows, battered and bruised, but offering Rainstorm a silent nod of gratitude. Freija sat with her wings draped loosely around her, the fresh bandages visible beneath the feathers. Kimiko remained almost motionless, one leg stretched before her, her expression as unreadable as ever. Adrian shifted carefully, unable to hide a wince as he settled into a more comfortable position. Across the fire, Nefertari folded her hands neatly in her lap, her head inclined toward the dancing flames.

Rainstorm chanted low in a mix of Wakasa and Earth Navajo. Her voice soothed the wind; her smoke circled their wounds. She passed around small bowls with warmed mixtures tailored to each species – some to drink, some to apply.

Each accepted their bowl in silence.

Lilith looked into hers, the reflection of flame caught in the dark gel. "Thank you, Rainstorm," she said at last, her voice lower than usual. "You keep us together."

Rainstorm smiled faintly. "You gave us something to stay together for."

Closing Reflections

As the fire dimmed and the smoke drifted skyward,

the team finally rested. Lilith paced once around the group, then paused, standing still against the distant howl of alien wind.

She felt the warmth of the fire behind her. The cold of space still ahead.

She wasn't sure what came next. But for now... just now... they had survived.

And survival was enough.

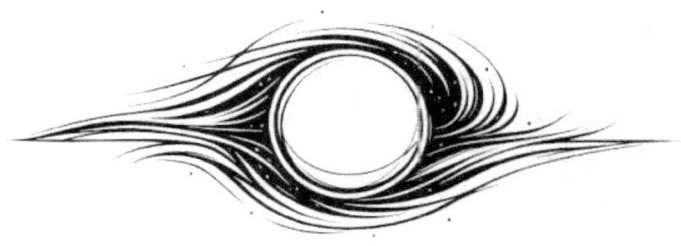

Chapter 38:

Crossroads of Resolve

The days passed slowly, marked by healing, quiet meals, and a growing tension that settled over the group like a mist. For a full week, the Scorpion remained hidden in the long shadows of the remote planet, tucked beneath the protective cliffs that wrapped around a windswept plateau. The sun rose and set with indifferent rhythm, and still, Lilith hadn't called a mission briefing... until now.

The Crimson Alliance gathered in the Scorpion's living area, the soft hum of ship systems a familiar background note. A faint breeze from outside still carried the earthy scent of the herbs Rainstorm had used in their triage ceremony. The past few days had been mercifully uneventful. Now it was time to decide what came next.

Lilith stood at the center of the room, facing the others. She looked composed – her wounds mostly healed; her wings folded tightly behind her – but something in her posture had shifted. She no longer stood as if her fire alone could scorch away every threat. Now, she stood like someone carrying the weight of the consequences.

Nefertari tapped a key on the console, and the holomap flickered to life. The decoded data chip projected a schematic of an enormous structure nestled between two mountain ridges back on Jaze.

"This," she said, her voice low, "is what we found on the chip. A weapons facility. Large enough to destabilize orbital infrastructure. According to the packet logs, it's still being assembled."

"And here," Adrian added, highlighting another marker, "is where Necra herself is located – several hundred kilometers away in a fortified base." He looked around the room. "Separate targets. Same planet."

A silence followed.

Lilith stepped forward slowly. Her voice was quiet, almost uncertain. "We can't hit both. Not at the same time. If we go after the weapon, she could vanish. But if we go after her... the weapon may become operational."

Rainstorm folded her arms. "Either path comes with risk. We don't know how soon that thing is scheduled to be operational."

Freija, seated with her wings carefully folded over her shoulders, looked up from the display. "We were almost killed last time. And even with this intel, it's a guess at best. She could be moving again."

Grilka scoffed. "If we hesitate, we lose our advantage. You want to dismantle her empire? You cut off the head."

Kimiko said nothing at first. She leaned forward, studying both data points on the projection. "We can plan for either, but we'll need full cooperation. And stealth."

Lilith didn't respond right away. She was staring down, hands clenched at her sides.

When she finally spoke, it was with an edge of raw emotion: "You were all nearly killed. Because of me. Because I pushed too hard. Too fast." She looked each of them in the eye. "I made decisions based on instinct, not strategy. And I let you walk into a bloodbath."

"No one made me fight," Rainstorm replied calmly. "We all accepted the mission. We're soldiers, Lilith."

"Still," Lilith said, her voice shaking slightly, "I've always believed in strength. In facing things head-on. But I... I don't know if I'm the leader you deserve anymore."

The room was silent for a beat.

Adrian leaned back, his chair creaking. "You're damn right we almost died. But that wasn't because of bad leadership. That was because we walked into the lion's mouth with our heads held high – and that lion bit back." He smirked slightly. "But we got what we needed. And we're still here."

Lilith's eyes flicked toward him.

"Let's vote," she said softly. "Do we go after Necra... or the weapon?"

Everyone looked at one another. Freija nodded first.

"Necra," she said simply. "She's the mind behind the machine."

Grilka grunted. "Same. I want her to know exactly who brought her empire to its knees."

Rainstorm raised her hand. "I think we should investigate the weapon. But I'll go with the group."

Kimiko hesitated, then finally said, "Weapon. Knowledge is power. But so is unity."

Adrian cracked his knuckles. "I say Necra; I'm tired of running."

Nefertari stood quietly for a moment. "The weapon is dangerous, yes. But she is the one who would wield it. Necra."

Lilith was going to be the tiebreaker. She finally said in a soft voice, "I agree with taking out Necra first. That would cause a lot of chaos and then we can see about the weapons next after the dust settles."

Four to three.

Lilith nodded, absorbing the vote. The room was still, the decision hanging heavy.

"I won't pretend this will be easy," she said, her voice growing steadier. "But we go together. We fight as one. And this time… we finish what we started."

There was no cheer, no dramatic rally. Just the nods of warriors who had already been through fire – and knew more waited ahead.

Lilith turned back to the console. "Prepare for infiltration. I want plans drafted by tomorrow morning. We're not walking blind again."

As the team dispersed, the hum of the ship resumed. Outside, the alien sky darkened into dusk. In the silence of that fading light, Lilith lingered by the holomap – her shadow stretching long over the projected flames of Necra's empire.

And for the first time in days, her wings did not tremble.

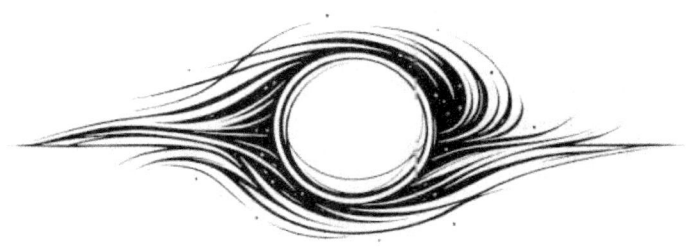

Chapter 39:

The Plan for the Queen

The holotable inside the Scorpion's living quarters flickered with new energy, updated schematics casting dull blue light across the faces of the Crimson Alliance. Night hung silent outside the vessel, the stars distant and indifferent. But inside, tension sizzled like static.

Lilith stood at the head of the table, her wings draped like a mantle of shadow and ember. Gone was the self-doubt that had haunted her in the days following their injuries. The fire was still there – cooled, tempered, but sharp as ever.

"All right," she began. "This is it."

Nefertari tapped the conscle, and the holographic image of Necra's stronghold materialized in full 3D relief – towering walls of obsidian, layered defenses, a central spire glowing red with internal power.

"This is the location confirmed by the data chip. Necra's primary base of operations is buried beneath the cliffside city of Tharnix on Jaze," Nefertari explained. "Half-fortress, half-laboratory. There's a full underground complex beneath the visible structure."

Rainstorm tilted her head, studying the terrain. "Those exterior towers are anti-air, I assume?"

"Correct," Nefertari replied. "The compound's air

defenses are strong – linked to a network of motion-tracking cannons and sensor mines. A direct assault from above would be suicide."

"Which means we go in from below," Lilith said.

Kimiko stepped forward, her eyes sharp. "There's a drainage aqueduct on the lower eastern slope – apparently abandoned, but still structurally sound. If we follow that system, we can bypass most of the exterior walls and emerge near the inner sanctum."

Freija tapped the map. "What's guarding the aqueduct?"

"Thermal mines," said Adrian, grimacing. "And likely pressure sensors embedded in the floor. We'll have to crawl through sections. Quietly."

Grilka grunted. "No room for a brawl, then. Until we find her."

Lilith nodded. "Once we're in, everything changes. The mission splits into three phases. First, infiltration. We use the aqueduct to get inside. Second, confrontation. I'll go after Necra personally. Alone, if I must. Third, extraction. Adrian, Freija, and Nefertari will clear our exit route and ready the Scorpion."

"I don't like you going alone," Rainstorm said. "You're strong – but this is Necra."

"I won't be truly alone," Lilith said softly. "I'll take Kimiko and Rainstorm with me into the inner sanctum. You'll be my shadows. But if I call for space – give it. If I fall, either finish it… or run."

The room went silent.

Finally, Adrian leaned back in his chair, boots crossed on the table. "Okay. So what's our distraction? This place is built like a fortress. We're not sneaking six people through the front gate unnoticed."

Freija smirked. "That's where I come in. I'll take the skies. Pull some attention to the western defense towers – draw their eyes up."

"And I'll help by planting decoys and false signatures along the southern ridge," Nefertari added. "They'll be chasing ghosts while we slip through the pipe."

Grilka crossed her arms. "What about the interior layout?"

Nefertari tapped a few keys. A red glow expanded beneath the main structure. "Here. The sanctum is built into the rock core. The data chip shows a singular access hallway – heavily defended and likely shielded. Once Lilith confronts her, the compound's alert state will spike."

"We need to be ready to move," Kimiko said. "The moment Necra is neutralized… if she is… then we'll have limited time before reinforcements arrive from off-world."

"I'll have the Scorpion circling at low altitude, masking our signal behind the canyon's magnetic fields," Nefertari said. "We'll need a launch window – maybe five minutes."

Lilith looked around the table. "This isn't just a fight. This is the moment her empire falls, or we do. We don't get a second chance."

Grilka cracked her knuckles. "Then let's make the first one count."

Adrian offered a rare nod of seriousness. "I'll prep the Shadow for low-altitude interference and close support. No retreat unless you call for it."

Rainstorm moved closer to the table. "We'll bring her down. And we'll bring each other back."

Lilith looked each of them in the eyes. "We're not the same team that started this war. We've bled, we've changed… we've grown. And now we finish it."

The map dimmed.

The room exhaled.

Outside, the wind swept gently across the plateau. Far in the distance, somewhere beyond the darkened peaks of Jaze, Necra sat upon her throne, oblivious to the storm approaching her doorstep.

Lilith turned toward the corridor. "Prep for infiltration. We leave at first light."

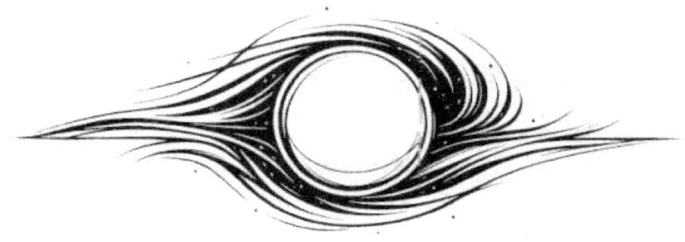

Chapter 40:

Shadows Over Tharnix

The Scorpion ascended slowly into the purple sky, engines humming with controlled purpose. Below, the quiet meadow that had helped to heal their wounds disappeared behind soft clouds and swirling mist. It had been a week since the battle – their bruises and injuries fading but not forgotten.

Lilith stood at the helm with Nefertari at navigation as the vessel cleared orbit. The planet's warmth receded beneath them, replaced by the cold promise of vengeance among the stars.

"Are we ready?" Lilith asked.

Nefertari nodded. "Everyone's strapped in. Course is plotted."

Adrian's voice came through the comm from his fighter, the Starlight Shadow, which cruised alongside them. "Locked onto your vector. That fortress isn't going to know what hit it."

Nefertari checking her display, "No anomalies on the route. We're clear to jump."

Lilith's voice was calm. "Then we jump."

A pulse rippled through the void as both ships

engaged warp. The stars stretched into long streams of silver. For a moment, it felt like the universe held its breath.

Arrival: Orbit Over Jaze

Jaze loomed like a half-swallowed ember – a planet of cragged canyons, deep volcanic ridges, and endless shadows. On the dark side of the world, tucked into a tectonic rift, was the city of Tharni – Necra's stronghold.

From orbit, it barely registered as more than a black blemish on scorched terrain, but as the Scorpion dropped into low-atmosphere flight, the scale became clear.

Obsidian towers spiked from the ground like fossilized bones. Massive heat sinks vented steam into the sky. Nestled between red stone cliffs, the fortress pulsed with internal energy, shielded and hidden – but not invincible.

Freija stood beside Lilith in the cockpit. "This place… feels wrong."

"Because it is," Lilith said. "But we don't confront it. Not yet. We find our way in."

Phase One: The Setup

They landed miles away, shielded by jagged ridges and ambient rock storms that played havoc with long-range sensors. The ground trembled faintly beneath their feet – Jaze was restless.

Rainstorm and Grilka exited first, scouting the perimeter in silence. The winds howled faintly over the canyon walls.

"This planet doesn't want us here," Grilka muttered.

"Good," Rainstorm replied. "Neither does Necra."

Nefertari unfolded a holo-map against the side of the Scorpion's hull. "Eastern aqueducts are still active. Most traffic enters and exits from the upper port gates. If we're going unseen, the aqueduct is our best chance."

Kimiko leaned in, her voice low. "Aqueduct tunnels lead to the service sublevels. If we're careful, we can reach the throne complex's lower sections undetected."

Lilith nodded. "Then that's our route."

She looked at Adrian and Freija. "You two fly wide. Hit the upper towers. Don't get shot. Don't overcommit. We just need noise."

Adrian saluted with mock flair. "Making noise is my middle name."

Freija's wings snapped once. "They won't see us coming."

Phase Two: Aerial Distraction

As night crept over Jaze, Freija soared into the upper atmosphere – barely visible against the darkening sky. Adrian flew parallel, looping above the fortress like a hawk scouting prey.

Below, motion lit up on enemy sensors.

"Eyes on us," Adrian said. "Anti-air guns are waking up."

Freija dove low, blasting a frost beam against a watchtower's sensor node. Sparks erupted, and alarms began to echo across the compound.

Adrian followed up with a sharp strafe, sending precision disruptors dancing along a landing pad. No deaths – just confusion.

Inside the stronghold, soldiers scrambled to defensive positions. Spotlights cut through the dusk, scanning the skies.

"Don't get cocky," Nefertari warned from the Scorpion, tracking their flight. "They're locking onto you fast."

Freija dodged a missile with a barrel roll doing a mock Adrian phrase. "Cocky is my middle name."

Phase Three: Ground Infiltration

With the fortress guards distracted by the commotion above, the rest of the team crept toward the aqueduct entrance: a cracked pipe half-buried in rubble and steaming runoff. The entrance stank of corrosion and chemicals.

Rainstorm moved first, testing the structure. "Stable."

Lilith followed next with her swords strapped across her back. Behind her came Kimiko and Grilka. Nearby at the helm, Nefertari waited.

The aqueduct was tight, damp, and pitch black – save for the faint glow from the cracks in Lilith's skin and Kimiko's blinking visor. They moved like shadows, careful not to trigger any echoes or vibrations.

"Sensor fields ahead," Kimiko whispered. "Stepping pattern matters. Follow my lead."

They tiptoed in unison, avoiding specific plates and broken sections. One misstep and the whole sublevel would light up.

Lilith paused only once, turning her head slightly toward Rainstorm behind her. "If I fall… you lead them out."

"You're not falling," Rainstorm said firmly. "Not today."

Phase Four: Positioning

Back in the sky, Adrian pulled his fighter into a sudden stall, flipping around a barrage of flak fire. "Getting hot out here."

"Wrap it up," Lilith whispered into comms. "We're inside."

Freija called back. "Copy. Heading east for the loop. They're still chasing us."

At that moment, the infiltration team reached the sublevel entrance beneath the command citadel. The walls vibrated faintly with the weight of machines above.

Kimiko scanned a sealed hatch. "No guards. No sensors. This is where we split."

Lilith's wings unfurled slightly. "Adrian, Nefertari – prepare for extraction routes. Rainstorm, Kimiko, you're with me."

Grilka turned to follow a parallel route toward the upper corridors. "I'll cause a mess in their munitions cache. Let's give Necra a night to remember."

Freija's voice cut through the silence one last time: "Whatever happens… finish this."

Lilith gave a final nod and stepped through the darkened threshold.

The descent had begun.

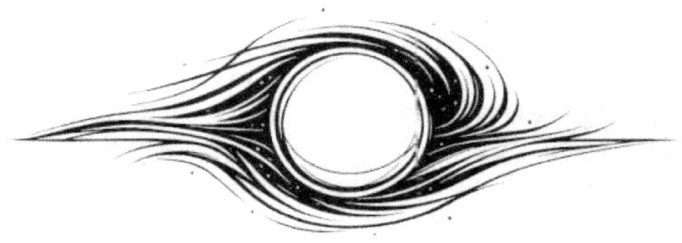

Chapter 41:

The Citadel's Core

The corridors of the inner citadel whispered with power.

Lilith moved through them like a silent flame, Kimiko at her flank and Rainstorm just behind. The metal walls were etched with jagged, angular script – not meant for reading, but for dominance. Each turn they took plunged them deeper into the heart of Necra's fortress. The air grew heavier, humid with a heat that pulsed from the floors. There was no dust. No sound. Only silence and warning.

"This place was built to intimidate," Rainstorm muttered, adjusting her disruptors. "Even the spirits won't speak here."

Kimiko gestured to a panel along the wall – motion detectors, barely visible to the naked eye. "Trip the wrong one, and we'll be the next inscription."

Lilith didn't answer. Her eyes were fixed ahead, her breath measured. The burn on her shoulder ached with each step, but her mind was elsewhere – on a feeling clawing its way into her soul. Something familiar. Something wrong.

They passed an arched threshold and stepped into a vast hall.

Massive pillars reached toward a vaulted ceiling so

high they faded into blackness. Pools of glowing blue light illuminated angular thrones set into the walls – empty now but clearly meant for command. At the far end, a narrow set of steps climbed toward a throne that dwarfed even the hall. Unlike the others, it was alive with energy – pulsating with veins of molten crystal and shifting shadows.

And standing before it… was Necra.

She turned slowly, the edges of her obsidian robes gliding over the floor like a liquid shadow. Her crown shimmered with faint arcs of green lightning, and the spectral glow of her eyes narrowed when they landed on Lilith.

NECRA

For the briefest moment, neither moved.

Then Necra tilted her head, her voice a silken echo across the chamber. "So. It's true. Another hellborne walks the stars."

Lilith stepped forward, her boots striking the stone like thunder. "I didn't come to be counted."

Necra's lips curled into a slow, unsettling smile. "But you *were* counted. Do you know how many centuries I've ruled without meeting another of your kind who wasn't broken, tamed... or dust?"

She descended the stairs, every step elegant and deliberate. Her aura pressed down like gravity.

"I smelled sulfur when you entered orbit," she said. "I thought it was the remains of the last fool who challenged me. But now I see..." Her smile vanished. "You wear your father's fire."

Kimiko's grip tightened on her blade, but Lilith raised one hand – not in warning, but to calm.

"You know Belzoth," Lilith said.

Necra's voice chilled. "We all knew him. A tyrant. A relic of a time before time. He ruled through fear, bred monsters, and never understood evolution." She studied Lilith with something like curiosity. "Yet here you stand... proof that even hell's fire can forge something new."

Rainstorm stepped closer, silent but tense. Lilith didn't flinch. Her fiery gaze locked with Necra's.

"Evolution?" Lilith echoed. "You built this fortress with bones and blood. You call it progress, but it's only decay."

Necra descended the last step. They were only ten paces apart now. Close enough to strike. Close enough to die.

"I built an empire," Necra said coldly. "I turned broken worlds into order. Obedience. Legacy. What have you built, Hellborne?" Her voice grew sharper. "A gang of traitors? A team of orphans with nothing to lose?"

Kimiko's voice was low. "Watch your tongue."

Necra's head turned sharply toward her, but Lilith stepped forward, blocking her gaze.

"I've built something you'll never understand," Lilith said. "Loyalty. Purpose. And when this is over, you'll be nothing but a warning to those who think cruelty is strength."

Necra's eyes blazed. "You don't know what you've awakened."

"No," Lilith said. "But I know who I am."

Silence stretched again – this time deeper. Charged. The throne pulsed behind Necra like a heartbeat.

At last, Necra turned.

"We will meet again, daughter of Belzoth," she said. "But not here. Not yet." She began to ascend the stairs, voice distant. "You're not ready."

Rainstorm whispered, "Now?"

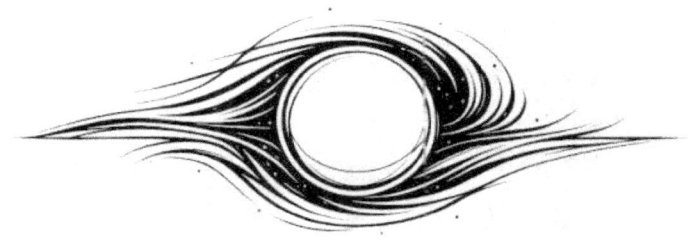

Chapter 42:

Crimson Shattered

Lilith's fiery gaze remained locked on Necra – but she sensed it first.

A shift in pressure. A presence behind the pillars.

A deep, resonant voice rolled across the chamber like thunder breaking stone.

"I knew the air stank of arrogance."

From the shadows emerged Agramor, a towering demon, easily a head taller than Lilith. His skin was molten crimson, cracked like volcanic rock around his shoulders and neck. Two jagged horns jutted back from his crown like a war-helm, and his eyes glowed a deep, baleful yellow. His chest was armored in spiked black obsidian, and in one clawed hand he held a cleaver-sized broadsword with a jagged edge that hummed with latent fury.

He strode forward slowly, every step shaking the floor.

"Another of the Hellborne," he sneered, voice low and brimming with disdain. "I thought you were all dead, or hiding beneath your father's skirts."

Lilith turned toward him, stepping forward. "Agramor."

AGRAMOR

He stopped a few paces in front of her and tilted his head. "So… Belzoth sired a daughter who thinks herself worthy of standing before a queen."

"I'm not standing before her," Lilith said coldly. "I'm standing against her."

Agramor's lip curled. "Then die on your feet."

Without another word, he stepped in front of Necra and drew his sword, the obsidian edge igniting with black flame. The air sizzled around it. Necra did not flinch. She simply watched, an amused glint in her eyes.

Lilith unsheathed her own twin swords, their infernal heat hissing against the chamber's cold stone floor.

And then they clashed.

Steel met steel with a crack like lightning, and the shockwave sent dust and debris tumbling from the ceiling. Lilith struck first, her blades spinning in tight arcs, darting for Agramor's joints. He blocked with monstrous strength, his single sword easily absorbing her flurry. He retaliated with a brutal overhead slash, forcing her to sidestep. The blade tore through the floor like paper.

Lilith ducked low, slashing at his leg. Sparks flew, but Agramor's armor held. He snarled and backhanded her, sending her skidding across the stone, her boots scraping against molten cracks.

"You fight like a child," he spat. "All rage. No purpose."

Lilith rose, blood trickling from the corner of her mouth. "That's all it'll take to end you."

She launched again, this time combining fire with speed. Her wings flared, and her blades became twin arcs of searing light. She struck with one, feinted with the second, twisting midair –and scored a deep gash across Agramor's chest.

He roared – not in pain, but in glee.

And then he struck back.

A massive swing caught her mid-roll. One sword flew from her hand. Agramor pressed forward, pummeling her defenses with relentless force. His blade crashed against her blade again and again, driving her back toward the center of the throne room. Her movements slowed – her shoulder, still injured, began to falter.

He kicked her squarely in the chest.

Lilith hit the ground hard, her last sword clattering out of reach. Agramor stalked over, placing a heavy boot on her back to pin her down. With a mocking grin, he kicked both swords across the floor, sending them spinning far away.

"Look at you," he rumbled. "Broken. Like your father. Like your realm."

Kimiko moved.

She darted forward, twin katanas flashing. Agramor turned just in time to block her first strike, then caught her second blade with his bare hand. With a roar, he lifted her by the throat and slammed her into the far wall, shattering stone as she crumpled to the floor.

Lilith tried to rise, arm shaking, blood in her mouth.

Agramor loomed over her. "Let me show you how demons die."

He reached into the air with his off-hand and snapped the jagged edge of his own horn. The tip gleamed with molten magic – a personal relic of power. With a sick, satisfied smile, he stabbed it directly into Lilith's chest.

The force knocked the breath from her lungs.

Her body arched. Her eyes flashed once... then went still.

Agramor let the broken horn fall from her body with a wet clatter. She collapsed to the stone floor, her wings twitching once, then going limp. A slow pool of black and red spread beneath her.

Necra descended from the throne.

She peered down at Lilith's still body and turned to Kimiko, who lay half-conscious against the wall, blood streaking her cheek.

"You should have run," Necra said softly. "But I'm glad you didn't. Watching you lose was more... satisfying."

Rainstorm stood frozen near the archway, trembling.

Necra and Agramor passed her without pause, chuckling softly.

"We'll leave you the corpse," Necra said. "You can bury your little rebellion properly."

The doors sealed behind them with a hiss of cold air.

Rainstorm ran.

She fell to her knees beside Lilith, hands trembling as she turned her over. The wound was deep... unnatural. The shard of horn had pierced clean through.

"Lilith?" she whispered.

No response.

She pressed her hand against Lilith's chest.

No heartbeat.

"Lilith..." she said again, voice breaking.

Tears blurred her vision.

The demon was dead.

And so was all hope.

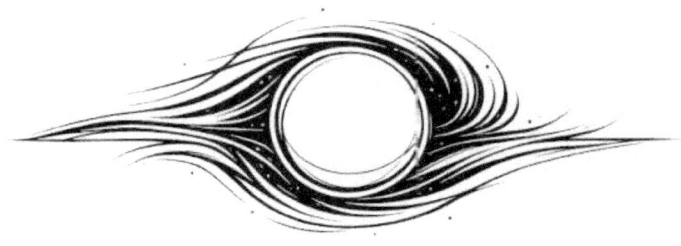

Chapter 43:

The Astral Passage

Lilith drifted.

At first, there was only the sensation of motion – not falling, not rising, just… movement. She felt no pain, no heat, no cold. The agony of her last battle was gone. In its place was silence.

Then came the light.

It shimmered like a tunnel spun from pure starlight, vast and spiraling, with waves of color and sound weaving together in gentle rhythm. Her body, or what remained of her, glided forward through it – weightless, formless, and yet somehow whole. The burning rage that had always lingered at the edge of her thoughts was absent. There was only peace.

And awe.

As the tunnel of light widened, she emerged into a realm unlike anything she had ever known. It was beautiful – indescribably so. A vast expanse of floating crystalline structures and glowing rivers of energy stretched across a silver-blue sky that pulsed with awareness. Every sound was music. Every movement echoed with meaning. Beings of pure light drifted between the spires, some with humanoid shapes, others more abstract – wings of gold, halos of motion, bodies made of thoughts.

Lilith paused, astonished.

"This… this can't be real," she murmured aloud, her voice soft and resonant in this space. "The Astral Realm?"

A figure of radiant light approached – neither male nor female, but somehow both. Its voice was melody and gravity woven together.

"You stand in the place between worlds," the being said gently. "Few reach this realm. None of your kind ever have."

Lilith blinked. "My kind?"

"You are the first demon to step foot here in all of eternity."

More beings gathered, drawn by the anomaly. They circled her, not in menace, but in reverence. Her crimson aura pulsed against their radiant forms, a contrast of darkness amidst luminescence. And yet, they did not shrink from her.

"You are not bound by your birth," another being spoke. "You are not condemned by your origin. You are here because something within you transcended."

"I…" Lilith faltered. "I don't understand. I've killed. I've fought. I've burned through lives for freedom, for vengeance. I'm not… worthy."

"There is no worth here. Only resonance," the first being replied. "You've walked through fire and shadow. You've chosen others over yourself. And when the moment came, you gave everything – not for power, but for purpose."

Lilith felt her core tremble.

"Am I dead?"

"You are beyond death. But not beyond choice."

Hours… days… perhaps lifetimes – seemed to pass as the beings showed her visions. Not just of her past, but of her potential. What she had been. What she could become. They spoke of unity, of transformation, of rising above the chains of one's design. Her horns, her wings, her blood – they did not define her. Her actions did.

"You are still becoming," the voices sang together.

"Still changing. And your journey is not complete."

Lilith's voice was barely a whisper. "What am I now?"

"A bridge."

She looked down at her own form – more luminous now, not entirely light, but no longer pure shadow either. Her wings pulsed with faint halos at the edges, and her fire no longer burned – it radiated.

"You must return," the beings said. "There are those who still need you. The realm of matter calls for you."

A door of light opened behind her – an archway carved from stars.

Lilith turned to the beings one last time. "Will I remember this?"

"You will remember enough. And what you forget, your soul will carry forward."

She stepped toward the doorway.

Down the tunnel of light, she fell – faster now, fire and memory trailing behind her like a comet across infinity.

As she neared the end, she saw them – two familiar figures crouched beside a broken body.

Her body.

Kimiko held her hand tightly, her face pale and stricken. Rainstorm knelt beside her, chanting softly, her palm pressed over Lilith's unmoving heart. Grilka is blowing into her mouth.

Lilith's spirit hesitated for only a breath.

Then, like lightning drawn to a conductor, she plunged downward – back into the world of pain, love, and unfinished destiny.

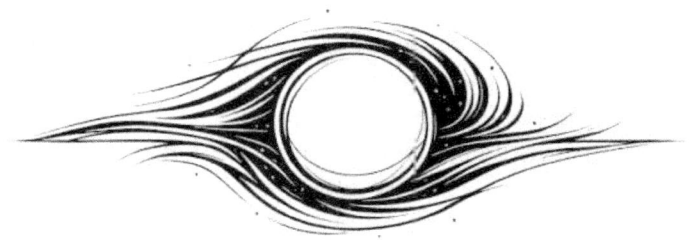

Chapter 44:

Breath Returned

The chamber echoed with silence.

Rainstorm dropped to her knees beside Lilith's lifeless body. The scorched stone beneath her knees radiated residual heat from the battle just moments before. Lilith's body lay still, splayed in a twisted heap of crimson limbs and dark armor, her fiery swords extinguished, her wings slack and heavy like torn banners after a storm.

Blood pooled beneath her ribs where Agramor's horn had found its mark.

Rainstorm's hands trembled, but her mind focused with the trained clarity of a Wakasa healer. She pulled a pouch from her belt and opened it with swift fingers, revealing vials, herbs, and salves she had gathered since their arrival on the healing planet. Her gaze narrowed.

"She's not breathing," Kimiko whispered, standing over them, her eyes wide in disbelief. "She's... dead."

"No," Rainstorm murmured. "Not yet. Not while I can still call her back."

From her pouch, she selected a silver leaf the color of moonlight and a pinch of ground yellow root. She crushed them together in her palm and added a single drop of distilled water. The mixture steamed faintly, releasing a sharp, aromatic vapor.

She smeared it over the wound on Lilith's chest – dark, cauterized edges around a mortal puncture. The balm hissed on contact, but Lilith did not stir.

Rainstorm placed her hands over the wound and closed her eyes. Her voice dropped into a chant – low, rhythmic, ancient. Each syllable carried a frequency that vibrated in the air, drawing warmth toward her fingers. Her palms pulsed with ethereal heat.

"Earth, fire, breath and bone…
Bridge the realms to call her home…"

Kimiko knelt beside her, watching, the wind from her tight braids brushing softly against Rainstorm's shoulder. "Can this work?"

Rainstorm didn't answer. Her chant deepened.

"Strength of stone, blood of sky…
Refuse the soul that dares to die…"

Still no breath. No flutter of eyelids. No twitch of a finger.

Rainstorm's calm began to fray.

She pressed her hands to Lilith's sternum and began chest compressions – slow, steady, and brutal. "Come on," she hissed through gritted teeth. "You've survived worse."

She counted quietly. At thirty, she tilted Lilith's head back and leaned close to breathe into her mouth. The exhale was shaky but full of will.

Kimiko leaned in, folding Lilith's wings delicately out of the way. Her voice was sharp, trembling, but resolute. "Lilith, if you can hear me... you don't get to go yet. You *do not get to leave us like this.*"

More compressions. More breath.

Lilith's lips remained pale, her chest unmoving. Her once-fiery skin was losing its glow, a dullness creeping along her edges like ash over embers.

Then, a shadow blocked the faint glow of the chamber entrance.

Grilka stomped in, blood streaked across her face and arms, her knuckles bruised, one of her gauntlets dented. She stopped cold when she saw the scene – Lilith motionless, Rainstorm weeping silently as she continued CPR, Kimiko pale and silent like a specter beside them.

"No. Nope. Not happening." Grilka dropped to her knees opposite Rainstorm.

She grabbed Lilith's face in her large, calloused hands. "This is not how demons die!" she bellowed. "You're a warrior, not a candle snuffed out by the wind!"

Without warning, Grilka leaned down and pressed her mouth to Lilith's, delivering a full, primal breath. Not one, but two.

Rainstorm blinked in stunned silence as Grilka sat back and slammed both fists gently but firmly on Lilith's chest. "If yelling doesn't work," Grilka muttered, "maybe shaking the soul does."

Kimiko tilted her head, half-horrified, half-stunned.

Then it happened.

A faint twitch in Lilith's hand.

Barely noticeable. But real.

Rainstorm leaned in. "Again!"

Grilka repeated the motion – another breath, another slam of her fists. "Come on, you flaming horned *badass*, don't make me *cry!*"

Lilith's body convulsed.

A choked gasp tore from her throat.

Her chest rose – sharply, suddenly, like the first breath after drowning.

Kimiko scrambled back. Rainstorm's hands froze. Grilka blinked hard, unsure whether to scream or laugh.

Lilith's eyes opened.

Not just open – burning. Molten gold spiraled into fiery red. They flared with a strange brilliance, a mixture of confusion and purpose, as though she had seen something vast and returned carrying a sliver of it in her soul.

She inhaled again, this time stronger. Her fingers clawed at the stone beneath her. Her wings twitched.

Kimiko stared at her, voice cracking. "Lilith…"

Rainstorm's lip quivered. "You were gone…"

Grilka sat back, eyes wide, then smacked her hand over her face. "You owe me one hell of a drink."

Lilith pushed herself upright, slow and shaky. Her muscles trembled under her weight, her breath coming in short bursts. She looked at each of them in turn – Kimiko's stunned silence, Rainstorm's tear-streaked face, Grilka's oddly tender smirk.

Her voice was hoarse. "...Did someone… kiss me?"

Grilka raised her hand. "Mouth-to-mouth. Emergency protocol. Totally professional."

Rainstorm choked on a laugh.

Kimiko blinked rapidly, then exhaled. "You… died."

Lilith looked down at her chest, where a blackened wound still smoldered faintly. She touched it, flinched, then whispered, "No. I traveled."

The other three women froze.

Lilith looked up, eyes glowing. "I've seen something… something no demon ever has."

The chamber remained quiet, save for the sound of their shared breaths.

Lilith sat upright, spine straight, wings slowly unfurling behind her like a banner reborn.

And for the first time since the mission began Rainstorm, Kimiko, and Grilka were at a loss for words.

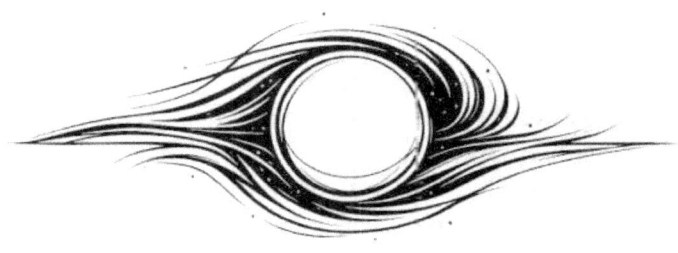

Chapter 45:

Signals In the Smoke

Lilith's body still trembled from the ordeal. Though her eyes were open and her heart did beat once more, every movement felt as though it was being pulled through thick, burning tar. Her limbs were sluggish, her breath short but her spirit surged with something new.

Grilka knelt beside her, sweat and blood caking her skin, and without a word, she slid her arms under Lilith's shoulders. "Come on, Captain," she grunted. "You're not lounging here any longer."

Lilith coughed weakly, managing a faint, rasped smirk. "I wouldn't call this… lounging."

"Right," Grilka muttered, hoisting Lilith to her feet. "Just gracefully collapsing while soaked in your own blood. Very regal."

Lilith's legs buckled for a moment, but Grilka caught her, propping her against her own bulk like a shield wall. Kimiko and Rainstorm stood nearby, each holding one of Lilith's massive twin swords – flaming weapons so heavy that even seasoned fighters struggled to wield them with ease. And yet, without complaint, both women bore the burden, eyes locked protectively on their commander.

"She's not going to be able to swing these for a

while," Kimiko said, examining the scorched hilt of the sword she carried.

"Then we'll carry them for her," Rainstorm replied softly, adjusting the weight across her back. Her voice still trembled with emotion. "No one leaves those behind."

Grilka supported Lilith with one arm and activated her comm with the other. "Nefertari," she barked, "we need immediate extraction. Coordinates transmitting. And... Lilith's alive. She... she was dead. But not anymore."

There was a beat of stunned silence on the other end of the comms. Then Nefertari's voice came through, breathless and disbelieving. "What?"

"I said she died," Grilka repeated. "And now she's standing next to me. Don't ask me how. Just get the ship here now."

"Confirmed," Nefertari said quickly, her voice steeling into command mode. "Scorpion enroute. I will be waiting for you at the extraction point."

They began their trip going back through the tunnels to where they would be picked up.

A faint whine filled the air. High above, the dark clouds parted just enough to reveal the descending silhouette of the Scorpion, engines flaring with low-blue thrust as it dove rapidly toward the fortress's outskirts.

Lilith leaned heavily into Grilka, her strength waning again. Her fingers twitched, trying to reach for her swords, but Kimiko gently pressed her back.

"You don't need to prove anything," Kimiko whispered. "Not to us. Not today."

Lilith looked at her, then to Rainstorm, then to Grilka... and for a rare moment, she allowed herself to lean on them, literally and figuratively.

"We're still alive," Rainstorm said, watching the Scorpion draw closer. "That's what matters."

Grilka nodded. "And I'm not giving that demon bastard the chance to make us not."

The ship's ramp extended before it even touched the ground. The loading bay door opened wide, light spilling into the shattered corridor of the citadel. Nefertari appeared at the top of the ramp, her gold-and-blue armor gleaming even in the haze of smoke. Her eyes locked onto Lilith, then widened.

"Stars..." she murmured. "You really did come back."

Rainstorm jogged forward, still carrying one of Lilith's swords. "Help us get her on board. We need to be gone before Agramor or Necra realize what just slipped out from under them."

The ground vibrated faintly, a distant rumble echoing through the stone. Whether it was structural instability or a signal of something more, no one wanted to stay long enough to find out.

Grilka and Nefertari hauled Lilith aboard while Kimiko and Rainstorm sprinted up after them, swords in hand. The moment the last foot cleared the ramp, the Scorpion sealed shut.

"Everyone aboard?" Nefertari called out from the cockpit.

"All accounted for," Grilka answered. "Burn us out of here."

The Scorpion's engines screamed as it launched from the plateau, leaving behind the ancient fortress – the site of Lilith's death, and now, her rebirth.

In the living quarters, Lilith lay back against a padded bench, her breathing shallow, her eyes closed. The others gathered around in tense silence. No one spoke for a moment.

Then Lilith's lips moved. "Don't... tell the others... yet," she whispered. "Let me explain it when I'm ready."

Kimiko crouched beside her and nodded. "We'll wait."

Adrian's voice buzzed through the internal comms.

317

"I'm already enroute to meet you guys. I picked up some odd seismic activity down there – don't think Necra or her pet demon will be far behind."

Grilka looked at the team. "Then let's vanish before they come looking."

Rainstorm glanced toward the viewports where Jaze's surface receded. "We'll rest. We'll heal. And then we finish this."

Lilith, half-conscious, let a faint smile curl across her lips.

They had made it out.

But the war was far from over.

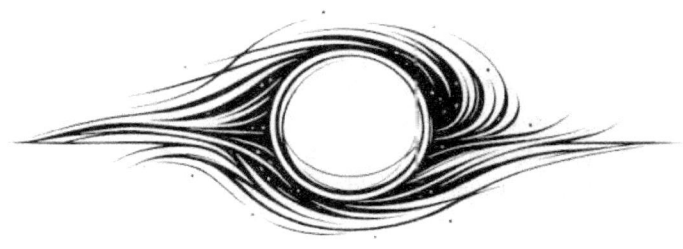

Chapter 46:

The Return of the Flame

The Starlight Shadow pushed through the thinning upper layers of Jaze's atmosphere. Inside the cockpit, Adrian's hands worked the controls in silence. His usual bravado was gone. The weight of what had just happened… what they had lost… pressed on his shoulders like gravity.

Beside him, Freija sat hunched over, her icy-blue wings folded close to her body, trembling ever so slightly. She hadn't spoken since they'd left the surface. Her face, streaked with soot and blood, was unreadable. But her fists were clenched in her lap, and her knuckles had turned pale.

"She died," Freija said softly, as if trying to convince herself. "Lilith died."

Adrian didn't look at her. "I know."

The silence returned – long, cold, and heavy.

When the Starlight Shadow approached the Scorpion, Adrian initiated docking procedures. The ship aligned with the larger vessel and sealed with a sharp hiss of magnetic locks.

The moment the airlock finished cycling, Freija launched herself forward.

She didn't wait for Adrian. She didn't ask permission. Her boots barely touched the floor as she sprinted through the access tube, her breath catching, her muscles straining despite her injuries.

The Scorpion's internal door slid open.

Freija stormed through it, heart pounding in her chest, her eyes scanning and then locking on.

Lilith was seated in the living quarters, upright but frail. Her crimson skin was pale, her body wrapped in field bandages, her posture still trembling from the ordeal. And yet... she was alive.

Freija didn't slow. She crossed the room in two bounds and threw her arms around her in a crushing, wing-encased hug.

"You *terrifying, stubborn, impossible* woman!" Freija breathed, holding her so tightly that Lilith gasped from the pressure. "You were dead. You were actually... and then Rainstorm... Grilka... and I thought..."

Lilith allowed the hug, even returned it weakly with one arm. "Not dead anymore," she murmured.

Freija pulled back only slightly, tears blurring the glow of her sapphire eyes. "We thought we lost you."

"You did," Rainstorm said softly, approaching from behind. Her expression was calm, but her voice held gravity. "She was gone. No breath. No pulse. I saw it with my own eyes."

Grilka, leaning against the wall with her arms crossed, nodded once. "I don't care what anyone says. We brought her back."

At that moment, Adrian stepped into the room, slower than usual. The levity he normally wore like armor was absent. His posture was straight, jaw tight, eyes dark. He didn't speak at first, just looked at Lilith as if confirming for himself that she was really there.

"Glad you're back," he said finally, voice quiet. "That... was too close."

Lilith met his gaze. "Thank you for not leaving."

He gave a faint, humorless smirk. "Not my style."

Kimiko stepped forward next to Rainstorm. "What happened?" she asked softly. "You looked at him... Agramor... and something changed. Then..." Her voice trailed off, eyes narrowing. "Then you died."

Rainstorm nodded again. "Agramor struck her. With his horn. Drove it through her chest." Her tone was flat, clinical... her hands still trembled at the memory. "There was nothing we could do."

Freija drew back a little, swallowing. "He was one of yours, wasn't he? A demon?"

Lilith nodded slowly. "Yes. Agramor is... old. Strong. One of the last of the elder demons bound by the Hellish Court. He served the great houses during the Second Reaping. I've only ever read about him."

"Well, he was real enough," Grilka muttered. "And brutal."

"But," Adrian said, gesturing slowly, "you're not dead anymore. So what happened?"

Lilith leaned back, closing her eyes for a moment. The breath she drew seemed heavier than the air around her.

"I don't know how to describe it," she began, voice barely above a whisper. "There was... light. A tunnel. I floated upward, like I had no weight. No body. Just... being. Then I arrived somewhere that wasn't a place."

The others listened in silence.

"It was... magnificent," she said slowly, her eyes become unfocused. "I can't tell you what it looked like – because it didn't *look* like anything. It *felt*. It *knew*. There were others – beings made of starlight and memory. They spoke without sound. They... knew me."

Freija sat beside her again. "Knew you?"

"They said I wasn't supposed to be there. That no demon ever had been." Her voice wavered. "They didn't understand how it was possible. Neither did I. But they weren't angry. They were curious. Kind."

Rainstorm's gaze narrowed in thought. "The Astral

Realm."

Lilith nodded. "I was there. They called it a convergence point. A place between all things. Where identity doesn't matter – only essence."

Kimiko, quietly kneeling nearby, asked: "Did they say why you were brought there?"

Lilith hesitated. "They said I was at a turning point. That my old self had died – by Agramor's hand. But that a new path was still open. They spoke of... transcendence. Of rebirth not through vengeance or fire, but through *awareness*. I wasn't summoned back. I *chose* to return. I don't know why, but I did."

Adrian leaned against the doorway. "Well, whatever made you come back... glad you did."

"It wasn't just for me," Lilith said softly. "It was for all of us. I felt something in that realm – like everything we do has an echo. Every action, a ripple in something vast."

There was a long pause.

"You've changed," Rainstorm said finally. "I can feel it."

"I have," Lilith admitted. "I don't know what I am now. Not just a demon. But not something new either. I'm in-between."

"Then we build from that," Kimiko said. "We keep moving forward."

Freija nodded firmly. "We still have Necra to face. We still have a war to end."

Lilith looked down at her hands, flexing her fingers slowly, as if unsure they still belonged to her. "I'm not the same leader who took us into that fortress. But I'll be the one who takes us out of it."

Grilka grunted. "You better. I'm not letting some resurrected wingless hell-skeleton think she won." She held out a fist.

Lilith smiled faintly and bumped it, weakly.

The tension broke. The room was still heavy, but it

no longer felt hopeless.

Lilith's journey had taken her to the brink of death –
and returned her not just alive, but transformed. Something
awakened in her in that realm beyond light and matter. And
though she couldn't yet name it, it burned like a second fire
behind her eyes.

The demon captain was reborn.

And this time, she would finish what she started.

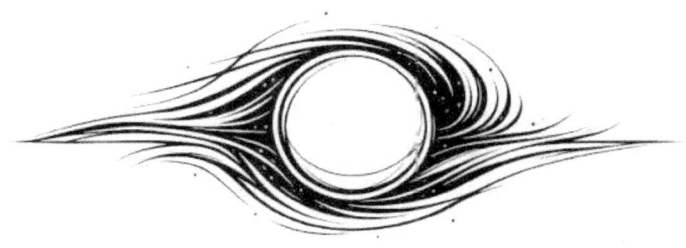

Chapter 47:

The Final Push Begins

The Scorpion hovered silently in high orbit above the burnt orange curve of Jaze. Inside, the air in the living quarters carried a different weight – not the heavy silence of mourning, but something tempered, steady… renewed. The team was gathered around the central holotable, the ambient blue glow casting long shadows over their tired but attentive faces.

Lilith stood at the head of the table, her breath still slower than usual, but she stood. Freija sat close by her wings folded tight to her back, her arm still bandaged. Adrian leaned against the wall, arms crossed and unusually silent. Rainstorm stood opposite Lilith, posture straight, arms behind her back like a sentry. Kimiko and Nefertari flanked either side of the table, both watching their captain with quiet reverence. Grilka leaned against a support beam, massive arms folded across her bruised chest, her gaze sharp.

Lilith reached forward and activated the chip embedded in the holotable. A soft chime sounded, and a series of encrypted files unraveled into the air – lines of movement, energy lines, facility structures, supply depots, transport convoys, relay beacons. Jaze's infrastructure lit up like veins of a dying beast.

"This," Lilith said, her voice still raw but stronger than it had been since her return, "is what we've been missing."

Adrian straightened slightly, nodding. "She's got an entire network of ghost systems. Hidden routes, supply caches, fallback strongholds. All the stuff we didn't see on the surface."

"Redundant infrastructure," Freija added, rotating one of the maps with a flick of her fingers. "She's built it so if one node fails, the rest adapt. Like a hydra. You cut one head, three more grow back."

Lilith tapped on one of the largest nodes. "Then we don't take off the heads. We go for the heart."

Kimiko stepped forward. "The network is linked by central command relays. If we hit the core relays – not destroy them, but reprogram them – we could disrupt her infrastructure without triggering her backups. It'll disorient her forces long enough for us to strike where it matters."

"Can we trust the data?" Rainstorm asked.

"It's encrypted at a level even Adrian needed help cracking," Nefertari answered, nodding to Lilith. "But there are signatures – command ID pulses, time-stamped logs. This came from Necra's inner circle. It's real."

Grilka gave a sharp nod. "So we take it all apart, piece by piece. What's our priority?"

Lilith looked up from the table, her gaze sweeping the team. For a moment, she hesitated – not from uncertainty, but from the gravity of her own presence.

She reached toward the display and changed the scope – zooming out from Jaze to the wider system, showing the three worlds that had already fallen under Necra's grip, and others in her path.

"When I was in the Astral Realm, they told me my purpose wasn't finished. That I had to return. I used to think power was about destruction, about control. But now... I see it's about *clarity*. About building something that lasts after the fire dies."

Freija stood slowly. "Then tell us what you need."

Lilith's molten eyes burned with quiet resolve. "We dismantle everything that feeds Necra's reach. Relay stations. Ghost ports. Intelligence hubs. One by one. Not to destroy, but to reclaim. And we leave behind something better."

Kimiko nodded. "We'll need coordinated strikes. Quiet insertions. No alarms."

Adrian finally smirked, just a little. "We'll make sure she never even knows we were there... until it's too late."

Grilka cracked her knuckles. "Give me a few structures to pull down with my own hands and I'm in."

"Good," Lilith said. "Then we begin."

She turned back to the table and traced a path across the central system. "We'll divide our next missions. One strike team per week. Surgical precision, no open warfare. Not yet."

As she outlined the targets, Freija leaned slightly toward Rainstorm. "She's different."

"She's *becoming*," Rainstorm whispered. "Like the fire inside her finally found direction."

When the meeting broke, the crew filtered out slowly – each with renewed purpose. Grilka wandered off to double-check the armory. Adrian returned to the Scorpion's flight systems. Rainstorm remained with Nefertari to run navigational simulations. Freija followed Lilith quietly down the corridor.

Kimiko paused at the holotable one last time. She tapped the edge and whispered, "Let's see how far this fire can spread."

Lilith stood alone on the observation deck moments later, her reflection flickering in the dark glass.

For the first time, she didn't just feel like a commander.

She felt like a *leader*.

And it had only just begun.

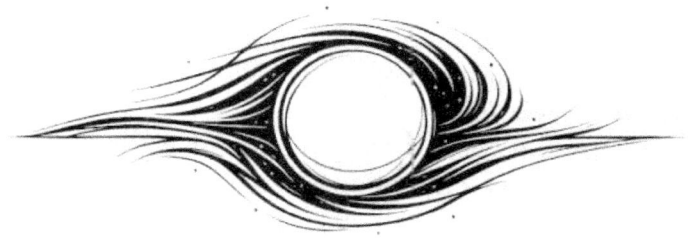

Chapter 48:

Relay Point Zero

The Scorpion drifted low over the shattered rock valleys of eastern Jaze, cloaked in a refractive shimmer. Its engines ran whisper-quiet, adapted for stealth. In the dim-blue light of pre-dawn, the jagged terrain looked more like the bones of a dead world than a functioning battlefield. But somewhere beneath those dead ridges, Relay Point Zero pulsed like a hidden nerve – a relay hub so deeply buried that even Jaze's command towers didn't acknowledge it on official maps.

Inside the ship, the briefing was short and quiet.

Rainstorm stood in front of the side monitor, arms folded, voice measured. "Relay Point Zero is buried under two kilometers of reinforced basalt and alloy. No overhead entrances. Just one sub-level access shaft – accessible through a fractured cavern on the northern slope. Adrian will fly us in and hold a hover above the valley mouth. Kimiko and I will descend through the shaft."

Lilith, standing beside the holotable, nodded but said little. She trusted them.

Kimiko while reading her twin katanas, "We don't trigger alarms. We slice in, reroute the relay's core output to a loopback signal, and then we vanish. It'll make it look like nothing's changed."

Adrian gave a half-smile from the cockpit ladder. "And I'll be your taxi out of hell if it goes sideways. Try not to need me."

"You'll be on hovering slightly above the canyon," Rainstorm said. "Hold position unless I call in."

"Copy that," he said, his usual sarcasm muted under a rare edge of seriousness.

They suited up in silence. No jokes. No fanfare. Just a shared sense of clarity. The kind that came after death had brushed too close to them all.

The Descent

The Scorpion hovered just above the broken ledge that hung over the northern cavern. Dust spun beneath its belly like a storm caught in slow motion. From inside, Rainstorm and Kimiko stood at the open ramp, both harnessed with mag-cable rigs strapped to their hips.

Rainstorm offered a hand to Kimiko. "You ready?"

Kimiko didn't hesitate. "Always."

They stepped off together.

Their descent was slow, controlled, the mag-cables reeling out with a soft *whirrrrr*. Below them, the cavern's walls were slick with old lava flow and laced with broken support pylons from some long-abandoned mining operation. The further they dropped, the darker it got — until their helmet lights were the only thing piercing the gloom.

"Thirty meters to entry point," Rainstorm said into the comms.

"Pressure readings are good," Kimiko replied. "Tunnel is stable."

They touched down inside a narrow metal chamber – half-natural, half-mechanical. To their right, a reinforced steel door stood shut, bearing no insignia, no interface.

Kimiko unslung a cable tool and pressed it to the corner seam. A faint *tick-tick-tick* later, and the panel hissed open – just enough for them to slip through.

They moved inside without a word.

Inside the Relay

The corridor beyond was narrow and choked with wiring. Orange emergency lights blinked faintly above – enough to navigate, but not enough to see the threat ahead.

"Switch to infrared," Rainstorm whispered. Both toggled their lenses.

The relay's core was four levels down – a central chamber buried beneath network terminals, coolant reservoirs, and AI-routing channels. Each step they took, their boots made no sound. Each breath came slow and deliberate. Any wrong move could trigger the entire site's security system.

Kimiko paused. She raised a hand.

A heat signature blinked to life – a guard, sitting motionless in a side chamber, cradling a disruptor rifle. He hadn't moved in several minutes.

"Pulse rate's too slow," Kimiko murmured. "He's asleep."

Rainstorm crept to the doorway, peeked around the edge, then returned. "Confirmed. Let's keep going."

They passed three more sleeping guards in similar states – barely responsive, drugged, or rotated out for rest cycles. Either way, it gave them a window.

At the base of the facility, the relay core flickered in rhythmic pulses, its central spike glowing blue with artificial nerve energy. The room thrummed faintly – like a heart.

Rainstorm moved to the central control node. "Begin upload."

Kimiko inserted the data spike – a black shard coded by Nefertari to mimic one of Necra's internal sync signals. It initiated a loopback sequence across the facility's communications systems, diverting packet flow into harmless feedback loops.

"We've got seven minutes," Kimiko whispered. "Before their logs start misfiring."

Rainstorm tapped her comms. "Adrian. Extraction in ten."

"Already warming up the engines," Adrian replied. "No movement up top."

Just as the final sequence processed, a screen lit up. One of the sleeping guards' biometric tags suddenly spiked.

"Movement," Kimiko hissed. "Third floor."

Rainstorm stiffened. "We've got to move now."

Extraction

They climbed fast – up maintenance ladders, past silent coolant fans, through vent shafts. As they reached the second floor, the tremor of bootsteps echoed below.

"They're not asleep anymore," Rainstorm said grimly.

"Still no alarms," Kimiko replied. "But that won't last."

At the surface shaft, Adrian's voice snapped in over the comm. "Just got a motion ping on the canyon ridge. You've got thirty seconds."

Rainstorm grabbed Kimiko's rig and fired the mag-cable. They were hauled up into the open sky just as three guards burst into the tunnel below. They shouted, but didn't fire – either confused or still unsure what had happened.

Kimiko and Rainstorm landed hard on the Scorpion's ramp, Adrian already spinning the ship skyward.

"Everyone in?" he asked.

"Go," Rainstorm barked.

The Scorpion banked hard and vanished into the morning cloud cover.

Above Jaze

In the silence of the cockpit, Lilith watched the

Scorpion's readouts. The relay's systems hadn't tripped. The logs showed no trace of external intrusion. The loopback was successful.

Relay Point Zero had become an echo chamber. One of Necra's key nerves was now singing a false lullaby – just as planned.

Lilith turned from the console and walked into the corridor, her voice echoing toward the rest of the ship.

"One down."

She didn't smile.

But her fire, once lost, now burned with purpose.

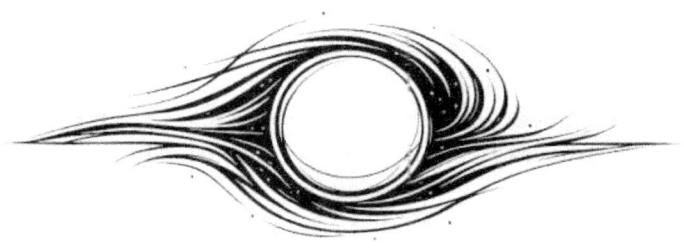

Chapter 49:

Sever the Signal

The volcanic moon Dharvox loomed beneath them like a simmering ember, its cracked obsidian surface veined with molten rivers that pulsed like arteries. From orbit, it appeared almost lifeless – just another rock. But nestled within the fractured bedrock lay the Black Spire: Necra's most clandestine intelligence hub, a subterranean fortress laced with surveillance nodes, encryption vaults, and a single command uplink capable of coordinating her forces across three systems.

Within the Scorpion, tension rippled through the team like static. Lilith stood in the ship's forward bay, her gaze locked on the projection of the Black Spire hovering above the holotable. Her fingers moved with calm precision, drawing circles around key entry points.

"We go in two teams," she said. "Adrian and Kimiko will infiltrate through the shielded utility conduits beneath the eastern ridge. Freija and Grilka will scale the exterior defense columns and disable the uplink's satellite dish. Nefertari will jam outbound transmissions. Rainstorm and I will monitor from orbit and coordinate the strike. Once the virus is planted, we pull out immediately."

"Stealth and sabotage," Kimiko said softly. "I prefer

335

this kind of mission."

Adrian checked the loadout on his belt. "As long as the exits stay open, we won't need a Plan B."

Grilka snorted. "Says the guy who *lives* in Plan B."

Lilith cracked the faintest smile. "Everyone's got their role. Let's execute it cleanly."

The Scorpion dipped low into the dense volcanic atmosphere, its hull shimmering against the rising heat as it approached the jagged outcropping that concealed the entrance to the Black Spire. From above, the Spire appeared as little more than a narrow fissure between the cliffs – but its sensors ran deep. Getting in would be hard. Getting out would be harder.

Beneath the Surface – Kimiko & Adrian

The utility conduit reeked of sulfur and ash. Kimiko pressed her back against the wall, barely breathing as a sensor drone buzzed past the access tunnel's opening. She gave a hand signal to Adrian, who crouched behind a coolant valve, disruptor drawn but silent.

"Ten seconds," she whispered.

Adrian raised his brows but nodded. When the drone passed again, Kimiko moved – slipping through the gap like a shadow. Adrian followed, muffling a grunt as he twisted through the narrow passage behind her.

The corridor led them to a reinforced access hatch. Adrian unhooked a compact terminal from his belt and began slicing the encryption code while Kimiko covered him, eyes sharp on the junction behind them.

"You know," Adrian muttered as he tapped the terminal, "this would be a lot easier if Necra didn't encrypt her doors with six layers of sadistic genius."

Kimiko didn't look back. "You're the sadistic genius in this hallway."

The lock clicked open.

"Flattering," he said. "But I prefer charming rogue."

Inside was a maintenance control room lit by red emergency strobes. Conduits fed into a central server tower lined with sleek black data drives.

"There," Kimiko said. "That's where we upload the virus."

Adrian crossed to the core and popped a panel open. His fingers danced across the console. "Uploading. Should take ninety seconds."

The moment the data stream began, alarms flared. Defense panels snapped open across the room. Kimiko pivoted, swords drawn in a breath. "They know we're here."

Surface Strike – Freija & Grilka

Far above, on the jagged cliff face of the Spire's outer shell, Freija's wings beat furiously against the dry wind. Climbing a fortress mid-eruption wasn't how she pictured her day, but the view had its appeal.

"Remind me again why we couldn't just blast the damn dish?" Grilka grunted, hauling herself up the side of the communications tower like a mountain goat in armor.

"Because we're not destroying it," Freija replied. "We're rewriting its transmission paths. Subtlety, remember?"

Grilka scoffed. "I'm subtle. I'm climbing without punching anything."

"Yet."

They reached the top of the dish platform. A rotating antenna hummed with energy, sending pulses of data into the sky.

Freija planted the relay tap while Grilka disabled the shielding with a controlled power drain. A burst of static flickered through the air, followed by a dull hum.

"We're in," Freija said into the comm. "Uplink is vulnerable. Ready for virus injection."

Command Coordination – Lilith & Rainstorm

Back on the Scorpion, Lilith and Rainstorm stared at the holotable's projection of the fortress. Lights flickered across the displays as feedback from each team came in.

"Virus upload at 72%," Rainstorm reported.

"Freija and Grilka are holding the relay line," Lilith said. "Nefertari, initiate comms jam."

From the cockpit, Nefertari responded. "Activating now."

A sharp static hiss surged through the airwaves. Across the compound, red warning symbols vanished from Necra's systems as their uplinks were severed mid-stream. Confusion spread like wildfire through her command network.

Ambush – Underground

Back in the control room, armored guards burst through the far wall. Kimiko moved like a phantom – slicing through the first attacker before he could raise a weapon. Adrian fired at the second, dropping him with two shots.

"They're not pulling punches!" Adrian shouted.

"Keep them off me," Kimiko ordered, "we're at 96%!"

Three more charged. Kimiko parried one, slashed the next, and took a shoulder hit from the third. Adrian dove and tackled him off her back.

"Done!" Adrian yelled, slamming the terminal closed. "Virus uploaded!"

"Extraction now," Kimiko said, dragging Adrian toward the access tunnel.

Retreat

On the surface, Grilka's fist slammed into a final power converter, shattering its shielding. "Signal's down!"

Freija twisted the uplink spike loose. "We need to

go… now."

All teams converged at the western extraction point where the Scorpion descended amid smoke and lightning. The hatch opened with a shriek, and Rainstorm stood ready, her tomahawks spinning in her hands.

Kimiko and Adrian scrambled in first, bloodied but breathing. Grilka carried a scorched Freija over one shoulder.

Once inside, Nefertari yanked the throttle and angled the ship into a hard escape vector. Below them, the Black Spire flashed erratically. Consoles exploded. Lights died. The web of Necra's coordination shattered silently.

They didn't stay to admire the view.

Aboard the Scorpion

The Scorpion stabilized in orbit. Inside, the team sat in silence, the low hum of engines beneath them.

Adrian exhaled. "That hub's offline. She won't be directing anyone through that system again."

Lilith nodded slowly. "We've severed her vision. Next, we target her voice."

Kimiko cleaned her blade in the corner, quiet. Grilka's grin was satisfied but faint.

Rainstorm turned from the console. "She's reeling now. This was precision. And it worked."

Lilith looked out the viewport, eyes still glowing faintly.

"One strike at a time," she said. "That's how we break her."

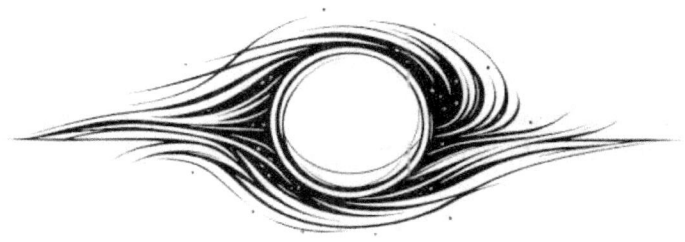

Chapter 50:

An Alliance of Light

Lilith stood at the Scorpion's central holotable, the flickering display still casting ethereal shadows across her face. The data chip had revealed a thousand routes, dozens of relay points, and too many battlefronts still burning across the quadrant. But in the quiet that followed their last mission, her eyes lingered on something else – a remote planetary system highlighted in soft violet.

"Zyntar," she murmured aloud.

Rainstorm turned to her and asked, "What's that?"

Lilith zoomed in. A lush, mineral-rich world orbiting a few parsecs beyond the Jaze system. High electromagnetic readings. Ancient defense tech. A series of local signal encryptions – small, but consistent.

"It's one of the few places Necra hasn't touched," Lilith said. "Their planetary defense tech shows them to be highly advanced."

Freija entered the room, scanning the glowing symbols. When she saw the name, her posture straightened. "Zyntar? You want to go there?"

"You know it?" Lilith asked, surprised.

Freija nodded slowly. "I do. I've never been there myself, but Icelandia has maintained peaceful relations with the Zyntarians for years. They keep mostly to themselves and are cautious around outsiders, especially tall ones. But they're brilliant. Their technology is elegant, their engineers unmatched. If we could earn their trust, we'd gain far more than warriors. We'd gain strategy, precision... hope."

Lilith gave a small nod. "Then we go."

"Freija was smiling ear to ear at the thought of new people joining the team." Then she said, "Let me fly us there."

Lilith replied, "Have at it."

Freija took over in the pilot's seat, and shortly after, they were dropping out of hyperspace. Nefertari was in the co-pilot's seat. The holographic display showed a small purple and green planet spinning slowly in the void. Its atmosphere shimmered with hues of violet and amber, marking it as unique compared to the barren wastelands they had seen before.

After waking from a nap Adrian asked, leaning against the frame of the cockpit door. "What is this place?"

"Zyntar," Freija replied, her tone serious for once. "It's home to the Zyntar, a race of purple-skinned people. They're small, around my height, and very insular. They don't trust outsiders... especially taller ones." She gave Adrian and Lilith a pointed glance.

Adrian smirked. "Guess I'll sit this one out, huh?"

Lilith folded her arms, her fiery eyes scanning the planet. "They're rebels, fighting against Necra's forces. If we can convince them to work with us, it could turn the tide."

Freija shrugged. "Good luck with that. They're terrified of anyone over five-two."

Adrian laughed. "Well, you're their perfect diplomat, Freija. Just don't let them see Lilith or Grilka... they might faint."

Lilith ignored the joke, turning to Freija. "You'll take the lead. Nefertari and Rainstorm will back you up. Kimiko can stay close but out of sight until needed. I'll stay on the ship for now, but if anything goes wrong, I'll step in."

Freija nodded, adjusting her icy-blue wings. "Understood. Let's hope they don't try to shoot first."

The Scorpion descended toward the planet, its engines humming softly. As they approached a sprawling compound hidden within the dense jungle canopy, Freija glanced over her shoulder. "Wish me luck."

Adrian grinned. "Luck? You've got this, ice queen."

Freija smiled faintly as she exited the cockpit, Rainstorm and Nefertari following close behind. The jungle seemed to come alive as they stepped out of the ship, its vibrant colors and strange noises both beautiful and unsettling.

The trio approached the edge of the compound, the towering canopy above filtering golden sunlight across the vibrant terrain. Freija glanced up at Nefertari and Rainstorm, her voice steady but firm. "Remember, I'm the lead here. These people are afraid of taller beings. Don't speak unless spoken to and let me do the talking."

Rainstorm gave a faint nod, adjusting the ceremonial sash she wore as part of her disguise. "Got it, boss."

Nefertari, whose height made her stand out even more, smirked faintly. "As you wish, commander. Just don't let them mistake your wings for weapons."

Freija shook her head slightly. "Thanks for the vote of confidence." She turned toward the gates of the compound, raising her hand in a non-threatening gesture. "We're here to speak with your leader. We have a mutual interest in defeating Necra."

The gates creaked open, revealing several Zyntarian guards, their purple skin shimmering under the sunlight of their red sun. Their wide eyes darted nervously between Nefertari and Rainstorm before settling on Freija, who matched their stature. One of them, a female guard with ornate markings on her face, stepped forward. "State your purpose."

Freija straightened, her icy wings folding neatly against her back. "We're here to offer a partnership. Your fight against Necra is our fight as well. Let us speak with your commander."

The guard hesitated, glancing back at her companions before nodding. "Follow me. But know this – if your intentions are false, you will not leave Zyntar alive."

Freija inclined her head. "Understood."

As they followed the guard through the compound, Nefertari leaned down slightly, whispering to Freija. "Charming place. Let's hope they don't decide to turn on us before we even meet their leader."

Freija shot her a look. "Just stick to the plan."

The compound was a blend of natural beauty and utilitarian design. Structures made of vibrant, polished wood were interwoven with the jungle, almost as if grown rather than built. Freija couldn't help but admire the ingenuity, though she remained focused on the task at hand.

Finally, they were led into a large chamber where a small figure sat on an elevated platform. The Zyntar admiral of military forces, clad in intricate armor of deep violet and gold, watched them with sharp, calculating eyes. Freija stepped forward, bowing slightly. "Admiral, my name is Freija. We've come to discuss an alliance against Necra."

The admiral's gaze flicked over Freija, then toward Nefertari and Rainstorm, who were about three to five inches taller. "Your companions are... tall," he said, his tone cautious.

Freija smiled faintly. "They are princesses from a planet across the realm called Earth. Rainstorm is the princess of the Navajo Nation, a powerful tribal society. Nefertari is the chantress – it's like a princess – of an ancient Egyptian kingdom, renowned for its regalness, strength, and wisdom." Both women nod respectfully as they are called out. "Their titles and courage reflect their roles as protectors of their people."

The admiral's eyes narrowed as he leaned forward. "And what assurances do we have that you will not turn on us once our usefulness is exhausted? And why would royalty align themselves with a cause so distant from their own kingdoms?"

Freija held his gaze, her tone steady and earnest. "You have my word and my actions. I have fought against Necra's forces, and my people have suffered because of her. If we do not unite, none of us will survive."

The admiral's gaze softened slightly but remained skeptical. "You speak with conviction, but words are easy. What proof do you bring of your deeds?"

ADMIRAL ILYAN

Rainstorm stepped forward cautiously, producing a

holotablet to show him of their recent battles against Necra's forces. Nefertari lowered her head and crossed her arms respectfully as Freija activated the recording. Images of their team's daring exploits flickered in the chamber, showing their destruction of enemy outposts and rescue of enslaved populations.

The room fell silent as the recording ended. The admiral's calculating expression turned thoughtful. "You are brave. But bravery does not always equal wisdom. Tell me this, Freija: why should we risk our people to aid you when we are already barely holding our own ground?"

Freija's icy-blue eyes hardened with determination. "Because Necra's reach will not stop here. Even if you survive today, she will come again, stronger and more relentless. Alone, your people will fall. But with us, you stand a better chance. Together, we are stronger. And my companions understand the cost of protecting their people and have chosen to fight not just for their worlds but for all free planets threatened by Necra."

The admiral was silent for a long moment before nodding slowly. "You speak with the wisdom of one who understands loss. Very well. I will consider your proposal. For now, you are welcome in our compound. But do not break our trust."

Freija bowed slightly, folding one hand across a loose fist. "Thank you, Admiral. You won't regret this."

A New Alliance

Freija exited the chamber with Nefertari and Rainstorm following close behind. As soon as they were out of earshot of the Zyntar guards, Nefertari leaned down, a teasing smirk on her face. "Princess of an ancient Egyptian kingdom, huh? Didn't know you were so creative."

Freija shot her a sideways glance but didn't lose her stride. "It worked, didn't it? Besides, it's not entirely a lie. You carry yourself like royalty, and you are a chantress."

Rainstorm chuckled softly "And I suppose calling me a princess wasn't too far off either? You're lucky I find that amusing."

Freija grinned briefly. "You're both warriors and leaders. That's all the truth I needed."

They approached the gates of the compound, where the jungle once again loomed before them. The guards nodded curtly, allowing them to pass without issue. The trio made their way back to the Scorpion, their steps quick but calm, not wanting to show any unnecessary haste.

Inside the Scorpion, Adrian was lounging near the entrance to the cockpit, his arms crossed as he watched them board. "Well? Did they throw you in purple jail, or did you charm them into submission?"

Freija ignored the sarcasm and turned to Lilith, who was waiting near the holomap display. "The commander has agreed to consider an alliance. He's cautious but receptive. I think we made a solid impression."

Lilith nodded, her fiery eyes reflecting both relief and determination. "Good work, Freija. The Zyntar will be an invaluable ally if we can secure their trust. For now, let's regroup and plan our next steps."

Adrian raised a hand mockingly. "Do these plans involve me getting some kind of purple diplomatic immunity? I'd like to avoid being shot at by tiny purple people."

Rainstorm rolled her eyes as she moved toward the galley. "You'd better hope they don't see your height as a threat when we go back."

Freija smirked as she sat down at the table. "Let's just say they might like me a little more than you. But don't worry, flyboy. You've got us to vouch for you."

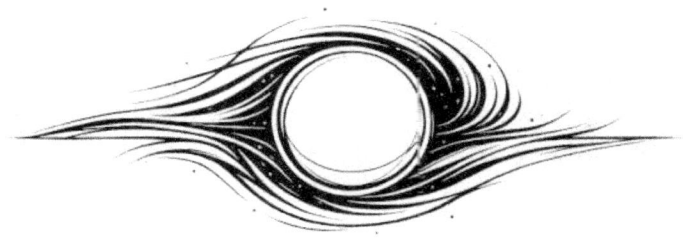

Chapter 51:

Joining Forces

The Zyntarian War Hall was unlike anything the Crimson Alliance had seen. Its architecture was a harmony of nature and technology – sunlight filtered through translucent ceiling vines, casting refracted light across the polished obsidian floor, while crystalline panels floated in midair, responding to Admiral Ilyan's gestures like waves responding to the wind.

Lilith stood at the center of the circular room, flanked by her team. Across from her stood Admiral Ilyan, clad in ceremonial violet and gold armor, his stature small but commanding. At his side stood Captain Varek, and behind him, his two elite officers – Commander Tarin, a sharp-eyed tactician with a scarred jawline, and Lieutenant Commander Zela, a quiet but deadly figure.

"We are ready to proceed," Ilyan said, his voice crisp but respectful. "You've earned our trust. What is your proposal?"

Lilith nodded and activated the holotablet. A full schematic of Necra's eastern supply hub unfurled before them – a glowing red sprawl of energy conduits, defense towers, and internal silos.

"This is a pivotal outpost," Lilith began. "A

command relay and munitions warehouse disguised as a resupply depot. Take it out, and we sever one of Necra's oldest arteries." She glanced around the table. "But we don't just destroy. We infiltrate, disable, and extract information. We dismantle her from the inside out."

She zoomed in on four key sectors.

Team Alpha – Infiltration and Communications Disruption

"Adrian and Kimiko will lead this team. Their mission is to infiltrate the outer communications hub, bypass security systems, and download movement logs for all recent off-world deployments."

Adrian smirked and leaned on the table. "Tight corridors, disruptor traps, high-value secrets. My kind of party."

Kimiko gave a short nod, her expression unreadable. "We won't be seen."

Team Beta – Armory Assault

"Captain Varek, Tarin, and Zela will target the internal armory vaults. They're to gather intel on heavy weapons logistics, confiscate high-yield explosives, and disable anything that can be used against us in future engagements."

Varek gave a short salute. "We'll clean house and leave nothing salvageable."

Tarin grinned. "I've been waiting to crack one of Necra's vaults since this war started."

Team Charlie – Supply Disruption and Evac Readiness

"Nefertari, Freija, and Grilka will monitor troop movements from a hidden drop point outside the base's main perimeter. Their task is to intercept, delay, or reroute any transport vehicles leaving the site, and sabotage the food and medical convoys. Should the need arise, they will provide emergency extraction support for any compromised teams."

Grilka rolled her shoulder with a satisfied grin. "Sabotaging supply lines is even better than smashing faces. We'll get it done."

Freija adjusted her wing brace quietly. "We'll move as shadows."

Team Delta – Leadership Extraction and Sabotage

"Rainstorm and I will make entry through the sub-tunnels beneath the command hall," Lilith said. "We believe a high-ranking lieutenant of Necra's remains stationed at this facility. We extract him. If we can't... we make sure he doesn't talk to anyone again."

Rainstorm stepped forward, expression calm. "I've studied the terrain. We'll adapt on the fly and make sure they don't see us coming or leaving."

Admiral Ilyan studied the holomap, then looked at Varek. "Captain, your team is prepared?"

Varek nodded. "We're ready."

Ilyan turned to Lilith. "You've coordinated this well. But remember, the strength of an alliance is not in its plan, but in its execution. Maintain comms. Get in, get out. No heroics unless necessary."

Lilith's voice was even. "Understood, Sir."

Adrian muttered under his breath, "We'll try to keep the heroics under control. No promises."

Freija smirked and Grilka elbowed him lightly. "For once, follow the plan, flyboy."

Nefertari stepped forward. "We'll report in every thirty minutes. Each team has an encoded channel. If any go dark, fallback begins immediately."

Ilyan gave a sharp nod. "You have Zyntar's full support. Strike swiftly and let them see the shadows move before they even hear your name."

The lights dimmed slightly as the holomap shut down. Lilith turned to her team. "Let's move."

One by one, the four strike teams filtered out of the War Hall into the jungle sunlight beyond.

Their ships waited at the ready. Gear had been loaded. Timers had been synchronized.

The Alliance had been formed.

Now, it was time to act.

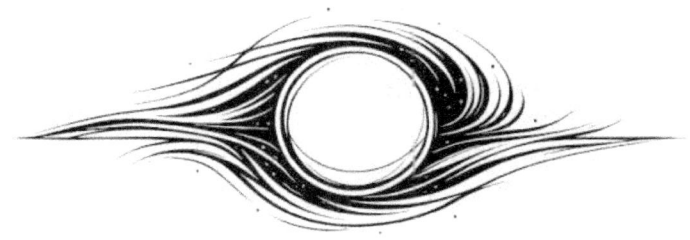

Chapter 52:

Ghosts in the Signal

Ten members of the Crimson Alliance – along with three ships visible in the distance – huddled in a secluded rendezvous point not far from the enemy outpost. Hidden beneath dense foliage and rocky outcroppings on a barren plateau, the team's tension was palpable yet united. The Scorpion, the Starlight Shadow, and the Astrell, Varek's ship, were parked in the background, their silhouettes barely discernible under the starry sky.

Lilith stepped forward and, with a commanding tone that belied the warmth in her eyes, addressed the assembled team. "Everyone, tonight we stand on the edge of destiny. Our mission is clear: we strike at the heart of Necra's operations and prove to every world that our alliance is unbreakable. May fortune… and your skills… guide you."

A ripple of nods and murmurs of resolve passed through the group. With a final round of encouraging looks and a few whispered jokes exchanged between teammates, the teams prepared to depart. The ground squad dispersed in four coordinated groups while Rainstorm and Lilith remained behind for their specialized insertion. Before splitting up, Lilith's gaze swept over the team one last time. "Stay sharp. Trust in your training. We'll reconvene at the rendezvous point once your objectives are complete."

Nightfall in the Communications Sector

Adrian crouched low beside a jagged stone ridge, the darkened terrain below stretching out in hushed patterns of shadow and metallic glint. Beside him, Kimiko adjusted the straps on her black satchel, her katana sheaths pressed tight to her back, barely a whisper in the darkness.

The communications hub stood like a hunched beast, low to the ground but bristling with transmitters and blinking antennae. Spotlights occasionally swept the perimeter, cutting harsh circles into the night. No walls. No gates. Just disruptor trip fields and patrolling drones… and a whole lot of problems.

Adrian tapped his earpiece. "Alpha, in position."

Kimiko replied softly, "Confirmed. Beginning infiltration." She barely moved her lips, but her words were clear, calm, and razor focused.

They slid down the ridge in silence, gravel muted by thin, padded boots. Adrian kept his disruptor holstered, opting for a small portable hacking spike he cradled like a dagger. Kimiko drew no weapons. Her presence alone was a blade.

At the outer edge of the compound, they halted behind a pile of discarded supply crates. A trip field shimmered faintly just ahead, its pulse invisible to the naked eye but clear through their visors.

Adrian raised the hacking spike. "Time me."

"Eighteen seconds," Kimiko whispered.

He grinned and plunged the device into the exposed access panel, fingers flying over the embedded keypad. Beads of sweat began to form on his forehead as static whined in his comm. The spike chirped once, then the shimmer faded.

"Seventeen-point-eight," Kimiko said, already moving.

They crossed the invisible boundary in tandem and ducked beneath a satellite dish humming with encoded pulses. The signal tower loomed nearby – a squat, multi-level structure with glassy walls, glowing faintly from within.

Adrian held up a hand. "Two guards. South-facing entrance. Patrol pattern. I distract; you disarm?"

Kimiko vanished into the shadows without answering.

Adrian sighed. "I'll take that as a yes."

He rolled a small holo-flare from his pack and lobbed it toward the opposite corner. It popped with a faint hiss, spilling an iridescent mist across the gravel. Both guards perked up, one raising a scanner.

"What is that?" one muttered, stepping away from his post.

The other turned, too late. A soft thud echoed, followed by the dull slump of a body hitting the ground. The second guard spun only to find Kimiko behind him. She pressed two fingers to his neck and he collapsed, unconscious.

Adrian winced. "You know, for once, I'd like to actually see how you do that."

Kimiko simply replied, "No, you wouldn't."

Inside the Tower

The interior of the communications hub pulsed with faint green light. Dozens of consoles blinked in methodical rhythms, their hum muffled by acoustic shielding. Adrian crouched at the primary data terminal, plugging in a second spike while Kimiko stood watch near the stairwell.

"Necra's got this place wired tighter than a mercenary's budget," Adrian muttered. "This is going to take longer than expected."

"You have four minutes," Kimiko replied. "That's when the next patrol cycle returns."

"Four minutes?" Adrian scowled. "You trying to make this exciting, aren't you?"

A soft chirp indicated the terminal was accessing internal logs. He keyed in the encryption from the data chip Lilith had given him, and one by one, secure files began to filter through his screen.

"Holy stars… She's been mapping civilian escape routes from four occupied planets. Targeting them for sabotage. Transport convoys, med ships, and refugee vessels. It's not just military…"

Kimiko's voice cut in. "Adrian. Movement. Above us."

She tilted her head toward a steel catwalk spanning the second floor. Two boots clanked softly across the mesh.

Adrian hit a button to suspend the download. "Can't risk corrupting the files. Keep them busy."

Kimiko didn't answer. She was already gone.

A shadow dropped from the catwalk a moment later – silent, efficient, and brutal. The soldier didn't even scream as Kimiko wrapped an arm around his throat and brought him down in complete silence. She lowered him gently, then glanced toward Adrian. "Continue."

Adrian blinked. "I swear you're half ghost."

"Focus," she said simply.

The Data and the Exit

The terminal gave a final chime. "Done," Adrian said. "Full logs, three-month routing records, satellite tags, encryption keys. We've got enough to cripple her entire logistics arm."

"Then we go," Kimiko said.

They backtracked swiftly, avoiding a new patrol near the west wing. As they slipped into the open again, the comms tower flashed with a low red light – an alert. One of the unconscious guards had been discovered.

"Time's up," Adrian said.

They sprinted for the outer perimeter. A spotlight swept their path, but Adrian lobbed an anti-thermal grenade that exploded in a bloom of heat signatures in every direction. Alarms erupted, but their real escape was already underway.

From above, the Starlight Shadow dropped fast – engines glowing in near-silent descent. Adrian keyed his wrist beacon.

The cargo hatch opened mid-air, and Kimiko leapt cleanly into the cargo hold, flipping backward and landing in a crouch. Adrian followed a half-second later, rolling to his feet as the hatch sealed behind them.

"Team Alpha to command," Adrian panted into the comms. "Package secured. Exfil complete. Returning to rendezvous."

"Copy that," came Nefertari's voice. "Team Charlie is in motion. Team Beta just reported engagement near the vault sector. Stand by."

Kimiko moved to the side console and slid the data spike into a secure lockbox.

Adrian slumped into the pilot's seat and finally grinned. "Well. That was the quietest near-death mission I've ever had."

Kimiko didn't respond. But for just a moment… she smiled.

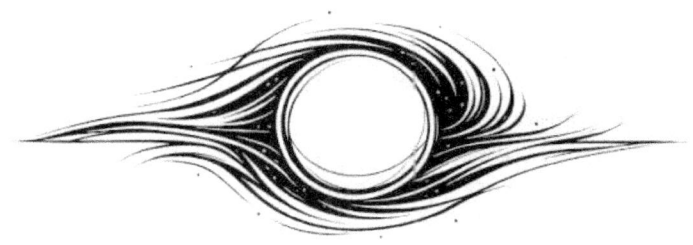

Chapter 53:

Team Beta – Explosives and Evasion

Under the cloak of darkness, Team Beta crept toward the enemy armory – a nondescript, fortified building amid the sprawling stronghold. Varek led the way, his lean purple-skinned form moving with military precision. Alongside him were his two trusted teammates: the rugged Tarin and the sharp-eyed Zela. Their mission was clear: infiltrate the armory without a single shot fired, download the manifests of armory shipments, and liberate every explosive device and round they could get their hands on. In a plan designed for stealth and minimal violence, every move was calculated.

Varek's low voice crackled through their comm, "Remember, we're ghosts tonight. Silence and speed. Tarin, Zela – stick together."

Tarin grunted, his eyes glinting with determination, while Zela adjusted her grip on her compact sidearm. They approached a narrow service door at the armory's rear, its lock humming softly under a thin layer of dust.

Inside, the corridor was dimly lit and nearly empty. Varek guided the team swiftly along the hallway. Their footsteps were muffled by scattered crates, and they paused at intervals to disable any sensor that dared blink to life. Varek produced a slim hacking tool from his belt and bypassed the security system in mere seconds. "Doors unlocked. In and out, quietly," he whispered.

The armory's inner sanctum was a treasure trove of military supplies – rows of ammunition, neatly stacked explosive charges, and a database terminal blinking softly in the far corner. Zela's eyes lit up as she surveyed the neatly arranged arsenal. "This is our jackpot," she murmured, her voice barely audible.

CAPTAIN VAREK

Varek split up the tasks: he and Zela would extract and download the digital manifests from the terminal, while Tarin was to secure as many physical explosives and ammo as possible into separate three large bags. The plan was designed for speed and stealth, so every second counted

After Varek and Zela downloaded the data, they began to place explosives in critical locations around the armory setting the time for two hours in advance ensuring when everything explodes that they are far gone.

COMMANDER TARIN

In the meantime, Tarin methodically began to fill the first bag, tucking in every explosive charge and round he could find, ensuring it was packed tight. The bag soon reached its weight limit, bulging with carefully organized munitions and ammo. With a satisfied grunt, he moved to a nearby stack of crates where a second bag awaited. He repeated the process with practiced efficiency, stuffing it until it too was filled to capacity.

LT COMMANDER ZELA

Then, as he glanced around, Tarin's keen eyes caught sight of a trove of additional items in the distance that he hadn't anticipated – rare explosive devices, high-caliber rounds, and even some advanced detonators that he'd been reluctant to leave behind. His heart raced at the thought of the extra firepower, and without hesitation, he edged toward the far side of the armory. There, hidden behind a row of unmarked storage boxes, lay a small supply of these valuable extras.

He set down his first two heavy bags and moved deeper into the armory with his third bag, eager to secure every last piece of equipment. He said over the comms, "The first two bags are ready to go."

Varek said softly over the comms, "Manifest download is complete. Setting charges now."

Carefully, he began to fill the third bag, his gloved hands moving swiftly as he retrieved the additional items. The quiet thrill of success surged through him until a distant sound made him freeze.

A faint clatter echoed down the corridor – a patrol was entering. Tarin's pulse quickened; his instinct screamed that this was no ordinary shuffle of footsteps. He paused, holding his breath, as the muffled voices of guards grew steadily louder in the background. His third bag was still only half-full, the extra supplies scattered around him on the cold floor.

In that suspended moment, Tarin's mind raced. The additional items, his secret stash of explosives and ammo, were now a liability if he was discovered. He quickly stuffed the remaining gear into the third bag, ensuring it was as inconspicuous as possible. His eyes darted to the door as the patrol rounded the corner, their presence cutting through the silence like a knife.

"Team Beta, status?" Varek's voice crackled softly over the comm, unaware of the tension building behind Tarin's back.

Tarin's fingers trembled as he clutched the heavy bag. "I'm... I'm almost done here. Just securing the last of it," he whispered urgently into his comm, his voice low and edged with worry.

Before he could finish, the patrol's footsteps grew nearer, and he caught a glimpse of a guard's silhouette through a gap in the doorway. The guards were armed and alert, moving methodically along the corridor. Tarin's heart pounded as he realized he'd inadvertently isolated himself from his team.

With adrenaline surging, Tarin pressed himself flat against the wall, the third bag clutched tightly in his arms. His mind raced – he had to find another exit or risk being caught in the act. He scanned the dimly lit room for a secondary door or a maintenance corridor that might offer a discreet escape.

The armory was cluttered, but his eyes locked onto a narrow side door partially hidden behind a row of supply racks. Silently, he edged toward it, every footstep measured and light. His hands shook as he fumbled with the handle, praying that it wouldn't betray his position with a creak.

At that moment, the patrol's voices echoed in the hallway, their presence imminent. With a final, quiet click, the door opened, and Tarin slipped through into the maintenance passage beyond. He paused in the shadowy corridor, heart hammering as he listened to the guards' footsteps approach the armory once more.

Determined, Tarin activated his comm, his voice barely above a whisper: "This is Tarin. I'm separated. Need extraction ASAP." The urgency in his tone was unmistakable.

A tense silence followed before Varek's reassuring voice crackled back: "Copy that, Tarin. Hold your position; extraction incoming."

The suspense of the moment was palpable as Tarin waited in the narrow corridor, clutching his third bag full of salvaged explosives and ammo, now the culmination of his meticulous gathering. He knew that every second he delayed increased his risk, but he also trusted that his team would come through. In the distance, the sound of approaching guards faded as they were diverted by a distraction set up by Varek's squad.

Finally, after what seemed like an eternity, the

extraction signal arrived. Adrian's fighter descended silently over the compound, its engines humming as it prepared to land. Tarin took a deep breath, relieved that his risky maneuver had paid off – albeit with the lingering sting of his greed and the near miss with the patrol.

Within moments, Adrian's ramp lowered near Tarin's position. Tarin quickly gathered his gear and sprinted toward the extraction point, his every step echoing with tension and relief. Adrian, already bracing for pick-up, secured Tarin aboard his fighter. With Kimiko in the co-pilot's seat, Tarin would have to hold up in the cramped sleeping quarters. He put the extra gear on the other bed.

As the fighter ascended and rejoined the main rendezvous, Tarin's tense expression softened just a bit when he caught Adrian's concerned yet amused glance through the cockpit window. "Next time, leave nothing behind," Adrian teased, his tone a blend of reprimand and camaraderie.

Tarin grinned sheepishly, nodding. "I guess I learned that the hard way."

In the midst of the extraction, Varek and Zela regrouped with their team, their mission in the armory successful despite the brief scare. Varek's leadership and Zela's marksmanship had ensured that the vital data and explosive assets were secured. Even though Tarin had momentarily separated from them, the extraction was a success, reinforcing the unity and resilience of Team Beta and the two different teams acting together when needed.

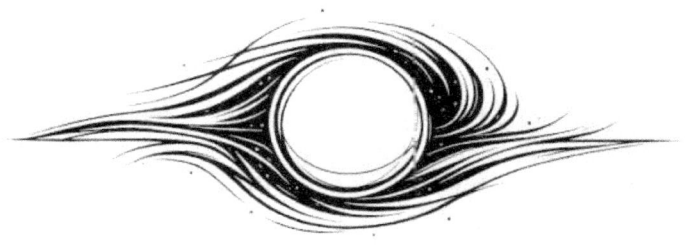

Chapter 54:

Team Charlie – Sabotage in the Shadows

Outside the towering walls of Necra's eastern outpost, the night was unnaturally quiet. Wisps of fog drifted along the forest floor, swirling around tree roots and the occasional twisted scrap of war debris. Team Charlie moved like ghosts through the overgrowth, silent but focused – three warriors with wildly different strengths, unified by a shared mission: cut off the outpost's lifeblood before it could feed the war machine inside.

Grilka led the trio, massive shoulders hunched as she cleared a path with quiet precision. Freija, her icy wings tightly folded behind her, followed close behind, light on her feet and constantly scanning the treetops for sentry drones. Nefertari brought up the rear, a rifle slung across her back and her long, regal strides precise and deliberate. The faint glow from her handheld tracker illuminated pulsing energy blips ahead – supply transports, timed like clockwork.

"There," Nefertari whispered, tapping the display. "A convoy moves along the ridge path every forty minutes. We'll intercept the next one before it reaches the perimeter gate."

Grilka cracked her knuckles, her grin faintly visible in the darkness. "It's been too long since I tossed a truck off a cliff."

"Try not to enjoy it too much," Freija said softly, pulling a small frost canister from her belt. "This has to look like a systems malfunction. We don't want to alert the base until we're long gone."

They positioned themselves on a cliffside overlook, where vines grew thick and the sound of distant engines began to hum in the air.

"Ten minutes," Nefertari said. "Let's prep."

Grilka moved to the ridge's edge, picking two large boulders and carefully moving them to the edge of a tall embankment. "One push, the whole convoy tumbles."

Freija laid frost charges beneath a bridge strut a few meters down the path. "If the boulders fail, these will freeze the supports and shatter the bridge as soon as they cross. We only get one shot."

Nefertari crouched low, pulling a field spike from her satchel. She drove it into the ground, syncing it to Adrian's atmospheric comms array. "This will scramble their outbound transmissions for five minutes once the trap is sprung. Just enough time to make it look like equipment failure."

The convoy approached – three large hover haulers glowing with internal light, followed by two scout bikes. Onboard, crates marked with Necra's symbol glinted under the search beams: food rations, power cores, medical supplies. Grilka's eyes narrowed.

"On my mark," she whispered. "Three... two..."

The bikes passed. The first truck reached the bend. Grilka shoved the first boulder. It tumbled silently at first, then crashed downward with explosive force – striking the truck square in its side. The vehicle jerked, spun, and toppled over the cliff edge.

The second driver swerved.

Too late.

Freija triggered the frost charges. The air screamed with cold as the bridge beneath truck two flash-froze and then collapsed into sparkling shards. Both vehicles went down in a cascade of ice and fire.

"Third truck's reversing!" Nefertari called out, already raising her rifle.

"No need," Grilka muttered. She bolted forward, massive legs carrying her like a cannonball. With one leap, she landed on the retreating truck's hood, punched through the windshield, and yanked the driver out with one hand.

"Truck secure," she grunted. "Cargo intact. Now what?"

Freija landed beside her, frost forming at her boots. "Rig it to explode if they come looking. We've got enough proof of sabotage now."

Nefertari moved to the rear compartment, scanning the crates. "Food and water. This will hurt them. But let's leave a message."

She pulled a Crimson Alliance emblem from her belt – a red dagger in a circle – and placed it atop the shattered crate pile.

Freija raised an eyebrow. "Bold."

"We need Necra's officers questioning where their grip ends," Nefertari replied. "Doubt can win battles too."

They melted back into the forest, moving toward the secondary site – a hidden junction terminal that controlled outbound drone patrols and regional energy distribution.

Freija arrived first, disabling the motion sensors with a flick of her frost dagger. Grilka yanked off the panel cover and shoved her entire hand into the conduit, twisting wires until sparks spat from the core. Nefertari planted a virus injector into the control port and activated a twenty-minute loop of static drone signals – buying time for the others.

"We've cut the supplies and cloaked their comms," Nefertari said. "They won't know what's hit them until it's too late."

"Then let's disappear," Freija said, wings unfurling as she took to the air.

Grilka and Nefertari followed close behind, navigating a hidden escape route up the rocky ravine and toward their rendezvous point on the Scorpion's north ridge.

They arrived just as the horizon began to glow faintly. The mission had taken less than two hours, but its impact would echo across the battlefield.

Freija leaned against the hull, eyes scanning the rising light.

Grilka dropped her gear with a thud and muttered, "Next time, let's hit a munitions depot. Feels more satisfying."

Nefertari allowed a faint smile as she keyed into the encrypted channel. "Team Charlie reporting in. Objective complete. No casualties."

Lilith's voice came back immediately. "Understood. Rendezvous confirmed. Alpha and Beta are already complete. We'll wait for Delta's signal, then exfil together."

Freija closed her eyes briefly. "Three teams down, one to go."

In the hush that followed, none of them spoke.

The war still raged.

But tonight, the shadows had struck first.

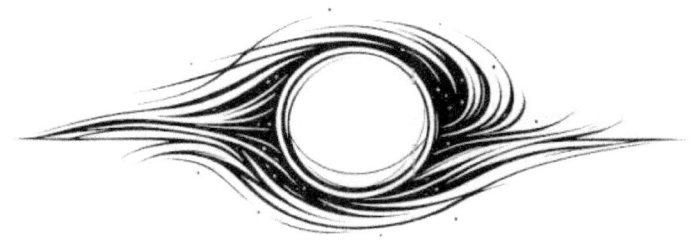

Chapter 55:

Team Delta – Close Call in the Shadows

Lilith and Rainstorm moved in tandem, stepping over flickering power conduits and ducking low-hanging cables. The air was thick with static, and the soft hum of active servers echoed through the stone-and-metal belly of the outpost.

"We're close," Rainstorm whispered, pointing to a locked control hatch ahead. "Command uplink chamber should be just beyond this."

Lilith nodded and stepped forward. Her fire-forged blades crackled with latent energy. "Stay alert. Necra's lieutenants aren't known for subtlety."

The two rounded a corner and walked straight into a trap.

From above, a flash grenade dropped between them, exploding with a blinding hiss. Lilith's vision blurred. Motion sensors flared inside her gauntlet – five hostiles. Rainstorm was already moving, deflecting incoming fire with one tomahawk as she threw the other down the hall. A scream followed.

Lilith spun, blocking a strike from a heavy soldier

clad in reinforced armor. His blade sparked against hers, sending shockwaves up her arm. She parried, ducked, and countered – her fiery blade slicing deep across his chest.

But she didn't see the second attacker coming from behind.

A lean, fast-moving soldier had flanked them in the chaos, slipping between fire-scorched pipes with a shock-staff aimed at Lilith's spine. Her senses were dulled just enough that she didn't hear his footsteps over the thrum of battle.

Rainstorm did.

From across the corridor, she pivoted mid-strike, hurled her tomahawk in a flat arc, and sprinted after it. The weapon buried itself in the man's side just as he lunged. He staggered but didn't fall.

He raised his staff again.

Rainstorm didn't hesitate. She surged forward, tackling him into the wall with such force that both of them collapsed. Her blade flashed… and it was over.

Lilith turned sharply, only now realizing how close she had come to death.

She stared at the fallen attacker, then at Rainstorm, who stood slowly, blood trickling from her lip, her shoulders heaving.

"You okay?" Rainstorm asked, brushing dust from her chest plate.

Lilith didn't answer immediately. She looked down at the ground where her own shadow stretched – and remembered the moment in the Astral Realm when the beings had told her: *Your purpose is not yet finished.*

But that didn't mean that she was immortal.

She approached Rainstorm and laid a hand on her shoulder.

"You saved my life," Lilith said, her voice quieter than usual. "I won't forget that."

Rainstorm gave a slight shrug. "We watch each

other's backs. That's what we do."

"No," Lilith said firmly. "That was more than instinct. That was a choice. And I'm still here because of it."

They stood in silence for a breath. Then Lilith glanced toward the corridor ahead.

"Let's finish this."

They reached the command sub-chamber shortly after – a smaller, reinforced office nested beneath the main stronghold. Inside, they found what they were looking for: crates of encrypted tablets, a minor lieutenant bleeding from a leg wound, and a digital node linked to a supply chain management AI.

Lilith interrogated the officer quickly and without cruelty. The man cracked faster than expected, offering up internal supply schedules, fallback routes, and confirmation that Necra was reassigning assets away from the outer colonies. With Rainstorm's help, they extracted the data node and disabled its beacon.

Alarms sounded faintly in the distance probably triggered by one of the other teams. It was time to go.

As they retraced their steps, the red emergency lights flared brighter. Shouts echoed from above. Rainstorm covered the rear while Lilith led the way, occasionally glancing back at her teammate with an expression more grateful than she could voice.

When they reached the extraction zone and the Scorpion swooped in low. The cargo ramp opened with a familiar hiss. Grilka was at the edge, disruptor drawn, watching for enemies. Freija waved them forward from the inside.

"Move!" she shouted. "We've got five seconds!"

Lilith and Rainstorm sprinted the final meters. Blaster fire rained overhead, but Nefertari had the ship rotating to shield the retreat. The ramp closed just as a volley of plasma exploded against the ridge.

Inside, Lilith collapsed against the wall, catching her

breath. Rainstorm dropped beside her, silent but alert.

The others crowded in moments later – Adrian and Kimiko first, both slightly battered. Grilka slammed the internal door shut.

"Everyone's back," Nefertari called from the cockpit. "We're clear."

Rainstorm looked over at Lilith. "Still think you're invincible?"

Lilith chuckled softly, pain flaring at her ribs. "Not anymore."

She turned toward the rest of the team, who were now gathering in the Scorpion's lounging area, adrenaline giving way to fatigue. But for now, they had succeeded.

Lilith glanced back at Rainstorm once more.

"One day," she said, "I hope I return the favor."

Rainstorm smirked. "You just focus on staying alive."

And as the Scorpion ascended into the stars, streaking toward their next rendezvous, the crew of the Crimson Alliance began to feel something rare.

Balance.

Even in chaos.

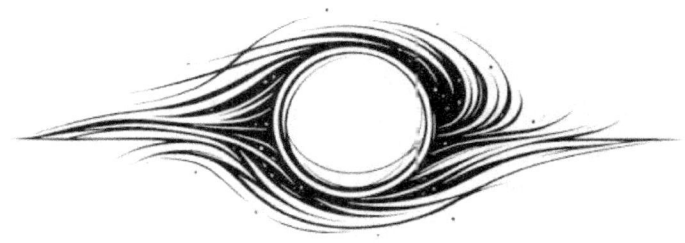

Chapter 56:

The Call Home

Varek sat in the dimly lit cockpit of his ship, which remained docked to the Scorpion via a secure airlock. The Zyntar vessel was small but agile, built for speed and maneuverability rather than brute force. The soft hum of the engines provided a steady background as he prepared his transmission.

The holographic interface flickered to life, the encrypted connection tracing its way back to the Zyntar home fleet. Moments later, a translucent image of Admiral Ilyan appeared before him. The admiral's deep purple skin was marked by years of experience, his piercing silver eyes scrutinizing Varek with keen intensity.

"Varek," Ilyan greeted, his voice steady but edged with expectation. "Report."

Varek took a breath. "The mission was a success. Our teams worked together without fault. Each objective was met, and the intel we gathered has revealed Necra's next move – she's mobilizing at Velyria."

Ilyan's expression darkened. "Velyria… That world has long been a strategic hold. If she is gathering her forces there, it means she's preparing for something far greater."

Varek nodded. "That's my assessment as well. But I

have to say, Admiral, I was skeptical of this alliance at first. The others are… well, taller than us, and their tactics are different. But they fight with discipline, intelligence, and precision. We complemented each other's strengths."

Ilyan studied him. "You are saying the alliance is worth committing to."

"I am." Varek straightened. "We've proven we can work as one. If we strike together, we may have a real chance at taking down Necra once and for all."

Ilyan was silent for a moment, considering. "If Necra is consolidating her forces, she will be expecting resistance. "We must act before she solidifies her position."

Varek leaned forward. "Can we count on reinforcements?"

Ilyan exhaled. "I will send word to the high council. If Velyria is the final battleground, we will send everything we can spare. An entire armada, if needed."

Varek felt a wave of relief. "That's what I was hoping to hear."

Ilyan offered a rare nod of approval. "You have done well, Varek. Continue to coordinate with the others. We will stand with you."

The transmission ended, leaving Varek momentarily lost in thought. He had always been a proud warrior of his people, but tonight, for the first time, he felt like he was part of something larger.

The fate of more than just his own people rested on this alliance.

A Moment Among Teammates

Stepping out of the cockpit, Varek made his way to the small common area of the ship where Zela and Tarin were already waiting. Zela sat cross-legged on a cushioned bench, absently polishing one of her long-range disruptors, while Tarin was leaning back against the wall, tossing a small explosive charge up and down in his palm.

"You look like someone just handed you a medal," Tarin commented with a smirk. "Good news from the admiral?"

Varek exhaled, his usual composed demeanor slipping just enough to show a hint of satisfaction. "We're getting reinforcements. Possibly an entire armada."

Zela let out a low whistle. "Now that's a rare thing. The council doesn't mobilize that kind of force unless it's serious."

"It is serious," Varek confirmed. "Velyria will be our battlefield. And if we don't take it, we may never get another chance."

Tarin gave a low chuckle. "Well, we'd better make sure we don't get squashed between all the giants on this team before then."

Zela smirked. "I'll admit, I wasn't too keen on working with taller species, but they proved themselves."

Varek crossed his arms. "Lilith commands respect. She leads with strategy, not just strength. Grilka? I've never seen someone handle ship weaponry like that. And Adrian – well, I'll give him credit, he knows how to get in and out of a situation without getting himself shot."

Tarin snorted. "He's also got a mouth on him. Never met someone so quick to joke while dodging plasma fire."

Zela smiles and shakes her head. "It's annoying, but effective. Keeps the tension down."

Varek leaned against the wall, a rare grin appearing. "And let's not forget Kimiko. She fights like a ghost – silent but deadly. And Freija? I swear, she's got the sharpest instincts I've ever seen."

Zela nodded in agreement. 'Still, it's a little strange, fighting alongside warriors who stand half a foot taller than us."

Tarin laughed. "Or in Lilith's case, nearly two feet taller."

They shared a chuckle, but there was an undeniable

sense of camaraderie forming between them. The tension that had existed at the start of this partnership was fading. The Zyntar had come into this alliance unsure, cautious of working with those unlike themselves. But now, they saw the value of their allies, not just as warriors, but as equals.

Tarin tossed the small explosive into the air once more before catching it with a grin. "Guess it's official. We're fighting with the giants."

Varek chuckled. "Yes, but at least this time, they're on our side."

Zela holstered her disruptor and stood. "Let's make sure we give Necra a reason to fear us *all* regardless if we are tall or short."

Varek nodded, his expression firm. "Agreed. Tomorrow, we plan for war."

The three warriors sat in silence for a moment, contemplating the battle ahead. The weight of the coming fight loomed over them, but for the first time, they faced it not just as Zyntar soldiers, but as part of something greater.

An alliance forged in battle.

And together, they would stand.

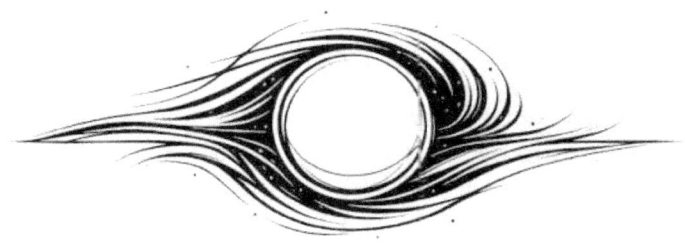

Chapter 57:

The Queen of Ashes

The war room deep within the volcanic fortress of Velyria pulsed with molten heat. Shadows danced across the obsidian walls, cast by veins of glowing lava that ran like arteries through the black stone. The chamber's centerpiece – a massive circular table carved from scorched iron – displayed a holomap of the region, though none dared speak as their queen stood before it, silent and seething.

Necra's eyes burned like twin embers, while fixating on the display. The projection of the sector flickered with updates – delay stations lost, comm-towers falling dark, outposts sending fragmented distress signals before cutting out entirely.

A single hooded messenger stood at the foot of the table, the hem of his cloak singed from the journey through the outer spires. His breath came in nervous gasps, sweat pooling at his brow despite the cool air enchantments meant to offset the room's heat.

"You said the relay at Otheon was impenetrable," Necra said at last, her voice low – calm, but with a deadly undercurrent. "You *assured me* it was beyond reach."

The messenger's voice cracked as he answered, "It… it was, my Queen. But we received word that… that several of our relay stations have gone silent. One by one. No survivors. No emergency beacons. It's as if they were dismantled from within."

From the far end of the chamber, General Valthar stepped forward. Massive and granite-skinned, his voice rumbled like distant thunder. "It wasn't sabotage. It was coordination. Targeted strikes. This wasn't a rebel skirmish… it was strategy."

Necra's gaze slid to him. "Are you suggesting someone has begun a campaign? *Against me?*"

Valthar bowed his head. "Not just someone. Multiple teams. Operating independently, yet striking with unified purpose. We suspect… the Crimson Alliance."

A sharp clink rang out as Necra's nails scraped across the metal surface of the table.

"They're scattered. Leaderless. I watched their forces fracture at Jaze." Her voice rose an octave, fury flaring. "How could they regroup under my nose?"

"They've grown quiet," came a new voice. General Serath, pale-skinned and armored in jagged red plating, leaned against a pillar of smoking basalt. "Too quiet. We dismissed it as retreat. But this – this is preparation. Retaliation."

Necra turned toward her. "And *you*, Serath. You were meant to monitor the sector. You oversaw the communication branches and satellite networks. How could this have escaped your notice?"

Serath stiffened. "Because they're not using our systems. Whatever they've done – it's outside of our grid. They're operating with stealth, precision… and new allies."

The word lingered in the air. *Allies.*

Necra's mind raced. She thought of the strange resistance cells that had been cropping up on the edges of her empire. Of the intercepted fragments of transmissions mentioning a species she didn't recognize. Zyntar?

No. Not just rebel cells. This was a bigger alliance.

Her blackened lips curled into a snarl.

"How many have we lost?"

The messenger flinched. "Four relay stations. Two intel hubs. One weapons depot in orbit around Korvax broke from its usual signal pattern – we believe it was compromised and purged. There are whispers that *a virus* is crawling through our systems, corrupting command pathways and rerouting control…"

Necra didn't wait for him to finish.

Her hand flashed forward – faster than any of them could react. In a blink, her nails pierced the messenger's chest. He gasped once, eyes wide in shock, before slumping forward onto the edge of the table.

"Enough whispers," she hissed, withdrawing her hand as the body hit the ground with a dull thud.

For a long moment, no one moved.

Then, Agramor stepped from the shadows. Towering, cloaked in warsteel, his eyes gleamed behind his helmet. "Let me lead the counter-strike."

Necra narrowed her eyes. "No. We do not strike blindly. That is what they want – to lure us out, spread our forces thin."

She turned back to the map. The flickering light of missing stations now formed a pattern.

"They think they can choke my command chain. Cut me off. Isolate me." Her voice grew cold, her anger razor-edged. "Then we'll show them what isolation truly is."

She glared at the three generals.

"Summon the Revenant Guard. Activate Protocol Abyss. We lock the systems down. Nothing leaves Velyria without my command."

The generals exchanged glances – this was a move of desperation, used only when Necra believed a siege imminent.

Valthar stepped forward. "And if they come here?"

Necra's eyes burned brighter. "Then they will know

what it means to face a Queen unchained."

She turned from the table, her cloak of scorched velvet billowing behind her.

"Let them come."

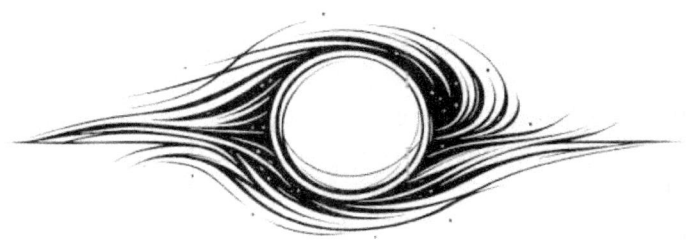

Chapter 58:

The Battle of Velyria Begins

The Scorpion hurtled through the void of space, its sleek form slicing through hyperspace like a blade through shadow. Inside, the atmosphere was tense – but focused. Every member of the team knew that once they dropped out of warp, there would be no room for hesitation. The battle for Velyria was no longer a distant goal. It had begun… and not as originally planned.

Lilith stood at the center of the living area, her fiery wings folded neatly behind her as she analyzed the glowing holomap of Velyria. Floating above the table, the projection displayed the enemy's reinforced fortifications, rerouted supply lines, and – most critically – the last three generals still loyal to Necra: General Serath, General Valthar, and General Agramor.

Adrian leaned against the wall with arms crossed. "So, we're taking out the generals before storming the fortress?"

Lilith nodded, her voice calm but commanding. "Necra has centralized her power on Velyria. But without her generals, she has no structure – no execution. We strike at her foundation first. Break that, and we leave her isolated."

Freija, perched casually on the corner of one of the seats, grinned. "So, what's the plan, fearless leader?"

Lilith adjusted the holomap, zooming in on troop movements and patrol arcs. "Each general controls a major segment of Velyria's defense. Serath oversees the stronghold's security grid. Valthar commands ground outposts and forward battalions. Agramor's securing reinforcements – mercenaries, fringe systems, unknown assets. If we take them down quickly, the rest of the structure collapses." Nefertari's arms were folded across her chest, her voice measured. "Divide and conquer. Logical. Who do we hit first?"

Lilith tapped a pulsing marker – an armored convoy cutting across a narrow ravine. "Serath. She's en route between strongholds. Mobile. Vulnerable. If we intercept before she reaches the command center, she falls with minimal resistance."

Kimiko narrowed her eyes. "And once she's down?"

"Valthar is next," Lilith replied. "He's proud. He won't go into hiding or retreat – he'll dig in. That makes him predictable. We take him before he fortifies."

Adrian raised an eyebrow. "And Agramor?"

Lilith's expression darkened. "He's the most dangerous of the three. If he senses the others are gone, he might flee – or retaliate with everything he has. Either way…" Her voice lowered. "We finish what was started."

The words hung in the air.

Adrian glanced toward her, his usual sarcasm falling away. "You've fought him before, haven't you?"

Lilith didn't answer immediately. Her eyes were fixed on the holomap, but the fire behind them flickered – not with anger, but with memory. After a pause, she gave a single nod.

"He's the one who killed you," Rainstorm said gently. It wasn't a question.

Grilka tensed at the admission, clenching her jaw.

"Then he doesn't walk away from this one."

Freija stepped closer, her voice soft but resolute. "You don't have to face him alone this time. We're with you. All the way."

Kimiko gave a quiet nod of solidarity. "We fight as one. That's what the Crimson Alliance is."

Nefertari met Lilith's gaze. "You've returned stronger, wiser... and not just in power. Whatever happened before – this time, *you* lead the ending."

Lilith looked at each of them in turn. For a moment, the stoic fire demon who had so often borne her burdens in silence allowed herself to feel the weight of their support. She drew a slow breath.

"Thank you," she said, her voice steadier. "He may have ended a chapter... but I decide how the story ends."

Adrian grinned, his tone lighter again. "Well, when you put it like that, guess we better make it one hell of an ending."

The ship's intercom crackled. "Exiting warp in five," Nefertari's voice announced.

Lilith's fiery gaze turned back toward the stars, the flickering holomap casting warm light across her face.

"Alright," she said, lifting her head. "Final checks. This is it."

The team dispersed. Kimiko inspected her blades. Grilka adjusted her holsters. Rainstorm closed her eyes for a moment, grounding herself. Freija's wings shimmered with quiet tension.

Lilith stood still in the center of the room, eyes closed, wings folded behind her like a phoenix at rest.

This time, she thought, *I am not alone.*

The Scorpion jolted as hyperspace collapsed around them, revealing the fire-veiled world of Velyria.

Lilith opened her eyes.

"Let's move."

The battle for Velyria had begun.

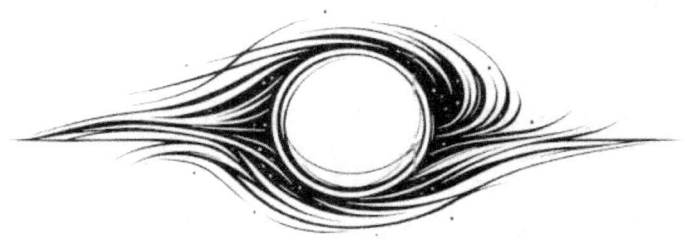

Chapter 59:

The Capture of General Serath

The Scorpion hovered silently in the shadows of Velyria's jagged cliffs, concealed beneath the overhangs of the barren, windswept terrain. Inside the dimly lit cargo hold, the team stood gathered around the central holo-table, the projected display outlining the target – a heavily fortified transport convoy en route to reinforce Necra's hold on the planet. General Serath, one of Necra's three remaining generals, was leading the operation personally.

"This is our first strike against Necra's generals," Lilith said, her fiery gaze sweeping over the team. "Serath is mobile, which means she's vulnerable. We take her out of the equation before she can regroup with the others."

Adrian leaned back against the wall, arms crossed. "So, what's the play, Captain? Fly in, grab her, and make a dramatic exit?"

"Something like that," Lilith replied. "We'll divide into three teams. Team Alpha – Varek and his squad – will create a diversion at the main stronghold to draw attention away from Serath's convoy. Team Beta – Freija and Nefertari – will provide air and ground support to ensure Serath doesn't receive backup. Team Charlie – Adrian, Rainstorm, Kimiko, and Grilka – will neutralize the

387

convoy's perimeter. I will take Serath myself."

Grilka grinned, cracking her knuckles. "Finally, some fun."

Rainstorm nodded, gripping her disruptors. "We do this quickly. The longer we're here, the harder this gets."

Lilith's fiery wings flared as she turned toward Nefertari. "Keep the Scorpion well-hidden and ready for extraction. Once I have Serath, we leave immediately."

Nefertari gave a firm nod. "Understood."

Lilith looked over the team once more. "This is the first of three. We take Serath, we break their chain of command."

Adrian smirked. "Then let's not keep her waiting."

The Setup

As the Scorpion approached the canyon pass where Serath's convoy was set to travel, Lilith and her team deployed into position. The rough terrain provided excellent cover, the deep rock formations shielding them from long-range scans.

Varek's squad made the first move. Explosions erupted in the distance, shaking the ground and sending plumes of fire and smoke into the sky. Over the comms, Varek's voice crackled through. "That should get their attention."

Lilith watched as Serath's convoy slowed, her guards scanning their surroundings for threats. "Beta team, move in."

From above, Freija streaked through the sky, her icy wings cutting through the wind. She spotted a cluster of enemy reinforcements moving toward the convoy's flank. "They've got incoming backup. Engaging now."

Below, Nefertari sprinted across the rocky terrain, her blasters taking out enemy scouts trying to regroup. "Clearing their perimeter," she reported.

Team Charlie was already in motion. Kimiko and

Rainstorm moved with calculated precision, eliminating guards with swift, silent efficiency. Adrian and Grilka took point, unleashing a barrage of fire to keep the remaining troops pinned.

Lilith stood at the edge of a high rock formation, eyes locked onto Serath's transport. The general was inside, shielded by the convoy's strongest security. With a deep breath, Lilith spread her fiery wings and launched herself into the air.

The Attack

Lilith descended like a meteor, landing atop Serath's transport with a resounding clang. The armored vehicle swerved violently as guards scrambled to react. Without hesitation, she plunged her flaming sword into the roof, carving a molten opening.

Inside, General Serath, an emerald-skinned warrior in intricate battle armor, glared up at her, drawing a curved blade. "You dare?!"

Lilith didn't hesitate. She grabbed Serath by the collar and yanked her out of the transport, launching into the air just as the vehicle lost control and crashed into a ravine below.

Serath struggled, her fists pounding against Lilith's armor. "You think you've won?" she hissed. "Necra will—"

Lilith tightened her grip. "Save it. You're coming with me."

The Escape

Below, the battle raged as the remaining guards fought to free their captured general. Grilka and Rainstorm covered Kimiko and Adrian as they moved to secure the retreat.

Adrian's voice came through the comms. "Lilith,

we're clear for extraction. But we've got incoming – multiple aerial units!"

Freija's voice followed. "I've got them. Just get Serath out of here."

As Lilith soared back toward the Scorpion, she spotted enemy gunships closing in. Nefertari maneuvered the ship into position, the airlock opening just as Lilith reached it. She tossed Serath inside before landing herself.

The moment Lilith was aboard, the hatch sealed shut, and Nefertari punched the thrusters. The Scorpion rocketed skyward, leaving the battlefield behind as enemy forces scrambled to react.

Serath sat on the floor of the cargo hold, restrained and glaring. Adrian leaned against the wall, grinning. "Welcome aboard, General. Hope you like the accommodations."

Lilith stood over her, her eyes burning with determination. "You're the first. The others will fall soon enough."

Serath remained silent, but the flicker of fear in her gaze told Lilith everything she needed to know.

The rebellion had begun its final war.

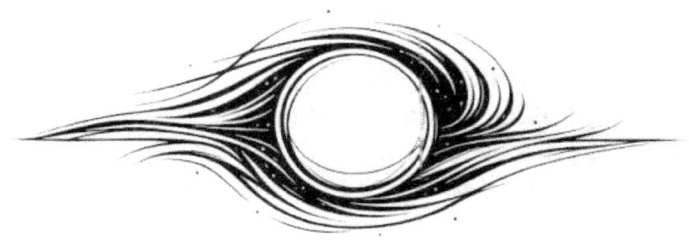

Chapter 60:

Serath's Interrogation Begins

The Scorpion floated silently in the upper atmosphere of Velyria, its engines humming faintly as it drifted in a secure orbit. Inside the dimly lit hold, the tension was palpable. General Serath was bound securely to a reinforced chair in the cargo hold. She was barefoot and wore only a T-shirt and short pants. She sat rigid with defiance. Her emerald-green skin glistened under the faint light, and her sharp, calculating eyes scanned her captors with cold disdain. Her uniform was nowhere to be seen.

Freija, with her characteristic charm and grace, stood leaning against the holo-table in front of Serath. Her icy-blue wings folded neatly behind her, and she gave the general a disarming smile.

"General Serath," Freija began, her voice light and friendly, "you've been causing us quite a bit of trouble, you know? But hey, I'm not here to talk about that." She leaned in slightly, her tone conspiratorial. "I'm here to help you."

Serath's sharp features didn't waver. "Help me?" she asked, her voice dripping with sarcasm. "By tying me to this chair? Quite the hospitality."

Freija grinned. "See? Now we're talking. I like that sarcasm – it means we're starting to connect."

Serath rolled her eyes. "If you think I'll betray Necra, you're delusional."

Freija shrugged, pacing lightly. "Betray? No, no, no. We're not talking betrayal. Think of it as... hmmm... reassessing priorities. Maybe realizing that working for the queen of death isn't exactly a long-term gig."

The Good Cop Routine

Freija continued her lighthearted approach, pulling up a chair and sitting across from Serath, her hands resting casually on her knees. "You know," she said, "I've heard stories about you. Fierce tactician, a leader your troops admire. It's impressive. But here's the thing – Necra? She doesn't care about any of that."

Serath's lips twitched, but she remained silent.

Freija tilted her head, her tone softening. "Do you know what Necra said about you when we intercepted her communications? 'Replaceable.' That's the word she used. Replaceable. After all your years of loyalty."

Serath's jaw tightened, a flicker of doubt crossing her face before she quickly masked it.

"See?" Freija leaned forward, her voice lowering. "That got to you. Because you know it's true. Necra doesn't care about you. But here's the difference – we do. If you work with us, we can protect you. You could be a part of something bigger, something better."

For a moment, Serath hesitated, her expression softening. But then, she straightened, her resolve hardening. "Spare me your false sympathies. I am loyal to my queen."

Freija sighed overly theatrically, shaking her head. "You're making this way harder than it needs to be."

Enter the Bad Cops

The heavy clank of boots echoed through the hold as Lilith and Grilka entered. Lilith's fiery wings flickered ominously, casting long, menacing shadows across the walls. Grilka loomed beside her, her massive frame exuding raw strength and intimidation.

"Well, looks like the good cop didn't get very far," Lilith said, her voice low and cold as she folded her arms and stared down at Serath. "Guess it's time for a different approach."

Freija stood, raising her hands in mock surrender. "She's all yours, Captain."

Grilka cracked her knuckles loudly, the sound reverberating through the cargo bay. "You know, General, I've crushed warriors twice your size in the pits of Valkorr. You're not exactly intimidating."

Serath's composure faltered slightly, her eyes darting between Lilith and Grilka.

Lilith stepped closer, her fiery gaze boring into the general. "Here's how this is going to work. You're going to tell us what we need to know – Necra's movements, her next targets, everything – or we'll let you go… in orbit."

Serath's lips curled into a sneer. "Empty threats. I've faced worse."

Lilith smirked faintly, her voice dropping to a menacing whisper. "Oh, I don't make empty threats… I make promises. You're lucky I don't drop you back into Necra's lap myself – broken and humiliated."

Breaking the General

Grilka stepped forward, towering over Serath. "You think this is some game? Let me show you what Valkorrans do to traitors." She grabbed the edge of the table and flipped it effortlessly, the metal crashing loudly onto the floor.

Serath flinched, her mask of defiance cracking slightly.

Lilith circled around the general, her tone icy. The talon of her left wing touched the woman's face. "Necra doesn't value you. You're expendable to her. She'll toss you aside the moment you're no longer useful. But us? We value strength, loyalty, and intelligence. You could be useful – if you cooperate."

Serath remained silent, but her resolve was visibly weakening.

Grilka leaned in close, her voice a low growl. "You think Necra cares about you? She doesn't. You're just another pawn. And pawns don't survive long in this game."

Serath's gaze flickered, the weight of their words sinking in. "You don't understand," she said finally, her voice trembling slightly. "Necra... she'll destroy me if I betray her."

Lilith crouched in front of her, her fiery gaze unrelenting. "Necra will destroy you whether you betray her or not. But we? We're offering you a way out. A chance to survive."

The General's Surrender

The silence stretched on growing more tense in the air. Finally, Serath exhaled shakily, her defiance crumbling.

"Fine," she said, her voice barely above a whisper. "What do you want to know?"

Lilith straightened; her expression triumphant but controlled. "Everything. Necra's plans, her strongholds, her weaknesses."

Serath hesitated for a moment before nodding. "I'll tell you what I know."

Grilka stepped back, folding her arms with a satisfied grin. "Smart choice."

Freija, watching from the corner, gave a small clap. "See? Told you she'd come around."

Lilith turned to Freija, raising a brow. "Your optimism is overwhelming."

Freija smirked. "That's why you keep me around."

Lilith turned back to Serath, her voice firm. "Start talking."

And with that, the team leaned in as General Serath began to divulge the secrets that could finally bring them closer to Necra's defeat.

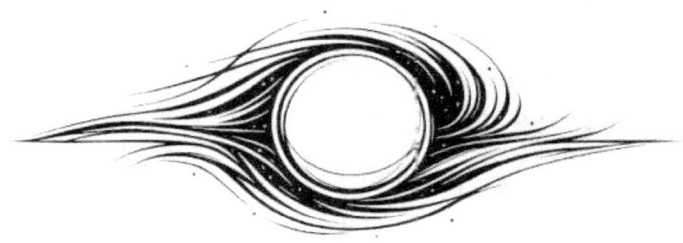

Chapter 61:

The Capture of General Valthar

The Scorpion hovered above the darkened plains of Velyria, hidden among the swirling shadows cast by the planet's red-tinged sky. Inside, the team was focused, each member preparing for their role in the mission to capture General Valthar. Known for his cunning and ruthlessness, Valthar was a dangerous adversary and Necra's most trusted general.

Lilith stood near the central holo-table, her fiery wings casting flickering light across the room. "Valthar is overconfident," she said, her voice calm but commanding. "He's been moving between outposts, consolidating his forces. Our intel says he's stationed at the eastern command base for the night."

Kimiko stood to the side, adjusting her dark, sleek attire. Her usual serious expression was tinged with a hint of discomfort. "You want me to be the bait."

Lilith nodded. "Valthar is known to have a weakness for intrigue. Your presence will disarm him. You'll lure him out of the stronghold."

Kimiko raised an eyebrow. "And if he doesn't fall for it?"

Nefertari, who was leaning casually against the wall,

smiled. "That's where Rainstorm and I come in."

Rainstorm, seated nearby, was sharpening one of her tomahawks. "We'll handle him if he resists. But the goal is to capture him alive. Lilith needs his information."

Kimiko crossed her arms. "Fine. Just don't leave me hanging out there too long."

Lilith gave her a firm look. "We won't. But timing is everything. Nefertari, Rainstorm, be ready."

The Approach

The Scorpion landed quietly in a ravine just outside the command base, its engines purring softly as it powered down. Kimiko exited first, her movements graceful and precise. She moved through the shadows, her dark outfit blending seamlessly with the night.

Nefertari and Rainstorm followed at a distance, their weapons at the ready. Nefertari carried a sleek plasma rifle slung over her shoulder, while Rainstorm gripped her tomahawks with disruptors on her side, her face painted with the intricate designs of her people.

The command base loomed ahead, its perimeter lit by dim, flickering lights. Guards patrolled in pairs; their movements were deliberate but predictable. Kimiko watched them carefully, calculating her approach.

"Remember," Nefertari whispered through the comms. "Draw him out. We'll handle the rest."

Kimiko didn't reply. She was already moving, her steps silent as she approached the entrance.

The Allure

Inside the command base, General Valthar sat in his private quarters, sipping a dark, bitter liquid. His scarred face was a mask of arrogance, his confidence bolstered by years of unchallenged power. He glanced up as the door slid open, his sharp eyes narrowing at the unexpected visitor.

Kimiko stepped inside, her demeanor poised but inviting. She gave a slight bow, her voice calm and measured. "General Valthar, I bring a message."

Valthar leaned back in his chair, his curiosity piqued. "And who might you be?"

"A messenger," Kimiko replied smoothly. "One with a proposal that may interest you."

Valthar gestured for her to continue, his eyes scanning her intently. "Go on."

Kimiko stepped closer; her movements deliberate. "Your position here is precarious. The rebels are gaining ground, and Necra's forces are stretched thin. But there are those who see you rise above the chaos."

Valthar smirked, his confidence unwavering. "And you're offering me... what, exactly?"

"An alliance," Kimiko said, her tone silky. "One that ensures your survival – and perhaps more."

Valthar chuckled, rising from his chair. "You're bold, I'll give you that. But why should I trust you?"

Kimiko tilted her head, her expression unreadable. "Trust is earned, General. I'm here to start that process."

Valthar took a step closer, his curiosity now mixed with intrigue. "You've got my attention, messenger. Let's talk."

The Ambush

As Valthar followed Kimiko out of the room, his suspicion began to grow. He glanced around the corridor, his sharp instincts sensing something amiss. "Where are we going?"

"To a secure location," Kimiko replied smoothly. "One where we can speak freely."

They exited the building, stepping into the cool night air. The base was quiet, the guards stationed far enough away not to notice their movements.

Suddenly, a shadow moved in the darkness. Nefertari

emerged from the shadows, her rifle aimed directly at Valthar. "Not another step, General."

Valthar froze, his eyes narrowing. "A trap."

Rainstorm appeared on his other side. "Surrender, and this doesn't have to end badly."

Valthar's hands clenched into fists, his defiance flaring. "You think you can capture me so easily?"

Nefertari smirked. "We already have."

The Struggle

Valthar lunged forward suddenly, aiming for Nefertari. She sidestepped with practiced ease, slamming the butt of her rifle into his midsection. He staggered but didn't fall, his hand reaching for the sidearm at his belt.

Before he could draw it, Rainstorm was on him, her tomahawk striking the weapon and sending it skittering across the ground. Valthar swung at her, but she ducked, delivering a swift kick to his knee that brought him to the ground.

Kimiko moved quickly, her movements fluid and precise. She twisted Valthar's arm behind his back, pinning him to the ground. "You're outnumbered," she said coldly. "Don't make this harder than it needs to be."

Valthar growled but stopped struggling as Nefertari aimed her rifle at his head. "Smart choice," she said.

The Extraction

The team moved swiftly, dragging Valthar toward the Scorpion. He continued to resist, but his strength was no match for Rainstorm and Kimiko's combined efforts. Once aboard, Nefertari secured him in a reinforced chair in the cargo hold, locking his restraints tightly.

As the Scorpion ascended into the night sky, Valthar glared at his captors. "You'll regret this," he spat. "Necra will crush you all."

Kimiko leaned in close, her voice icy. "We'll see about that."

Rainstorm folded her arms, her expression calm but resolute. "You're in our hands now, General. And we have questions.

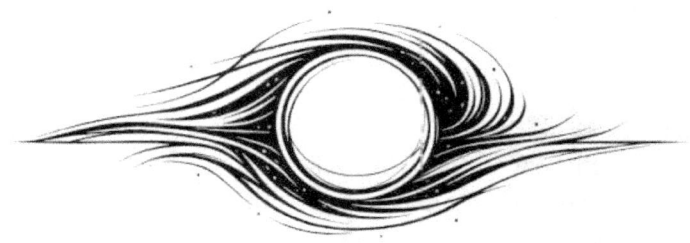

Chapter 62:

The Interrogation of General Valthar

The Scorpion floated silently in orbit above Velyria, its reinforced hull shielding it from the faint pulses of the planet's waning defenses. In the cargo hold, General Valthar sat shackled to a heavy chair, his yellow skin glistening under the dim lighting. His sharp eyes scanned the room, landing briefly on General Serath, who sat silently in the corner, her once-defiant gaze now subdued. She was wearing soundproof headphones and a blindfold. He had also been stripped of his uniform and shoes as he sat in a T-shirt and underwear.

"You," Valthar sneered, his voice dripping with contempt. "You've given in, haven't you?"

Serath didn't respond, her expression unreadable. Lilith's fiery figure stepped into view, her wings casting flickering shadows across the walls. Grilka followed closely, her hulking frame a menacing counterpoint to Lilith's commanding presence.

"Serath made the smart choice," Lilith said coldly, her fiery gaze locking onto Valthar. "But you? You're going to make this hard, aren't you?"

Valthar leaned back in his chair, feigning nonchalance. "What makes you think I'll tell you anything?"

Lilith smirked faintly. "Because we've been through this before, and we always get what we want."

Setting the Stage

Lilith paced in front of Valthar, her fiery wings flickering with restrained energy. Grilka stood to the side, her arms crossed, her piercing orange eyes fixed on the general.

"You're going to answer our questions," Lilith said, her tone steady but laced with menace. "We want to know Necra's next moves, her remaining strongholds, and any weaknesses in her forces."

Valthar chuckled darkly. "You think I'd betray my queen? You're more delusional than I thought."

Grilka stepped forward, cracking her knuckles loudly. "I've broken men twice your size in the pits of Valkorr. You'll talk. It's just a question of how much pain you'll endure."

Valthar raised an eyebrow. "Intimidation? Is that the best you can do?"

Lilith stopped pacing and leaned in close, her fiery gaze inches from his face. "No, General. This is just the beginning."

The First Round

Lilith began with calculated questions, her tone sharp and deliberate. "How many troops does Necra have stationed in the southern quadrant?"

Valthar smirked. "I don't know what you're talking about."

Grilka moved closer, her massive shadow looming over him. "Wrong answer."

Without warning, she slammed her fist onto the table beside him, the metal denting under the force. Valthar flinched, though he quickly masked it with a sneer.

"You think brute force will scare me?" he asked, his voice tinged with mockery.

Lilith tilted her head, her fiery wings flaring slightly. "No, but watching your defenses crumble might."

Grilka walked over to Serath removing one side of the soundproof headphones.

Lilith turned to Serath, who had been silently observing. "Tell him what you told us."

Serath hesitated for a moment, then spoke quietly. "I told them about the supply lines and the relay stations. They already know more than you think."

Valthar's composure faltered, his sneer replaced with a flicker of doubt. "You betrayed us."

Serath's gaze hardened. "Necra would have done the same to us."

Grilka returns to Lilith, leaving one of Serath's headphones off.

Cracks in the Armor

Lilith seized on the moment of doubt. "You see, Valthar, we already have plenty of information. You're just here to fill in the gaps."

Valthar scowled. "You're bluffing."

Grilka leaned in, her voice low and menacing. "Are we? Because if you don't talk, I've got a few... creative ways to make you reconsider."

Lilith placed a hand on Grilka's shoulder, her tone shifting to cold confidence. "We don't have to bluff, General. We've dismantled your defenses, captured your allies, and turned your queen's plans into rubble. You're already losing."

Valthar's jaw tightened, his defiance slipping further. "You don't know what you're up against."

Lilith smiled darkly. "Then enlighten us in what we don't already know."

Breaking the General

The room fell silent for a moment, the weight of the confrontation pressing down on Valthar. Finally, he exhaled sharply, his defiance cracking under the pressure.

"Necra's forces are regrouping in the northern quadrant," he admitted reluctantly. "She's consolidating her troops for a final stand."

Lilith exchanged a glance with Grilka, her expression triumphant but measured. "And her strongholds? Where are they?"

Valthar hesitated, then continued. "There's a hidden base near the volcanic ridge. It's heavily fortified. That's where she's keeping her reserves."

Grilka grinned, her sharp teeth glinting in the light. "See? That wasn't so hard."

Lilith stepped back, her fiery wings dimming slightly as she turned to Serath. "Does that line up with what you told us?"

Serath nodded. "Yes. It matches the intel I provided."

Lilith's gaze returned to Valthar. "You made the right choice, General. But if you're lying, you'll wish you hadn't."

The Aftermath

As Lilith and Grilka left the cargo hold, they exchanged a brief glance of satisfaction.

"He broke faster than I expected," Grilka said with a smirk.

Lilith's lips curled into a faint smile. "Everyone has a breaking point. You just have to know how to find it."

"Still," Grilka added, her tone more serious, "we've got to be careful. Necra's not going to take this lying down."

Lilith nodded, her fiery gaze steady. "She won't. But now we have the upper hand. And we're going to make sure she knows it."

Back in the living quarters, the rest of the team waited, their expressions tense but hopeful. Lilith relayed the information with confidence, her team's determination reigniting as they prepared for the next step in their fight against Necra.

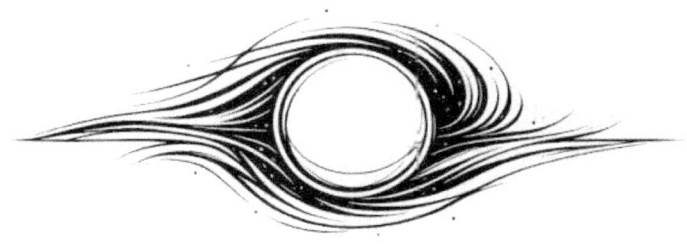

Chapter 63:

The Battle with General Agramor

The Scorpion sliced back into Velyria's ravaged atmosphere. The once-proud planet was fractured – its command chains shattered, its leaders captured or broken. Only one remained.

General Agramor.

This time, there would be no capture. This time... Lilith would face the demon who had once ended her life.

Inside the living quarters, the team stood silent around the holo-table. The map of the last stronghold flickered with interference, as if the planet itself trembled at the presence buried within it.

"He knows we're coming," Kimiko said, her voice low and unreadable.

Lilith stood tall, wings folded tight behind her, her arms crossed. "Good. Let him."

Adrian glanced across the room. "Word's already out. We took Serath and Valthar. Agramor's going to dig in hard and hit harder."

Rainstorm, sharpening one of her blades, said softly, "He's not just defending Necra. He's doing this for pride. For legacy."

Lilith's eyes never left the projection. "He's doing it

because he thinks I'm still the same." She raised her gaze slowly, meeting her team's eyes one by one. "But I'm not."

There was a pause. Kimiko took a half step forward, her tone careful. "You don't have to face him alone."

Lilith turned to her, calm but resolute. "Yes, I do."

Kimiko hesitated. Her last encounter with Agramor – being hurled aside like debris – still haunted her. She gave a sharp nod and stepped back. "Then we'll get you there."

Grilka cracked her knuckles. "You beat death once. Make sure this demon doesn't get a second chance." Lilith's lips curled faintly. "He won't."

Storming the Fortress

The Scorpion descended toward the broken remains of the Black Fortress. Its outer walls had collapsed, scorched and cratered, but the subterranean heart remained untouched. That was where Agramor waited.

The team moved swiftly through the ruins. Varek's squad had already disabled exterior turrets and landmines. As they breached the main access tunnel, resistance met them in a last, feral wave – fanatics loyal only to Necra's bloodthirsty cause.

Kimiko darted through the chaos, katanas a blur. Grilka and Adrian provided cover fire, mowing down defenders as they fell back. Freija took to the air, raining frost from above, while Rainstorm and Nefertari handled the flanks with grim efficiency.

They cleared the last barricade, a wall of twisted steel and stone. Beyond it, the sealed chamber of the stronghold pulsed with dark energy.

Lilith stepped forward, sword in hand. "Stand back."

No one argued.

She raised her flaming blade and drove it into the lock. The door hissed open – revealing a cavern lit with molten veins running through black stone.

And there he stood.

Agramor. At eight feet of shadow-forged muscle, his horns curved like blades, his double-axe weapon humming with cursed energy. His crimson eyes locked on her. A sneer spread across his face.

"Well, well," he growled, stepping forward. "The Hellbourne rises again. I thought I killed you already."

Lilith didn't flinch. "You did."

Agramor tilted his head. "Then why come back for more?"

"Because this time," Lilith said, stepping into the chamber, "I know who I am."

The Battle Rekindled

Without another word, Agramor lunged.

Lilith met him head-on, her dual swords crossing his massive axe. Sparks screamed through the chamber as metal clashed against fire and fury. His blows were monstrous – each one shaking the stone under her feet. But Lilith didn't retreat.

She adapted.

She parried, stepped aside, cut through the arcs of his rage. His strength was unchanged… but she was not.

He swung low. She vaulted over him, twisting mid-air to slash across his back. He roared, spinning, only to find her already at his flank, cutting again.

"You've improved," he spat, staggering as he caught his balance.

Lilith's wings spread wide, the flame within her eyes burning brighter than ever. "I've evolved."

Agramor's fury boiled over. He slammed her backward, sending her skidding into a wall. Pain flared in her ribs – but she didn't cry out. She rose slowly, deliberately.

The last time she fell to him, she died afraid.

This time, she stood without fear.

Agramor charged again. Their blades locked once

more – but Lilith dropped low, dodged his backswing, and slashed deep across his side. He bellowed in pain, twisting wildly.

"You think this will change anything?" he snarled. "You're still a traitor to the realm!"

Lilith's expression didn't waver. "I didn't betray the Hellish Realm. I outgrew it."

With a powerful flare of her wings, she launched herself upward. Agramor tried to follow – but he was too slow. She dropped like fire from above, both blades igniting as she struck.

Agramor screamed as her swords tore across his chest. He fell to one knee, still gripping his weapon.

"You... little... worm!"

He swung blindly – but Lilith was already gone from his line of sight. She reappeared behind him, crouched and waiting.

She let him raise his weapon.

Let him feel the illusion of control.

And then... she struck.

The Ending Blow

Lilith dropped her blades.

Agramor blinked.

Her talon on top of her left wing – deadly, hell-forged, razor-sharp – punched clean through his chest from below.

His body froze, mouth slack in disbelief.

Lilith leaned in, her voice a whisper in his ear.

"You killed the girl I was. But I'm not her anymore."

She twisted.

Agramor's mouth opened in a final snarl... then nothing.

As she drew her talon free, his body dropped like a felled beast. His soul, black and snarling, began to disintegrate... dragged screaming into the Hellish Realm from which it came. This time as one of the damned.

Aftermath

Silence filled the chamber.

Lilith stood alone over the remains, smoke curling from her shoulders. Her breath steady. Her mind clear.

The team entered moments later, weapons raised – but they were no longer needed.

Freija let out a long, low whistle. "Damn."

Adrian stared. "Remind me never to get on her bad side."

Kimiko's gaze lingered on the corpse. "He tossed me like I was nothing."

Lilith turned to her, gently. "You weren't nothing. He was just too blind to see your strength."

Grilka clapped a hand on Lilith's shoulder, surprisingly soft. "You okay?"

Lilith nodded once. "I am now."

She looked at the smoldering remains one last time.

"We're done here," she said.

She turned toward the exit.

"Let's finish the war."

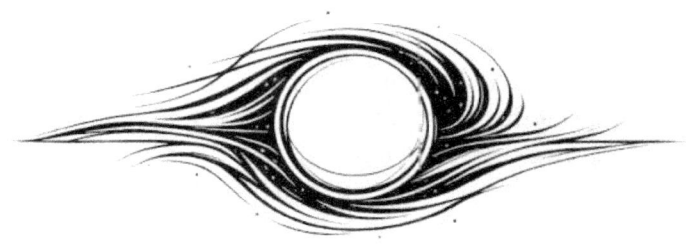

Chapter 64:

The Final Ground Assault

The Scorpion hovered in the shadows above the shattered remains of the Black Fortress, its engines idling in near silence as the crew gathered in the living quarters. They had come a long way.

Three of Necra's generals were now either captured or dead. The fortress had taken heavy losses. The tide of battle was shifting.

But they weren't done.

Lilith stood at the head of the table, her fiery wings partially unfurled, casting a faint crimson glow that danced over the faces of those assembled. Her molten gaze locked onto each of her crew in turn – Crimson Alliance and Zyntarian alike.

"This is it," she said, her voice edged with steel. "Serath and Valthar are out of play. Agramor is dead. The backbone of Necra's command has been shattered. But if we think she's going to roll over and surrender, we're fooling ourselves."

Freija leaned against the wall, arms crossed over her chest, her icy-blue wings flexing slightly. "Which means she's going to be twice as dangerous now."

Lilith nodded. "She'll be rallying everything she has

left for a final stand. But we're going to cut off her legs before she can move."

Kimiko, sharpening one of her katana blades, spoke up without looking up. "Cut off the head, and the body dies. That's what this has always been about."

"We're close," Rainstorm said from her spot near the doorway, her voice calm and grounded. "But she still has control over the power grid and communications array. As long as those stay up, she can coordinate defenses and call for backup."

Adrian, sprawled lazily across a chair with his boots on the table, let out a dry laugh. "So what you're saying is: we break stuff. Finally, a mission I was born for."

Lilith smirked. "Exactly. We take out both, and she's blind, deaf, and defenseless. Then we strike hard and finish this."

The Plan

Lilith gestured to the holo-map. Two glowing red markers hovered above key locations – one buried beneath the fortress, the other near the outer perimeter.

"The power grid runs through the sub-levels. Kimiko and Zela, that's your target."

Kimiko gave a silent nod, sliding her katana back into its sheath with calm precision. Zela, beside her, cracked her knuckles. "We'll make sure the lights go out permanently."

Lilith turned to Grilka and Rainstorm. "The communications array is mounted in an old relay tower to the east. It's guarded, but once you disable it, the entire stronghold will descend into chaos."

Grilka grinned, adjusting the strap of her rifle. "So, we break in, break stuff, and blow it sky-high? Love it."

Rainstorm gave a slight smile. "We'll leave nothing standing."

Lilith turned toward the holoprojector as a new

shimmer flickered to life – Varek's image, transmitted from the Astrell, hovering just above the table.

"Tarin and I will stay with the ship," Varek said, his arms folded. "The moment your teams confirm the targets are down, we launch. No reinforcements in, and no survivors out."

Tarin's voice came in from just off-frame. "We've already mapped the airspace. Once the comms go dark, they're cut off. Velyria will be a cage."

Lilith nodded. "Good. We also have those explosives stolen from Jaze. Use them to ensure the power grid and relay can't be brought back online."

Adrian gave a slow nod. "Let me guess: once those go boom, we all regroup and go full sledgehammer on Necra's front door?"

"Exactly," Lilith replied. "But only on my signal. Timing has to be perfect. We don't want any piece of this to trigger early."

Freija's wings twitched as she stepped closer. "And what about the rest of us?"

Lilith's smirk widened slightly. "We prepare for the final assault."

Final Preparations

The team broke into groups, each member preparing for what would likely be their last mission of the war.

In the weapons hold, Kimiko adjusted the straps of her sheaths while Zela carefully inspected the Zyntarian explosives. Her movements were deliberate, focused.

"You sure about the charge timing?" Kimiko asked without looking up.

Zela grinned. "Don't worry. I'm not new to making things explode exactly when they need to."

Across the corridor, Grilka and Rainstorm checked their equipment. Rainstorm ran her fingers over the curved handles of her disruptors, while Grilka tapped her rifle's magazine against her palm.

"First time taking out a communications array?" Rainstorm asked.

Grilka shrugged. "Nope. But I've blown up enough towers that it's probably the same idea."

Rainstorm gave a quiet chuckle. "Good enough."

Onboard the Astrell, Varek and Tarin sat in the pilot chairs, reviewing tactical routes and orbital positioning.

"Once we get the green light, we go in fast," Varek said, eyes fixed on the navscreen. "No mistakes."

Tarin grunted. "And if they scramble a counterforce?"

Varek's lips curled. "They'll be vapor before they break the clouds."

A Moment Before the Storm

Lilith stood alone on the Scorpion's observation deck, staring down at the broken surface of Velyria. The stars beyond were still and distant, but below... below was a reckoning. The last war of a long, bloody campaign.

Freija entered quietly, leaning beside her against the railing.

"You're thinking too much again," she said.

Lilith huffed a breath. "Can't help it. We've lost too much already."

Freija looked out the window. "And if we win... if we finish this... we get to start deciding what comes next. That's worth fighting for."

Lilith was silent for a moment, then nodded. "This is the endgame."

Freija straightened. "Then let's end it right."

Lilith turned, the fire in her eyes steady.

"Let's go."

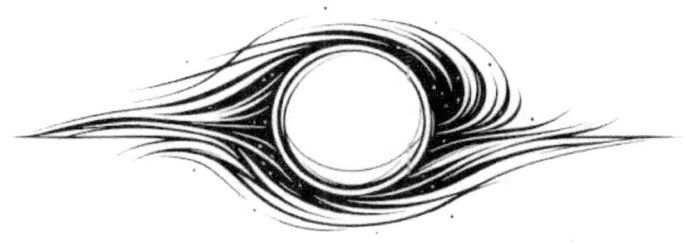

Chapter 65:

The Battle for the Command Center

The narrow corridor pulsed with flickering red warning lights as Kimiko and Zela advanced deeper into the fortress. Shadows stretched along the walls, cast by failing security lights, giving the entire stronghold a haunted, uneasy atmosphere. The first power relay they sabotaged had already thrown parts of the enemy's defenses into disarray, but they had more work to do.

Moving with the silence of wraiths, Kimiko took point, her katanas still sheathed as she relied on stealth. Zela, fingers poised over a portable hacking device, trailed just behind, her mind already calculating the quickest way to disable the fortress's main energy grid. The mission demanded both precision and efficiency – qualities both warriors excelled at.

Ahead, two of Necra's guards patrolled the corridor near their next target: the second power relay. Kimiko flicked her wrist, sending a small sensor jammer spinning across the floor. It landed between the guards with a faint click, momentarily disrupting their comms and motion sensors. The moment their heads turned in confusion,

Kimiko struck.

She sprinted forward, drawing one of her katanas in a single fluid motion. The first guard barely had time to react before she spun behind him, slicing across his back with her blade. He crumpled without a sound. The second guard raised his rifle, but Zela was already moving. She surged forward and caught his wrist, twisting it sharply and using his own momentum to slam him into the wall. With a precise elbow to his throat, she knocked him out cold.

Kimiko and Zela exchanged a brief nod confirming their flawless execution.

Without hesitation, Zela knelt by the power relay, fingers flying over the console. She overrode the security measures in seconds, bypassing the system's firewall while Kimiko stood watch. From her satchel, she retrieved a small charge. The panel beeped once, and Zela grinned. "Power to the northern defenses is offline," she whispered.

Kimiko tapped her comm. "We're clear. Moving to the next relay."

After the second power relay was down, much of the power across the fortress began to falter. At that time, both Kimiko and Zela retraced their steps back to the rendezvous point.

Rainstorm and Grilka: The Communications Relay

Across the fortress, Rainstorm and Grilka stalked toward the central communications array, a massive tower of blinking consoles and long-range transmitters. The enemy relied on it to coordinate air and ground forces. Destroying it would leave them blind to allied movements.

Reaching a vantage point just outside the control center, Rainstorm peered through her laser disruptor's scope, taking stock of the guards. Five soldiers patrolled the lower entrance while two marksmen stood on raised platforms watching for intruders.

Grilka whispered, "You take the left. I'll handle the

right."

Rainstorm didn't reply... she simply acted.

In perfect synchronization, both warriors fired. Two guards fell instantly, silent blasts searing through their helmets. A third spun around, eyes wide, but before he could shout, a second shot from Rainstorm's disruptor took him in the throat. Grilka fired twice more, dropping the last two with effortless ease.

Only the snipers remained.

"Hold," Rainstorm whispered, pressing against the wall as a high caliber shot struck the pillar beside them, sending concrete dust into the air. A sniper had spotted them.

Grilka ducked behind cover, pulling out her rifle. "I see him." She adjusted the scope, tracking the enemy's movement.

The sniper repositioned, believing himself to be in the clear.

Grilka smirked. "Bad choice."

She exhaled once, steadied her aim, and squeezed the trigger.

The sniper jolted as the well-placed shot dropped him from his perch. His body tumbled to the ground below.

Rainstorm let out a breath. "Nice shot."

Grilka gave a cocky shrug. "Was there ever any doubt?"

The second sniper's keen eyes caught her. He fired once but missed by mere inches. His finger hovered over the trigger, and for a long, tense moment, Grilka found herself pinned behind a low concrete barrier. Each second stretched out painfully as the sniper's gaze stayed fixed on her, his weapon humming with lethal promise.

Seeing Grilka in distress, Rainstorm instantly pivoted. "I'm moving to flank him!" she hissed into her comm, her voice edged with urgency. In a fluid motion, Rainstorm darted to the side, her steps silent as a shadow. With her keen, hawk-like vision, she gauged the sniper's position and trajectory. As he prepared to take the next shot, Rainstorm sprang forward, silently outflanking him from the opposite side of the platform. In one well-timed motion, she raised her disruptor, and with precise, rapid-fire shots, she tore through the sniper's cover. The sniper's shocked expression flickered before he crumpled – an expertly executed neutralization that saved Grilka from a deadly crossfire.

Even as Rainstorm secured the area, Grilka recovered from her pinned position. With a curt nod toward her comrade, she rejoined the fight, checking that the sniper was truly down. "Nice flank," she muttered into her comm, and together they advanced further into the array area, their combined sharpshooting ensuring that every potential observation post was silenced before it could alert the enemy reinforcements.

Once they reached the main communications relay, they set explosives all around the structure. With a 10-minute timer set to each charge, it gave them enough time to retreat after activating the countdown. Once set, both Rainstorm and Grilka retraced their steps back to the rendezvous point.

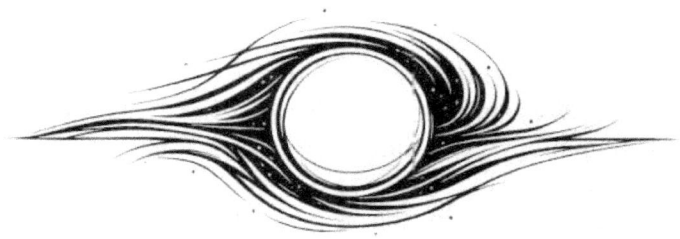

Chapter 66:

Necra's Fury

The throne room of Necra's fortress was an imposing chamber of black stone and jagged obsidian pillars, lit only by the eerie glow of blue flames set into sconces along the walls. Shadows stretched unnaturally across the floor, swallowing the trembling figure kneeling before the Queen of Death.

Necra sat in absolute stillness, her pale fingers tapping slowly against the armrest of her throne. Each tap echoed through the chamber like a war drum counting down to destruction.

"You mean to tell me," she said at last, her voice so calm it sent an icy chill through those gathered, "that all three of my generals are gone?"

The officer kneeling before her swallowed hard. His uniform was damp with sweat, his body shaking as if the weight of his news might crush him before she ever got the chance.

"Y-yes, my queen. General Serath and General Valthar were taken by the rebels. General Agramor has been... slain."

A dangerous silence settled over the room.

Necra did not move.

The officer's breath came in short, panicked gasps.

He licked his lips, forcing himself to continue. "My queen... the communications array has been completely destroyed. We cannot send orders to the fleets still under your command. We cannot request reinforcements. The fortress is... cut off."

The tension in the room thickened. The flames flickered violently as if reacting to the storm brewing beneath Necra's deathly still exterior.

"And the power grid?" she asked, though her tone suggested she already knew the answer.

The officer flinched. "Sabotaged. The rebels detonated the power relays. The entire system is down – no way to refuel ships, no shields, no outer defenses. Even life support is failing in the lower sectors."

The cold stillness in the throne room shattered.

Necra stood.

The heavy obsidian chair groaned under the sudden shift as she rose to her full height, her black armor catching the light in a way that made her seem even more monstrous.

Her jaw clenched, eyes blazing with contained fury. She stepped forward slowly, deliberately, the metallic click of her boots on the stone floor ringing in the cavernous space.

A muscle twitched in the officer's jaw. He did not dare move.

She stopped a foot away from him. "They have taken everything from me."

He flinched as she spoke, her words carrying no mercy.

Her gaze bore into him as if she could flay him with sight alone. "And what, dear officer, is your suggestion?"

The officer's throat bobbed. "M-my queen, perhaps we should... regroup. We still have forces scattered throughout the system. We can ..."

SMACK.

The sound of bone meeting metal reverberated through the throne room as Necra slapped him across the face with the back of her armored hand.

He collapsed onto the floor, blood dripping from his split lip.

She towered over him. "Regroup?" she mocked. "What use is regrouping when we have no fleet to command, no generals to lead, and no way to coordinate a counterattack?"

The officer gasped, coughing violently as he tried to push himself up.

Necra wasn't finished.

She grabbed him by the collar of his uniform, hauling him up with surprising strength. His boots barely scraped the ground.

"You think I need your pathetic strategizing?" she hissed. "You think I don't already know what must be done?"

She threw him down, sending him sprawling across the cold stone floor.

He groaned, clutching his ribs as he struggled to breathe.

The other commanders and officers in the room watched in tense, fearful silence. None of them dared to intervene.

Necra took a slow breath, lifting her chin. "We are not beaten."

The officer on the ground dared to glance up, his lip trembling.

"We still have troops. We still have resources. We still have fear," she declared.

Necra turned to the remaining commanders, her piercing gaze pinning them in place.

"They believe they have won." She sneered. "They believe I will cower in the dark, licking my wounds, like some weakling."

Her voice rose, filled with venom. "I am the Queen of Death. I do not cower. I do not run."

She gritted her teeth, fists clenching at her sides.

"They took my fortress. They took my armies. But they did not kill me."

She turned back to the officer, who had managed to crawl to his knees, panting.

"You are right about one thing," she said, tilting her head. "We must gather what remains. But we do not retreat."

She bent down, gripping his jaw in an iron hold, forcing him to meet her gaze. "We do not run. We make them think they have won."

She let go of his face with a shove. "And then... when they think their victory is assured, we strike."

She stood straight, turning to her commanders once more. "Ready the remaining ships. Call in every favor, every debt owed. We may have lost a battle, but we will remind them …" her lips curled in a wicked smile, "… why I am feared."

The officers hesitated for only a moment before bowing their heads.

"Y-yes, my queen," one finally answered.

The rest quickly followed.

Necra exhaled slowly, rolling her shoulders. The rage inside her did not subside – it burned hotter, deeper.

As the officers scurried away to carry out her orders, Necra turned toward the massive holo-display. The map of Velyria flickered, and the red markers of her strongholds diminished.

It did not matter.

She wasn't finished.

She wasn't beaten.

Her lips curled into a slow, cruel smile.

"Let them come," she whispered to herself.

"They have no idea what awaits them."

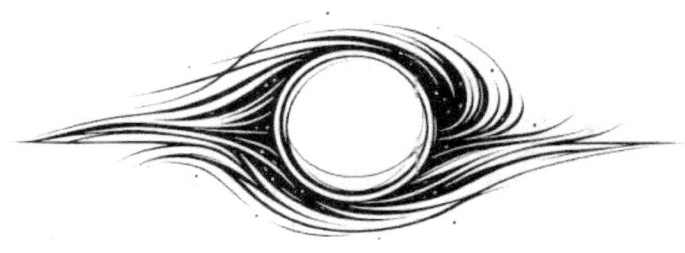

Chapter 67:

The Aerial Battle – Chaos in the Skies

Varek was the first to sense the rising storm. In the cockpit of Astrell, he stared intently at his sensor displays. Suddenly, his eyes widened in alarm as dozens of enemy fighters burst from the swirling clouds that shrouded the fortress below. "All units, this is Varek on Astrell – enemy interceptors incoming in multiple vectors! Prepare for immediate engagement!" he barked into the comm system. His voice, low and steady yet edged with urgency, cut through the static and reached every allied pilot in an instant.

The threat was swift and relentless. In the Starlight Shadow, Adrian's practiced hands flew over the controls as he banked the ship low, skimming just above the rugged canyon floor. He grinned despite the danger, his eyes glinting with adrenaline. "I'm taking a detour through these canyons," he quipped, maneuvering his fighter with such precision that two enemy ships, unable to follow his sudden, tight turns, careened wildly and tumbled into the canyon depths, their fiery wreckage disappearing into the shadows below. For Adrian, each evasive maneuver was a delicate dance with death—a testament to years of solo flights through hostile territory.

Meanwhile, aboard the Scorpion, Nefertari kept her

gaze fixed on the swirling sensor readouts, her fingers deftly adjusting the ship's thrusters. The Scorpion was their heavy hitter – a robust, if scarred, vessel that had already seen more battles than most. Her calm was almost meditative, yet the sharp alert on her console made her heart pound. "I have someone on my tail," she murmured, barely audible over the hum of the engines. A dark silhouette flitted on her rear sensor display, clearly an enemy fighter that had locked onto her signal.

At that critical moment, Lilith and Freija took to the skies in her direction. Lilith, with her majestic, fiery wings unfurled in a sweeping arc, and Freija, with her icy-blue plumes catching the glimmers of starlight, moved as a coordinated pair. Their mission was clear: to neutralize the advanced interceptors and prevent any enemy craft from homing in on the Scorpion. "Freija, I see a fighter on my tail," Lilith reported calmly, her voice crackling through the comm. "Keep your eyes peeled and prepare to engage."

Freija's response was a steely whisper: "Copy that, Lilith." With a burst of energy, she veered sharply toward the threat. Her wings sliced through the vacuum with such speed that a crisp sonic boom marked her rapid approach. She emerged from a bank of swirling dust and, with a fluid, almost balletic motion, launched a volley of ice-charged laser bolts at the enemy fighter. The bolts, glistening with a lethal blue frost, hit their mark with uncanny precision. The fighter's engines sputtered as its hull was rapidly coated in a thin layer of ice, causing it to wobble uncontrollably. In a spectacular display of teamwork, Lilith swooped in immediately, her flaming swords igniting with infernal heat, and delivered a decisive slash that split the fighter's engine compartment. The enemy ship shuddered violently and then exploded into a dazzling fireball, its remnants scattering like dying embers in the dark.

Back aboard Astrell, Varek was not idle. His eyes never left his sensor panel as he monitored the progress of the aerial skirmish. "Freija, excellent work!" he called out, his voice brimming with approval. Just then, an unexpected blip appeared on his screen – a solitary enemy vessel, small and sleek, darting in from the left in a surprise attack on Astrell. The craft had not been detected by the earlier sweeps, and it had come in fast. Varek's fingers flew over the controls as he attempted to bring the intruder under his radar lock. In the blink of an eye, the enemy fighter closed in dangerously, its weapons primed to fire.

Sensing the imminent threat, Freija acted without hesitation. While still trailing behind Lilith's formation, she veered sharply to intercept the intruder. With calculated precision, she released a concentrated burst of frost energy that expanded into a shimmering barrier, forcing the enemy fighter to slow its advance. The vessel hesitated. Seizing the opportunity, Varek's Astrell adjusted its vector to assist Nefertari's Scorpion; together, they provided overlapping fields of suppressive fire that took out the enemy ship.

Just as the situation began to stabilize, the intensity in the sky increased dramatically. The enemy's formations began to splinter as reinforcements swarmed in from multiple directions. Now, a full-scale dogfight erupted in the void over Velyria. The Starlight Shadow was embroiled in a chaotic ballet of maneuvering fighters. Adrian banked low through the rugged canyons, his ship dodging bursts of laser fire that threatened to tear it apart. Every twist, every loop was a battle against gravity and enemy precision. He skillfully used the rocky outcrops as cover, his fighter's thrusters pushing him to the limits of control. "I'm in a tight spot here," he grumbled into the comm, his voice laced with both adrenaline and humor, "but I'll be the last one flying if I have to."

Meanwhile, Lilith and Freija continued their coordinated assault, a dazzling display of dichotomy as their opposing powers clashed with enemy fire. Lilith's flames danced through the sky, setting enemy fighters ablaze in a riot of orange and red, while Freija's icy blasts created a shifting landscape of frost and shattered metal. Together, they wove through the enemy ranks, their movements synchronized as if choreographed by an unseen conductor. Their synergy was evident – each time one faltered, the other compensated seamlessly, ensuring that the combined assault remained unbroken. The enemy's dogfight escalated in intensity; the black void was lit intermittently by bursts of laser fire, explosions, and the brilliant glows of plasma bolts colliding with shield generators.

Amidst the chaos, Varek's Astrell found itself drawn into the fray as well. From his vantage, he observed the unfolding aerial chaos with a mixture of awe and concern. The enemy fighters, now in full force, swarmed like locusts, their numbers overwhelming the isolated craft. Varek's voice, calm yet urgent, came over the comm: "Attention, all airborne units! I'm picking up a formation of at least a dozen enemy fighters fast approaching our port side. Take cover and be prepared to maneuver!" His words were met with immediate responses from the other allied pilots.

Adrian let out a low, determined laugh. "I'm getting a tail of two here, but they're nothing compared to what's coming!" He banked sharply, using the canyon's walls to obscure his movements. Yet the enemy was relentless, their collective fire began to force him into a dangerous, open flight path.

Back aboard the Scorpion, Nefertari kept her focus razor-sharp, her hands dancing over the controls as she adjusted the ship's trajectory. The Scorpion, though massive and battle-worn, proved to be a stalwart platform in the chaotic fray. However, even with Varek's support and Nefertari's seasoned piloting, the skies were becoming increasingly perilous.

As the dogfight raged, the allied ships found themselves outnumbered. Enemy fighters dove in from the east, their formation tight and menacing. Varek's Astrell executed a daring maneuver, skimming along the Scorpion's hull as if in a death spiral. With a swift pull of the throttle, Astrell's thrusters roared to life, and the ship banked hard, its sleek frame cutting through the enemy ranks. In a breathtaking display of aerial acrobatics, Varek managed to lure two enemy fighters into a narrow canyon formed by the rocky outcroppings below, forcing them to crash against the unforgiving walls of Velyria's surface.

In the midst of this intense aerial ballet, Lilith's and Freija's formation was suddenly compromised. As they flew in tandem, a squadron of enemy interceptors closed in unexpectedly from above. Their rapid approach sent a chill through the allied pilots. Freija, always the first to react, veered sharply to the left, her wings slicing through the dark as she fired a precise, ice-laden burst that intercepted one of the incoming fighters. The impact was catastrophic, the enemy ship erupted in a blaze of frosted fire, its debris scattering onto the rocky surface.

But the intensity didn't let up. The enemy's numbers swelled as additional fighters joined the assault, their collective fire turning the once-calm space into a veritable storm of energy bolts and exploding missiles. Adrian, now locked in a desperate dogfight with the remaining enemy craft, narrowly avoided a barrage that rattled his fighter to its core. He ducked behind a massive outcropping, using every ounce of his skill to weave in and out of danger. "Not today, death machine," he muttered, adrenaline fueling every maneuver.

The allied ships began to feel the strain. The Scorpion's shields flickered under sustained enemy fire, and even Varek's Astrell, with its advanced defenses, struggled to maintain its position.

The team was becoming increasingly outmatched and outgunned.

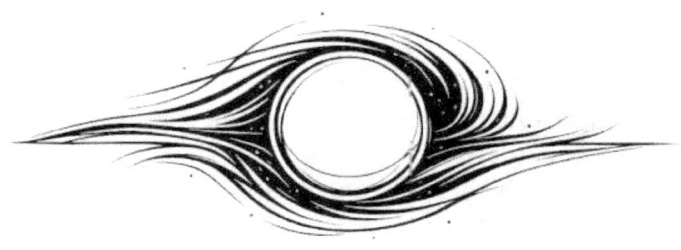

Chapter 68:

Ilyan to the Rescue

When the allies were starting to realize this could be it, a miracle happened.

A crisp message burst over the comms, the voice of Admiral Ilyan cutting through the chaos: "Captain Varek, I hope I am not too late!" The words were filled with both urgency, hope, and relief. Varek's eyes lit up behind his controls as he responded with barely contained excitement, "Admiral, your timing is impeccable. We're in the thick of it… Thank you!" His voice reverberated with relief and determination, a beacon of support amid the raging dogfight.

Varek turned to the communications with the allies, "Lilith! The armada has arrived!"

The Zyntarian fighters, part of an incoming armada, swooped in to provide additional cover. They moved in perfect synchrony, their craft weaving intricate patterns as they intercepted enemy fire with swift, coordinated strikes. With their support, the allied formation gained a temporary reprieve. Varek's Astrell, reinvigorated by the arrival of his kin, executed a series of high-speed maneuvers, its thrusters blazing as it pushed back against the enemy's onslaught. In a dazzling display of aerial warfare, the Zyntarian fighters fanned out, each engaging a target with ruthless efficiency, their laser cannons painting the void with streaks of violet light.

As the dogfight raged on, the combined might of the allied forces began to turn the tide. Lilith and Freija, soaring above the battlefield, coordinated their strikes with precision. Lilith's fiery swords clashed with the enemy's metal hulls, her every movement a blend of grace and lethal power. Freija launched targeted bursts that froze enemy systems, rendering their craft immobile. Together, they created an intricate web of fire and ice that enveloped the enemy fighters, each shot from their weapons carving a path of destruction through the enemy ranks.

Adrian's Starlight Shadow, nimble as ever, maneuvered through the chaos with a reckless abandon that belied his meticulous training. He exploited every gap in the enemy formation, drawing them away from the other allied ships. His fighter's engines roared as he performed hairpin turns and sudden drops, each maneuver a calculated risk that kept his adversaries off balance. "Come and get me!" he shouted over the comms, his voice a blend of challenge and exhilaration. His antics, though dangerous, bought precious moments for his team.

Despite the chaos, Varek's Astrell maintained a disciplined formation, its sensors locked onto the enemy's weak points. Varek coordinated with his incoming Zyntarian allies, their voices merging in a chorus of tactical precision. "Focus on the rear engines of those fighters!" he instructed. "We'll disable them one by one. Maintain your formation and watch your flanks!" His commands cut through the noise, his calm authority a stabilizing force in the midst of the storm.

The enemy's countermeasures began to falter under the relentless assault. As explosions rippled through their ranks, several enemy fighters were forced to retreat, their formation breaking apart as they attempted a hasty withdrawal. But the battle was far from over—the enemy was regrouping for one final, desperate push. In the midst of this renewed assault, a stray missile narrowly missed Lilith's, grazing the edge of her wing. The impact sent a shockwave of searing pain, but she fought through it, her determination burning as fiercely as her weapons.

It was at that moment of heightened peril that Freija, ever vigilant, detected a new threat emerging from the edge of the battlefield. A lone enemy fighter, cloaked by the chaos, had been slowly gaining on Astrell from behind. Freija's eyes widened in alarm. "Varek, we have an unidentified vessel tailing you!" she called, her voice urgent. In an instant, she adjusted her flight path and surged forward, her icy-blue craft weaving through the enemy's line. With precise timing, Freija intercepted the intruder, a nimble fighter with erratic movements – and, with a burst of concentrated frost energy, she disabled its propulsion system. The enemy ship shuddered and then plummeted, tumbling uncontrollably toward the surface. "Got it!" she exclaimed over the comm, a triumphant note lacing her tone.

The tide of the battle had now fully shifted. With the enemy fighters increasingly disorganized, the allied ships pressed their advantage. The combined firepower of the Starlight Shadow, Astrell, and Scorpion, augmented by the freshly arrived Zyntarian armada, began to erode the enemy's resolve. In a dazzling aerial display, Varek's Astrell executed a series of tight, coordinated maneuvers with its newfound allies, forcing several enemy fighters into an inescapable spiral that culminated in their disintegration against the rocky surface of Velyria.

Admiral Ilyan's earlier message echoed in Varek's mind as the final enemy formations fell back. *I hope I am not too late,* had been his urgent call, and now, with the allied forces emerging victorious from the chaos of battle, Varek couldn't help but respond with unbridled excitement. "Admiral, we've done it – thanks for the reinforcements! Your armada arrived just in time. We've turned the tide here!" His voice, laced with relief and triumph, resonated through the comms, a testament to the power of unity in the face of overwhelming odds.

The battlefield, once a chaotic canvas of fire and ice, began to settle into a fragile calm. Enemy fighters lay scattered, their wrecks illuminated by the fading glow of explosions, while the allied ships regrouped in formation. Lilith and Freija, still soaring high above the remnants of the conflict, exchanged a glance that spoke of hard-won respect and quiet camaraderie. Their combined assault had not only neutralized the enemy's air defenses but had also sown chaos among their ranks – chaos that would prove decisive in the final phase of the operation.

Adrian, having evaded pursuit through his daring canyon maneuvers, rejoined the formation. He allowed himself a brief, exhausted chuckle as he reported, "I've seen some close calls, but I'm still in one piece… barely!" His lighthearted banter belied the gravity of the situation, yet his voice carried a note of resolve. Every pilot, every ship in the allied fleet had contributed to the victory, and now, with the enemy's forces in disarray, the final battle for Velyria was imminent.

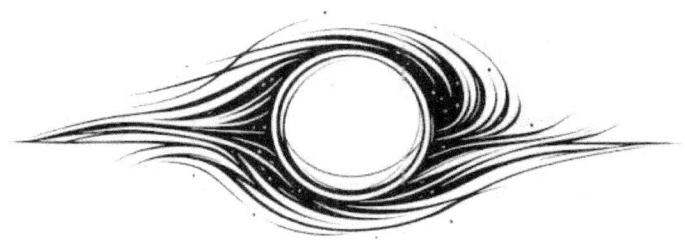

Chapter 69:

The Final Push

The cargo bay of the Scorpion was alive with activity. Lilith and her team stood gathered around a holo-display, the air thick with tension as the final battle loomed ahead. Admiral Ilyan had patched through from his command ship, his grim expression flickering on the display as he outlined their mission.

"This is it," Ilyan said, his voice steady but urgent. "We've broken their aerial defenses, and with their power and communications down, the stronghold is vulnerable. But make no mistake – Necra isn't going down without a fight."

The holo-map rotated, showing the fortress's inner layout. Lilith's eyes narrowed as she studied the path to Necra's throne room, located in the heart of the stronghold, connected to a large antechamber. It was likely the last defensive holdout before reaching the Queen of Death herself.

Ilyan tapped a control, highlighting key routes. "We suspect most of the remaining forces will be concentrated here, outside the throne room. Necra has no way to call for reinforcements, so she'll be using every last soldier she has to protect herself. Expect tight corridors, fortified choke points, and likely a few surprises."

Varek, arms crossed, leaned in. "My crew and I will handle ground support. We'll keep the escape routes open and make sure you're not cut off. Once you push in, we'll hold the perimeter and intercept any stragglers trying to flee."

Lilith nodded. "Good. Ilyan, you coordinate from above. Keep our exit clear. If Necra has any last-ditch gambit, I want to know about it before it turns into a problem."

Ilyan smirked. "Wouldn't expect anything less from you."

Lilith turned back to her team. "Alright. Grilka, Nefertari, Rainstorm – you three run point. We'll be moving fast, and I want you to clear resistance before we even have to slow down."

Grilka cracked her knuckles with a wolfish grin. "That's what I like to hear."

Rainstorm adjusted the strap on her blaster rifle and gave a solemn nod. "We won't let anything stand in your way."

Nefertari smirked. "Let's make this quick."

Lilith then turned to Kimiko. "You'll move ahead, in the shadows. I want updates on enemy positions before we walk into anything nasty."

Kimiko gave a rare half-smile, flipping a throwing knife between her fingers. "You'll never see me, but I'll see everything."

Adrian, who had been uncharacteristically quiet, adjusted his gun holsters and smirked. "Guess that makes Freija and me your official Lilith bodyguards."

Freija snorted. "Please. I'm there to make sure you don't do something stupid."

"Like what?" Adrian asked, feigning innocence.

Freija rolled her eyes and smiled coyly. "Like breathing."

Lilith shook her head but couldn't help a smirk.

"Both of you – stay close and cover my flanks. If anything moves on me while I'm handling Necra, put it down."

With a final nod, Lilith turned back to the holo-map. "This is it. We take Necra down tonight. No second chances."

The tension in the room was electric. Each of them knew they were walking into the lion's den—but that was exactly where they belonged.

Storming the Fortress

The entrance to the stronghold loomed before them, a massive set of iron doors already blown open from the initial bombing run. Smoke and dust curled in the air, obscuring their vision as they moved swiftly into the ruined corridors.

Kimiko had vanished ahead, already melding into the shadows.

Lilith's earpiece crackled. "First hall is clear," came Kimiko's voice, barely above a whisper. "Two guards ahead at the next junction. Armed, but unaware."

Lilith smirked. "Rainstorm, Nefertari – lights out."

Rainstorm dropped to one knee, lining up her blaster sight. Nefertari stood beside her, both aiming in perfect sync.

Two shots – one to the chest, one to the head.

The guards didn't even make a sound before they collapsed.

"Next corridor," Kimiko's voice came again, moving ahead. "A group of six. Armed, armored. Might put up a fight."

Grilka grinned. "I hope so."

The team advanced, moving swiftly through the corridors. When they reached the next intersection, the waiting guards opened fire.

"Take cover!" Lilith shouted, diving behind a stone pillar as blaster fire tore through the walls.

Grilka and Rainstorm rolled behind overturned

crates, returning fire.

Kimiko suddenly dropped from above, landing in the middle of the enemies like a phantom.

Two quick slashes, and the first two guards collapsed.

Another turned his weapon, but before he could react, Kimiko vanished again, rolling into the shadows.

"What the …" the soldier began.

A dagger flashed, embedding itself in his throat.

As he fell, Grilka and Rainstorm finished off the rest, their blasters kicking up sparks against armor before finding their marks.

Freija and Adrian covered the rear, ensuring nothing followed them in.

"Move!" Lilith ordered, stepping over the bodies. "Keep pressing forward!"

Kimiko's voice whispered in their ears. "We're getting close. The next section is the final corridor leading to the antechamber. A dozen guards, positioned defensively."

Lilith growled. "That's nothing."

Final Corridor

As they approached, alarms blared.

The guards had fortified the hallway, taking cover behind overturned tables and barricades.

Lilith glanced at her team. "Nefertari, Rainstorm – take high shots. Grilka, keep them pinned down."

"On it," Nefertari said, shifting position.

Rainstorm and Nefertari moved to higher ground, perching on the rafters like snipers.

Grilka let out a war cry, charging ahead with a barrage of fire.

The guards panicked, turning their weapons toward her.

That was their mistake.

Nefertari and Rainstorm fired at the same time.

One by one, the guards dropped.

Kimiko darted forward, clearing stragglers with precise knife work.

Adrian chuckled. "I almost feel bad for these guys."

Freija shot him a look. "You're enjoying this too much."

"Tell me I'm wrong."

Lilith smirked but kept her eyes forward. "We're at the doors."

Kimiko appeared beside her. "Guards neutralized. The antechamber is clear."

Lilith exhaled slowly. *She had walked into death once before and came back stronger. This would be no different.*

Lilith scanned the faces of her team – warriors, survivors, friends. This was more than a strike force. This was a family forged in battle. "Inside that room, Necra is waiting for us."

She then unsheathed her fiery swords, the glow illuminating their faces.

"We end this. Now."

The team nodded, weapons ready.

Lilith pressed a hand to the door.

With a deep breath, she pushed it open.

And the final battle began.

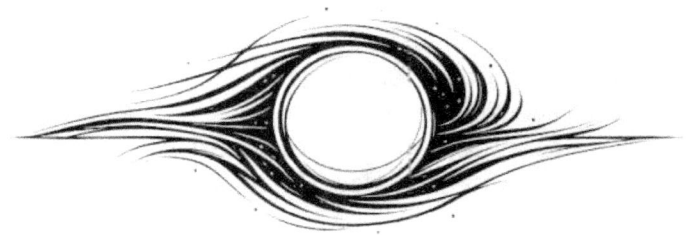

Chapter 70:

Hello Necra, Nice to Meet You

Lilith, Freija, Kimiko, and Adrian entered the throne room. The heat of battle still clung to their armor, the scent of scorched stone and fire thick in the air. Behind them, Nefertari, Grilka, and Rainstorm stood guard at the door watching for any last defenders.

Lilith stepped forward, her fiery wings unfurled, casting a flickering glow across the charred chamber. Her twin fiery blades burned with a focused fury, their light illuminating the cracked black tiles beneath her boots.

Across the throne room, Necra stood waiting. She was a figure of deathly poise, her dark armor absorbing the faint light, her death swords pulsing with malevolent energy. There were no wings to carry her – only her raw, terrifying presence.

A smirk crept across Necra's lips. "So… the Hellbourne walks again."

Lilith's eyes narrowed. "Surprised?"

"Agramor killed you. I was there; I saw it," Necra said plainly. "You shouldn't exist."

"I'm not the same person that he killed," Lilith replied. "I died. But I came back… better."

Necra scoffed. "Better? You still wear fire like it's a

crown. But I see the cracks. I hear the hesitation. You've been softened."

"I've changed," Lilith said, voice low and even. "And that's why you've already lost."

Necra's smile vanished. "Let's test that."

With a furious cry, Necra charged forward.

The First Clashes

Their swords collided in a blinding clash of flame and darkness, the resulting shockwave splintering tiles beneath their feet. Necra's strikes were fast and brutal – each swing calculated to end the fight in seconds. But Lilith was ready.

They moved in a blur, steel ringing against steel, fire sparking against shadow. Lilith's blades forced Necra back step by step, her power no longer driven by rage… but by resolve.

"You're stronger," Necra admitted, voice clipped. "But you lack the killer's edge."

Lilith's fire surged as she countered with a sweeping arc. "I don't need it. I have something you never did… purpose."

The Aerial Advantage

Lilith kicked off the ground, wings flaring wide as she launched into the air. Heat rolled from her back in waves as she gained altitude, her swords gleaming in the overhead torchlight.

Necra snarled and hurled a blast of dark energy upward, forcing Lilith to dodge. But the queen of shadows remained grounded, unable to follow.

From the skies, Lilith rained down fiery slashes, forcing Necra to block and retreat behind shattered pillars. Necra fought back fiercely, her dark energy searing into the air, but it could not match the mobility of wings.

Lilith used her aerial advantage to control the tempo, diving low, striking hard, then rising again out of reach.

"You fight like a goddess," Necra growled, breathing hard. "But you bleed like the rest of us."

Lilith dove again, blades crossing as she struck. The momentum knocked Necra back into her throne, splintering it into rubble.

The Ground Struggle

Necra quickly recovers and snarls at Lilith while pointing her sword of death at her.

Necra approached and again and swung. Her blade slicing across Lilith's thigh leaving a trail of searing pain. Lilith gritted her teeth, her wings flaring as she propelled herself backward to gain some distance.

"You're slowing down," Necra mocked, advancing with deliberate steps. "The flames of rebellion can only burn so long before they're snuffed out."

Lilith wiped the blood from her leg, her fiery eyes never leaving Necra's. "You talk too much."

With a burst of speed, Lilith closed the distance between them, her swords moving in a whirlwind of fiery strikes. Necra blocked and dodged, her movements precise but strained under Lilith's relentless assault. One of Lilith's blades grazed Necra's shoulder, the flames searing through her armor and drawing a hiss of pain.

Necra retaliated with a powerful burst of dark energy, the shockwave throwing Lilith backward. Before she could recover, Necra was upon her, her blade descending in a deadly arc. Lilith rolled to the side, the sword striking the ground where she had been moments before.

Desperation Sets In

The fight began to take its toll on both women. Lilith's movements grew heavier, her wings flickering as their flames dimmed. Necra's strikes, once precise and calculated, became wild and desperate. The battlefield bore the scars of their clash – craters of molten rock and fields of twisted shadows.

"You're finished," Necra snarled, her blade aimed for Lilith's heart.

Lilith dodged at the last moment, her wings carrying her upward in a burst of flames. She descended with a spinning slash, her blade colliding with Necra's and forcing her to retreat. The two combatants circled each other, their breaths ragged, and their bodies battered.

The Climactic Struggle

Summoning the last reserves of her strength, Lilith launched herself at Necra, her swords blazing brighter than ever. Necra met her charge with equal ferocity, their blades colliding in a deafening explosion of light and shadow. They fought with everything they had left, their movements a blur as they exchanged strike after strike.

Necra managed to land a devastating blow, her sword slicing across Lilith's side and drawing blood. Lilith staggered but refused to fall. She retaliated with a powerful upward slash, her blade carving a fiery arc that struck Necra's leg. The flames seared through her armor, forcing her to her knees.

"You're done," Necra hissed, her voice trembling with rage and desperation.

Lilith's gaze was steady, her resolve unshaken. "Not yet."

Necra lunged with a final burst of energy, her blade aimed for Lilith's throat. But Lilith twisted at the last moment, her wings flaring to propel her behind Necra. In one swift motion, she pressed the fiery blade of her sword to Necra's throat.

The Surrender

Necra froze, her body trembling with exhaustion. Slowly, reluctantly, she dropped her sword, the dark energy dissipating into the air. For a moment, the battlefield was silent, the only sound the ragged breathing of the two combatants.

"You've won," Necra said, her voice filled with venom and resignation. "For now."

Lilith didn't lower her sword. "Your reign is over, Necra. Surrender your forces, or I'll end this here."

Necra staggered backward and fell to her knees, her once-imposing form reduced to a shadow of its former power. Her death swords, symbols of her unyielding strength, lay on the scorched ground. The fire in her eyes dimmed as she clutched her side, blood seeping through her armor.

Lilith advanced cautiously, her fiery swords burning low, her body trembling with exhaustion. "It's over, Necra," she said, her voice firm but weary. "Surrender, and your forces will be spared."

Necra chuckled, her laugh hollow and defiant. "Surrender? To you? I am eternal... I am ..."

A swift motion cut her words short. Kimiko, silent and unseen, stepped from the shadows, her katanas gleaming in the faint light. With precision honed over years of training, she thrust her blades through Necra's chest. The strike was clean, swift, and final.

Necra gasped, her defiance giving way to a flicker of disbelief. She looked down at the blade embedded in her chest, then up at Kimiko, her once-dominant aura now replaced by a fleeting vulnerability.

"You..." Necra rasped, her voice a faint whisper. "What makes you... Think you're different? That you won't... become like me?"

Kimiko held her gaze, her voice steady and cold. "Because I fight for others, not for myself. And unlike you,

I know when to let go."

With a sharp motion, she withdrew both blades. Necra collapsed to her hands, her strength gone. She cast one last glance at Lilith, then at the rest of the team gathered in the distance, before her eyes closed, her body slumping lifelessly to the ground.

Kimiko stood still for a moment, her katana dripping with blood, before turning to Lilith. Her voice was calm but resolute. "Sometimes, there's no room for redemption. She made her choice."

Lilith, still catching her breath, nodded solemnly. "And you made yours."

The battlefield was silent, save for the faint crackle of embers in the distance. Necra's reign was over, her death marking the end of her tyranny. The team stood together, their victory hard-earned but bittersweet, knowing that even in triumph, sacrifices had been made.

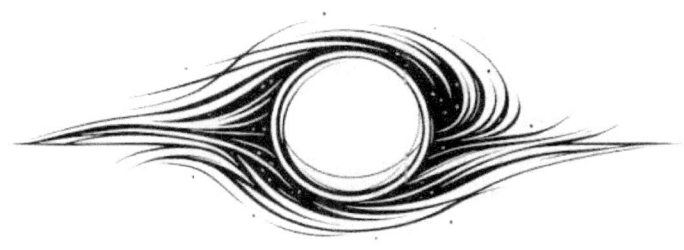

Chapter 71:

Rebuilding What Was Lost

The sunlight over Velyria was warm and golden, a stark contrast to the crimson skies of war that had hung over the planet for so long. The battlefield had been cleared, and the command center, now under rebel control, was being transformed into a hub for reconstruction. The echoes of tyranny were fading, replaced by the hum of rebuilding efforts.

Inside the command center's main hall, Adrian, Rainstorm, Nefertari, Grilka, and Kimiko stood at the forefront, facing the subdued higher-level commanders who had surrendered after Necra's demise. Varek, Tarin and Zela flanked the team, their Zyntar presence lending an added air of authority.

Adrian, leaning casually against a table but with a sharp glint in his eye, was the first to speak. "All right, let's make this simple. You folks ran this place into the ground. Your queen is gone, your armies are scattered, and frankly, you don't have much choice but to listen to us. So, here's the deal."

Rainstorm stepped forward, her demeanor calm but commanding. "Velyria and the other planets you've oppressed will not heal on their own. You've broken them, and now you will help rebuild them. That is your penance."

One of the commanders, a grizzled man with deep scars across his face, raised his hand cautiously. "And if we refuse?"

Grilka snorted, stepping forward with her arms crossed, her imposing figure towering over the seated commanders. "Then you'll get a firsthand experience of what it's like to rebuild from a prison cell – or worse. Trust me, I can make sure of that."

The commander swallowed hard, nodding quickly. "Understood."

Nefertari's Commanding Speech

Nefertari stepped forward, her golden-blue armor catching the faint light of the room, making her seem larger than life. Her regal bearing was undeniable, and the room seemed to still as if all eyes turned to her. She clasped her hands behind her back, the epitome of control and authority, and surveyed the gathered commanders with an unyielding gaze.

"When you look around this room," she began, her voice steady and deliberate, "what do you see? Power? Authority? Strength? No. What you see is the hollow shell of a broken empire. A reign that once thrived on fear and cruelty has now been reduced to ash. And why? Because the very foundation it was built upon was flawed."

Her words hung in the air like a blade poised to strike. The commanders, once proud and defiant, now seemed smaller under her piercing gaze.

"Your queen is gone," Nefertari continued, her voice rising with intensity. "Her lies, her greed, her thirst for destruction – none of it could stand against the united strength of those who refused to be crushed under her rule. She thought herself invincible. She thought her grip on this galaxy was eternal. And yet here we stand, victorious, because we fought for something greater."

She paused, her eyes sweeping across the room to ensure her words were sinking in. "But make no mistake – your surrender is not forgiveness. Your past cannot be undone. The lives lost, the families shattered, the worlds destroyed… those scars will never fade. What matters now is what you do from this moment forward. Will you choose to wallow in your defeat, clinging to the remnants of a fallen empire? Or will you rise and rebuild, not for power, but for the people you have wronged?"

Her voice grew sharper, more commanding. "This galaxy does not need tyrants. It needs leaders who understand that true strength comes not from fear, but from justice. True power lies in the ability to uplift, to heal, to unite. If you cannot grasp that, if you cannot rise to this challenge, then step aside and make way for those who can."

She stepped closer to the commanders, her golden eyes locking onto the grizzled leader who had dared to speak earlier. "But if you choose to accept this responsibility, know that you will not be alone. We will ensure you succeed – not because we trust you, but because the people of this galaxy deserve better than the chaos you've left behind."

The commander flinched under her gaze, but Nefertari didn't relent. "Let me be clear. This is not an opportunity for redemption – it is a demand for action. You will rebuild the worlds you've destroyed. You will restore hope to the people you've abandoned. And you will do so under our watchful eyes."

Her tone softened slightly, though it remained firm. "This is your chance to rewrite your story. To turn a legacy of destruction into one of rebuilding. It will not be easy, and it will not be quick. But it will be worth it."

She straightened, her presence towering, her voice unwavering. "I am Nefertari, a warrior, a chantress, and a protector of those who cannot protect themselves. I do not command through fear or oppression. I command through purpose. And I will not tolerate failure."

The room was silent, the weight of her words pressing down on every soul present. The grizzled commander, visibly shaken, stood slowly and bowed his head.

"We hear you," he said quietly, his voice tinged with humility. "We will do as you ask."

Nefertari nodded, her expression unreadable. "You will do as is needed. And the galaxy will judge you by your actions."

The remaining commanders stood as well; their defiance replaced by grim determination. Nefertari had planted a seed of purpose in their hearts – a spark of hope in a galaxy that desperately needed it.

The Commanders' Surrender

The room was heavy with silence, the commanders exchanging uneasy glances. The weight of Nefertari's words, coupled with the looming presence of the rest of the team, left no room for defiance. Finally, the scarred commander who had spoken earlier stood.

"We have no choice," he admitted, his voice tinged with defeat. "We've lost. And if this is the price for our survival… we will pay it."

One by one, the other commanders rose, their postures slouched in submission. Some looked bitter, others resigned, but a few showed faint glimmers of resolve, as if the idea of rebuilding offered them a sense of purpose they hadn't felt in years.

Nefertari inclined her head slightly, acknowledging their surrender. "Then begin now. Organize your teams, distribute resources, and rebuild. The people of Velyria, Jaze, Luthor, and the other planets are waiting."

As the commanders were led out to begin their new assignments, Nefertari turned to the grizzled leader. "Know this: we will be watching. Every step of the way."

The commander hesitated before nodding.

"Understood. You'll see no trouble from us."

Nefertari stepped back, allowing the group to leave under the watchful eyes of the team.

Reflection Amongst the Teams

As the room emptied, Adrian let out a low whistle, breaking the tension. "Damn, Nefs, that was impressive. I almost felt bad for them… almost"

Nefertari raised an eyebrow at the nickname but chose not to comment. Instead, she replied, "Sometimes strength is in restraint. They needed to know we mean business, but we also gave them a chance to redeem themselves."

Kimiko, who had been silently observing, nodded. "They'll need constant monitoring. But fear can be a powerful motivator, especially when tempered with purpose."

Rainstorm, leaning against the wall with her arms crossed, added, "They're broken, but broken things can be mended. With time and effort."

Grilka chuckled, crossing her arms. "And if they screw up, we'll just knock them back in line. Easy enough."

Adrian smirked. "Spoken like a true enforcer. Remind me not to get on your bad side."

Lilith's Approval

Lilith stepped forward, her fiery wings casting a faint glow over her team. "You all did well. This was a battle fought with words instead of weapons, but no less important. Their surrender marks the beginning of something new… a chance to rebuild not just Velyria, but the galaxy."

She turned to Nefertari, her voice steady. "Your words carried the weight of justice, Nefertari. You've proven why you are a true leader."

Nefertari inclined her head. "It's not leadership

without a team willing to see it through. We're all part of this victory."

Lilith nodded, a faint smile playing at her lips. "And together, we'll make sure it lasts."

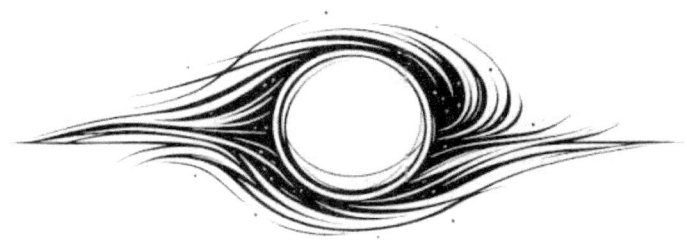

Chapter 72:

The Bonds Forged in Fire

The Scorpion's living quarters was quiet, save for the hum of its systems as the ship hovered above the rebuilding of the command center on Velyria. The team sat together for the first time in days, the weight of their victory against Necra mingling with the reality of what came next. It wasn't just a victory – they had altered the galaxy's future. But with change came decisions, and one member of the team was preparing to make a monumental one.

Nefertari stood near the center of the room, her golden armor gleaming faintly despite the countless scratches and dents it had sustained. Her regal posture betrayed a hint of hesitation, but her voice was steady when she finally spoke.

"My friends," she began, her gaze sweeping across the team. "This battle has been unlike any other I've fought. We didn't just win a war; we planted seeds of hope. But the people of Velyria are fractured. Their wounds run deep, and they need someone to guide them as they rebuild."

The room was silent as her words sank in.

Nefertari continued, her voice firm but tinged with emotion. "I've decided to stay. My duty for now lies here, with these people. They need a leader, someone who understands the weight of responsibility and the power of unity."

Adrian was the first to break the silence. He leaned back in his seat, arms crossed, and smirked. "You know, Nefs, you just love being in charge, don't you?"

Freija, perched on the edge of the galley counter, chuckled. "She does have a knack for commanding a room."

Nefertari allowed herself a small smile. "Leadership is not a privilege; it's a responsibility. And it's one I cannot ignore."

Grilka, sitting cross-legged on the floor, let out a sigh. "Well, I guess someone has to keep these people in line. If anyone can do it, it's you."

Kimiko, standing in the corner with her arms folded, nodded in agreement. "Your strength and honor are exactly what they need. You're making the right choice."

Rainstorm stepped forward, her quiet presence filling the room with calm. "Your decision is noble, Nefertari. The spirits would approve."

Adrian glanced at Rainstorm, his usual sarcasm tempered with sincerity. "You think the spirits approve of her ditching us?"

Rainstorm responded, "I do. It's for a higher purpose."

Parting Words

As the group stood, Nefertari approached each member of the team, offering a handshake or a warm embrace.

To Grilka, she said, "Your strength is unmatched. Keep them safe."

To Kimiko, she said, "Your precision and wisdom will guide them."

To Rainstorm, she said, "Your connection to the spirits is a beacon for us all."

Freija grinned as Nefertari approached her. "Try not

to get too bored without me around."

Nefertari smirked. "I'll manage. But your energy will be missed."

Finally, she stood before Adrian, who opened his arms. "I don't usually do hugs, but this is a clear exception."

Nefertari laughed softly and took his embrace. "Take care of them, Adrian."

He grinned. "Don't worry. I'm the glue that holds this mess together."

Rainstorm's lips curved into a faint smile. "I think the spirits approve of anyone brave enough to follow their path."

Nefertari turned to Lilith, whose fiery wings were dim but still radiant in the room's soft light. "Captain, you brought me into this fight. You showed me a galaxy worth fighting for. For that, I will always be grateful."

Lilith's molten gaze met Nefertari's. "Your strength and wisdom carried us through some of our darkest moments. You were more than a fighter, Nefertari. You were our foundation."

Nefertari said one last word to Lilith. "Will you let my family know where I am and what I will be doing?"

Lilith returned, "I think they will be very proud of what their daughter has become. Of course, I will inform them."

With that, Nefertari smiled.

Lilith's Final Speech

As Nefertari prepared to leave the ship, Lilith stepped forward, her fiery wings unfurling slightly. "This journey wasn't just about defeating Necra. It was about finding purpose, about building something greater than us."

She turned to Nefertari. "You're doing just that, Nefertari. You're leaving your mark, not just on Velyria, but on all of us."

The golden warrior nodded. "And you all will

457

continue to leave yours. Wherever you go, whatever battles you face, know that you'll always have an ally here."

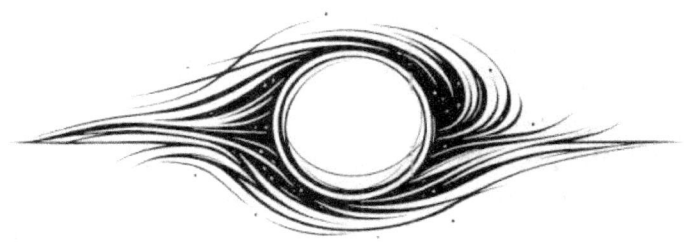

Chapter 73:

Finale

The Scorpion drifted in the tranquil expanse of space, its engines humming softly as the team gathered in the main living area. The battle was over, and Necra was defeated. The oppressive weight of her reign was gone, replaced by a cautious sense of relief as Nefertari would help rebuild what was destroyed. The group sat in a loose circle, exhaustion etched on their faces but pride evident in their eyes.

Lilith stood in the center, her fiery wings dimmed but still striking. Her gaze swept over the crew – her team. Each of them had risked everything, and each had delivered when it mattered most. These weren't just warriors; they were family.

"This moment," Lilith began, her voice resonant and firm, "belongs to all of us. We've accomplished something extraordinary, something no one else could. We didn't just defeat Necra... we've given the entire galaxy a chance to heal. And we did it together."

Her fiery gaze softened. "I want to thank each of you. Not just for your bravery, but for your commitment to this mission and to each other. I would be honored if you'd stay with me. The galaxy will still need us, and I can't imagine doing this without you."

"We lost a sister, but for a worthy reason. Nefertari will be missed… but she'll change an entire quadrant with her strength and grace."

Freija's Reflection

Freija leaned against the wall, her icy wings folded neatly behind her. She crossed her arms, a faint smile on her lips. "You know, I wasn't sure about this team when we started. I've always been... independent. Flying solo suited me. But this? Being part of something bigger?" She paused, her voice growing softer. "It's been incredible.

The room was quiet as Freija continued. "Lilith, you believed in all of us, even when we doubted ourselves. That means more than I can say. If you'll have me, I'm staying. The skies are always brighter when I know I'm not flying alone."

Adrian chuckled from his seat. "Not flying alone? That's rich, coming from the one who insists on soaring at Mach 2 every chance she gets."

Freija rolled her eyes but grinned. "And yet, somehow, you manage to keep up – barely."

Kimiko's Reflection

Kimiko sat quietly. She looked up, her calm expression betraying a flicker of emotion. "I've spent my life in the shadows, working alone. It was safer that way. No one to rely on, no one to betray you."

She paused, her voice steady but filled with depth. "But this team has shown me that trusting others doesn't make you weaker. It makes you stronger. You've all taught me something I never thought I'd learn – that it's okay to rely on people."

Kimiko's gaze met Lilith's. "I'm in. Wherever you lead, I'll follow."

Grilka snorted from across the room. "And here I thought ninjas didn't do feelings."

Kimiko's lips curved into a small smile. "Even ninjas have hearts. Some just hide it better."

Rainstorm's Reflection

Rainstorm stood near the corner. She adjusted the ornate tribal necklace around her neck, her expression contemplative. "Before this mission, my loyalty was to my people, my tribe. It still is. But I see now that my strength can serve a greater purpose."

She glanced around the room, her voice softening. "This team has become another tribe for me. A family. And I've realized something: fighting for the galaxy doesn't mean abandoning my roots. It means honoring them in a bigger way."

Rainstorm looked at Lilith. "I'm with you. As long as you'll have me."

Grilka's Reflection

Grilka stood near the kitchen, her orange hair wild and untamed from the recent battles.

She crossed her arms, a smirk tugging at her lips. "I'm not one for speeches, so I'll keep it simple. I've fought in a lot of battles, and I've fought with a lot of people. Most of them weren't worth remembering."

Her smirk faded, replaced by a rare moment of sincerity. "But this crew? You're worth it. You've got my back, and I've got yours. That's all I need."

Adrian, seated nearby, piped up. "Don't go soft on us, Grilka. It's unnerving."

Grilka rolled her eyes. "You wish."

Adrian's Reflection

Adrian was sprawled across one of the chairs, his

arms crossed behind his head. He grinned, his usual sarcasm evident. "Well, I guess someone has to stick around to keep you all entertained. Let's face it… I'm the best pilot you've got. And you'd miss me."

The crew chuckled, but Adrian's grin softened as he sat up. "But seriously, this team? You're the real deal. I've flown a lot of ships and worked with a lot of crews, but none of them felt like this. You've got my loyalty. Can we work on the sleeping arrangements? I mean, I've been crammed into bunks with snorers. You know who you are."

The team burst into laughter, Rainstorm and Grilka both mock-glaring at Adrian.

Lilith's Closing Words

Lilith waited for the laughter to die down before speaking again. "You've all made your choices, and I couldn't be prouder to lead this team. Together, we've done the impossible. And together, we'll face whatever comes next."

Freija leaned forward, her expression curious. "So, what's the plan, Captain?"

Lilith smiled faintly, her fiery wings flaring slightly. "We rest. We heal. And then… we see where the galaxy needs us next."

The Bond of a Team

As the crew dispersed to the barracks and cockpit, the sense of camaraderie was palpable. Each member reflected on their journey; their bonds deepened by the trials they had faced together. Lilith lingered on the observation deck, staring out at the endless expanse of stars.

Adrian appeared beside her, his usual grin in place. "You know, for someone with fiery swords and wings, you're not half bad."

Lilith smirked. "And for someone who never stops

talking, you're tolerable."

Adrian quipped back with a smile and a sideways hug, "I can take that."

Lilith closed her eyes for a brief moment, the warmth of the stars reflecting in her mind as flickers of memory – Agramor, Necra, the team's first real mission. There was peace in the silence. And purpose in the path ahead.

The Scorpion soared onward…

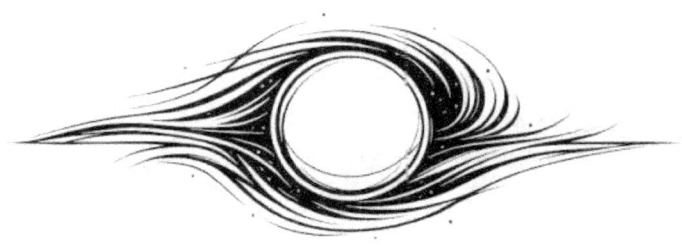

Epilogue 1:

Zyntar's Praise to the Team

The great crystal amphitheater on Zyntar shimmered like a living jewel beneath the twin moons. Thousands of Zyntar citizens had gathered in rows of glittering tiers. Lanterns drifted overhead like stardust, casting radiant patterns across the stage. The air was reverent, electric. One month had passed since the fall of Necra and the liberation of Velyria – and now, the heroes who had changed the fate of the quadrants were being honored with the Crystal Star of Bravery, Zyntar's highest award.

Standing tall in the center of the stage were the members of the strike team – Lilith, her wings folded but still radiant with ember-light, flanked by Freija, Adrian, Grilka, Rainstorm, Kimiko, and Nefertari. To the left stood the Zyntar crew of the Astrell: Varek, calm and focused; Tarin, stoic and silent; and Zela, proud and beaming.

Admiral Ilyan, dressed in ceremonial robes of deep crimson and starlight silver, stepped forward to address both his people and the heroes.

"Citizens of Zyntar – and every world that can now breathe free," he began, voice firm and rich with pride, "we gather not to mourn what was lost, but to honor what was saved. And we owe that salvation to the brave beings before

465

you. Warriors who did not come here for glory or recognition. They came for justice. And they gave us hope."

A hush swept through the crowd. The Admiral continued.

"These fighters are giants – not just in size," he said, drawing laughter and nods, "but in courage. Lilith, born of fire and myth. Grilka, the strength of a mountain. Adrian, whose ship is barely outpaced by his sarcasm. Rainstorm, whose soul speaks to forces older than time. Kimiko, silent as a shadow but deadly as light. Freija, our goddess of speed. And Nefertari, the shield of the fallen. You are now the legends of Zyntar."

He turned to Zyntar warriors. "But legends are also born in the stars. Varek, whose mind cut through defenses no blade could breach. Tarin, who stood unshaken in the heart of battle. And Zela, whose hands built what we needed when we needed it most. You are our own – and today, you stand among the galaxy's finest."

The applause thundered like a storm of light. Then Ilyan opened a box from a table next to his podium pulling out a Crystal Star of Bravery medal. One by one each hero approached starting from the end with Nefertari.

Nefertari bowed with royal formality. "You opened your arms when we had nothing. For that, you'll always have my sword."

Kimiko bowed with solemn grace. "Your quiet resolve matches my own. In that, I found kinship."

Rainstorm bowed low, her voice calm. "To the people of Zyntar, I give thanks. Your strength reminded us of who we are."

Grilka bent one knee and crossed her arms proudly. "You're small, but you're scrappy. I like that."

Adrian, grinning widely, bowed deeply and whispered, "Try not to cry, Ilyan. I get emotional too, sometimes."

Ilyan smirked. "Somehow I doubt that."

Freija simply gave a wink and the closest thing she could manage to a formal Zyntar salute. "I'll always fight for the ones who flew beside me."

Lilith approached last. She dropped to one knee – her enormous frame humbling itself before the tiny Admiral. She bowed her head as he placed the medal around her neck.

"You showed us that fire can light the way," Ilyan said softly. "Even when the path was lost."

Lilith's voice was low but strong. "You gave us sanctuary when the galaxy had none. And reminded us that hope is never too small to matter."

Then Ilyan turned to the three Zyntar crewmembers.

Zela stepped forward and saluted proudly. "You believed in us. You gave us purpose. And you reminded me why we build."

Tarin, rarely one for words, bowed and offered only, "It was an honor. And I'd do it again."

Varek gave a respectful nod, his voice clear and steady. "My loyalty was always to my people. But now, I know it belongs to something greater. Thank you for showing me that."

As the final medals were placed, the entire amphitheater erupted into cheers. Fireworks burst into silent brilliance across the sky, and the Zyntar banners unfurled across the towers behind the stage.

Admiral Ilyan raised one hand. "From this day forward, let all who stand in darkness remember hope flies on wings of fire and ice, speaks in shadows, stands tall with strength, and shines even in silence."

The heroes stood side by side, medals gleaming. And as the stars glittered above, they knew this moment would live forever – not just in history, but in every heart that beat freely from this day forward.

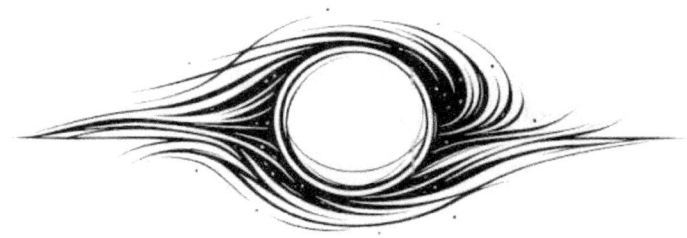

Epilogue 2:

Damnation

A ragged breath escaped Necra's lips as she stirred, her body cold, yet burning from the inside out. She tried to lift her hand, but it felt impossibly heavy, as if her limbs were shackled by invisible chains.

Something was wrong.

No, everything was wrong.

She thought she had died. She remembered the final moments – Lilith standing over her, the heat of her enemy's fire swords blazing in the night. She had fought with all the fury of a queen unwilling to surrender, but in the end, it hadn't been Lilith's flames that delivered the fatal blow. No. The sting of cold steel, silent and merciless, had come from the shadows. Kimiko. That wretched assassin had ended her life with no fanfare, no moment of final defiance – just the swift, clean efficiency of someone who saw her as an obstacle to be removed.

The memory sent a wave of rage coursing through her, and with a sudden, desperate inhale, Necra's eyes shot open.

She immediately wished they hadn't.

The sky above her swirled in endless, suffocating shades of crimson and black, as though the very air was stained with blood and sorrow. The world around her pulsed with heat, but it was not the warmth of life, it was oppressive, thick, filled with the acrid scent of sulfur and something deeper, something wrong.

Hell.

Her fingers twitched against the ground, but it was no earth she had ever known. The surface beneath her was slick and pulsing, like the flesh of some great, living beast. The sound of distant, echoing screams filled the air, weaving through the infernal wind like a sorrowful melody played on broken strings.

Slowly, painfully, Necra forced herself upright, her breath coming in ragged gasps. Her once-imposing armor was tattered and cracked; her death swords gone. She felt hollow, as though something essential had been stripped from her.

A slow, rumbling chuckle rolled through the air. Deep, resonant, filled with amusement.

"Finally awake, are we?"

Necra turned sharply, her breath catching in her throat.

Seated upon a throne of jagged obsidian, his crimson skin illuminated by the glow of the tormented souls writhing in the chasm behind him, was a figure of nightmare and legend. His horns curved back like the crescent of a blood moon, his eyes burning embers set deep within a face carved from shadows and fire. Smoke curled lazily from his nostrils as he exhaled, and a slow, knowing grin spread across his face.

Belzoth.

Her pulse pounded against her ribs. She had heard whispers of him, stories of the Demon Lord who commanded the abyss itself. Lilith's father. But standing before him now, she realized the stories had been... lacking. No words could capture the sheer weight of his presence, the way the very air trembled around him.

"You..." Necra swallowed, forcing herself to stand straighter despite the trembling in her legs. "Why am I here?"

Belzoth smirked, his massive form shifting slightly in his throne. "Oh, come now, my dear. Do you truly not know?" He tilted his head, feigning curiosity. "You lost. You died. And now... you are mine."

Necra clenched her fists, her nails digging into her palms. "I am a queen," she spat. "I will not bow to you."

Belzoth let out a rich, velvety laugh. "A queen?" He rose from his throne, his towering frame moving with a grace that was unnatural for something so massive. He stepped toward her, his presence alone pressing against her like an unbearable weight. "Tell me, Necra... what is a queen without a kingdom?"

Her lips parted, but no words came.

"You ruled through fear," Belzoth continued, his voice smooth and deliberate, like the slow drip of poison. "You built an empire on the bones of the weak, but the moment you fell, your name began to rot like spoiled fruit. Your loyal subjects surrendered. Your armies abandoned you." He leaned down slightly, his flaming eyes inches from hers. "You are nothing, child."

Necra's breath hitched.

"You always were."

A chill unlike any she had ever known crawled up her spine, and for the first time in her existence, doubt crept into her heart.

"You disappoint me, Necra." This voice was different. Softer, feminine, but filled with something worse than wrath... disappointment.

Necra turned, and there, stepping from the shifting darkness, was a woman as ethereal as she was terrifying.

Isolde.

Lilith's mother.

A queen of shadows, draped in midnight and adorned with silver filigree that caught the flickering, hellish light.

Her violet eyes, sharp as daggers, fixed upon Necra with quiet contempt. Unlike Belzoth's blazing inferno, her presence was cold, like the whisper of death before a final breath.

"You thought yourself untouchable," Isolde murmured, gliding forward with the grace of a wraith. "Yet here you stand, stripped of power, of purpose. Tell me, Necra, do you understand now?"

Necra stiffened. "Understand what?"

Isolde's gaze never wavered. "That you were never strong. Only cruel."

Necra flinched as though struck by an unseen blade.

"You built nothing," Isolde continued, her tone like the slow unraveling of a tapestry. "You inspired nothing. And so, when you fell, there was no legacy, no mourning. Only silence."

Belzoth chuckled. "She's rather good at this, isn't she?"

Isolde didn't acknowledge him, her focus entirely on Necra. "You tormented my daughter. You sought to break her, to erase her. And yet, it was you who was erased instead. Fitting, don't you think?"

Necra's nails dug into her palms, her breath coming in sharp gasps. "You think you can lecture me?" she hissed, but there was no power in her voice, only desperation.

Isolde tilted her head. "Lecture? No. I merely wish for you to understand what eternity holds for you."

Belzoth grinned, stepping back toward his throne. "Ah, yes. The part where we tell you your fate." He gestured broadly. "Necra, Queen of Nothing, Ruler of Ash... welcome to your new kingdom. No throne. No armies. No name. No voice."

Isolde's lips curled in something almost like amusement. "We will not torture you. There will be no grand spectacle of suffering. No dramatic trials or poetic redemption."

Belzoth leaned forward, his grin widening. "No, we've given you something far worse."

Necra's breath caught.

"We've forgotten you," Isolde whispered.

A ringing silence filled the air.

Necra shook her head. "No... no, that's not..."

"Your name will fade," Belzoth said smoothly. "Your legacy will wither. No stories will be told of your conquests. No records will remain. Even those who once feared you will move on... will forget you ever existed."

Isolde's voice was like silk over steel. "You will not be remembered. You will not be feared. You will not be anything."

Necra stumbled back. "You can't!"

"But we already have," Belzoth finished, his smirk cutting like a blade.

The air pressed against Necra's chest, the weight of nothing closing in around her.

No escape.

No legacy.

No memory.

She screamed.

But in the endless, burning void, her voice made no sound.

And no one heard her. Her importance and legacy were now forgotten... forever.

ABOUT THE AUTHOR

K.A. Dunlap is a storyteller with a passion for epic sci-fi adventures, fierce heroes, and high-stakes battles that shape the fate of worlds. With a background in storytelling, he has crafted a universe filled with unforgettable characters, intense action, and deep, emotional narratives that keep readers on the edge of their seats.

Inspired by the vastness of space, the resilience of warriors, and the bonds forged in battle, K.A. Dunlap weaves stories that blend cinematic action with heartfelt moments of triumph, loss, and redemption. His works explore themes of leadership, loyalty, and the enduring fight against tyranny – all set against the backdrop of a galaxy teetering on the edge of chaos.

When not writing K.A. Dunlap can be found be found exploring what this world has to offer. He enjoys good stories, especially in the sci-fi world.

The adventure is just beginning!

To learn more about the Crimson Alliance Universe go to: https://www.TheCAU.net.

Contact K.A. Dunlap @ KADunlap@TheCAU.net

CONTINUE INTO THE CRIMSON ALLIANCE UNIVERSE

The Crimson Alliance Universe includes full-length novels, interludes, tales, and micro-tales that expand the adventures of these characters.

Origins (2-chapter character driven back stories)

Every hero has a beginning. The Crimson Alliance Origins series explores the formative journeys of the seven warriors who will one day unite to form the Crimson Alliance whose choices help shape the future of Icelandia. Each Origin story can be enjoyed on its own while revealing the events, challenges, and defining moments that forged these unforgettable characters.

Frigid: The First Accord

Frigid and her slightly younger twin sister, Freija, enter the Aerial Command Academy determined to earn their place through discipline, leadership, and perseverance. After surviving the academy's final Gauntlet, Frigid faces an even greater challenge when visitors from another world arrive on Icelandia, placing the future of her people and their first step toward the stars in her hands.

Adrian: I Guess I'm Part of a Team, Again

Adrian Flynn has spent years flying alone, trusting only himself and the ship beneath his hands. When an unexpected encounter forces him to reconsider the life he has built, he must decide whether joining a team is worth risking old wounds.

Lilith: Rebirth
Lilith comes from a realm where power is everything and nothing truly changes. When she crosses into the Material Realm, she discovers something entirely different: worlds worth protecting, people worth trusting, and a purpose greater than herself.

Grilka: Tuff Enuff
When a transport vessel is destroyed during a pirate attack, Grilka finds herself stranded alone on a hostile moon with limited supplies and no guarantee of rescue. As heat, isolation, and exhaustion push her to her limits, she must rely on the determination and resilience that have defined her since childhood.

Tala Redhawk: Vision Quest
Tala Redhawk was a young girl facing one of the most important traditions of her people. Sent alone into the sacred canyon on a vision quest, she must learn to endure silence, uncertainty, and the forces of nature as she discovers the path that will shape the rest of her life.

Kimiko: The New Path
Kimiko has spent her life mastering the paths of the ninja and the samurai, relying on discipline, precision, and self-reliance to overcome every challenge. When a chance encounter forces her to question whether some battles require more than a single blade, she must decide how she will face the future.

Nefertari: Birth of Chantress
Nefertari is an unproven leader seeking to earn the respect of her people. When a violent faction attacks a remote shrine under her care, she must rely on faith, discipline, and courage to protect those trapped inside and discover what it truly means to lead.

Freija: The Living Storm
Raised beneath the frozen skies of Icelandia, Freija constantly challenges the limits of flight and tradition. Her journey from reckless royal flyer to respected instructor changes the future of Icelandian aviation.

Collect all eight Crimson Alliance Origins.

Ensemble Novel
A Demon's Rebellion: The Rise of Lilith
The first full novel of the Crimson Alliance Universe. Lilith must unite an unlikely team of warriors from different worlds to challenge a growing threat that endangers the galaxy itself.

Interludes (Character focused novels)
Cold Front: Echoes in the Frost
When a mysterious force awakens on Icelandia, Freija, Frigid, and Kimiko must uncover the truth before an ancient power reshapes their world forever.

Sunlight and Shorelines: This Was Supposed to be a Vacation
A simple vacation turns into a dangerous mystery when Adrian and Grilka uncover a conspiracy hidden beneath the paradise world of Ona.

Tales (10-chapter story)
Smuggler's Gambit: When the Skills End and the Luck Begins
When Adrian Flynn is approached by fellow smuggler Kevan Dralis with a lucrative delivery opportunity, the job appears straightforward and highly profitable. Needing a third pilot to complete the run, they recruit the mysterious Rafe Juno and set course for what should be a routine operation. But when hidden agendas, dangerous cargo, and unexpected enemies emerge, the three smugglers discover that some jobs are far more dangerous than the credits are worth.

The Tournament of Snowfall: The Evolution of a Princess

For over a century, Frigid stood in the shadow of her twin sister's achievements, content to focus on duty rather than competition. When she is called upon to represent Snowreach in the legendary Tournament of Snowfall, she must confront her fears, discover her own strengths, and learn that true victory comes not from surpassing others, but from becoming the person she was always meant to be.

Old Wounds: The One Who Returns

When a championship house faces defeat, an aging warrior answers a call she never expected to receive. As Grilka steps back into the hexagon after years away, she must prove that some lessons are never forgotten and that true strength is measured by more than points alone.

Micro-Tale (5-chapter story)
The Night of a Thousand Lanterns: A Lesson of Release

A peaceful festival in rural Japan becomes the setting for friendship, rivalry, and unexpected challenges as Kimiko, Freija, and Adrian celebrate beneath the lantern-lit sky.

www.ingramcontent.com/pod-product-compliance
Lightning Source LLC
Chambersburg PA
CBHW071339020726
47502CB00001B/156